BOOKS BY MARC ALAN EDELHEIT

GUARDIANS OF THE DARK
Off Midway Station

COMMAND DECISION
Forged in Battle

FANTASY

THE STIGER CHRONICLES
Book One: Stiger's Tigers
Book Two: The Tiger
Book Three: The Tiger's Fate
Book Four: The Tiger's Time
Book Five: The Tiger's Wrath
Book Six: The Tiger's Imperium
Book Seven: The Tiger's Fight
Book Eight: The Tiger's Rage
Book Nine: The Tiger's Battle

STIGER: TALES OF THE SEVENTH
Book One: Stiger
Book Two: Fort Covenant
Book Three: A Dark Foretoken

THE KARUS SAGA
Book One: Lost Legio IX

Book Two: *Fortress of Radiance*

Book Three: *The First Compact*

Book Four: *Rapax Pax*

Book Five: *Brothers of the Line*

THE ELI CHRONICLES

Book One: *Eli*

Book Two: *By Bow, Daggers & Sword*

Book Three: *Lutha Nyx*

THE WAY OF LEGEND: WITH QUINCY J. ALLEN

Book One: *Reclaiming Honor*

Book Two: *Forging Destiny*

Book Three: *Paladin's Light*

THE CLAIMED REALM

Book 1: *Legacy's Edge*

Book 2: *A Call to Arms*

SCI-FI

BORN OF ASH

Book One: *Fallen Empire*

Book Two: *Infinity Control*

Book Three: *Rising Phoenix*

NONFICTION

Every Writer's Dream: The Insider's Path to an Indie Bestseller

OFF JAVELIN STATION

MARC ALAN EDELHEIT

SECOND SKY

Published by Second Sky in 2025

An imprint of Storyfire Ltd.
Carmelite House
50 Victoria Embankment
London EC4Y 0DZ

www.secondskybooks.com

The authorised representative in the EEA is Hachette Ireland
8 Castlecourt Centre
Dublin 15 D15 XTP3
Ireland
(email: info@hbgi.ie)

ISBN: 978-1-83618-738-7
eBook ISBN: 978-1-83618-737-0

PROLOGUE
GARRETT

Surprise shuddered violently beneath him, a deep, grinding tremor that Garrett felt in his very bones through the command chair. The impact rippled across the deck, rattling consoles and sending a few unsecured items clattering to the floor. Overhead, the bridge lights flickered wildly before emergency circuits kicked in, flooding the space with a sterile white that carved sharp shadows across the faces of the crew working at their stations.

Garrett tightened his grip on the armrests, willing himself to stay calm and in control, even as another groan, signaling a secondary explosion, raw and deep, rumbled up from the wounded ship's core. His jaw clenched. It felt personal—every hit, every jolt—as if *Surprise* herself were crying out in agony. And Garrett felt each one as if it were a blow to his own body.

"Shields at forty-two percent," Keegan called, his voice taut with the strain of the moment.

Garrett's gaze snapped to the holographic tactical display, its swirling projection showing the chaos of the fight. Red icons swarmed across the board, tracking missile vectors streaking toward his battered task force like a cloud of enraged wasps... Their own volley had been launched moments earlier, and it was burning downrange toward the enemy. The exchange had become a punishing and prolonged affair, something he had not wanted but had planned for when he'd jumped into the system.

"Thank you," Garrett replied, his voice clipped, controlled as he acknowledged the report. On the display, impact markers flared across *Surprise*'s aft quarter. Almost immediately, the ship shook again as the rest of the enemy's staggered volley hammered home.

"Six missiles made it through the point defense screen," Keegan reported grimly after the shaking subsided. "Moderate bleed through aft. New fires on Deck Sixteen. Damage control has been dispatched. After shields now at thirty-eight percent."

"Scratch one cruiser!" Krebs barked. "Two destroyers down, Commodore. Another's dead in the water... her gravitic drive is fluctuating... she's falling out of formation." There was a pause. "She's... gone too."

A flicker of satisfaction stirred within Garrett, but it was fleeting. His gaze shifted to the broader tactical plot and his heart sank. His task force... the ships he'd brought to this distant star system... they were being torn apart, one after another, and they hadn't even been in-system for more than five hours. Already, half his force was gone, crippled ships limping away from the fight or reduced to wreckage tumbling through the void.

Worse was the mounting damage to *Surprise* herself. With every passing volley, his ship was being hurt. Garrett exhaled slowly, steadying himself as the crushing weight of command settled even heavier on his shoulders. He had known when he rose this morning it was going to be a long day. Now he understood, it was going to be far longer than he'd ever imagined.

ONE

GARRETT

"Transition complete," Lieutenant Heller reported. "Wormhole has closed. We are no longer in the Midway System. We're in the deep dark, sir."

Garrett sat at Shaw's station, his gaze sweeping over the battle-scarred bridge. The acrid stench of burnt composites, melted circuitry, and singed fabric still clung to the recycled air, a reminder of the chaos that had unfolded here not long ago. Blackened consoles and deep gouges in the bulkhead walls spoke to the ferocity of the battle—and the desperate struggle to hold the bridge against the enemy.

The ship felt like a wounded beast to Garrett. And yet, somehow, they had made it. He leaned forward slightly, his fingers brushing the edge of the console as if grounding himself to reality. The transition out of Midway had been unnervingly smooth—utterly devoid of the gut-wrenching lurch common to jump points, or the brutal, disorienting shove of the crude beacons humanity relied on to rapidly traverse star systems. Those primitive yet powerful constructs always left an aftertaste of nausea in their wake, the human body protesting against the raw forces used to fold and bend space in a way that seemed unnatural.

But this? Garrett struggled to reconcile what he'd just experienced—or rather, what he hadn't. There had been no sensation of motion, no telltale shudder in the deck plates. It was as if the ship had simply slid through space, undisturbed, like a shadow moving across a wall on a sunny day.

He glanced at the glowing displays. The HTD—the holographic tactical display—was a blank slate, its readings wiped clean the moment they entered the wormhole and transitioned through and into the deep dark. For the first time in a long while, Garrett felt disoriented, not because of where they were, but because of how seamless the transition had been. If it weren't for the absence of telemetry and the vast, star-speckled void now visible on the forward viewscreen, he might have doubted they'd left Midway at all.

"Lieutenant Cassidy, report... What are you seeing?" Garrett's voice carried across the bridge. He made sure to keep his tone steady and firm. He turned toward his sensor and electronic warfare officer, who was hunched over her console, clearly working. The soft glow of the HTD cast shifting patterns on her face as she studied the stream of data flickering in before her as the ship's active sensors swept the space about them, probing for contacts and returns.

She straightened slightly and turned as she glanced over at him. "We're in deep space, Commodore," she confirmed. "That much is certain. I'm working to triangulate our position now but am having some difficulty doing that due to the positions of the stars and how far we have traveled. I am in the process of establishing relevant points of reference. Sensors are actively building a composite of our surroundings, but so far, there are no contacts within immediate threat range—just, as one would expect, there are random fragments of rock, ice, and dust drifting nearby. I am picking up what seems to be a gravitational distortion approximately six to seven million kilometers off our starboard beam. Sweeping it now." She paused, tilting her head as she scrutinized the display some more. "It appears to be a rogue micro-planetoid, mostly gaseous in nature. Mass readings are consistent with that profile. No energy signatures, no indications of artificial constructs. As far as I can tell, there is no threat to the ship that I can detect. It's not even moving in our direction."

Garrett gave a brief nod, but his attention lingered on Cassidy's report. Even out here, beyond the edges of star systems, true emptiness was an illusion. The term *space*, he mused, was a woefully inadequate descriptor—a lazy misnomer perpetuated by those who seldom contemplated the intricacies of the void. The space between solar systems, the so-called deep dark, was a vast expanse teeming with untamed phenomena: rogue planets, micro-planetoids, wandering ice giants, asteroids, ancient debris from long-dead stars, and the occasional artifact of some forgotten cosmic collision. There might even be complex and intelligent life out in the deep dark, but no one had found it yet.

He leaned back in the chair, letting his eyes drift to the main viewscreen. The star-studded void stretched endlessly, an ocean of silence pierced only by the faint hum of the ship's systems, at least on his bridge. He thought about the gravity distortion Cassidy had mentioned and considered it for a moment.

"Alert the science team of the rogue planet," Garrett said. "They might find it interesting and worth studying while we are here. Also, launch an investigative probe to scan and study the planetoid."

"Aye, sir," Cassidy replied.

Garrett tapped the edge of the chair's armrest, his mind turning over the data he had. Out here, far from the gravitational cradle of a star system, they were a small, fragile speck navigating an untamed expanse.

He keyed a command on his console, initiating the ship-wide tone that signaled they were standing down from general quarters. He could almost hear and feel the collective sighs of relief from both his crew and the evacuees they had taken aboard at Midway.

"Mister Heller," Garrett said, turning his attention back to the bridge, "work with Cassidy to determine an absolute fix on our location and confirm we've landed where we expected to be."

"Aye, aye, sir," Heller responded promptly.

Garrett tapped a command to open a channel, and a secondary screen flickered to life. The image resolved into the familiar face of his chief engineer, Commander Sing La Tam. The man looked every bit the part of someone who had wrestled with disaster and lived to tell the tale... just barely at that. His hair was disheveled, standing at odd angles as if it hadn't seen a comb in days. The utilitarian ship suit he wore was torn at the right collar, a hastily applied patch covering the damage to ensure functionality and survivability in the event of a sudden and unexpected decompression event.

But it was the bruise on his right cheek that drew Garrett's attention. It had deepened to an ugly purple since their last conversation, the edges tinged with sickly green. The injury was another reminder of just how close they'd come to losing the ship entirely through the enemy's boarding action.

"Sir, how can I help?" The chief engineer's voice was heavy with exhaustion, his eyes rimmed with fatigue. He looked like he was teetering on the edge of collapse... The only thing keeping him up were his hands leaning on something as he stared into the camera.

"Commander," Garrett said, his tone softening just slightly. "What's the status of the gripper drive?"

"We're somewhere else—not in Midway—and she's still in one piece. I suppose that means we're alive," Tam responded, his tone carrying a mix of relief and exhaustion. "Call it confirmed progress."

Resisting a scowl, Garrett gave a faint nod. The last few hours had been a maelstrom of frenetic activity: final preparations to escape the warzone, frantic loading of supplies, equipment, and desperate evacuees who had clung to their chance of salvation by boarding *Surprise*. He felt his own weariness pressing in upon him. His temper was short, a byproduct of the exhaustion he felt, though he did not show it. "I was hoping for something a little more definitive than that, Tam."

The engineer exhaled heavily. He glanced downward at something out of sight—likely an engineering display console or a hastily cleared workbench where a data tablet lay. The man squinted. "The gripper drive functioned within expected—hell, I might even say normal—parameters." He paused, rubbing at his bruised cheek as he looked back up at Garrett. "I would have expected something, like nausea, but the transition was smooth, like skating on perfect ice. I'd like to request time to study the drive thoroughly, make absolutely certain there are no issues before we risk another transition. We're working with untested —well"—he flashed a crooked grin—"I guess it's tested now— but still essentially new systems. I need to pull everything apart, metaphorically speaking, and examine it all to decide if it is safe to proceed."

"How long do you need?"

Tam bit his lip in thought, his brow furrowing. "Can I get at least forty-eight hours?" His gaze softened slightly as he continued. "And, Commodore... I know you might find this surprising, but I need some rest first, and yes, contrary to popular belief, I do occasionally sleep."

Before Garrett could respond, Heller's voice broke through. "Commodore," he called from his station. "We're right where we expected to be—two hundred fifty thousand AU from Midway, exactly on point, with no more than a meter's deviation."

Garrett refocused on the screen, meeting Tam's tired gaze. "Congratulations. The drive worked flawlessly. We're right where we are supposed to be."

Tam's grin widened, though it was cut short by a wince as the movement clearly aggravated his bruised cheek. "I knew it would," he replied, the quiet pride in his voice unmistakable. He made a fist and shook it. "I bloody knew it!"

"You've got your forty-eight hours," Garrett said with a firm nod. "We need to stand down, rest, recover, and take stock of everything before we proceed. We might even stay here longer. I need time to get our house in order."

"Thank you, Commodore," Tam said, his voice carrying a note of genuine gratitude. "I will use the time allotted well... and more if you give it, after I get some sleep."

Garrett leaned forward slightly, gesturing at the screen, his index finger pointing directly at Tam. "Make sure you see medical too," he said, his tone leaving little room for debate.

Tam waved a dismissive hand, his grin half-hearted now. "I'm fine, Commodore. Really. I've seen worse from a bar fight."

Garrett's eyes narrowed, and his voice took on a sharper edge. "That was not a suggestion, Tam. It was an order. Go see Doctor Neelan and have yourself checked out before you get some rest. That bruise looks worse every time I see you."

Tam hesitated for a moment before sighing in resignation. It came out as a heated hiss. "Yes, sir, I'll make time to visit our good sawbones before I collapse in exhaustion."

Satisfied, without another word, Garrett terminated the channel. The screen went dark. He rubbed the back of his neck, feeling the tightness in his muscles—an ache that had grown persistent; one born of stress, fatigue, and the relentless strain of command. The stim he had taken earlier had run out, and he was starting to feel the aftereffects.

His gaze drifted to the forward viewscreen, where the stars stretched endlessly. Each point of light felt like a distant promise, that now, with the gripper drive, was a reachable goal. He let out a slow breath and focused back on his duty.

"Lieutenant Keeli," Garrett called. He straightened in his chair, pushing aside the fatigue gnawing at the edges of his focus. "Put me on the 1MC, and ensure the ships mated with *Surprise* are included."

"You're on, Commodore," Keeli replied after a brief pause. "Everyone should be able to hear you."

Once more, Garrett resisted the urge to scowl. The title felt foreign, as if it belonged to someone else. *Commodore.* Just a few hours ago he'd been a mere job captain, a finisher—one destined to never command a commissioned warship. But he knew there was no time for hesitation or self-doubt. He had to own it, for great responsibility had been placed in his hands. He inhaled deeply, centering himself as he thought about what to say, what he needed to communicate.

His mind wandered briefly to the chaos of the past hours— the surprise attack on the Midway Star System, the desperate battle against the enemy fleet, the brutal fight to repel the boarders who had stormed *Surprise*, and the deadly struggle on the bridge and in the corridors beyond. The image of Tyabni, his tactical officer, lying dead, flickered in his mind. Tyabni was gone now, along with so many others. Even his second in command, Shaw, had been injured and was now in medical recovering.

"This is the cap—commodore speaking," Garrett began. He hardened his tone, doing his best to fill it with confidence. "We have successfully jumped away from Midway, and we are now in deep space, two hundred fifty thousand astronomical units from our last position. I'm pleased to report we've left the enemy behind. Sensors confirm there are no immediate threats in the vicinity. For the moment, we are safe."

He paused, letting the words hang, giving everyone a chance to absorb the statement and what it meant.

"We will stand down for the next few hours," Garrett continued, "to take stock and recover before preparing for our next jump. Get what rest you can, while you can."

He paused again, his gaze sweeping over the bridge as he considered his next words. "To the evacuees we've taken aboard *Surprise*, we are aware of your needs, and we will ensure you are settled and receive food, water, and medical attention. Please be patient with us as we work to address those needs. To all department heads: see to your stations, and ensure your teams are taken care of. Put in place a rotation schedule to stand crew down."

Garrett glanced at his station's screen, the digital clock glowing faintly against the darkened backdrop. "We will hold a meeting for all department heads at thirteen hundred." That was twelve hours away—enough time to allow Garrett to snatch some much-needed rest himself. The thought of sleep felt almost indulgent, but he knew he couldn't keep running on fumes forever. He and everyone else required a break.

"To the captains of the ships now attached to *Surprise* and part of our newly formed task force," Garrett added, "stand down, rest, see to your people, and await further orders. They will come soon enough."

He paused, letting the silence stretch for a moment. "To everyone, know, for the moment, we are safe. Take comfort in that. Commodore Garrett out."

"You're off," Keeli said quietly, her voice breaking the stillness that followed.

Garrett exhaled slowly, leaning back in his chair as a fresh wave of exhaustion washed over him. The bridge was quiet again, save for the low hum of the ship's systems and the soft beeps of the consoles. He rubbed his temples absently, his thoughts already turning to the tasks ahead and what he needed to do. He felt a dull headache coming on.

Garrett glanced down at one of the monitors embedded in his console. With a few taps, he pulled up his mail queue, his eyes narrowing as the screen populated with messages. The count at the top made him grimace—over six hundred unread messages. A handful were marked *PRIORITY*, their red tags glaring against the rest of the list.

One in particular caught his eye. The sender was listed as Captain Norwood, captain of the battlecruiser *Palestro*. The subject line was succinct but telling: *SENIORITY AND COMMAND, LET'S DISCUSS SOONEST!!!*

Garrett exhaled heavily, the sound more resignation than frustration. Norwood... Garrett had only ever encountered the man in social gatherings on Midway Station. Those interactions had been far from positive. Like many other starship captains, the man had been condescending toward Garrett's rank and role as a job captain. He had found Norwood stuffy, distant, cold, and stuck-up.

Garrett had no doubt the captain of the *Palestro* had already scrutinized the ad hoc task force's structure, angling to assert himself as the most senior captain in grade, which, he likely was... That would make him Garrett's second in command. How would that complicate matters? What type of working relationship would they have?

The timing, though, was telling—Norwood had sent the message less than a minute ago, likely the moment Garrett's broadcast concluded. Shaking his head, Garrett leaned back in his chair, letting his hand hover over the delete option for a moment before pulling it away. This wasn't something he could ignore, but right now, the ship—and the evacuees packed into every available space—took precedence over Norwood's jockeying for position. There would be time to deal with pecking orders and egos later.

He stared at the screen for a moment longer, his fingers drumming lightly on the console. Sorting through six hundred messages felt like an impossible task, and one he was not ready for...

With a resigned sigh, he flagged Norwood's message for later review and closed the mail queue. The screen returned to a display of the ship's systems, a detailed schematic showing the health of *Surprise* and the smaller vessels now docked with her.

Garrett cast a glance toward his cabin, his sanctuary in theory, but one that held no immediate promise of rest. The sealed orders waiting within were the priority for the moment. He pushed himself to his feet, every movement a reminder of how thoroughly the past hours had worn him down. His joints protested, his muscles ached, and a deep weariness had settled in his bones. For a fleeting moment, he felt like an old man.

"Mister Heller," Garrett called.

"Sir?" Heller turned in his chair, looking back toward Garrett, his expression alert despite the drawn features that betrayed his own exhaustion.

"I have sealed orders to read," Garrett said. "I am not to be disturbed unless it is an emergency. In the interim, you have the bridge. Make sure you are stimmed up. You might have command for a while."

"Aye, sir," Heller responded with a quick nod.

Garrett turned and made his way toward his quarters. The marine stationed outside snapped to attention the moment Garrett approached. Garrett barely acknowledged him, his mind already on the task ahead. The hatch to his cabin hissed open. He stepped through, and as it slid shut, the sounds of the bridge disappeared, leaving him enveloped in silence.

For the first time in hours—perhaps longer—he was truly alone.

The room was dimly lit, the ambient glow from the overhead fixtures casting long shadows on the walls. Garrett paused, his gaze sweeping over the small space. He imagined going to his cabin and dropping onto his bed, letting the world fade away, and sleeping for what felt like an eternity.

But there was no time for that. A harsh taskmaster, duty called. It always did.

His eyes landed on the secure bag sitting squarely on his desk where he had left it, a plain reminder of the responsibilities that waited. He moved toward it. His sealed orders waited, along with the bag. He had no idea what Fleet wanted him to do... the target he was to hit. The word *Indigo* flashed in his mind, unbidden but persistent. Admiral Yenga had let that morsel slip. The word lingered, pulling at his thoughts.

What is Indigo?

More importantly, where is it? Is that the target?

He reached the desk and pulled out the chair. Sitting down, Garrett pulled the secure bag to him, the synthetic material cool under his fingers. He pressed his thumb against the scanner, the faint beep and click of the lock disengaging, breaking the silence in the office.

Inside, nestled securely, was the tablet. He pulled it free and placed it on the desk before him and eyed it for a long moment. Garrett activated it, and the screen lit up. He would finish reading the rest of what Admiral Gray had sent. Then, he'd read his sealed orders, the ones Yenga had given him.

Garrett leaned forward, his tired eyes narrowing on the tablet's display. Whatever came next, he would face it head-on. But deep down, a part of him couldn't shake the feeling that *Indigo* was just the beginning of something far larger—and far more dangerous—a place that would ultimately test him in ways he could not imagine.

TWO

TABBY

"We are safe. Take comfort in that. Commodore Garrett out." The channel went silent, and the light on the console blinked off, signaling it had been cut.

"Damn," Tabby muttered under her breath, letting out a slow exhale. Closing her eyes, she leaned back in her flight seat, the harness straps automatically pulling tight against her shoulders, and listened to the mechanical whine of the landing struts deploying. Her assault boat, *Max*, trembled slightly as the mechanisms engaged, the vibrations running through the deck plates beneath her boots and seat. She could feel it through her flight suit.

Surprise's departure had been timed to the second, and Tabby's assault boat had touched down on the landing deck mere moments before the Mothership's transition out of the Midway Star System. Opening her eyes, she watched on the small monitor to her right as the external cameras tracked their descent into the hangar bay. *Max* was being moved. The crane was in motion, guiding the assault boat down from the landing bay toward the deck with methodical exactness.

There was a sharp and heavy metallic clunk as the boat

made contact, the entire craft rocking briefly as the crane released its grip and the landing struts took *Max*'s full weight.

"We're down," Sanchez confirmed, her voice firm but tinged with a weariness Tabby keenly felt. "Magnetic grapples in place. We're locked in, ma'am."

Tabby nodded, though her eyes remained fixed on the monitor. She could not see much. The angle of the camera was wrong. From what she could see, the hangar deck loomed large, its cavernous space filled with the organized chaos of a working dock. Tabby stretched. She had been in her seat for hours, longer than she could ever recall. Her entire body felt stiff.

As she double-checked the readouts, Tabby shifted her attention away from the monitor, confirming the assault boat was securely docked and locked in place. She'd long since learned, in the military, it was always worth double-checking nearly everything, for mistakes were easily made. The magnetic locks were holding steady, and all systems registered nominal.

"Commence system shutdown procedure," Tabby ordered.

"Commencing," Sanchez replied as she leaned into her console, methodically working through the checklist. "Reactors powered down to safe levels. Gravitic drive is... offline. Weapons in safe mode. PDS in safe mode." There was a long pause as Sanchez worked on the final steps. She exhaled softly, her voice carrying a note of satisfaction. "System shutdown complete. *Max* is cold and safed, ma'am."

With those last words, the assault boat fell abruptly silent, as if *Max* had dropped into a deep sleep. The gentle hum of the reactors had faded, and with it, the subtle vibration that had been coursing through the boat ceased. Even the air handlers powered down, silencing the faint, ever-present background hiss of air circulating through the cabin. The stillness was startling, the kind of quiet that pressed against the ears and made every other sound seem amplified and overly loud.

Tabby tugged off her flight gloves and placed them on the

armrest to her left, flexing her fingers as she turned her attention to Chen, who sat slumped forward at his station. His helmeted head hung low, and his body remained motionless, reduced to eerie stillness. A quick glance at the vitals displayed on her console told her he was still alive, his biometrics steady but unnervingly subdued. He'd been that way since the rough beacon jump in Midway. Tabby thought it a direct result of the enemy hijacking the beacon network. His suit was delivering first aid and keeping him hydrated.

She closed her tired eyes, the lids heavy, and immediately saw the bulk of her squadron, flying straight toward the dreadnaught, like Chen, unresponsive, even as she screamed at them to wake up, to break off before it was too late. She cleared her throat, opened her eyes, and shook away the nightmare that had become reality.

Her brow furrowed as she spoke. "Have you notified the CAG that we require medical assistance?"

"Aye, ma'am," Sanchez replied without hesitation, her voice carrying an edge of concern. "As instructed before we landed. They should be on their way."

Before Tabby could respond, a loud bang echoed through the cabin, followed by another, then another. It was a rhythmic, hammering knock that rang through the hull, emanating from the ship's hatch.

Tabby leaned forward and keyed in a command, initiating the opening sequence for the outer hatch. A faint hissing sound filled the cabin as the air pressure equalized with that of the hangar deck beyond the boat. The sound was subtle, but the shift in pressure was enough to make her ears pop.

Several seconds later, the hatch unlocked with a metallic clunk as the internal bolts retracted. It swung inward before sliding smoothly to the right, revealing the floodlit environment of the hangar deck. A cacophony of noise flooded in: shouts, clangs, machines in operation, engines running...

Standing on *Max*'s ladder just beyond the hatch, a marine leaned into view, his eyes scanning the interior of the assault boat. He quickly located Tabby, his gaze locking onto her. The armband on his sleeve marked him as a corpsman, the word MEDICAL emblazoned in bold, block letters. That was odd... she'd never seen a marine corpsman before. They were usually Navy personnel attached to marine units.

"I am Corporal Hillman, temporarily attached to the medical division. How can we help, ma'am?"

Tabby lifted her hand and pointed toward Chen. "He needs assistance."

The marine climbed inside the boat. He navigated his way forward, crouching beside Chen's station, immediately beginning a quick assessment with a handheld scanning device, which he had detached from his belt.

"What happened to him?" Hillman asked, glancing back at Tabby as he reattached the scanner.

Tabby hesitated, the weight of her memories surfacing once more. Her squadron... almost all gone. She forced herself to focus, shrugging off the haze of grief and guilt that threatened to suddenly overwhelm her, for they had all been her responsibility... Mama's little ducks. "He didn't handle the beacon jump well... something the enemy did—it screwed with the damn thing. Sanchez and I woke up, he didn't."

Most of her squadron hadn't even had the chance to realize what was happening. She supposed they had died in their sleep, unconscious, never waking, never being able to fight back, just never having a chance. In a way, that was a mercy, for Tabby had to continue on with the knowledge she had led them to their deaths. She swallowed hard, forcing the lump in her throat down. "It was a bad jump, up range. I don't know exactly what it did to him, but it hit us all hard, the entire squadron."

"I understand, ma'am," the marine said, his tone respectful but brisk. He signaled to another marine who had climbed into the boat behind him. "Let's get him out of here. We can start treatment on the hangar deck—more room for us to work and get him stabilized before we transport him to medical."

The second marine moved forward, joining the first and helping to unstrap Chen from his harness. Together, the two marines lifted him carefully, ensuring his head and neck were supported as they maneuvered him out of the cramped confines of the boat and to the ladder.

Tabby, her jaw tight, watched them carry Chen toward the open hatch. The reality of what they'd been through hit her again, a fresh wave of grief and exhaustion washing over her in near equal measure. She pushed it down, locking it away for later. There would be time to grieve. For now, there was work to be done. She had the survivors of her squadron to look after.

Sanchez unbuckled and pulled herself to her feet as Chen was carried and manhandled out of *Max*. Tabby rubbed at her tired eyes. She felt a hand on her shoulder and looked up.

"We lived, ma'am," Sanchez said softly, her tone carrying a mix of relief and quiet reassurance. "That's what matters right now. We lived. Take comfort in that..."

Tabby nodded wearily. "I know," she replied, though the words felt hollow.

"That was all you, ma'am. You got us through the storm," Sanchez added. "I don't think anyone else could have done that. More importantly, we hit them hard. We hurt them... paid them back for the others."

Tabby nodded again. It didn't make her feel any better. Almost her entire squadron was gone. As Sanchez turned and made her way toward the hatch, Tabby began unhooking her own restraints, the clasps sounding loud as they clicked open and fell free. She pulled herself to her feet, and watched as Sanchez climbed out of *Max*, disappearing onto the ladder that led down to the hangar deck.

As was her custom after a long flight, Tabby lingered for a

moment, standing in the cockpit and letting her eyes roam the familiar interior of her assault boat. The controls, the displays, the worn padding of her seat—of all their seats... The assault boat felt like an extension of herself.

Despite her mental exhaustion and grief for those they'd lost, a small, wry smile tugged at the corners of her mouth. She felt an undeniable fondness for *Max*, the powerful little machine that had carried them through hell and beyond.

To most, *Max* was just a mechanical construct, an amalgamation of steel, composite, wires, cabling, and complex systems designed for one purpose: war. But to Tabby, he was something more. He had a personality—not in the artificial intelligence sense, but in the way she'd come to know and trust... his quirks, his capabilities, his limits. He wasn't just a tool.

Max was one of the crew.

She ran her hand over the edge of the console, the cool surface grounding her in the moment. The cockpit was quiet now, save for the faint creaks of the hull settling. It was a fragile peace, one she doubted would last. With a final glance around, she squared her shoulders, steeling herself for whatever came next.

"Thank you, *Max*," Tabby murmured, her voice quiet but sincere. She ran her hand one last time along the edge of the console before turning toward the hatch. Reaching out, she gripped the rim of her boat's outer hull, steadying herself as she began to climb out. But just as she pulled herself onto the ladder, she froze, her breath catching in her throat.

The sight before her was... impressive and shocking.

The hangar bay was massive—unbelievably so. It stretched out in every direction like a cathedral to machinery and flight. The ceiling loomed high above, at least a hundred meters overhead, with beams of light cutting through the faint haze of exhaust, ozone, and recycled air.

Rectangular in shape, the hangar extended almost farther

than her eyes could follow. From end to end, it had to be over a kilometer long, maybe even more. Tabby wasn't certain. Cradles and garages for a wide range of craft lined the towering walls from deck to ceiling. They were stacked in neat vertical rows that seemed to climb toward infinity, and almost all were full.

The deck was a maze of activity. Craft of every type and make were scattered across the expansive floor: sleek shuttles; angular fighters; dart-shaped interceptors; sturdy, predatory-looking assault boats like her own; torpedo bombers; and even lumbering automated haulers, big cargo transports, and delivery drones from Midway Station. There was even a couple of civilian passenger craft, complete with viewport windows.

The variety of craft in view was staggering.

Hundreds of deck crew bustled about. Shouts echoed through the cavernous space as people called out orders, coordinated movements, and signaled to one another for some purpose. The cacophony, from machines to engines to people's voices, was near deafening, yet it somehow carried a rhythm—a controlled madness born of necessity. It was the same or really an extension of the chaos she had witnessed during the desperate hours leading up to their departure, as *Surprise*, in a mad dash, had taken aboard hundreds of craft and countless tons of supplies.

Tabby's eyes scanned the hangar, searching instinctively for the familiar markings of her squadron—the 712th Nighthawks, the survivors. Her heart sank as she realized they were nowhere to be seen. For all she knew they could be in a separate bay. They'd all followed landing vectors, so she knew they were aboard, but the absence hit her like a physical blow, a painful reminder of just how much she had lost. She swallowed hard, forcing herself to focus on the scene before her.

The enormity of all she saw was difficult to process. It defied belief that this hangar was not a component of a fixed station but rather a part of a starship—a vessel so massive it dwarfed anything humanity had ever constructed before. *Surprise* was a marvel of engineering, her very existence speaking to ambition and necessity in equal measure, not to mention desperation for her race's survival.

A sudden blare of sirens pulled her from her thoughts, the sharp wail cutting through the noise of the hangar. Flashing lights bathed the bay in rhythmic bursts of amber, drawing her gaze upward. Above, a massive hatch slid aside, revealing a crane in motion. The crane was lowering an interceptor toward an open space that had been cleared on the deck. Several marines in yellow jackets stood around the space, keeping people and automated equipment safely back.

For a long moment, Tabby watched, amazed as the crane carefully lowered the sleek craft to the deck and set it down upon its landing gear. The fighter rocked lightly, shocks absorbing the impact and weight as the crane released and began to ascend again.

She shook herself free of the spectacle and looked down the ladder, which dropped to the deck, three meters below. Chen had been placed upon a stretcher. His helmet had been removed, and the right arm of his flight suit had been cut away. Two marines were hunched over him, working to set up an IV, while another waited. The sight of Chen's ashen face was enough to give her pause.

He was white as a sheet.

Sanchez, biting her lower lip, was standing just off to the side, watching the marines work. Her face carried a deeply worried expression. Letting go an unhappy breath, Tabby climbed down the ladder, dropping the last half-meter to the deck.

"All right," the marine medic said as he leaned back and stood. He was holding a bag of fluid up in the air. A tube ran from the bag to Chen's arm. "The IV's in place. Let's get moving."

The other two marines positioned themselves at either end of the litter and bent down, readying themselves.

"On three. One... two... three... *lift*," one of the marines said. The stretcher lifted, rocked for a moment, then steadied.

The medic turned to Tabby.

"He'll be brought to the trauma center at main medical. That's Deck Thirty-Six, Section Two. We will take good care of him, ma'am," Hillman said.

"See that you do," Tabby said.

"Yes, ma'am." The corpsman nodded. With that, they started off, rapidly moving through the confusing jungle of craft, and carrying Chen from view.

From down on the deck, the hangar felt like an immense labyrinth. The sheer number of craft packed so closely together was staggering, their hulls crowded with barely a meter or two separating them. They stood literally shoulder to shoulder. Every direction Tabby turned, her view was blocked by another vessel, the bulk of their frames towering overhead, *Max* included.

The closeness of the craft created a claustrophobic effect. Tabby couldn't see farther than a few meters in any direction before her line of sight was cut off and obstructed by another parked craft. The air was thick with the metallic tang of grease, propellant, and ozone, mingling with the faint but ever-present hum of idling and operating machinery.

"What now?" Sanchez asked, her voice cutting through the background din of the hangar. She glanced around, her expression a mix of confusion and frustration. "I've grown accustomed to ground crews greeting us on stations or ships, providing guidance. Where do we go, ma'am?"

Tabby followed Sanchez's gaze, scanning the chaotic scene around them. The absence of a ground crew didn't surprise her —not given the current state of things. Their final approach and subsequent landing had been a whirlwind of frantic orders, last-second adjustments, a barely controlled rush to bring everyone still in space aboard before the ship left the system and jumped out.

Since the enemy had attacked, chaos had been the only constant, and their landing had felt more like the culmination of a desperate sprint than a routine and ordered operation. She shrugged, her weariness dulling the sharp edges of her thoughts.

"Let's grab our go bags and find someone with authority, someone who can make decisions," Tabby said as she bent down and picked up Chen's discarded helmet. "I'm sure there's a place for us somewhere in this madness."

She turned back toward her assault boat, only to stop short. For a moment, she simply stared at *Max*, really looking for the first time since climbing out and down to the deck. The sleek and smooth lines of her beloved craft were pitted and heavily scarred, bearing the unmistakable signs of their ordeal. Scorch marks streaked much of the armored hull, blackened trails that crisscrossed the boat's surface like battle scars. And they were scars... there was no denying that.

Sanchez stepped up beside her, letting out a low whistle as she too surveyed the assault boat.

"Wow," Sanchez said, shaking her head. "There's a lot of damage here, more than I'd expected."

Tabby nodded slowly. "I've seen ground crews fix worse. Besides, *Max* is still flightworthy." She waved a hand at the craft. "That's mostly superficial."

"If you say so, ma'am," Sanchez replied more than a little skeptically. "You're the pilot."

Tabby opened her mouth to respond, but the words didn't come. She was suddenly too exhausted to muster the energy for a witty retort. Instead, she gave a small shrug and started forward, moving toward the cargo compartment beneath *Max*'s belly. Sanchez followed close behind, the two of them silent as they approached the rear of the craft.

The compartment hatch bore its own share of battle scars. The surface was heavily pitted, with a long, deep gouge running straight down the center. Tabby reached out, her fingers brushing the damaged armor. It had held, but the sight of it sent an involuntary chill down her spine. She vividly recalled the frantic flight through the edge of the debris field, the chaotic swirl of wreckage that had battered *Max*'s hull. The scratch might have been from that, or perhaps it was something worse—a near miss from an enemy point defense cannon, the remnant of a kinetic round that had made its way through the energy shields. The thought sent her stomach twisting, but she shoved the feeling aside.

Tabby keyed open the hatch, which slid aside with a smooth hiss. Inside the cargo compartment, their gear was neatly strapped down and stowed. Six bags in total—two for each of them. The go bags, the ones she was interested in, contained essentials: a spare uniform, personal items, toiletries, and the basics needed for short-term stops.

Tabby leaned in, placed Chen's helmet inside, then unfastened the nearest bag, marked with Sanchez's name, and handed it over. Without a word, Sanchez slipped the straps over her shoulders. Tabby followed suit, retrieving her own go bag and settling it across her back before keying the cargo hatch closed. The mechanism engaged with a faint click, sealing their remaining gear inside *Max* for later retrieval.

The go bags were meant for brief stays, just enough to keep them comfortable until they could return to the ship. But as Tabby glanced around the bustling hangar, she knew this wouldn't be a short stop. They weren't just passing through. She could feel it in her gut—they'd be here for the duration. For better or worse, *Surprise* was now their home.

"Once we're assigned quarters, we can come back for the rest later," Tabby said.

Sanchez gave a brief nod, her face unreadable as she

adjusted the straps on her shoulders to make the load more comfortable.

"Let's go find someone who knows what the hell is going on," Tabby said, her tone tinged with determination. "Then we'll connect with the rest of the squadron." Silently, she added, *What's left of it.*

With that, Tabby set off in the direction the marines had taken Chen, weaving her way through the dense forest of craft and the throngs of crew bustling about the hangar. Sanchez followed close behind, the two of them navigating the narrow gaps between parked ships and supply carts. The air was thick with noise—shouting voices, the clang of tools on metal, the rumble of engines—but Tabby tuned it out, her focus fixed on the path ahead and finding someone who could make decisions for her and her squadron.

THREE

STROUD

Stroud stood with his hands firmly planted on his hips, his posture rigid as he stared through the isolation glass into the cell. The glass composite, a relic of old-school design, was one-way—opaque from the prisoner's side but crystal clear from his. Despite the array of modern surveillance systems at their disposal, which they were actively using—from cameras to sensor tech that could track even the subtlest shifts in body temperature—the glass offered a certain visceral satisfaction. It allowed him to observe unfiltered, a silent and unseen witness to the man pacing inside. More than that, it gave him an instinctive read, a personal and up-close sense of the man's mood and intent in a way that a monitor or video feed could not.

The prisoner was one of the six survivors they had taken alive after the failed boarding attempt to seize *Surprise*. The rest of the enemy had fought with a ferocity that left no room for negotiation, let alone surrender, clearly preferring death to capture. Even when cornered and offered the chance to lay down their arms, they had fought to the bitter end or died by suicide rather than give up.

Stroud's lips pressed into a thin line, his expression and feelings grim as he took in the man's agitated movements. Beside him, Sergeant Major Burns mirrored his mood, the senior NCO's face set in a deep frown, his arms crossed tightly over his broad chest.

Inside the cell, the prisoner paced with restless energy, his steps quick and erratic. His mouth moved constantly, forming words that were lost to the soundproof walls. His gestures were wild, his hands slicing through the air as if emphasizing points in an argument only he could hear. The man's face was gaunt, his cheeks hollowed, and his eyes darted about, never settling for long. Even through the glass and silence, his agitation was plain.

Burns reached out and tapped a control on the console beside them, activating the speaker. The soft hum of the system engaging was followed by a burst of sound as the prisoner's raspy voice filled the observation room.

"Misguided... you are all misguided," the man croaked, his voice hoarse, the edges of his words frayed as if he'd been speaking—or shouting—for hours. "Terribly, horribly misguided. You have eyes but you see not the light. You see not the blue, the true blue, the beautiful light of truth. Open your eyes before it is too late!"

Stroud's brow furrowed as he listened, his mind turning over the cryptic words. The prisoner's tone carried a strange intensity, almost fevered, and his old-fashioned phrasing added an unsettling edge to his rant. He seemed utterly consumed by whatever doctrine or belief drove him, his conviction radiating through every syllable despite his obvious physical exhaustion.

"How long has he been going on like that?" Stroud asked, glancing over at Burns.

Burns leaned slightly closer to the glass, his eyes narrowing. "Since we brought him in," he muttered. "Doesn't seem like he's slowing down anytime soon either."

Stroud sucked in a deep breath and let it out slowly, his eyes narrowing as he studied the prisoner more closely. The young man pacing the confines of the cell couldn't have been older than eighteen, maybe twenty at most, his short-cropped brown hair lending him the appearance of a fresh recruit. Muscular and fit, he had the build of a soldier, someone accustomed to rigorous training and discipline.

If not for the circumstances, Stroud might have mistaken him for one of his own marines. Yet the words spilling from his mouth were unlike anything Stroud had ever heard from his men—disjointed, fanatical, and laden with cryptic fervor.

The orange jumpsuit hung loosely on the prisoner, though the right pant leg had been cut short, exposing the heavy bandages wrapped around his thigh. A second bandage covered his temple, just above his right eye, where dried blood had seeped through the edges of the dressing. Despite his injuries, the man paced the cell like a caged animal, his motions jittery and erratic, almost as if he were on drugs or coming down off a high of some kind.

The cell itself was sparse—barely more than a steel box. A narrow bunk was bolted to one wall, its thin mattress offering little in the way of comfort. A toilet and a compact shower occupied the opposite corner, their presence practical but sterile. No personal touches, no amenities, there was nothing to humanize the space. It was a place designed for confinement and nothing else.

"You have been led astray," the prisoner called out, his voice rising as he stared up at the ceiling before turning toward the glass. His bloodshot eyes seemed to search for something beyond the walls of his cage. "I know you can hear me. I know it! Why hide like cowards? Come and face me!"

"He hasn't stopped since he woke up from surgery and got thrown in there," Burns said sourly.

Stroud turned his attention back to the prisoner, who was now gripping the edge of the bunk with white-knuckled intensity, his body trembling with emotion. "You are ruled by false prophets," the young man continued, his raspy voice cracking under the strain. "Evil men and women, and you don't even know it. They have led you astray."

Stroud's expression darkened. The conviction in the prisoner's words was unsettling, not just because of their content but because of the raw intensity behind them. Whatever ideology the young man followed, it clearly consumed him. He wasn't just a soldier—he was a zealot of some kind.

"Honestly, he's kind of repetitive," Burns said. "Could be the meds the doc gave him."

"Maybe," Stroud responded. "Are the other prisoners the same way?"

"No," Burns replied. "They're in rough shape and currently secured in medical. They're not saying much of anything, at least not yet. Doctor Neelan has them fully sedated. Their injuries are more severe, bordering on fatal."

"I see," Stroud said, his tone contemplative as he glanced at his sergeant major. "They're under guard?"

"A heavy guard, sir," Burns confirmed. "We're not taking any chances with them. Neelan and his people performed thorough scans on each, and it turns out they've got some interesting implants embedded in their heads and throughout their bodies. A few of them have a more intensive set of implants, perhaps a specialist upgrade for leaders of some kind... officers. We're not sure yet."

"What kind of implants?" Stroud asked, his curiosity piqued. He turned fully toward Burns. "Do we know what they do?"

Burns shifted his weight slightly, his expression grim. "They're not like anything in the databases," he said, his voice lowering as though the information carried a certain gravity. "Neelan's not sure what they do, but they're bio-powered— much like our own tech— different... clearly alien in their design."

"Alien?"

"The doctor has suggested the implants are more advanced than Confederation tech. His initial impression is that humans did not make them. But more study will be required. He made that plain."

Stroud's jaw tightened as the implications sank in. Bio-powered implants were standard among their own forces, but the idea that their enemies had access to potentially superior technology was troubling. He glanced back toward the cell, watching the prisoner move with that strange, agitated energy as he paced about.

"Neelan's running deeper scans," Steele added. "He thinks some of the implants might be inactive, but we can't be sure. Until we know more, the med bay, 15-A, where we're keeping the prisoners, is locked down tighter than a bank's safety deposit vault. And to be certain, I've even posted men with powered armor nearby... just in case."

Stroud turned his gaze back to the prisoner, his expression hardening as he studied him pacing in the cell. He watched for a long moment, his thoughts a maelstrom.

"A day ago," Stroud began quietly, his voice barely audible, "if you'd told me our enemy was human... and that they spoke perfect English..."

"Hydrogen breathers they are not," Burns added, his tone dry but laced with bitterness.

Stroud frowned, his mind brimming with questions that seemed to multiply with each passing second. How had Fleet, with all its vast resources and intelligence services, failed to uncover the true face of their enemy? Or worse, had they known all along and concealed the information? That smacked of betrayal.

"I think they knew," Burns said, as though plucking the thought directly from Stroud's mind. His voice was low, steady, and edged with suspicion. "Someone did. And they said nothing. That's my guess, my gut feeling. They hid this."

Stroud shook his head slightly, his gaze never leaving the prisoner. "I'm not so certain about that," he said, his words carefully measured. The young man continued his agitated pacing, his limp becoming more pronounced. He was clearly tiring. The pain and discomfort of his wound was beginning to show.

"The Conclave is the real truth, the only truth," the prisoner suddenly yelled, his voice cracking with raw emotion. He turned toward the ceiling as if addressing some unseen entity. "You're all blind to the light! If you had only made the pilgrimage... if you had only seen what I saw... the blue... that perfect blue... I beg you... listen to me!"

Stroud folded his arms, letting out a long breath as he gestured toward the cell with a slow wave of his hand. "I think this might be something new," he said after a moment. "A conquered people's children, human slaves, maybe... the brainwashed, more likely..."

"And if it's not? What then?" Burns asked, his tone blunt and unyielding. He glanced at Stroud, his jaw set. "What if Fleet did know the truth and chose to say nothing, or worse, they lied?"

Stroud exhaled sharply. It sounded explosive in the small observation room. "I don't even want to contemplate that," he admitted, his voice tight. "Not for one moment. For now, until we know more, we give Fleet the benefit of the doubt, understand me? I don't need unfounded rumors spreading about the ship. If you hear them, you quash them posthaste."

"I understand," Burns said, "but rumors have a tendency to spread all on their own and grow in the telling, no matter how much one tries to stamp them out."

Inside the cell, the prisoner's pacing paused for a brief instant before he thrust a hand toward the glass, finger seemingly pointed at them, his face twisted in fervent desperation.

"Listen to me... the Conclave is the only truth, the right of things, the only path to tread," he shouted, his hoarse voice echoing faintly through the speakers. "Open your eyes! Welcome the Conclave and the Union! Do it, before it is too late... before the tide comes in... and all are washed away."

The intensity in the prisoner's words sent a chill down Stroud's spine. Was the tide the Push? The young man's conviction was unsettling, his fanaticism radiating through every word. Stroud exchanged a glance with Burns. Whatever this Conclave was, it wasn't just an enemy force—it was something far more insidious, something they did not yet understand.

"Are we recording this?" Stroud asked, his eyes still fixed on the prisoner, who had resumed his frantic pacing, muttering half-coherent phrases under his breath.

"We are, sir," Burns confirmed with a curt nod. "Every bloody and crazed word he utters."

"Good," Stroud said, his tone firm. "I want the intelligence company to analyze everything he's saying. Even if most of it sounds like gibberish, there might be something buried in there worth knowing." He paused, his gaze sharpening. "Also, make sure they have the scans Neelan performed, the ones detailing the implants. When things calm down, we're going to need medical to take a closer look at those and see what we can learn from them. After the fight for the ship, we should have... what, several hundred bodies?"

"At least, yes, sir," Burns said, his voice steady. "That should be plenty to work with. Oh... we took aboard additional assets that might be useful. There's an interrogation unit, a platoon with the 164th Battalion. I'd recommend bringing them in on this. They're experts, sir—they'll get answers, even out of a madman like him."

Stroud glanced at Burns, considering the suggestion. The prisoner's erratic behavior and fevered ravings weren't likely to yield much under traditional questioning, but a dedicated interrogation unit was a different story. They had the tools, the training, the patience, and the experience to extract information, from even the most hardened subjects.

"That sounds reasonable," Stroud said after a moment. "Make it happen."

"Aye, sir," Burns replied crisply.

Stroud turned back to the prisoner, watching as the young man raised his hands toward the ceiling, his voice rising again in a hoarse crescendo. "The Union will bring the light! The Conclave is the way! You will all see—when the sky turns blue as can be, you'll see all that's holy!"

"Did you find anything useful on his person?" Stroud asked. "Or on any of the others?"

"Yes, sir," Burns replied, stepping forward. He motioned to a metal table positioned to the left of the viewing port. A small tray rested upon it. Burns picked up the tray and carried it back to Stroud, offering it with a steady hand.

Stroud took the tray and looked down at the contents. The first item to catch his attention was a small holographic photo that had been thumbed off. He picked it up carefully, activating the still frame with a soft tap. A three-dimensional image sprang to life, displaying a woman and a young child, perhaps two or three years old. The woman was close to the prisoner's age. They stood together on a sunlit beach, their smiles directed toward the camera, the child's small hand clutching the woman's dress. The scene was simple, intimate, and strangely disarming.

He studied the image for a long moment. The beach, the warmth of the sunlight—it could have easily been a scene from any number of Confederation worlds.

"Interesting," he murmured, his brow furrowing slightly.

"I thought so too," Burns said. "Each of the prisoners and dead we've searched so far has had at least one photo on their person. They all share a common theme."

"Family?" Stroud asked, glancing up.

"Yes, sir," Burns confirmed, his tone grave. "Something to fight for."

Stroud nodded thoughtfully, setting the holographic photo back onto the tray. His fingers moved to the next item—a silver necklace with a circular pendant. Picking it up, he turned the pendant over in his hand, studying its design. The pendant displayed a large blue circle with three smaller silver circles branching outward, connected at equal intervals. The pattern was strange, unfamiliar.

"All of the enemy we've searched have had that necklace," Burns said. "We're not sure what it represents. Neelan had a few thoroughly scanned, the science team too, but they couldn't find any digital imprints or hidden functions, such as an external implant or communication device separate from the standard kit the enemy had on their persons. It could be some type of dog tag, though I'm not sold on that. No, these two items are personal, as is that string bracelet." Burns pointed at the last item on the tray. "The rest is standard-issue gear, the kind of things we hand out to our boys and girls. We've secured those and are analyzing them."

"The Conclave is the only truth," the prisoner rasped, interrupting their conversation. His hoarse voice rang out as he raised his gaze toward the ceiling again. "You are all so blind... so blind."

Stroud's eyes shifted from the pendant to the prisoner, watching the young man for a long moment. His pacing had slowed, but his fervor had not. The way he spoke, the conviction in his tone—it all hinted at something deeper, more sinister. Stroud turned the pendant over in his hand once more, considering Burns's earlier words.

"It's a religious symbol."

"With how he's been going on, that's certainly a possibility, sir, a strong one I think," Burns admitted, though his expression remained skeptical. "But at this point, we just don't know for certain. The enemy is still a mystery. For all we know, the Union could be their nation and the Conclave the ruling body, a theocracy of some sort."

"That might be it," Stroud said. "But..."

"But we just don't know," Burns finished.

Stroud set the necklace back on the tray before handing it back to Burns. The sergeant major returned it to the table as the colonel shifted his attention back to the prisoner. Though interrogation would be necessary to confirm his theory, Stroud was certain the necklace was more than just a keepsake or identification tag. It carried real significance—whether that was religious, ideological, or both. The colonel shook his head slightly, a faint sense of unease creeping into his thoughts. Whatever the pendent represented, it was tied to something much larger than the prisoner himself.

"How's everyone getting settled?" Stroud asked, turning away from the prisoner.

"It was a bitch of a process. Still is, though we're beginning to make headway," Burns replied, his voice tinged with the weariness of someone deeply entrenched in the effort. "We picked up more than seven thousand marines from Midway. Getting them all squared away and settled is taking time. Some were on leave, others in the middle of a transfer... all now thrown together, all from different commands. About eighty percent of them arrived without arms or equipment, just the clothes on their backs. It's going to take some real organization to reform them all into combat-capable units."

"Yeah," Stroud muttered, exhaling heavily. "We're to be a cobbled-together force, all now part of what Fleet labeled the 3rd Special Missions Group."

"And you, sir," Burns said with a grin, rocking slightly on the balls of his feet as if the news amused him, "are now a full bird colonel and in command of said Special Missions Group's marine contingent. I'm right proud of you, sir. Once more, you have exceeded my humble expectations and failed upward."

Stroud let out a low grunt, the sound carrying a mix of amusement and resignation. His promotion had been a battle-field brevet, handed down before *Surprise* had left the system. There hadn't been time to argue, even if he'd wanted to, which he didn't. This was a challenge, and Stroud enjoyed such tests.

"Funny how there were senior officers—colonels and even generals—aboard Midway Station, but they stayed put," Burns remarked, his grin fading as his expression grew serious once more. "I have a feeling they were ordered to remain behind. Care to comment on what you know about that, sir?"

"Stationside officers," Stroud responded evenly, "mostly in supply or support roles. I was told they weren't suited for a combat command, so there was no need to have them aboard *Surprise*, where they might try to interfere or pull rank... complicate matters."

"And who told you that, sir?" Burns asked, his eyes narrowing slightly. His tone had taken on a harder edge.

"Admiral Yenga," Stroud said simply.

"My opinion of the admiral just increased a tad." Burns tilted his head slightly, his gaze sharpening. "And what else did the good admiral have to say? Inquiring minds wish to know, sir."

Stroud regarded Burns silently for a long moment. He trusted the man implicitly. Burns was as solid as they came. Stroud considered telling him more about the conversation and the secret brief that had accompanied it. But after a moment's internal debate, he settled for sharing only a fragment of what he'd learned and now held close to his chest. "I was told our captain... commodore now, is one tough son of a bitch."

"I already knew that, sir," Burns said. "I saw the grit in the man's eyes on the bridge after the fight. I also made a point of reviewing the security footage... watched the commodore in action when the enemy blasted their way through the hatch. I saw everything I needed to in the moments that followed. He is a man worth his weight in salt."

Stroud gave a small nod, his thoughts briefly drifting back to the footage he too had reviewed. Garrett's actions had been decisive, instinctive, almost surgical in their execution. The man had fought like a seasoned veteran and without hesitation, but there was more to him than just combat prowess. Yenga had shared insights about Garrett that Stroud wasn't ready to voice—not yet. Bottom line... the Confederation needed the man, and Stroud would give everything to support him.

"Commodore Garrett is cool under fire," Burns continued. "Cold-blooded, even. That gives me a warm and fuzzy feeling, sir."

"Me too," Stroud admitted, though he quickly decided it was time to steer the conversation in another direction. "Any problems getting people settled?"

"The marines or the civilians?" Burns asked, his brow lifting slightly.

"Both," Stroud said.

"There are always problems, sir, but we're managing," Burns said plainly. "When it comes to our own, we'll need to order everyone, the marines of course, into scratch battalions—I'm thinking maybe six in total. Trouble is, we didn't bring aboard nearly enough lieutenant colonels or majors to put a bow on everything. But we've got plenty of NCOs to help keep people in line, at least for the time being."

Stroud nodded.

"I haven't had time to scan the service records of those who came aboard yet," Burns continued, "so I don't know which officers have combat experience, what their specializations are, or whether they're worth a damn in a fight or capable of effectively leading others." The sergeant major paused and glanced down at the deck before looking back up. "Some of what Fleet sent us feels… haphazard."

"There was no time for a more organized effort," Stroud said. "The station was already being stormed, with the enemy moving from deck to deck and component to component. We got many of those who were not yet engaged in fighting. But, bottom line, they're all marines and they all get the same basic training."

"That, they are, sir. We can work with that."

"Sergeant Major, I know we can."

With nearly enough personnel to form a division, the task ahead was a monumental one—something that would normally fall on a general's shoulders. The thought of what was expected of him was daunting. But, Stroud knew he could handle it. He just needed time to get that job done. He only had one real question. Would he have that time before *Surprise* went into battle again? That was an answer he did not have.

"Send me the service records on all senior officers who came aboard, those ranked captain and above," Stroud said firmly. "I'll start reviewing them immediately. Then you and I will sit down and plan how to organize these *scratch* battalions. I was given latitude to promote those I think capable and that includes NCOs to officers, so check those records too… look for anyone of quality."

"The files on the officers will be in your inbox within the hour," Burns assured him. He hesitated, his expression growing more serious. "There's also the shipboard contingents to consider, those of the task force now attached to *Surprise*. Technically, sir, you're the senior marine present and on station, which means they'll report to their ship captains first *and* then to you. Our responsibility will include training, supply and equipment requisitions, limited disciplinary matters too, and the doling out of replacements. On the bright side, we might find some capable officers among them, ones we can use to lead the new battalions or perhaps support them in an executive role. That might create certain complications... but make no mistake —a lot of this is going to fall on your plate, sir."

Stroud's mouth tightened into a grim line as he processed the information. His responsibilities were growing at a pace far beyond anything he had anticipated. What was once manageable was rapidly expanding into a sprawling command that required immediate structure and decisive action. He also got the warning lingering in Burn's words. If he poached any of those officers, the ship captains would not be happy. But there would be no helping that. Stroud needed to organize his expanded command and quickly. If that meant stepping on some toes, so be it.

"I understand," Stroud said after a long moment.

"Good that you do, sir," Burns replied with a faint smirk. "Because as your headaches grow, so do mine. And I don't much like headaches."

Stroud's lips twitched into a grin. "They will grow, won't they, your problems that is? Why Sergeant Major, I can't tell you how much that pleases me. I'm not in this alone. I am so thrilled you're here to help me carry this burden."

Burns let out a dry chuckle and flashed a grin at Stroud. "Glad to be of service, sir. It is my absolute pleasure to be here at your side, helping to shoulder your responsibilities."

"I'm sure it is," Stroud said dryly. "I have no doubt it brings you endless delight."

Burns gave a faint smirk. "You've got no idea, sir." He paused, glancing down at the deck before looking back up. "Oh, one more thing. We've had several thousand civilians volunteer to help."

"Volunteers?" Stroud raised an eyebrow. "Really?"

Burns nodded. "That's right. Before we left Midway, Commodore Garrett put out a call and asked if any of the evacuees wanted to step up and lend a hand... well, if they were interested, to make themselves known. Turns out, quite a few of them do want to help. Commander Shaw sent me a list. Truth is, most are scared, angry... and some of them want to feel like they're doing something other than just sitting around and cooling their heels."

Interest piqued, Stroud leaned forward slightly. "Go on. Share your thoughts. How can we put them to use?"

"I was thinking," Burns continued, "after our... *thrilling* departure from Midway, what with being boarded and taking enemy fire... well it might not be the worst idea to have extra hands employed in damage control, medical support, or simply carrying stretchers. Odds are, we're going to be in another fight soon enough... maybe sooner than any of us want or expect."

Stroud considered that. "That's going to require training... supervision... coordination."

"I know," Burns admitted. "But it could make a material difference—and, honestly, they *want* to help. I've personally spoken with a few. Some of them need it... something to do, anything really. For many of those we took aboard, Midway was their home. They'd lived there their entire lives. It's gone now, and they've lost friends, loved ones... everything they knew."

Stroud gave a thoughtful nod. "All right. I like it. The idea has merit. Let me discuss it with Major Ramirez and get his thoughts on the matter. Then we'll run it up the flagpole to the Commodore."

"The true faith is coming for you!" the prisoner bellowed, his voice raspy and overused, but still fanatically insistent. He banged his fist against the reinforced glass, the sound echoing sharply in the observation room and drawing their attention. "There is no stopping it! No putting it off! After centuries of war, surely you can see that. We are coming! The truth is coming for you all!"

Stroud regarded the man with a look of disdain. His fervor was unsettling, but it wasn't the first time he'd faced zealots.

"I think you might be right, sir," Burns said, shaking his head. "This is a religion. I've always disliked religious fanatics. They just rub my ass the wrong way, like bad toilet paper on hemorrhoids." He paused, his tone softening slightly. "Don't get me wrong, sir. I'm as religious as the next man and believe in god sure enough. I have my own personal savior, but this"—he waved a hand toward the prisoner, his expression hardening—"this is extremism, the kind I've seen on some of the trouble worlds. You know of the ones I'm speaking of, Constantinople, Meridon, Jedda, worlds that had to be pacified so we could all focus on the Push."

Stroud gave a sharp nod, his expression grim. "I do. Let's get this bastard interrogated properly," he said, his voice growing cold. "Wring him out like an old sponge. I want everything he knows about the enemy— and I mean *everything*. Even the inconsequential details"—he gestured toward the table holding the tray of personal items—"like where that picture was taken, who's in it, the significance of the necklace. I want it all."

"Aye, aye, sir," Burns said, straightening his posture. "I'll see it done, and soon."

"Good." Stroud spared one last look at the prisoner, then turned on his heel and left the brig, his mind already on reviewing the records of those officers freshly come aboard. He had a shipboard marine expeditionary unit to form and organize, a volunteer Corps to recruit, and that was just the start of all he had on his plate.

FOUR

GARRETT

Several hours had passed since Garrett had left the bridge. He sat alone in his office. The digital clock on his built-in desk console ticked silently onward. The tablet Admiral Gray had sent him lay next to it.

Garrett leaned back slightly in his chair, his fingers tracing the edge of the desk as he let out a quiet breath. Exhaustion had clawed at him earlier, the relentless haze of sleeplessness threatening to dull his focus. Reluctantly, he'd fought back with yet another stim. He knew he'd pay for it later—the crash would hit him like a jackhammer—but right now, he couldn't afford to let fatigue slow down his thinking. The stim had done its job, cutting through the fog in his mind and leaving him sharp, alert, and unnervingly clear-headed.

The feeling was almost eerie, as if his body's natural rhythms had been temporarily hijacked. The burn behind his eyes was gone, his muscles no longer ached, and his mind raced at breakneck speed. He'd devoured the orders he'd been given, pored over every line and phrase, dissecting the implications of Yenga's directives, not to mention the information Gray had sent him.

To say he was floored by what he'd learned felt like the understatement of the century. And now, he couldn't shake the feeling he was standing on the precipice of something far larger than himself.

How to proceed?

That was the question he kept circling back to, the knot he couldn't untangle. Yenga had left that part entirely up to him, handing over the reins without a roadmap or clear instructions, just an objective, one he must overcome and defeat... 66-Lima... Indigo.

Command was never meant to be easy, but this—this was something else entirely. It wasn't just the responsibility of leadership; it was the burden of knowledge, the weight of truths he couldn't unlearn.

Garrett let out a slow breath, his fingers steepling as he rested his elbows on the desk. He'd never imagined that command would come with such a heavy load, a price that seemed destined to cost him everything in the end. But here he was, and there was no turning back. Even if he could, Garrett wouldn't.

The office around him felt smaller than it should have, the usual sense of comfort replaced by a quiet tension, a realization of what was ultimately to come. The walls seemed to close in, their presence a reminder of his isolation, the loneliness of command. The hum of the ship's systems vibrated faintly through the floor, the hiss of air circulation, a subtle background constant to his thoughts.

"Shit," Garrett muttered under his breath, rubbing his jaw as he leaned back in his chair. His fingers brushed over the coarse stubble on his chin, a reminder of how long it had been since his last shave.

The soft chime of an incoming comm call broke the stillness a heartbeat later, the tone distinct and unmistakable—it was from the bridge, but it was not an alert, signifying an emergency that required his personal and immediate attention. Garrett straightened, shaking off his thoughts. With a subtle mental nudge of his implants, he accepted the call.

"What is it?" Garrett asked, his tone sharper than he intended, an edge of irritation creeping into his voice at the unwanted interruption.

"Sorry to bother you, sir," came Keeli's response from the other end. "Captain Norwood from the *Palestro* is calling."

"Again?" Garrett asked, his voice tightening. "I told him, I would get back to him."

"Yes, sir. He says he's written you several notes and that you have yet to respond to any of them."

Garrett let out a slow, exasperated breath. This was the second time Norwood had attempted to comm since Garrett had left the bridge, each time insisting they speak immediately concerning seniority, as though the world depended on it.

Couldn't the man wait a few hours?

Garrett had already turned away two close friends with history: Tina and Jason. Both were captains of their own starships and had been attached to his command, his task force. He needed space to think and devise a general plan. Gray's information, along with Yenga's orders, loomed large in his mind, demanding careful consideration and deliberation before he took his next steps... before he issued orders, and everyone began moving in one direction.

"I'm sorry, sir," Keeli repeated, her tone apologetic. "He's quite insistent."

"Is it an emergency?" Garrett asked, his irritation deepening. "Is there something wrong with his ship?"

"Ah... no, sir," Keeli replied after a slight pause. "I asked. He said everything was fine in that respect."

"Then tell him he must wait," Garrett said firmly. He didn't need to check his mailbox to know that a long list of people wanted his attention. "I will get to him soon enough."

Keeli hesitated. "But, sir, he says he insists and will not take no for an answer, not this time."

Garrett pinched the bridge of his nose, letting out another heavy breath. "As commodore of this task force, I am telling him no," he said, his tone steely. "If this is not an emergency concerning the safety of his ship, he, like everyone else, can wait." Garrett suddenly realized he was being unkind to Keeli as she was taking the brunt of his frustration and likely Norwood's too. This was not her fault. She was just in the middle. He softened his tone. "Kindly inform him that this is a direct order from me. I will get back to him as soon as I am free. Is that understood?"

"Yes, sir," Keeli said, though the reluctance in her voice was evident. At the same time, she sounded relieved. "I will pass along your orders, sir."

"Thank you." Before she could say more, Garrett terminated the call. The silence that followed felt heavier than before. Had Shaw been here and not in medical recovering from a wound, he would have kept Norwood at bay until Garrett was ready for him along with the rest of the captains of the task force.

Deep down, Garrett knew he should have taken the captain of the *Palestro*'s call. He should have spent the twenty minutes that would be needed to placate the man's ego and address whatever concern he had when it came to seniority among the other captains of the task force.

But he couldn't bring himself to do it—not yet. His thoughts were too tangled, the decisions before him too monumental. Every moment was needed to process what Gray and Yenga had handed him, to sort through the implications and decide how best to proceed.

Garrett exhaled heavily and unhappily. With his implants, he opened a comm channel back to the bridge, audio only.

"Sir?" Keeli asked.

"Have you responded to Captain Norwood yet?"

"I was in the process of doing that," Keeli said, sounding relieved at the interruption.

"Put him through to my personal console," Garrett said. "I will handle it."

"Yes, sir." Keeli seemed genuinely relieved. "Thank you, sir."

Garrett cut the channel, and a moment later, Norwood's image flared to life on the display. Just the sight of the man's haughty look, his perfectly groomed hair, and immaculate uniform was enough to irritate Garrett; also how he stared down his nose at others he thought inferior, which he was doing.

"Ah, Captain," Norwood began, "thank you for taking my call. I would like to talk with you about—"

"It is 'Commodore'," Garrett said, cutting the man off.

"If you say so," Norwood said.

Garrett raised an eyebrow at that, his irritation rising to new levels. "Captain, Fleet says so. I am the commodore. There is none other. I understand you are interested in talking about seniority."

"That is correct. I do wish to speak with you on that matter," Norwood said. "It is fairly important, and I think we should consider a change in—"

"Captain," Garrett said, raising a hand, "I am very busy at the moment. There is a tremendous amount I need to handle. I will deal with that matter soon enough."

"I don't believe this can wait," Norwood said plainly.

"Captain, it can and will wait," Garrett said firmly. "More importantly, you will hold off until I am ready to address the matter. Kindly stop badgering my personnel. Soon enough, I will call a meeting of the other captains. At that point, we can discuss seniority and get everything sorted properly. Is that understood?"

Norwood's jaw flexed. He gave a curt nod. "We will discuss it before the other captains, then?"

"Excellent that we understand one another. Garrett out." He terminated the call. Norwood's image vanished. It felt good to cut the conversation short, to put the pompous ass in his place. But at the same time, Garrett knew he was making a mistake. He should have been more diplomatic, because ultimately, he needed all of his captains to pull in the same direction and not against him. Later, he would have to smooth things over.

Garrett let out an unhappy breath, his chest rising and falling as he exhaled slowly. Something about Norwood had always rubbed him the wrong way, and he supposed it always would.

His gaze drifted back to his official orders from Fleet, displayed on the console before him. He'd gone through them several times with a fine-toothed comb. The words seemed to taunt him, their implications heavier with each reread.

How do they know Indigo is the place to strike?

The question gnawed at him. *How could Fleet be so certain that an attack there would make a material difference in the war?*

Garrett frowned, his thoughts racing. *Are they just guessing?* The possibility unsettled him. *Or is this some desperate gambit to finally deal a significant blow to the enemy, using* Surprise *as their... Yenga's weapon of opportunity?*

He clenched his fists briefly, his knuckles brushing against the cool surface of the desk. The lack of clarity infuriated him, but more than that, it filled him with doubt.

It was what that implied about the war, about their enemies, and about the lengths Fleet was willing to go to score a significant win. Garrett shook his head, his frustration mounting. His eyes shifted to Gray's tablet, the compact device sitting silently on the desk. What she had sent him was perhaps even more important, critical even to the future of the war and how going forward it would be waged.

His gaze returned to the console, to the blunt finality of the orders from Fleet. Taking a partially completed starship to Indigo, with a scratch crew cobbled together in desperation...

How could anyone think that wasn't suicide?

If Fleet's intelligence was correct, the potential reward was monumental, a decisive blow that could finally shift the war in their favor. But if they were wrong... Garrett didn't want to finish the thought. The consequences were too dire, too catastrophic to entertain. *Would a strike there end the war, or would it make it worse?*

The buzz of the hatch startled Garrett, snapping him out of his thoughts. He jumped slightly, his heart skipping a beat as his irritation flared. For a moment, he simply stared at the hatch, his teeth clenching. The interruption wasn't just unwelcome—it was intrusive, shattering the fragile bubble of concentration he had managed to build. After a long, exasperated breath, he forced himself to respond as the buzzer sounded again.

"Come."

The hatch slid open with a soft hiss, and Garrett blinked, his irritation giving way to surprise as the figure on the other side stepped into view.

"Am I disturbing you, sir?"

"Shaw!"

"In person." Lieutenant Commander Shaw's shoulder was heavily bandaged, the white dressing peeking out from beneath his uniform at the collar. His arm was secured in a sling, and his usually composed expression was tinged with the pallor of someone still recovering from a significant injury. Yet, despite his obvious discomfort, there was a determined set to his jaw. The hatch closed, leaving the two men alone.

"What are you doing out of sick bay?" Garrett asked. "I was

told you'd be there another day or two before moving to your quarters. I had planned, when time allowed, to come visit."

Shaw shook his head, his posture stiff. "I couldn't just sit there and do nothing, sir. Not when there's a mountain of work piling up. Everyone's running themselves ragged, and there I was, stuck in sick bay, being useless—hell, worse than useless—taking up a bed someone else could use."

"You were shot," Garrett reminded him, his tone carrying both concern and a hint of admiration. He knew Shaw was tough but seeing him like this—pushing through the pain and exhaustion to return to duty—spoke to the man's character. "That's not something you walk or shrug off."

"I forced Neelan to discharge me," Shaw admitted, a faint grimace crossing his face as he shifted his stance. "He wasn't happy about it—put up quite the fight, actually—but I wasn't taking no for an answer. Told him I'd walk out on my own when he and his staff weren't looking if he didn't let me go."

"I see," Garrett said after a moment, gesturing toward one of the chairs opposite his desk. "Please, sit. Make yourself comfortable."

"Thank you, sir." Shaw moved to the chair. He pulled it back with his good arm, the motion slow and deliberate, and, back held rigid, carefully lowered himself into the seat. His face tightened with pain as he settled, a small grunt escaping, despite a clear effort to mask it. Once seated, he leaned back slowly as he found a position that wouldn't aggravate his injury.

"You look like you haven't gotten any sleep, sir," Shaw said after he'd settled in.

"And you look like you've been shot," Garrett countered, allowing a faint smirk to tug at the corners of his mouth. It was good to see Shaw up and about. "How are you feeling?"

"I won't lie—even with the meds, it hurts," Shaw admitted. "I requested basic pain pills. No narcotics or anything that could mess with my thinking." He sucked in a breath, the effort causing a flicker of discomfort to cross his face. "I want to go back to work, to take my mind off this shoulder and make myself useful. I can carry some of the burden, sir, lighten your load."

Garrett leaned back in his chair, eyeing Shaw critically. It looked like it was taking all his effort to simply sit still in the chair. "You should be in your cabin or in sick bay, resting and recovering, not on the bridge," he said as he gestured to the sling. "Work can wait."

"I don't think so, sir," Shaw replied, his voice firm. "You need me. Heller and the other junior officers won't cut it. I think we both know that."

"I can manage till you are sufficiently recovered," Garrett said, though deep down he knew how much he needed the help, someone he could not only rely upon but who knew the ship and her capabilities. Shaw fit that bill.

"I know that, sir, but you look like shit," Shaw said plainly. "How long has it been since you slept?"

"Too long," Garrett admitted, rubbing a hand over his face. "I've stimmed twice now... so that's what, more than a day?"

"You're going to regret that," Shaw said, his expression grim.

"Don't I know it," Garrett muttered.

"And it's likely been longer since you got some shut-eye." Shaw's gaze shifted to the secure bag on the desk, his brow furrowing slightly. "I understand you've been holed up in here since we jumped away from Midway," he said. "I've even gotten several calls about it. People are starting to worry."

Garrett resisted the urge to scowl. He had spent too long locked away in his office. That much was clear now. His eyes flicked to the secure bag on the desk, its presence a reminder of the burden he carried.

"Are you okay?" Shaw asked, his voice tinged with genuine concern. Having worked closely with Garrett for months, their relationship had grown into a solid friendship. "You can confide in me."

"I'm fine," Garrett said curtly, though he could tell Shaw didn't believe him.

"Norwood doesn't think so," Shaw said, his tone careful but pointed.

Garrett looked up sharply, irritation rising within. "He called you? In sick bay?"

"He did..." Shaw said simply.

"He wants to establish a pecking order," Garrett said, interrupting before Shaw could elaborate further. His voice carried an edge, the frustration bubbling to the surface once more. "It's been just a few hours since we left Midway, and he wants to play politics with the other captains of the task force—measure who has the biggest dick."

Shaw said nothing at first, his calm gaze fixed on Garrett. After several seconds of silence, he spoke. "He asked me to talk to you. Said I should try to get you to call him back. I think he wants to help..."

"I just set him straight. Honestly, he's starting to piss me off," Garrett growled. His hand curled into a fist on the desk before he forced himself to relax. "He's like a child who can't wait to go to the park or toy store. I have far more important things on my plate than playing political power games with subordinates."

"Of course, sir," Shaw said, his tone neutral.

Garrett let out a heated breath, forcing himself to calm down. His jaw unclenched as he regarded Shaw with a steady gaze. After a moment, he leaned forward slightly and eyed the other man closely. "Are you certain you're up for work? I know our medical tech is advanced and that wonders can be accomplished in short amounts of time, but... be honest with me. You owe me that. Are you ready to get back into the saddle?"

"You know me, sir," Shaw replied, his tone forceful, almost defiant. "I was born ready. I can hack it. And if it gets to the point where I can't, you'll be the first to know."

Garrett studied him for a long moment before nodding. "Fair enough. You can return to work, but I want you to take it easy. You need to rest and heal. Make things worse for yourself and you won't be any good to me."

"Thank you, sir," Shaw said, inclining his head slightly. "Now, tell me the problem. Why have you been holed up for so long?"

"I've read our sealed orders. They're not at all what I expected." Garrett leaned forward, picking up the reader. The device felt heavier than it should have, a compact but potent repository of secrets. He activated it with his thumb, the interface lighting up with a muted glow, then leaned forward and handed it to Shaw. "First, I think you should read what Gray sent. This came just before the enemy attacked Midway. I didn't have a chance to look at it fully until a short while ago. Now that I have... well... read each message."

Shaw glanced at Garrett, his curiosity plain, then turned his attention to the tablet. As the information scrolled across the screen, his expression shifted from neutral to grim. After several seconds, he shook the tablet slightly in plain frustration. "This warning came a little too late."

"That's unimportant now," Garrett said, his tone dismissive. "Read the other two messages. They're what really matter to us."

Shaw's eyes narrowed slightly as he returned his focus to the tablet. After several heartbeats, he sucked in a sharp breath, his posture stiffening. He didn't grimace this time. Minutes passed, his features growing more severe with each word. Finally, he looked up, his irritation unmistakable as he tapped the tablet with a finger.

"Knowing the enemy was human might have helped sooner... maybe even saved lives," Shaw said, his voice edged with anger.

Garrett wasn't so certain about that point. "It's clear from the message and attached report they only recently discovered that particular truth—or at least Gray was let in on it."

Shaw's gaze dropped back to the tablet, his eyes scanning the lines again. "The admiral still believes aliens are pulling the strings, the hydrogen breathers."

"She also thinks the humans are either slaves or, worse, converts to their cause—brainwashed, conditioned, and now loyal to the enemy. Heck, it states their plants are all from conquered star systems, descendants. Regardless, we now have a fifth column to worry about, the enemy within. There's no telling how long they've had to infiltrate, or how deeply they've managed to embed themselves. In the Core, there's likely quite the hunt going on right now."

"I can imagine." Shaw's jaw tightened, his grip on the reader firm. "What's this about a test? Gray mentions it, but there are no real details."

"All that's further on, in the attached reports," Garrett said, motioning toward the tablet. "Intelligence Directorate has developed a blood test to identify possible agents. Apparently, they've had some success rooting them out in the Core worlds." He paused, tapping a finger on the desk. "It's based on genetic markers—specifically, the ones that trace a person's lineage to their next of kin and so on back down their ancestral line. The results aren't one hundred percent accurate, but it's good enough to track down infiltrators. Gray made sure she sent us full databases on all Confederation worlds. We can track someone's genetic lineage back several hundred years if needed for a cross-reference."

"So," Shaw said slowly, working the logic aloud, "descendants of those captured by the enemy in earlier Pushes would stand out. They'd have no direct and immediate link with someone currently living in Confederation space... say a mother, father or sibling. Their genetic line would trace back to a conquered world, right?"

"Exactly," Garrett said with a nod. "Even if they've assumed a false identity, their genetic code will not lie. They can't conceal that. We've also been provided with early colonial and sector data for worlds that, at the start of the war, fell into the enemy's hands. It's not perfect—there are apparently gaps in the records, especially from the Pushes before the Confederation came to be—but it's better than nothing."

Shaw sucked in a deep breath and slowly let it out, his gaze turning sharp. "We're going to need to test everyone aboard, aren't we?"

"We are," Garrett said, his voice grim. "And that's going to be a colossal endeavor. Between the civilian evacuees, and the military personnel we've taken aboard, all told, more than fifty thousand people will have to be screened." His eyes narrowed slightly as he leaned back in his chair. As if protesting, it creaked softly with the movement. "Everyone must be accounted for—including the crew. Each and every single person aboard *Surprise* will need to be tested and cleared."

Shaw let out a low whistle, shaking his head. "That's going to take time... a hell of a lot of time too. And it's not going to be popular either."

"I know," Garrett said, his tone edged with resignation. "But the risk of doing nothing is too great. If even one infiltrator is aboard, they could compromise everything—our mission, our safety, even the survival of this task force by sabotaging a critical piece of infrastructure."

"We'll need to prioritize key personnel first—bridge crew, engineering, marines, anyone with access to sensitive systems or information. Then we can move on to the general population and crew," Shaw said.

"Agreed. But we can't afford to drag our feet. The longer we wait, the greater the risk of an enemy agent doing something to jeopardize operations."

Shaw leaned forward. "Sir, this could get ugly. If we find

someone... if we confirm an infiltrator among us, it's going to create panic... and at the very least cause trust issues with the crew. We need a plan for handling that fallout."

"We do."

"Do you think we have the enemy aboard?" Shaw asked.

Garrett hesitated, leaning forward slightly, resting his elbows on the desk. "I—I just don't know," he admitted. "I want to say no, but Gray isn't certain how widespread the problem is —or, for that matter, how long the enemy has had access to Confederation space. Until the testing is complete, we simply can't trust anyone other than those we've worked with for an extended period and maybe not even then." Garrett shook his head. "If there *are* enemy agents aboard, there's no telling their agenda, their objectives, or what they're capable of doing in the coming days and weeks."

Shaw looked down into his lap, his jaw tightening as he thought matters through. Several heartbeats passed in silence before he spoke again. "We're going to have to involve Stroud and Neelan."

"We are," Garrett confirmed with a nod. "But the smaller the group that knows the truth of what and who we're after, the better. If word gets out prematurely, it could compromise every-thing, and maybe even encourage the enemy to strike."

Shaw tapped the tablet lightly, his expression grim. "I don't see how we're going to conceal this effort. Testing fifty thousand plus people, not to mention the crew, is going to raise questions. We'll need a cover story." He expelled a long breath. "This is a real headache."

Garrett barked a short, humorless laugh. "That isn't even the worst of it."

"No?" Shaw raised an eyebrow, his surprise evident.

"Go to the next note from Gray," Garrett said, gesturing toward the tablet.

Shaw hesitated for a moment, his gaze lingering on Garrett's face as though searching for a clue to the gravity of what he was about to read. Then he turned his attention back to the device, his fingers moving over the controls to bring up the next message. The screen shifted, and the new text came into focus.

The office fell silent as Shaw began to read. Garrett watched him closely, noting the subtle tightening of his jaw, the slight flare of his nostrils.

"Damn," Shaw muttered under his breath.

Garrett said nothing, waiting for the lieutenant commander to process what he was reading. He knew exactly what was coming—the revelation, the implications, the questions.

"Wow," Shaw breathed. He looked up from the tablet. "A jump point destabilizer? I don't see how this is bad news. In fact, I don't understand why it wasn't deployed sooner."

"It was successfully tested a few weeks ago," Garrett said, understanding Shaw had not finished the message, "halfway across the Confederation, in the Davros System. Fleet is already in the process of constructing more of the devices."

"That's really good news, then." Shaw's astonishment turned to a faint smile, his expression momentarily lighter. "If we can deploy these at key locations, critical jump points, we'll be able to stop the Push cold—end the war. The enemy won't be able to advance down system chains to attack us. They won't reach the Core."

"Yes," Garrett said, giving a small nod. "However, it may not ultimately prove to be the end of the war, but I think it's good news too."

Shaw's smile faded slightly as he caught the hint of tension in Garrett's voice. "With ships like *Surprise*, I suppose not. So how is this a problem for us?"

Garrett placed his hand on the console embedded in his desk and swiveled it around, angling the screen so Shaw could see it clearly. Garrett's expression hardened.

"What you're about to read," Garrett said, "you will share

with no one without my direct and express permission. Is that understood?"

Clearly wondering what was coming, Shaw met Garrett's gaze, his own expression sobering. "I understand. This remains between us until you say otherwise."

"Then read our orders regarding 66-Lima and what Fleet has termed Indigo Station, what they want us to do there."

Shaw adjusted his position, wincing slightly as he used his uninjured arm to scoot his chair closer to the desk. He settled down, and his eyes moved to the console, scanning the text as it scrolled across the display.

Garrett watched Shaw closely. He didn't need to read the orders again himself. Instead, he focused on Shaw's reactions. The tick in his jaw. The way his brows rose, then furrowed. The faint shifts in his posture.

Several times, Shaw glanced up at Garrett, his expression flickering between disbelief and dawning understanding, before turning back to the screen. Finally, he leaned back in his chair, shaking his head.

"Interesting reading, isn't it?" Garrett asked, breaking the silence.

Shaw opened his eyes, his expression now guarded but grim. "That's one way to put it. Fleet isn't just asking for the impossible—they're asking us to gamble everything on a plan that feels half-baked at best."

"They're asking us to trust the intelligence."

"Do you trust it?" Shaw asked, leaning forward slightly, his voice filled with cautious skepticism.

Garrett didn't answer immediately. The silence stretched, heavy and uncertain, before he finally spoke. "I don't have a choice, and neither do you."

"How do they know all this?" Shaw asked quietly, his voice barely above a whisper, as though afraid someone might overhear them despite the secure environment.

"There are several attached reports that will bear studying. I've only managed to skim those. One mentions data gathered from remote telescopes and sensor platforms. How they drew conclusions from those alone..." Garrett shrugged, the gesture as much an expression of doubt as resignation.

"They're relying on visual information?" Shaw pressed. "Speed of light? That's—"

"Given the location, potentially hundreds of years out of date," Garrett finished with a nod.

"Those must be some serious telescopes and sensor platforms."

Garrett gave a nod.

"There has to be another source."

"I agree, there likely is," Garrett said, his expression thoughtful. "But if so, it's not mentioned in these orders, or the attached reports. It's another layer of secrecy, one we're not privy to. Did you finish all of it?"

"No," Shaw said.

"Keep reading the general draft. You can study it in greater detail later, along with the attached reports. We both need to begin planning not only our approach, but the assault."

Shaw turned his attention back to the console. The man's lips pressed into a thin line as he continued to read. When he finally leaned back and let out a low whistle, the sound carried a mix of disbelief and reluctant acceptance.

"It won't be easy."

"What they want us to do," Garrett agreed, "is nothing short of monumental, and that's the problem."

Shaw jabbed a finger at the console, his frustration evident. "If this system, 66-Lima, is as heavily guarded as they think, it's likely a suicide mission. You do realize that?"

Garrett held his gaze, his own expression unreadable. "We haven't even begun planning yet; we've not really analyzed the target and how we can best neutralize it and then get what we need."

Shaw snorted softly, leaning forward again and crossing his arms on the desk. "Planning or not, sir, we're being sent into the fire."

"We are."

"And if we fail?"

"We won't... can't fail," Garrett interrupted, his tone harder than he intended. He straightened in his chair, his shoulders squaring as he met Shaw's gaze. "We can't afford to fail, not if this system is what they believe it to be... not now, not after everything that's happened."

"I don't like it," Shaw said, waving a hand toward the console. "It's clear now that our trial run with the gripper drive was only ever supposed to be a recon mission, to get a better picture of what is actually there... the orders even mention that."

"At least until additional Motherships become operational, and a larger fleet can be assembled to attack the target," Garrett said. "But now, given what's happened—given that the Push is on—Yenga has decided to make it a strike."

Shaw's gaze drifted back to the orders on the display. "This feels rushed. And it's obvious we're expendable to them."

"I agree on all points," Garrett said, his voice steady but grim. "But those are our orders, and we will find a way to execute them to their fullest, especially those that apply to the main objective."

"And of the secondary objectives?" Shaw asked.

Garrett gave a shrug.

"Does he know about the disruptor?" Shaw asked, glancing briefly at the reader before looking back at Garrett.

"Yenga?" Garrett hesitated for a moment, then shook his head slightly. "I'm not sure. I suppose so, but it is not explicitly stated or mentioned in our orders. When we talked, he didn't say anything about the disruptor either, and of course all of that was over comms. The enemy's already shown a capability to hack into systems, like the jump beacon network, which we thought secure. Yenga might not have wanted to mention it. There's so much we don't know."

"With the disruptor, there's no need for this attack," Shaw said, leaning forward slightly. He tapped the desk with a finger. "We have time—time to build more Motherships, time to assemble a real fleet. Take the war to the enemy and do the job properly."

"I don't think we have the time you believe we do."

"What do you mean?"

"Think about it," Garrett said. "With enemy agents operating inside the Confederation, there's a chance they already know how the drive on this ship works, or at least that we've built something revolutionary."

"That's assuming a lot."

"It is, but they certainly saw us jump out of Midway, didn't they? So, now they know we have a new type of drive technology. Even worse, after studying their sensor feeds, they might be able to figure out what we did and replicate it—make their own gripper drive—that is if they haven't already outright stolen the technology."

"Shit." Shaw's face darkened, his jaw tightening as he leaned back in his chair. "That's a scary thought."

"It's more than scary—it's terrifying," Garrett admitted, his tone hardening. "The advantage we've barely begun to exploit could vanish overnight... though I guess it will likely be a few years, not many, though. That's why I think the mission was changed from recon to one of attack. We need to make a difference now, and Yenga thinks that's the place to hit, the critical infrastructure to take out. He intends us to strike a crippling blow." Garrett paused. "But therein lies the problem. We have a choice to make."

"A choice on how to proceed, to plan our attack?" Shaw

asked, his tone cautious, as though trying to read between the lines.

"No," Garrett said firmly, shaking his head. "Our orders give us freedom of action—when, where, and how to strike the target system. Yenga made that much plain. The key to all of it is timing—when we choose to make our move."

"Okay," Shaw said. "That's understandable. So, what are you thinking? What is this choice, beyond how, when, and where?"

"I find myself thinking of the greater strategic picture, also hedging our bets," Garrett said, gesturing at the tablet that lay on his desk. "Especially as it relates to the Dows System and Third Fleet." Garrett nodded slowly, almost to himself as he voiced his thoughts. "I think we have an opportunity to save lives—to make an immediate difference. More important, Admiral Bryer has what we need to get the job done right, to increase the odds of mission success. That's what I've been considering for the last few hours... go straight to the target system or go get what we need first, then make our move.

"Do I think we can hit Indigo and take the target out, then extract successfully? Possibly. It will take significant planning on our part to pull off. Do I think a successful strike will be the start of something significant? Perhaps. Remember, the enemy controls *multiple* star systems. Intelligence estimates that number to be in the hundreds, if not thousands. Taking out one target, no matter how strategically important, won't end the war —not by itself. At least, I don't believe it will. It will slow things down, yes... for sure. I think, given time, the enemy will rebuild whatever we manage to destroy."

Shaw frowned, considering Garrett's words. "Fleet seems to think otherwise," he said carefully. "This strike might even get them talking to us."

"I know," Garrett said, leaning back in his chair and crossing his arms. "They must have access to intelligence they haven't shared—something they're holding close to the chest. Maybe there's a reason for that, like getting them to talk for the first time. Either way, we have a target, and they want it taken out. At the same time, with the Push underway and Midway in enemy hands, Bryer is effectively cut off—isolated."

Shaw sucked in a breath as the pieces clicked into place. His free hand shot out, a finger pointing at Garrett. Shaw jabbed the finger. "You want to build the disruptor and head to Dows... to Javelin Station, don't you? You want to give it to Admiral Bryer so he can protect himself."

"That's correct. I do." Garrett pointed at the tablet. "We have the technical specifications, and—I checked with Tam—what we need aboard to make several of the devices. There are sixteen settled star systems up that chain, with several million Fleet personnel—*and* civilians. If we go, we'd not only have the chance to aid Third Fleet, but also offload the civilians we've taken aboard before leaving for the target system. They are a consideration too." Garrett paused to suck in a breath. "And more vital—we would be able to pick up trained personnel, people who are better qualified to help us get the job done right. With a proper crew, a full marine contingent, the chances of successfully pulling off the mission increase, especially with a strong space wing for support. In addition to that, we could pick up greater weight in ships, several dreads, perhaps even a carrier or two... and trade off on some of the lighter ships we've brought with us. That way, when we drop into Lima-66, we have more firepower with us."

"Our orders allow us to requisition what we require. We could go deeper into Confederation Space," Shaw said, "stop by a Fleet base behind the front lines."

"They may not have all that we need," Garrett said, "especially ship and small craft-wise, not to mention the personnel. The advantages of going to Dows outweigh the disadvantages. The system is closer than the nearest major Fleet base, at least by a month or more. Bryer has everything on hand that we require... at least he should. I can't help but feel going there first is the right move, especially given what we are being asked to do... to accomplish."

"I see..."

"Right now, we don't even have a full crew or a complete small-craft support wing. Everything is ad hoc, personnel and units thrown haphazardly together. Yenga simply gave us what he could in the short time he had, and what was available at the station itself... and, well, it's not enough to do the job right. Not as I see it. Do you see matters differently?"

Shaw thought for a moment, then shook his head.

"Yes, we could complete the mission asked of us, but it would be more difficult, more challenging... dangerous... to the point where this ship's survival is far from guaranteed, let alone likely. Do you disagree with any of that?"

Shaw studied him, his gaze steady and searching. For a long moment, he said nothing. Then, with a faint grunt of amusement, he leaned back. "I think you've already made up your mind."

"What makes you say that?"

"I've known you long enough. You're just thinking it through—dotting the I's, crossing the T's. But deep down, you've already decided. We're going to the Dows System to get what we need. As you said, Bryer has everything we want and could ever need."

"Okay." Garrett leaned forward, resting his forearms on the desk. "Going to the Dows System, to Javelin Station, will delay our mission some. But I'm leaning in that direction, yes. It makes sense strategically—and morally. That's a secondary benefit. If we can give Admiral Bryer the technical specifications for the jump disruptor, it would hand him the tool he needs to hold the line, to preserve his fleet and his people, not to mention the civilians under his protection."

"Do you want my opinion?"

"You know I do," Garrett replied, leaning back slightly in his chair. "I always value it. I wouldn't have shared all of this with you otherwise."

"I say we go and save Third Fleet," Shaw said plainly. "Give them the plans for the disruptor, get the critical assets we require from Bryer, pry them loose if needed, then, carry out our mission and go loud in the heart of enemy territory, show them what *Surprise*, a properly outfitted Mothership, can really do."

Garrett didn't immediately respond, his gaze distant as he processed Shaw's words.

"What's the problem?" Shaw asked.

Garrett let out a slow breath. "Since the Push began at Midway, there's a good chance the enemy hasn't struck at Dows yet," he said carefully. "But if they have spies among us—and they clearly have some spread about the Confederation—they'll know Third Fleet is a powerful force, a unit to be reckoned with. I think the enemy will ultimately try to tie the bulk of the Third down by attacking the front line, punching Bryer in the teeth, and keeping him pinned and in place, occupied and unable to redeploy down the chain to Midway. Bryer could potentially attack there and complicate matters for the enemy."

Shaw considered this, rubbing his jaw thoughtfully. "They might do that. And if they have already hit Dows? What then?"

"We will have a difficult decision to make when we arrive. Can we help or do we jump away? Also, within days, maybe two weeks at the most, Bryer will receive word of the attack at Midway. If he's not already under attack by then, he might react. He could make a move toward Midway and counterattack or he could simply stay put and dig in. Either way, I think the time we have to act is limited..."

"So, the clock is ticking."

"Yes."

"What are the chances he'll concentrate all of Third Fleet in Dows to prepare for an assault?"

"It's a fortress system," Garrett said. "Being cut off, it makes sense for him to consolidate there, dig in, and force the enemy to come to him, to bleed them hard. A conservative leader would take that approach. That said, Bryer is known for being aggressive. If he goes for Midway, he will take all his toys with him—much of what we need—and hammer at the enemy there." Garrett paused to suck in a breath. "I think he'll act—and soon."

"Then why delay?" Shaw pressed, leaning forward. "Let's head there now, straight away, and find out what's happening firsthand. We can jump far enough out to get eyes on, to see if an attack is underway before heading deeper into the system."

"We can't leave yet," Garrett said.

"Why not?" Shaw asked, frowning.

"Because of the fifth column," Garrett said, his tone hardening. "They're a real danger to the ship, at least at the moment. Gray's report makes a note of their fanaticism. If we have enemy agents aboard—and we very well might—they must be rooted out first before we make a move. They could sabotage us mid-operation, mess with a critical system, including the gripper drive, at, say, the wrong moment." Garrett tapped his index finger on the desk. "Shaw, *Surprise* is the future, and right now the only operational Mothership in existence. She provides a capability the enemy simply does not yet have, the ability to strike targets deep in enemy territory, behind the front lines. Our first priority must be securing the ship. When that's done, only then can we move forward and travel to Dows to get what we need."

"All right, you've sold me," Shaw said after a moment's thought. "We need to go to Dows first. It is the logical next step, but we also need to be sure about the people we have aboard."

"That's how I see matters." Garrett gave a slow nod. "I don't want to go into battle with a crew I cannot trust or rely upon."

"That's going to take time," Shaw said. "At least several days to screen everyone."

"It will, and we will need to do it within that two-week time frame," Garrett admitted and then gestured at Gray's tablet. "We have to build the disruptor. That will also take a few days. I want to have one ready when we jump into Dows. If the enemy's already there and in the system, we may need to deploy it immediately."

"All right," Shaw agreed, "secure the ship, build the disruptor, and then head to Dows and get everything we need to secure mission success. That's the plan, then..."

"Yes," Garrett said. "That is exactly my current thinking."

"Let's go save Third Fleet's ass. They can thank us later."

Garrett suddenly grinned at that. "So, you don't think I am crazy for wanting to go to Dows first?"

"Commodore, I already know you're crazy." Shaw gave a light chuckle. "Hell, I've known it for some time. But you are my kind of crazy. It's why we work so well together."

It was decided.

"I suppose we are both nuts, then," Garrett replied.

"Let's not tell anyone, eh?" Shaw said. "It will be our little secret."

"That's a deal," Garrett said.

"You know," Shaw said, "when we pull off the raid on Indigo, everyone is going to know we are batshit crazy."

"If we live through it, we will deal with that then," Garrett replied.

Sobering, Shaw shifted his position in his chair, grimacing slightly. "Any other good news to share?"

Garrett thought for a long moment, then gave a nod. "Before we jumped out of Midway, Admiral Yenga sent us Lieutenant Commander Senica, along with a special operations unit that we might be able to use when we hit Indigo. He spoke highly of her and thought she'd be helpful in what's to come. She's an intelligence officer by trade and may have insights that could prove invaluable. She might even know more on the admiral's thinking."

"That's encouraging," Shaw said. "We may be able to use her elsewhere too. We're a little short on qualified senior-grade officers."

"My thoughts as well. I want you to send for her; Stroud, and Neelan too. We'll meet in an hour on the admiral's bridge to discuss and plan our next moves when it comes to testing everyone aboard."

"Understood, sir," Shaw said.

"Oh, and there's one more bit of news." Garrett's gaze softened as he regarded Shaw. "Effective immediately, you are officially my second in command," he said. "You've been promoted to full commander. I spoke to Yenga about that. He confirmed it before we jumped out of Midway. Congratulations."

Shaw blinked, a flicker of surprise crossing his face before he broke into a wry smile. "Second officer and a full commander to boot... Are you trying to sprinkle a little sunshine amidst the shit, sir?"

"You know it." Garrett grinned back at him, then glanced at the hatch to his personal cabin. "I'm going to grab something to eat, take a shower, and put on a fresh uniform. We'll meet and plan our next steps in an hour."

"I'll call Senica and Stroud to the bridge," Shaw said, pulling himself carefully to his feet. He grimaced from plain discomfort. "Neelan too, though he won't be happy about it. I'll get them all there."

"Good," Garrett said with a nod of approval. "After the meeting, make sure you find some time to rest. I don't want you overdoing it."

"I will, that is, if you promise to do the same, sir," Shaw said.

"It's a deal," Garrett said.

Shaw turned toward the hatch, his steps slow and careful. As he reached the threshold, Garrett's voice stopped him.

"And Shaw?"

Pausing, Shaw turned back, his hand resting lightly on the edge of the open hatch. "Sir?"

"It's good to have you back," Garrett said.

"Thank you, sir. I'm looking forward to pitching in and getting to work."

"I know you are," Garrett replied. With that, Shaw stepped out of the office, the hatch sliding shut behind him, leaving Garrett alone once more.

Garrett reached out and slid the console back around to face him, his fingers deftly navigating the interface, pulling up another window. A detailed map of the Dows System appeared, glowing faintly on the screen. His gaze settled on Javelin Station, the largest battle station the Confederation had ever constructed and the linchpin of the system's defense. Then his gaze went to the Beleris jump point. It led directly to enemy space. Nothing the Confederation had ever sent through had returned, not even unmanned stealth probes.

Despite settling on a course of action, Garrett felt a stab of concern.

When they arrived, what would he find? What would be waiting?

FIVE

TABBY

"Here you are, ma'am," the marine said as she stopped in front of an unremarkable hatch. There was nothing to distinguish it from the dozens of others lining both sides of the corridor. The marine's uniform tag identified her as PFC Taylor, and her tone carried a no-nonsense efficiency, along with a bored edge, as if she'd been doing this very same thing all day long, which Tabby supposed was very likely.

Taylor inputted a code manually on the glowing keypad beside the hatch. "These are the squadron leaders' quarters. There are six others like them, at least on this side of the ship, ma'am."

Taylor pulled out a handheld tablet. She tapped at the screen for a few moments and studied the result. Then she tapped some more. A soft chime sounded.

"All right," Taylor continued, glancing up at Tabby, "I've imprinted your personal identifier. Going forward, the hatch will open automatically for your ID tag. There's no need to use the keypad, but if the situation ever arises, you can manually open it by entering the last four digits of your Military Identification Number. Any questions, ma'am?"

"No," Tabby said.

It had taken far longer than she'd hoped to find someone in authority. After wandering the labyrinthine corridors that branched off from the hangar, she'd finally located a crew chief who'd directed her to the CAG—the Commander Air Group. The title was a relic of old Earth's naval aviation traditions. Unfortunately, the CAG had been too busy to see her, but an assistant had helped her connect with the surviving members of her squadron and arranged quarters for all of them.

Sanchez had left her a few minutes earlier with another rating, heading toward the flight crew quarters, which she'd been told was down this same corridor. The thought was oddly grounding—knowing they would all be on the same deck, just a short walk away. The rest of her squadron would end up there too, but it would take some time. They'd docked on the other side of the ship.

Tabby cast a quick glance down the corridor. It was broad, straight, and brightly lit, with dozens of personnel moving purposefully in both directions. Most wore flight suits, or the casual off-duty uniforms of flight crew. A few bulkhead wall panels were conspicuously absent, exposing bundles of colorful wiring and neatly routed cabling—a reminder *Surprise* was not yet a fully completed vessel.

What caught Tabby's attention most, though, was the lack of signage. There were no direction markers along many of the walls, or indicators overhead, no helpful plaques denoting where vital compartments or facilities lay. She realized that getting lost in the maze of decks was inevitable.

The hiss of the hatch opening before them drew her attention. She turned back to see the compartment beyond—a wide, well-appointed space. Several low tables and couches were arranged in conversational clusters. A small refreshment station, along with a kitchenette was built into the back wall, complete with a countertop and storage cabinets. The lighting was soft and muted, a welcome change from the harsh overhead panels of the corridor.

"Cabin 6-A has been set aside for your use, ma'am," Taylor continued. "The controller is also keyed to your ID tag and will open as you approach."

Tabby hesitated for a moment, glancing around once more, curiosity getting the better of her. She decided she did have questions. "How long have you been aboard?"

"Six months, ma'am," Taylor replied.

"What's that been like—serving on a Mothership?"

"Hectic," Taylor said with a faint grin. "When I came aboard, the ship was just a frame, with a skeleton crew and thousands of yard dogs crawling over every centimeter. Now she's almost fully operational and crazy huge. Occasionally, I still get turned around. It is very easy to get lost. In fact, expect to. There's plenty that needs finishing touches, but she's a good ship, solid as they come, and I'm proud to serve aboard her." The marine paused, glanced down at the deck, then back up. "You're gonna like her, ma'am. We've become attached to her."

Tabby noted the pride in the marine's voice and glanced down the corridor again. "Where's the mess? I could use something substantial to eat."

Taylor pointed farther down the corridor. "That way, aft, roughly two hundred meters. There's no sign, but you'll see people coming and going at all hours. You can also smell the food. Look for a double hatch. Chow's better than most ships, but the mess department is a bit overwhelmed at the moment. Meal selection is limited. I've been told that should change in the coming days."

Tabby nodded.

"The gym's the next compartment down," Taylor added. "Unlike on most carriers, there's no separate section for officers. It's a no-rank zone as well. The commodore decided that weeks ago. Some people jog in the corridors rather than on a treadmill. That's permitted."

"Commodore Garrett?" Tabby asked curiously.

"Yes, ma'am," Taylor said with a touch of what could only be described as reverence. "He's both the ship's captain and the task force's commodore."

Tabby's curiosity sharpened. She'd never heard of him before, but after what she'd witnessed, he clearly knew how to command this ship.

"He's a good one, ma'am," Taylor added. "When the enemy breached and stormed the bridge... word is he killed several enemy soldiers himself with only a pistol."

Tabby arched a brow, filing that piece of information away. Whether it was exaggerated or true, it clearly carried weight with Taylor and likely the rest of the marine contingent aboard *Surprise*. That spoke about their... now her leader's character. He was clearly a man to follow.

"*Surprise* also has a wonder weapon," Taylor said. "Word is it was used against the enemy, but I've not spoken to anyone who witnessed that..."

Tabby thought Taylor sounded almost disappointed.

"I saw it in action," Tabby said after a moment's thought.

"You did?" The young marine's eyes grew wide. "Really?"

"*Surprise* took out several capital ships with one blast. I'm still not sure how that was managed... The enemy were nearly two million klicks away and should have been well out of range."

Tabby noted Taylor was following her with interest. Gone was the sense of slight boredom. "We'd heard for months the ship had something special but anyone in the know kept their mouths shut."

"As well they should have," Tabby said.

"It was just rumor until a few hours ago. Then people started talking about it." Taylor paused. "So, it's real, ma'am?"

"It's quite real," Tabby assured her.

Just then the marine's earlobe illuminated and glowed faintly blue, signaling that she was receiving a call. She straightened and sucked in a breath. "I must go, ma'am. Duty calls. Can I help you with anything else?"

"I understand, and no, I'm good. Thank you for the escort, marine," Tabby said. "I can handle it from here. Carry on."

"Yes, ma'am." Taylor started to turn away. She stopped herself. "Oh, and welcome to *Surprise*." With those parting words, Taylor turned on her heel, and went back the way they'd come, her steps brisk and purposeful.

Tabby watched her go, a faint smile tugging at her lips. The marine's parting words lingered in her mind. Taylor was the first person who had properly welcomed her aboard, and it felt... genuine.

Turning, Tabby gazed into the squadron leaders' lounge, looking closer, studying it, a space that felt worlds apart from the utilitarian corridors of the Mothership. Larger and far more inviting than anything she'd seen on a standard carrier, the compartment had clearly been designed as a haven—an escape from the constant demands of command and leadership. The size and comfort level also told her the Mothership's deployments were expected to be long, and the planners had accounted for that.

Soft lighting bathed the room in a warm glow, giving it an almost homey atmosphere. Plush couches and chairs, upholstered in neutral tones, were arranged around low tables in clusters that seemed to encourage casual conversation or quiet reflection. A few were occupied. Low voices and muted laughter reached her out in the corridor.

The walls were lined with sleek storage cabinets, likely for flight gear since the hangar bay was less than fifty meters distant. There were display panels above the cabinets. These cycled through real-time feeds of what was clearly the Mothership's tactical situation, rotating images of squadron insignias, and archival photos showcasing the history of space aviation. There was even the accustomed scoreboard, though all the slots were empty. This particular display would track the squadron stats and metrics, ranking each.

The lounge, however, lacked personal decorations. She knew it was only a matter of time before each squadron leader would begin leaving their mark, filling the compartment with personality. It had always been that way on any carrier she'd ever served upon, and she had no reason to doubt it would be that way here, once everyone got settled.

Along the bulkhead walls, evenly spaced hatches marked with alphanumeric codes clearly led to the personal quarters. It took only a moment for Tabby to spot hers—a red composite plate reading 6-A, the last room on the left.

Still, she hesitated at the threshold. She was a stranger here. The faces in the room were unfamiliar, and for a moment, a pang of doubt gnawed at her. Then, her anger spiked, and she gave herself a mental shrug, banishing such thoughts. Like her, everyone here was a newcomer. And Tabby had nothing to prove to anyone. Also, there was the curious fact... *Surprise* was now her home.

She belonged on this ship.

She stepped inside. The hatch slid shut behind her with a soft hiss, and for a moment, the room seemed to take notice of her presence, stilling. Conversations faltered as heads turned her way, curiosity evident in the glances. The interest rapidly faded and feigned indifference became the rule, as they returned their attention to whatever they'd been doing just moments prior.

Tabby adjusted the packs, each slung over a shoulder, the weight of her personal gear feeling heavier than it should have. That was the fatigue. It pressed down on her, a bone-deep weariness that seemed to gnaw upon her soul. She was so tired she felt ready to drop where she stood.

Exhaling slowly, Tabby allowed herself to absorb the scene for a heartbeat longer. This was her new reality. And though the faces were unfamiliar now, she had no doubt that soon enough they'd all be competitors... to see who had the best squadron.

Deciding she'd wasted enough time, Tabby moved toward her new cabin. As she approached, the hatch emitted a soft chime, recognizing her ID tag as Taylor had said it would. The hatch slid aside with a smooth hiss, revealing a compact space.

The cabin was on the small side, but larger than what she had become accustomed to on other starships. A bed, tucked against the far wall, was already made, with a single regulation pillow. A desk with a fold-out terminal occupied the wall opposite the bed, the surface bare save for a recessed tablet docking port and a few integrated storage compartments. A narrow locker stood to one side. Another locker was located under her bed. Despite the cabin's utilitarian design, there was just enough room for personal touches—a few photos, perhaps a small memento or two—to make the space feel less sterile.

The hatch slid shut behind her, and alone, Tabby dropped her bags next to the hatch with a sigh of relief. Her gaze lingered on the bed for a long moment, the thought of sleep tugging at her like a siren's call. It had been more than two days since she'd slept in a bed or had a proper shower. The temptation to crash was strong, but she dismissed it with a shake of her head. Coffee and something to eat would have to come first, then she'd clean up and shower. Rest would come after.

On the back of the cabin hatch hung a narrow, full-length mirror. As Tabby turned, her reflection caught her eye, and she paused, her hand resting lightly on the hatch frame. For a long moment, she simply stared.

Her face, usually composed and sharp, looked drawn and

pale. Dark circles shadowed her eyes, making the steel-gray irises appear even more piercing. Fine lines she hadn't noticed before etched faint patterns around her eyes and mouth, the stress and lack of sleep carving its toll. Her short, dark hair was tousled and matted, a tangled mess—the direct result of wearing her helmet—that bore no resemblance to the neat style she usually maintained.

Tabby stepped closer, her fingertips brushing the cool surface of the mirror as if to confirm the image was real. She tilted her head slightly; a faint, raw patch on her jawline caught her attention, a bruise she hadn't even noticed. How had she gotten it?

Her eyes met her own reflection again, and something flickered beneath the exhaustion—something fierce and unyielding. A simmering anger burned low in her chest, coiled and restrained, but unmistakably present. It wasn't the kind of anger that erupted in an instant. It was the deep, steady kind that built over time, sharpened by loss and tempered by resolve.

She thought of her people—the Nighthawks. So many of them were gone now, their lives snuffed out in an instant. Friends, comrades, pilots who had flown off her wing, trusted her, and depended on her.

Tabby exhaled slowly, her breath fogging the surface of the mirror for a brief moment. The cabin was insulated from the lounge, and quiet, save for the faint hum of the ship's systems, but in her mind, the echoes of the battle still lingered—the hiss of comm channels, the barked orders... the screams of those needing help.

"You can't fall apart," she whispered to herself, the words low and firm. Her own voice startled her, breaking the silence. She straightened, pulling herself away from the mirror. The anger within her wasn't just grief—it was fuel. A reason to keep moving, to keep fighting, to keep leading.

She reached up, brushing a hand through her hair to smooth it into something presentable. The image in the mirror wasn't perfect, but it didn't need to be. What mattered was that she was still standing.

She activated the hatch with her implants and it slid aside, then she stepped back into the common area. The lounge had grown livelier in the few minutes she'd been away as more people had arrived, a dozen at least. Voices overlapped in a steady hum, punctuated by the occasional burst of laughter.

Clearly many of those present knew each other. Tabby let her gaze sweep across the space. She didn't recognize anyone. She knew she'd need to introduce herself sooner rather than later, but for now, she allowed herself a moment to simply take it all in. The squadron leaders here were her peers, each responsible for dozens of lives. Like it or not, she'd need to find her place among them. She knew she eventually would.

Settling into a new environment was never easy. But she was no stranger to this kind of transition—the quiet balancing act of observation and integration, learning the dynamics of a group before fully stepping into it. But truth be told, Tabby didn't give a shit what any of them thought about her. The anger she felt was mounting, growing, replacing the loss she felt, filling the void. The enemy had hurt the Nighthawks, hurt her, but she'd hurt them back in turn and, given the chance, would keep doing so.

She'd make them pay.

Glancing around again, she noted the fresh look of those present. How many had fought the enemy off Midway? She figured most had likely been transferred over from the station, without ever having fired a shot in anger. There hadn't been many small craft in space when everything had gone down. Her squadron and a handful of others had been the exception. If anyone had anything to prove, it was the people before her.

The kitchenette in the corner, where the scent of fresh coffee lingered in the air, drew her attention. The anger faded a little. Tabby made her way over to the kitchenette, the soft hum of conversation continuing behind her as she chose a mug from among a stack. Spotting the coffee carafe, she grabbed it and poured herself some of the dark and steaming liquid, the rich aroma wafting up to her. On the counter nearby were neatly arranged trays of muffins and cookies, alongside a basket brimming with paper-wrapped sandwiches. Each was labeled with its contents in clean, block lettering: HAM AND CHEESE, ROAST BEEF, PEANUT BUTTER AND JELLY...

She glanced at the food, her stomach twisting uncomfortably. After what she'd just been through, and despite being hungry, the thought of eating suddenly felt more like a chore than a necessity. Tabby decided to put it off. Still, at some point she knew she needed to refuel.

Reaching for a small container of sugar, she began stirring in a generous scoop, more than usual. She looked but did not see any hazelnut creamer. There was only one type. She stirred in a splash, the coffee swirling to a lighter shade of brown, and as she was just about to take a sip, she sensed someone approaching.

A tall man stepped into view, coming up next to her, his posture relaxed, confident. His face was hard-edged, with piercing brown eyes so dark they almost seemed black. His short-cropped brown hair added to the no-nonsense impression he exuded. Like her, he appeared near exhaustion, for she could easily read it in the lines around his bloodshot eyes.

"Devon Woodward," the man introduced himself, extending a hand toward her. "Of the Sky Sabers, SS-81. Just call me Dev, or by my call sign—Hotster."

Tabby paused, her eyebrows lifting slightly. "All right, Dev..." She hesitated, her lips twitching as she thought on his call sign. "Hotster?"

Dev shrugged. "It's what the flight instructors gave me."

"I suppose there's a story that goes with it," Tabby said.

"Isn't there always?" Dev's smirk grew into a grin, and he pushed his hand forward a bit further. His grave demeanor softened. "One day, maybe I'll even tell that story. That is, if we become friends."

"Tabby, of the 712th Nighthawks." She took his hand. His grip was firm, warm, and steady.

"Nighthawks, huh..." He snapped his fingers. "Say, that was you out there with us." Dev's tone shifted to one of genuine respect. "I saw you take out that carrier. That was some damn fine work."

Tired mind working, Tabby thought for a moment and then connected the dots. "Yours was the squadron that launched after us, off *Neptune?* You were escorting two shuttles. When we were called to defend *Surprise,* you were too."

"We were," Dev confirmed with a nod. "That's us."

"A pleasure to meet you, then," Tabby said.

"Likewise," Dev said. "That carrier attack was some nail-biting stuff. I've never seen anything like it—gutsy, too. Those assault boats of yours are tough."

Tabby hesitated. He'd likely have seen most of her squadron die helplessly but had been too polite to bring it up. Her thoughts snagged on the memories of those she'd lost. Their absence suddenly pressed against her chest with renewed vigor. At the same time, the anger spiked again. After a moment, she decided to take the compliment for what it was: honest and true. "Thank you. It wasn't easy out there..."

Dev sucked in a low breath and let it out. "No, it wasn't."

Tabby thought of the conversation a few minutes before with Taylor. "Your boys tore up those assault craft attacking *Surprise,*" Tabby added, returning the compliment. "But we didn't get all of them, did we?"

"No, we didn't." Dev glanced about the room. "Most of the other squadrons that managed to get into space around Midway did so after the fighting was finished. There was no one left for them to shoot."

He'd just confirmed what she'd suspected.

"Why don't you join us?" Dev gestured across the compartment. "We've got two hours before the staff meeting with the CAG, and then I expect things will get busy. About all we can do right now is sit around and wait, cool our heels." He paused and cracked his neck. "Rest doesn't really seem like an option at the moment..."

Her mug halfway to her lips, Tabby paused and blinked, as the realization of what he'd said hit home. "Meeting with the CAG? I didn't receive notice about that."

"It came through a short while ago, within the last half-hour," Dev said. "It's for all squadron leaders and should be on your personal tablet. You'll have to manually check it on a regular basis, at least for the time being—integration with all the new crew hasn't been fully set up yet. Until it's done, your implants won't get the auto-notifications."

She gestured back toward her cabin with her free hand. "My tablet's still in my bag. I just arrived. It took a while to find someone useful enough to steer me in the correct direction."

"I saw you arrive," Dev admitted, jutting his chin toward the main hatch, his tone casual but carrying an undertone of understanding. "You looked like you could use a friend."

Turning, he gestured with a hand and led her to a low table flanked by a pair of couches, one of which bore his abandoned coffee mug, which he took up as he sat. Unlike Tabby's freshly poured cup, which steamed, his drink had clearly long since cooled.

Seated on the opposite couch was a woman in a flight suit, her posture relaxed, but her sharp eyes had tracked their approach. Her rank insignia marked her as a flight captain. Tabby didn't recognize the patch on her right shoulder. That wasn't unusual. The Confederation was vast, with thousands of squadrons scattered across its many fleets, stations, and planetary bodies, each carrying their own insignia and unique traditions.

"Missy, this is Tabby from the Nighthawks," Dev said as he sank back into his seat, gesturing toward Tabby with a casual wave of his hand to do the same.

"Missy Davis," the woman said, extending her hand across the table. "Call sign Spot Rod. Eclipse Squadron, EC-09."

Tabby shook the offered hand and sat down on the opposite couch, her legs grateful for the reprieve. "Electronic warfare. Growlers?"

"That's us." Missy's gaze went to Tabby's flight suit and the right breast where Tabby was marked. "Call sign?"

"Tabby."

"Wait," Dev said, looking over at her, "your name and call sign are one and the same?"

Tabby gave a weary shrug. "It started as Tabby Cat, but it got shortened to just Tabby by the end of flight training." She turned her attention back to Missy. "How'd you end up on *Surprise?*"

"We were passing through Midway when everything went to shit. Now we're here—just like everyone else—feeling a bit dazed... wondering how it could have happened."

Tabby leaned back. The cushions yielded just enough to cradle her aching muscles, and for a moment, she allowed herself to relax, to sink into it. She closed her eyes, letting the quiet hum of the lounge fill the silence in her mind.

Exhaustion pressed down on her like a heavy blanket, the events of the past days catching up to her in full force. It would have been so easy to drift off, to let the weariness take her. But she couldn't. Not yet. She had a flash of the fighting, making the attack run on the damaged enemy carrier, the stress of the moment, the sound of her own ragged breathing in her helmet, the taste of the recycled suit air... the enemy's point defense fire streaking out toward *Max*. Her heart began beating faster. She sucked in a calming breath and let it out slowly. There was a meeting with the CAG in two hours—a critical one, no doubt. Rest, she now understood, would have to wait.

Almost reluctantly and with some effort, Tabby opened her eyes, her gaze sliding to the coffee in her hand. She took another sip, the bitter liquid burning slightly as it went down. It wasn't enough. She might need to stim just to focus and get through the meeting ahead. The thought wasn't appealing, but it wouldn't be the first time fatigue had demanded a chemical assist.

"It's been rough on all of us," Missy said, her tone weary as she glanced about the lounge. "Half the squadrons that came aboard are missing either pilots or craft, most the latter. Many of the squadrons who were sent over from Midway were in transit to rotational commands out on the Outer Rim with Third Fleet, their craft waiting for them at the destination. Very few are fully intact. It's a real mess, with a lot of confusion still swirling around. The CAG and her team are working overtime to bring order to things."

"None of this was expected," Dev added, his voice carrying a note of frustration. "Fleet was caught completely by surprise, and it shows."

"I was caught by surprise," Tabby admitted, shaking her head. Her thoughts drifted back to those first moments of chaos —the alarms blaring, her sudden awakening to the nightmare outside. She'd woke up in the middle of a battle with shipkiller missiles and point defense rounds flying everywhere. "The enemy hacked our jump beacon network. I didn't even think that was possible."

"No one did," Missy said bluntly, her lips pressing into a thin line. "Fleet got caught with its pants down."

The fight in space had been nothing like Tabby had ever experienced, let alone trained for. It was a maelstrom of near absolute confusion and desperation, a far cry from the orderly combat simulations she'd drilled for. She'd been taught to expect structure, strategy, and precision—not the frenzied, chaotic mess that the battle had become, a close-quarter fight with death at every turn.

There was a lesson there, one she was determined to learn.

"The enemy was boarding the station before anyone even knew what was happening," Missy continued, her voice edged with frustration. "Sure, we responded to the alert and reported back to barracks like we were supposed to, but once we got there, we were just standing around. No orders. No direction. Nothing. We were all left with our thumbs up our collective asses." She let out a breath, her hands tightening slightly around her coffee mug, which she cradled in her lap, as if seeking warmth and comfort from it. "We didn't have a clue what was going on, until word came down to transfer to this ship, via an old clapped-out cargo hauler. All I brought were my pilots and the packs on our backs. Until that moment, we were waiting for our ride out to Third Fleet. My squadron got aboard *Surprise*, but not our craft. I have no idea what we're supposed to do now."

"That seems to be a common theme around here," Dev said. "Uncertainty... a lot of it. The meeting with CAG will clear things up."

"It should," Tabby agreed, taking another sip of her coffee. The drink was hot and invigorating, chasing away some of her lingering exhaustion. She glanced around the lounge again, letting her gaze linger on the comfortable seating, the subtle lighting, and the faint hum of conversation. "These accommodations aren't bad, though, I might grow to like it here."

"It's quite cushy," Dev said with a grin. "Much better than the average carrier. And the rooms are larger too."

"They are," Missy agreed, lifting her coffee in a mock toast. "At least there is that."

"Even the basic crew have their own cabins," Dev added. "They have to share with someone, sure, but it's still a hell of a lot better than being crammed into a standard squad bay on a carrier."

Shifting slightly in her seat, Tabby caught the acrid scent of sweat, along with the faint smell of propellant that clung to her. It made her feel grimy. She glanced around the lounge once more, searching. "Where's the head and the showers?"

"Back there," Dev said, gesturing toward an unmarked hatch near the kitchenette. "There are six individual bathrooms, each with a shower. We are truly living in luxury."

Tabby frowned, her gaze following his finger. The hatch was unremarkable—no sign, no indicator.

"The ship's still missing a lot of the basics," Dev added, noting her expression. "Signs and stuff—things we take for granted on other ships—are absent in a lot of places. It'll take some getting used to. They were still putting the finishing touches on her when everything went to hell."

"You said we have about two hours before the meeting with the CAG?" Tabby asked, glancing between Dev and Missy.

"Less now," Missy said. "More like an hour and a half."

Tabby nodded, her thoughts turning inward. Her body ached, her mind felt sluggish, and the uncertainty surrounding the future loomed like a dark cloud. But one thing she knew for certain—first impressions mattered, especially when it came to new leadership. She had no intention of meeting the CAG looking and feeling like she'd just crawled out of an exhaust vent.

Standing abruptly, she drained half of her coffee in one gulp. "I'm going to hit the head, grab a shower, and clean up while I still have time. I'll catch up with you both later, perhaps at the staff meeting."

Dev and Missy nodded in unison but said nothing. Tabby crossed the lounge toward her cabin. Entering her quarters, she set the mug on the desk and opened one of her bags, the larger one. She pulled out a spare flight suit, its fabric crisp and clean, untouched by the chaos of the last few hours. As she began gathering her things, fresh socks, undergarments, and her toiletry bag, her mind wandered to the meeting ahead.

What could she expect? What would she learn?

The future was uncertain, but one thing was clear—this meeting would set the tone for everything to come, and she expected the ride ahead to be far from easy. Tabby knew that at some point soon, combat would be in their future. She was on a new type of warship, one designed to take the fight directly to the enemy. It would likely happen sooner rather than later.

"So be it," Tabby said, the anger simmering within, heating her. Whatever challenges lay ahead, she was determined to meet them head-on. That, and she'd make the enemy pay.

SIX

GARRETT

Garrett emerged from his office, stepping onto the bridge, into what could only be described as controlled chaos. Swarming with more than two dozen techs from engineering, the bridge was a hive of activity and noise.

The shattered remnants of Garrett's old command chair and station had already been ripped out and removed. In its place, a new station was being actively installed. Judging from what he could see, the technicians were making good progress too. From a glance, he estimated the job would be finished within the day, which was encouraging.

The battered, crumpled remnants and shattered pieces of the old bridge hatch had been loaded onto several construction sleds. The parts still attached to the bulkhead, the portions that had not been blasted away during the attack, were being physically cut loose with laser torches. Ready to be installed, a replacement hatch sat waiting farther down the corridor.

The marine sentry standing guard just outside Garrett's office snapped to attention as he passed. Garrett gave her a brief nod, before halting a few paces onto the bridge. His eyes swept the scene with a practiced gaze. Despite the ongoing repairs and the accompanying noise, his crew were at their stations and working. The atmosphere was steady, calm, and methodical— exactly how Garrett preferred it. Sitting at his helm station, Heller spotted him and turned. Garrett shook his head. He was not here to relieve the man, not yet. Heller gave a nod of understanding and turned back to his work.

After a much-needed shower, a clean uniform, and a hot meal, though he hadn't gotten any sleep, Garrett felt renewed. The stim coursing through his system left him feeling a touch jittery, but it had given him the energy he needed to power through. He was awake, alert, and sharp—a necessity given the coming meeting.

More importantly, Garrett had made his decision. They were going to the Dows System. Now, all that remained was to make it happen.

His gaze lingered on the HTD at the front of the bridge, studying it for a long moment. Nothing stood out to him as out of the ordinary. A combat space patrol had been launched, a close-in fighter screen, but beyond that, the ship was right where she needed to be. No threats were on the board. Then again, in the deep dark, Garrett did not expect any. Still, it was a precaution and always paid to be safe.

Satisfied everything on the bridge was well in hand, Garrett turned and made his way toward the admiral's bridge, located just behind the main bridge. The two were connected by a short, enclosed passageway designed for quick access between command centers.

He came to an abrupt halt a few steps before reaching the hatch. A man clad in light armor, a rifle held casually across his chest, blocked the way. The armor, though unpowered, was clearly reinforced with subtle modifications—a far cry from standard marine issue. Its dark matte finish seemed to absorb the light rather than reflect it, and the lines were sleeker, more angular.

The stranger's eyes, cold and calculating, locked onto Garrett. There was no salute, no snap to attention—just an appraising look that lingered a beat too long for Garrett's liking.

For his part, Garrett resisted the urge to frown but felt his jaw tighten. Who was this man? The lack of rank insignia and nameplate on his armor was notable, even suspicious. His gear hinted at something unconventional, and the absence of any identifying markers only deepened the mystery.

Garrett's thoughts turned to Admiral Yenga's earlier mention of special operators now assigned to the ship and his command. Was this one of them? If so, why had he been stationed on the bridge and without Garrett's direct knowledge? He disliked surprises, and this one left a bad taste in his mouth.

For a moment, Garrett considered questioning the man directly, but he thought better of it. The answers he wanted could wait for Shaw, who was already on the admiral's bridge. He started forward again, crossing the remaining distance between them. The man would either move aside or Garrett would have him moved.

The soldier didn't snap to attention or offer a word. Instead, he stepped to the left, granting Garrett access to the hatch. The lack of deference grated on Garrett's nerves. His scowl broke through, as the hatch opened with a faint hiss, revealing the short, utilitarian corridor that connected the two bridges. Garrett stepped through, the hatch behind him sealing automatically, cutting off the noise of construction work and activity from the main bridge.

The hatch ahead slid open, and Garrett stepped onto the admiral's bridge. Designed to function as the nerve center for fleet-wide operations, it was slightly larger than the main bridge. The space was a blend of cutting-edge technology and glaring incompletion. Bulkhead panels leaned askew or were missing entirely, exposing a tangled web of conduits and cabling that snaked along the walls and ceiling. As if someone had abandoned them mid-installation, in one corner, several panels were stacked in a precarious pile.

A cluster of tools lay scattered across the top of an open and empty shipping container, their arrangement haphazard. The scene felt frozen in time, the work left unfinished.

At the heart of the bridge stood a large circular display table. It was the centerpiece, built to tie directly into the HTD and project a three-dimensional holographic display of the space surrounding *Surprise*—along with the small fleet now under Garrett's command. For now, however, the table sat dark and inert.

Around the table, several workstations jutted from the floor in various states of assembly. Some were fully installed and operational, their screens displaying diagnostic reports, navigation data, or system overviews. Others flickered erratically, struggling through or frozen at incomplete loading and boot cycles. A tangle of disconnected cables spilled out from one terminal.

These stations were meant for the admiral's staff—aides and advisors who would monitor the fleet's status and provide tactical and strategic insight when required. But there was no admiral to command here, no aides to man these stations. This was Garrett's show and his alone. Circumstances had seen to that.

Shaw stood waiting near the central table. Beside him was a strikingly beautiful woman, her presence commanding in a way that was both subtle and undeniable. Her jet-black hair, tied back into a single braid, gleamed faintly under the lighting of the admiral's bridge. As if carved from stone by a master, her features bore the distinct hallmarks of Native American heritage, sharp and dignified, high cheekbones, hinting at her likely origins from Hahowis—a world settled by the indigenous people of Old Earth's North American continent.

The rank on her uniform marked her as a lieutenant

commander. This would be Senica. There was an understated elegance to her appearance, but also something else—cutthroat and blade-like—beneath the surface. Garrett could see it plainly.

Both she and Shaw turned toward him. Their conversation ended abruptly, the air shifting as her eyes met his. Senica's gaze was piercing, cold, and unnervingly analytical. There was no warmth in those dark eyes, no hint of deference or hesitation. Instead, he felt as if he were being sized up—measured and weighed with the clinical precision of someone who understood people not as individuals, but as potential assets or threats and how to best use them.

This was a dangerous woman.

He could sense it as surely as if she had drawn a weapon and pointed it at him. But Garrett was not intimidated, not in the slightest. Just off to Lieutenant Commander Senica's right stood another man clad in light tactical armor. His rifle rested at the ready—a silent promise of immediate action should the need arise. Like the one guarding the entrance to the admiral's bridge, he bore no rank insignia or nameplate. To the side and their left, Stroud and Burns waited.

"Lieutenant Commander Senica, I take it," Garrett said, stopping before the inert holographic table and looking across it at her.

She straightened to a position of attention. "As ordered, I am reporting aboard, sir. I would have presented myself earlier —and I attempted to do so—but I was informed you were unavailable. I made my presence known to Lieutenant Heller instead and was entered into the rolls."

"At ease," Garrett replied, his gaze shifting to the armed and armored man beside her. He hadn't moved a muscle, but his gaze was fixed upon Garrett.

"And who is this?" Garrett asked plainly, meeting the man's gaze.

"I am Brent, sir." His voice carried a rough, gravelly edge, as though worn from years of shouting orders or enduring harsh conditions.

"What's your rank, soldier?" Garrett asked. He could sense the same tightly coiled energy within Brent as he had in the guard outside. This man was dangerous too. His trade was killing. But there was precision here and absolute control.

"I don't have a rank, sir, other than team leader." Brent's stance remained relaxed, though there was an unmistakable readiness about him, as if he were a single heartbeat away from action.

"Team leader," Garrett repeated, tilting his head slightly as he thought on that for several seconds. "You stand outside the general military structure, then?"

"That's correct, sir. I report directly to the 3rd Special Missions Group. I have no other boss or supervisor outside of that chain of command."

Garrett's lips pressed into a thin line as he considered the implications of what the man had just told him. "Meaning you report to me?"

A faint shadow of a smile tugged at the corner of Brent's mouth, though it didn't reach his eyes. "You could say so, sir, yes. That would be a correct statement."

The commodore regarded the man for a long moment, weighing the situation. Special mission operators were rare, often deployed in situations where conventional military forces couldn't function effectively, or where a scalpel was needed instead of a sledgehammer. Their presence aboard *Surprise*, a warship, was both a reassurance and a question mark, especially when it came to his command of them.

"Going forward, sir," Senica said, drawing Garrett's attention, "I've taken the liberty of assigning Brent, along with several others from his team, as your personal guard. Wherever you go on the ship, they will accompany you. If for any reason you leave *Surprise,* they will form the nucleus of your escort and security detail."

Stilling, Garrett found himself incredulous. She'd already begun making decisions aboard his ship—and without consulting him. His eyes narrowed slightly, and one eyebrow arched as he fixed her with a pointed look. She wasn't even part of the ship's chain of command. "Care to explain yourself, Commander?" His tone was even, but there was an unmistakable edge to it.

"I have my orders, sir," Senica replied, her tone steady. "They come directly from Admiral Yenga. Next to the chief engineer—who has already been assigned his own protection detail from B Team—you are the most critical person aboard *Surprise.* You understand the ship and her capabilities like no one else. I'm simply following the admiral's instructions to best support the mission."

"Yenga ordered this?" Garrett asked.

"He did, sir," she said, nodding. "I have written orders if you'd like to review them."

Garrett's jaw tightened as he shifted his gaze to Stroud, searching for any sign of surprise or disagreement. This superseded his responsibilities, directly stepping on his toes. The colonel remained impassive, his expression calm and unreadable. Beside him, Burns mirrored his superior's demeanor, standing at ease and showing no reaction to the news. It became clear they had already been informed. Senica must have briefed them beforehand... Shaw too, likely just before his arrival.

"You don't have a problem with this, Colonel?" Garrett asked, his voice carrying a subtle challenge.

Stroud exhaled slowly, his posture shifting slightly as he considered his words. "I'm not exactly happy about it, sir, but after what I've been told concerning the enemy's infiltration of the Confederation, I understand the necessity of a personal escort"—the colonel's gaze flicked to Brent—"one beyond the capabilities of my marines. At the same time, it also frees up my people to focus on other jobs."

Garrett's irritation deepened, though he kept it from his voice. His gaze swung back to Senica, his thoughts churning. The fact that Yenga hadn't mentioned these orders to him directly was troubling. Perhaps there just had not been time, but it still felt like a breach of trust, even if the move was meant to ensure his safety. What else had Yenga tasked Senica with? What other instructions had his old friend given her that he hadn't been made aware of?

"Very well, Commander," Garrett said after a long pause, his tone carefully neutral. "For now, I'll defer to Admiral Yenga's judgment. But I'll be reviewing those written orders—and any others you might be operating under."

Senica inclined her head, her expression giving away nothing. "Understood, sir. I will share everything."

The hatch hissed open behind them, and in strode Neelan, the ship's chief of the medical department. He was an older man with thinning gray hair that clung stubbornly to his scalp. His perpetual scowl was firmly in place, giving the impression that he was either mildly irritated or seconds away from snapping at someone. Garrett had worked with Neelan enough over the past few weeks to suspect that this was just his natural state. His personality was an abrasive one, but he was good at his job.

"Neelan," Garrett said, preempting whatever complaint the doctor seemed poised to unleash as he took in the gathering and approached the table. "Thank you for coming."

Neelan folded over his chest. "Do you know how long it takes to get here from my office? It's not as if I work in the medical annex just off the bridge. We could have done this through a virtual conference. I have patients to tend to and tests that demand my attention. I am, after all, a busy man."

Garrett felt a flicker of irritation but suppressed it. The doctor's personality was as reliable as the ship's artificial gravity.

"We could have, but I thought it better to do this in person. Besides, I don't want anyone overhearing what we are about to discuss. The flag bridge is secure."

"Fine, but as soon as this is over, I'll need to get back to my duties," Neelan said, pausing just long enough to tack on a begrudging, "sir. I am still working on those test kits."

"What test kits?" Garrett asked curiously.

"The ones that Lieutenant Commander Senica tasked me to make." Neelan waved a hand at her. "What with all the wounded, it's not like I don't have enough to do at the moment, and that doesn't even begin to cover my regular duties along with those of my staff."

Garrett exhaled slowly, reining in his mounting frustration, and turned back to Senica. "You briefed the doctor concerning the fifth column?" His voice carried a sharp edge now.

"When I found you unavailable, I did brief him, sir," Senica replied, her voice calm and measured, as if she had anticipated his reaction. "He was instructed to keep the information to himself. In my judgment, securing this ship is a critical priority and there was no time to waste. Admiral Yenga explicitly ordered me to impress that fact upon you, sir, and take every action available to me to make that a reality."

Garrett felt his jaw tighten. It was becoming increasingly clear that Yenga's orders had granted her a great deal of autonomy. Still, she should have waited and checked with him before giving his people orders. That grated on Garrett. Before this meeting was over, she would either be working for him or not at all.

"The only people who know about this are currently in this room," Senica added, "along with both of Brent's teams. They were also instructed to keep this knowledge strictly to themselves."

"Going forward," Garrett said, "you will not share information concerning the enemy infiltration of the Confederation with anyone else, unless I give you explicit orders to do so. Is that understood?"

Senica straightened, her gaze meeting his evenly. "Yes, sir. That is perfectly clear. I will bring no one else in on this without your personal authorization."

Satisfied for now, but still wary, Garrett gave a short nod. While Senica's initiative might have been well-intentioned, he would need to keep his eye on her.

Garrett turned his gaze from Senica back to Neelan. "Have you examined the blood test? Do you think it will be effective?"

"I have," Neelan replied. "And I do believe it will be effective. I've already tested it on three of the prisoners in medical, and it works as intended. As we speak, I'm manufacturing enough testing units to meet the need, as it was explained—two thousand reusable kits. Nearly all my medical printers are focused on the task at hand. I should have the first test kits ready within the hour. Education on how to use them should be rather simple."

Garrett nodded. "Good. Stroud, your people will be conducting the testing."

"Yes, sir," Stroud said and looked over at Neelan. "My people won't have a problem operating these test kits?"

"Well, they are marines after all," Neelan said. "If there's a way to screw things up, you jarheads are capable of doing it." Neelan wagged a finger at the colonel. "But... the kits are quite simple and dare I say almost idiot-proof. They're designed to cross-reference genetic samples against the records provided. We will know in seconds if there's a hit. After the first kits are ready, I will walk you and anyone else you want through how they work. After that, you can teach others."

"That works," Burns fairly growled. It was clear he had not appreciated the doctor's comments.

Shaw crossed his arms. "We'll need a cover story. If word leaks about what we're really hunting, it could trigger the enemy into action—assuming they're among us—or worse, cause a panic."

"Thoughts on that?" Garrett's gaze swept the room, silently inviting input. For a long moment, the room was still. Then Burns cleared his throat, breaking the silence.

"We could use the Bloom shipment we discovered as a cover," the sergeant major suggested, looking over at Stroud.

Garrett's eyes snapped to Burns, surprise turning to anger. "You found Bloom on my ship?"

"We did, sir," Stroud admitted, straightening under Garrett's scrutiny. "The discovery was made just as the enemy attacked. I had intended to write a report, but there hasn't been time."

"The mule is still in custody and in the brig, sir," Burns added. "If we frame the testing as part of a broader crackdown on drug smuggling, illicit substances, it could serve as an effective cover story."

Shaw rubbed his chin with his uninjured hand, his expression plainly skeptical. "It's a bit thin as far as cover stories go, but it's better than nothing. Do we know how the Bloom got aboard?"

Burns hesitated, his gaze shifting once more to Stroud before answering. "Someone dropped the security system, sir. That means it has been compromised."

Garrett did not like the sound of that.

"Was that failure on the ship or the station?" Shaw asked.

"Unfortunately, on the ship, sir," Burns admitted, "around main medical."

"They hacked my ship?" Garrett growled, his anger rising like an incoming tide.

"It appears so, or a backdoor was coded into the software, sir," Stroud confirmed. "Either way, it's a bad business all around."

Garrett's jaw tightened. "This is unacceptable. Finding and fixing that vulnerability needs to be a top priority."

"I agree," Shaw said, glancing at Garrett. "Drug dealers compromising our security is bad enough. If the enemy found out about such a vulnerability... that becomes a whole other level of concern, especially after how they just proved they can access some of our critical infrastructure."

"I have people who can assist," Brent said, speaking up. "Two specialists—experts in computer systems and security. It may take some time, but they'll help root out any vulnerabilities."

"We'll provide additional resources as well," Garrett replied as he forced himself to calm down. It was supposed to be near impossible to compromise their security system. The fact that it had been done—and under his nose—was concerning. "This isn't something we can afford to approach half-heartedly. This needs to be fixed, and yesterday."

"I can oversee the effort, sir," Senica offered. "If you wish, I'll coordinate and supervise the team attacking the problem."

Garrett turned his gaze to Senica, studying her for a long moment. Yenga had spoken highly of her—praised her intelligence, capability, and work ethic. She had already shown a willingness to take decisive action, not to mention initiative, but that trait could be both an asset and a liability.

While he appreciated her resourcefulness, Garrett also knew the dangers of unchecked autonomy. He'd have to watch over her carefully. Still, his command was stretched thin, and senior officers with command experience were currently few and far between.

"Very well," Garrett said. "You'll head the effort. Pull Brent's specialists into the team and coordinate with engineering to lock down the ship's systems. You can have any resources you need. Find out how they got in and close that hole."

"Yes, sir," Senica replied with a nod, her expression unreadable. "I'll make it a top priority."

Garrett shifted his attention to Stroud. "We spread the word: every crewmember and evacuee is to be tested. The official reason? Bloom and other contraband were discovered during the evacuation from Midway Station. The search and subsequent testing is part of a broader effort to ensure the safety of everyone aboard."

Stroud nodded, his stance solid. "Understood, sir. I will get the word out."

Garrett paused, considering the practicalities of the operation. "If I recall correctly," he said, glancing back at Stroud, "we have dogs aboard, don't we?"

"Yes, sir," Stroud confirmed. "Six enhanced animals, trained to detect contraband and dangerous substances, including explosives. We also have specialized scanning equipment—drones, air sniffers, and similar tools that can be employed in searches."

"Good," Garrett said, a plan forming in his mind. "I want this hunt to look convincing. Every space and compartment on this ship gets searched, no exceptions. Put teams on it immediately. You can get started on that without test kits."

"Yes, sir, we can. We'll get on it right away," Stroud said.

"Excellent," Garrett replied. "Word will spread quickly, and anyone hoarding something like Bloom will panic. They'll either try to hide what they have or get rid of it altogether. But when the testing begins, people won't question it, especially if we uncover additional stashes of contraband. Conducting a thorough search beforehand will make the cover story more credible. It'll hold up under scrutiny, at least for a time."

Shaw nodded. "I think so too. It's a solid plan."

Garrett straightened, his gaze sweeping the room. "This needs to happen swiftly and efficiently. No slip-ups. Stroud, coordinate the searches and testing."

"And if anyone refuses, sir?" Burns asked, drawing Garrett's attention. The sergeant major's expression was grim. "What do we do if someone refuses to be tested?"

"That's non-negotiable and a nonstarter," Garrett replied, his voice firm and unwavering. "If anyone refuses, take them into custody and test them anyway. This is a matter of ship-wide security. We clear everyone—and I mean everyone—military and civilian. Is that understood?"

"It is crystal clear," Burns said with a curt nod.

"Sir," Stroud said, speaking up again. "There's another matter regarding the civilians I'd like to bring to your attention."

Curious, Garrett gave a short nod, signaling for him to continue.

"We've had several thousand step forward and volunteer to help out in any way they can," Stroud said. "I've discussed it with Major Ramirez and Sergeant Major Burns. We believe they could be of real value, especially in areas like damage control and casualty care if—*when*— we find ourselves in another engagement."

Garrett's expression shifted to one of interest, but he remained silent, allowing the colonel to continue.

"Many of those we brought aboard were employed by Construction Command," Stroud continued. "Civilians under contract, with experience in structural repair, systems maintenance, even medical support in field zones. We'd need to provide orientation, some basic safety, and technical instruction, but we think they can make a difference, especially when it comes to casualty care, first aid, transport, and triage."

Garrett weighed the idea, then gave a nod. "It has merit. Idle hands and anxious minds aren't good for general morale. If they want to contribute... fine." He paused, then met Stroud's gaze. "Every volunteer must be vetted, tested, and cleared, no exceptions. We can't afford any further lapses in security."

Stroud gave a sharp nod. "Understood, sir. We'll run full

background checks, physical assessments, the works, along with Doctor Neelan's test."

"I recommend we limit these helpers to noncritical areas of the ship," Shaw said, "just to be certain."

"That sound reasonable," Garrett said and turned his attention back to Stroud. "You are cleared to proceed. Keep me updated on the program and its progress."

"Thank you, sir, and I will."

Garrett shifted his attention to Senica, his gaze lingering for a few moments as he considered his next question. "How did the Confederation discover the enemy was operating among us? I assume you know more than what was in the briefing I received?"

"There was an incident on Arcadia Prime. A transport crash resulted in several casualties. One of the injured was severely burned and brought to a hospital. The medical staff couldn't identify her through standard procedures. She had no identity implant, so they ran a genetic test. That's when they discovered her genetic lineage had no direct and immediate link other than on a planet that fell to the enemy two Pushes ago."

"Two Pushes ago?" Garrett thought on what she'd just told him for a moment. "That would mean—what? Over a hundred years?"

"Correct, sir," Senica confirmed.

"If she didn't have an implanted tag," Burns asked, "how would she move around?"

"A tag was found near her person. It was not implanted and belonged to someone else—a Confederation citizen who had disappeared months earlier. The directorate believes she was using the identity to move about."

Neelan leaned forward slightly and placed both hands on the table, his voice tinged with curiosity. "She couldn't be questioned, could she?"

"She succumbed to her injuries before she could be properly interrogated," Senica replied. "Initially, Intelligence thought it was an isolated case, perhaps the work of one of the larger and more sophisticated criminal syndicates. But other cases and anomalies have surfaced. Each individual identified was linked with one of the conquered colony worlds."

"Did the Intelligence Directorate learn anything useful from those who were captured?" Garrett asked.

Senica shook her head slightly. "I'm not privy to the specifics, sir. What I do know is that the findings confirmed the presence of enemy agents, and ID has since expanded its screening protocols. A broader search... hunt is now underway in the Core."

"Sir," Stroud interjected, "it's worth noting Fleet personnel undergo exhaustive screening prior to being accepted into service. Any discrepancies in their records or backgrounds would raise immediate red flags."

"You're not wrong," Garrett admitted. "But this threat wasn't fully understood before, and we can't afford to take chances, not now. We have no idea how long the enemy has had access to our space, or how deep the infiltration might go. Fleet personnel, civilians, officers, or enlisted. Everyone aboard gets screened. No exceptions."

The room fell into an uneasy silence as Garrett's words sank in. The enormity of the task loomed over them, but so too did the urgency of its necessity. They couldn't afford to overlook any possibility—not with the stakes this high.

"While we're at it, sir," Neelan said, "I'll modify the testing protocols to include screens for illicit substances or residual traces in the blood." He nodded toward Stroud. "That includes Bloom. We can kill two birds with one stone and identify any addicts on the loose."

"Good thinking," Garrett said, giving a curt nod of approval. "Do it."

"We'll start with my marines, sir," Stroud said and looked

over at Burns for a moment. "Officers and NCOs will go first, followed by the rank and file. Once that's done, we'll move on to the crew and then the civilians."

"That sounds like a solid plan," Garrett said.

"What about the other ships in the task force?" Burns asked. "Do we test their crews as well or wait till *Surprise* is done?"

"As I see it, we don't have a choice," Garrett replied, his tone firm. "Their personnel will have access to *Surprise*. That means they get tested too, but you can begin with those on *Surprise*. No exceptions."

"Their captains aren't going to like that," Shaw said. "Their ships are their kingdoms. We will be stepping on their toes."

"I don't care if they like it or not," Garrett said flatly. "That's the order, and it's final. Drugs will not be tolerated under my command. That's the message I want sent, loud and clear. If they have issues with it, they can take it up with me." He paused, his gaze locking onto Stroud. "I also want an increased guard presence over all critical sections of the ship—reactors, engineering, the bridge, magazines, life support, and any other sensitive areas."

"Yes, sir," Stroud said. "I'll see to it immediately."

"I'd recommend testing those who come into regular contact with the captain and chief engineer first," Brent said, speaking up.

"I will make that happen too," Stroud said.

"Colonel, how long do you estimate the testing will take?" Shaw asked.

"With the number of test kits medical is preparing," Stroud replied, thinking for a long moment, "several days at the very least. A week and a half at most, depending on how smoothly things run. I am certain as time passes, we will get more efficient at it."

"That time frame should also give us a chance to investigate and potentially resolve the security system breach," Senica added. "We'll run that effort in parallel with the testing."

"We'll also need a reason for delaying our jump to the objective... the mission," Shaw said. "Our messaging has to be clear—especially since we'll be screening and testing everyone."

Garrett gave a short nod, thinking for a moment. "Skeleton crew, new personnel slotted into unfamiliar roles—positions they weren't originally trained for. That demands retraining, and retraining takes time. Getting our house in order—that's our excuse. Clear?"

"Clear," Shaw replied. "And it'll hold up, especially if the training looks legitimate, which it should be."

"We'll have each department draw up drill and instruction schedules," Garrett said. "I want ship-wide drills too. We use every minute to get ready for what's coming. When I meet with the captains of the task force, I will explain the real reason behind the delay and where we are going first."

Shaw nodded in agreement.

"Very good," Garrett said. "*Surprise* will remain in our current position until the testing is complete. I'm not taking this ship into battle or putting her at risk until I know for certain we don't have enemy agents aboard. This ship is not moving until I'm confident we've done everything in our power to secure her." Garrett turned to Stroud. "Have you begun questioning the prisoners?"

"The interrogation unit has just started, sir," Stroud replied. "At the moment, only one prisoner is in a condition to answer questions. The rest are too badly injured. They're either sedated or in medically induced comas."

"I wouldn't recommend waking them up just yet," Neelan interjected. "Their bodies need time to heal, or we risk losing them entirely."

"Also, sir," Stroud continued, "you should be aware each of

the prisoners we've examined so far, along with the dead, have extensive sets of implants."

Garrett's eyebrows rose slightly. "Is that right?" He turned to Neelan. "Have you had a chance to examine them?"

"It's true, sir," Neelan confirmed, a note of unease in his voice. At the same time there was interest and some excitement. "These implants are unlike anything I've encountered before. They're sophisticated—run throughout their entire bodies and appear to be highly interlinked. Frankly, they're very advanced and beyond our current level of technology. At this point, I can only speculate as to their purpose and function."

Garrett did not like the sound of that.

"The implants integrate seamlessly with their biology. They're not just simple augmentations; they've become, for lack of a better explanation, a part of them, the person. They may enhance strength, cognition, or even serve as communication tools, or do something else. I just don't know at this point. When I have the time, I plan to examine the implants we've recovered from the dead. Once I know more, I will let you know."

Garrett exhaled slowly, absorbing the information. Then, turning his attention to Senica, he asked, "What about the woman who was burned on Arcadia Prime? Did she have implants too?"

Senica frowned, frustration flashing across her face. "I don't have that information, sir. The details I received were sparse and focused primarily on her genetic anomaly. If implants were discovered, that information wasn't included in the brief."

"All right," Garrett said finally, glancing between Stroud and Neelan. "I won't keep you any longer. Get back to work. Let's get the testing done as rapidly as possible. Shaw, Senica, kindly remain behind. Everyone else is dismissed."

Stroud, Burns, and Neelan filed out. Brent remained. Garrett wasn't very surprised by that. He waited until the hatch slid closed behind the others before speaking again.

"Commander Senica," Garrett asked, his tone measured, "are you aware of our orders? Our destination and what we're expected to do there?"

"No, sir, I am not," Senica replied, her voice steady. "Admiral Yenga did not see fit to read me in on that part of the operation."

"What about the jump point disruptor?" Shaw asked.

She tilted her head slightly, a flicker of curiosity crossing her sharp features. She looked between the two of them. "I've never heard of it, sir, but it certainly sounds fascinating. I'd love to learn more."

"You will," Garrett said. It was clear now that Yenga hadn't told her everything. Did the admiral even know about the disruptor? Garrett was seriously beginning to wonder.

"Shaw, I want you to get with the science team and engineering once they've been tested and cleared. Begin working on manufacturing a disruptor. I'll send you the specifications that Gray shared. You'll personally oversee the project. If possible, I want the first device operational within the week."

"Aye, aye, sir," Shaw replied without hesitation.

Garrett shifted his attention back to Senica. Her dark, intelligent eyes remained locked on him, their intensity almost unsettling. He studied her for a long moment, weighing her capabilities. It was time to test her further—to keep her occupied and integrate her fully into the command structure.

"Effective immediately, you are now third officer," Garrett said, his tone firm. "You will command the Combat Information Center. Do you have any objections?"

"No, sir, I do not," Senica replied without missing a beat. A faint flicker of amusement softened her otherwise rock-cold expression. "I have experience in that department. I served aboard a battleship in that capacity. Besides, sir," she added with a small smile, "I enjoy information."

"Good," Garrett said, his voice resolute. "Work with Shaw.

Assemble a capable team and ensure the CIC is fully operational before we take the ship into harm's way."

"I'll see to it, sir," Senica replied with confidence.

"Excellent," Garrett said. He allowed a brief pause, his gaze darting between Shaw and Senica. "Now, let me bring you up to speed on our mission, the jump point disruptor, and"—he glanced meaningfully at Shaw—"our ultimate target."

Senica's expression shifted to one of focused curiosity. "I'm eager to learn about that, sir."

Garrett exchanged a glance with Shaw. Turning his attention back to Senica, he said, his voice low and deliberate, "Be careful what you wish for, Commander."

SEVEN

TABBY

"Be Seated." The tone of the woman's voice was sharp and commanding as she climbed up to the stage and took her place before the podium. The assembled officers took their seats. "I am Lieutenant Commander Knox, your CAG. If someone else hasn't already said so, welcome to *Surprise*."

Tabby leaned forward in her seat, her arms resting lightly on the armrests of a simulated leather chair. It was surprisingly comfortable, a rare touch of luxury in an otherwise utilitarian space. The briefing compartment was packed to capacity, with standing room only along the back wall around the main hatch. The latecomers had taken up positions there. Tabby, Dev, and Missy had arrived early.

The compartment itself was standard military fare; no frills, purely functional. Thirty chairs, bolted firmly to the deck, faced a raised platform and podium at the front. Behind it, an over-sized holoscreen displayed *Surprise*'s space wing insignia—a stylized depiction of a phoenix rising from a starburst. Knox had apparently chosen it. At least that was what Tabby had just been told by someone in the know.

Knox stood at the podium, her sharp eyes scanning the gathered squadron leaders. She was tall, her posture straight despite a noticeable limp that lent an unevenness to her movements as she had taken the stage. Her short brunette hair was neatly trimmed. A jagged scar cut across her chin. Rather than detracting from her presence, it added an edge of grit and resilience that seemed entirely fitting for someone in her position. Tabby found it almost comforting.

There was no mistaking the air of authority she carried. It was hard and no-nonsense. Her penetrating gaze swept the room, lingering briefly on each pilot, as if weighing their worth in an instant.

To Tabby's right, Dev sat relaxed, slightly slouched, one hand resting on his knee. To her left, Missy was sitting upright, her hands clasped in her lap, her expression focused. Both, like Tabby, were evaluating Knox as much as she was evaluating them.

Tabby's thoughts wandered briefly to the scar on Knox's chin and the limp that followed her steps. It wasn't hard to piece together that she'd likely endured a serious accident, one involving aviation that could easily have ended a career—or worse, taken her life. Yet here she was, commanding their attention with ease, her presence alone enough to demand respect.

Knox placed both hands on the edges of the podium and leaned forward, her gaze hardening as she continued. "We have a lot to cover today, and not much time to do it. So, let's get straight to the point."

The room settled into complete silence. Any whispering that had been going on stilled.

"I don't have time to dick around. Nor do you. I know you have questions. Save them. Now is not the time. I'll get to meet each of you in turn over the next few days, and then we can talk. That doesn't mean we're going to be taking long hot showers together and enjoying the quiet moments cuddling together in a bunk."

A ripple of laughter broke through the room. Knox didn't flinch or smile. She waited, her posture rigid, until the laughter faded into uneasy silence. Her gaze swept the room once more, pinning several squadron leaders in place like insects under glass.

"You may think I'm funny now, but let me make something crystal clear: I'm a taskmaster and I will not be easy on you. I will work you harder than you've ever been worked before. You will come to hate and loathe me, but I don't care." As if to let that sink in, she paused. "You may hold the rank of officer, but for the foreseeable future, you'll work like enlisted personnel. No exceptions. The days of being pampered are over."

That statement caused a wave of discomfort to ripple through the room. A few squadron leaders shifted in their seats, exchanging glances with their neighbors. Others simply sat frozen, waiting for more, their expressions unreadable.

Knox straightened slightly, her hands gripping the edges of the podium. "I'm going to bottom-line it for you: we are woefully short on ground crews. I have less than a third of the qualified personnel needed to service and maintain our small craft."

This time the reaction was audible. Chairs creaked, and scattered whispers sprung up. Tabby felt her jaw tighten. She shook her head slightly, for *Max* needed extensive work, and it was now clear who would be doing it.

Nothing is ever easy.

Knox's voice cut through the rising whispers like a scalpel. "The good news," she said, her tone laden with sarcasm, "is that every single one of you, along with your pilots, has received maintenance and repair training for your fighters, interceptors, torpedo bombers, assault boats, or shuttles, whatever it is that you fly. You may be rusty and out of practice, but it's time to put that training to use. From this moment forward, everyone is pitching in to get things done. There are no exceptions, no excuses. If you don't like it, the hatch is at the back of this compartment, and then I will find you a real shit detail, one you will hate even more than me."

Tabby glanced to her left. Missy had a grim look on her face. Dev, on her right, sat back in his chair, arms crossed, a faint smirk tugging at the corner of his mouth. He leaned closer to Tabby and whispered, "Looks like we're getting our hands dirty."

Tabby didn't respond. Her thoughts churned as she stared at Knox. She couldn't decide whether she would ultimately come to respect the woman on the stage or hate her guts as she said they would. But, one thing was certain, Knox was as direct as they came. The room settled into silence again. Whatever they had expected from this briefing, this certainly wasn't it.

"The ground crews we have are going to be overworked, fatigued, and stressed," Knox continued. "Hell, they are already exhausted. If I hear any of you have chewed out one of my people, your ass will be mine. If there's a problem, you come see me first." She tapped her chest with a finger. "I will handle it."

Knox paused, rubbing the back of her neck with one hand. Simultaneously, her gaze dropped to the tablet resting on the podium. She seemed to gather herself before looking back up, her eyes scanning the officers in front of her. Tabby felt the intensity of that gaze sweep across her, a reminder that Knox wasn't just speaking to a roomful of squadron leaders—she was addressing them individually.

"Now for the good news," Knox said. "Many of you arrived without your craft or are for whatever reason missing personnel. Before we left Midway, we managed to take aboard a substantial number of fighters, interceptors, and torpedo bombers. Those will be assigned accordingly."

The announcement sent a ripple of murmurs running through the compartment, though Knox continued without pause. "We also took on crated spacecraft that will require assembly before they're doled out. On top of that, we brought aboard a good number of qualified pilots. They'll be assigned to squadrons currently short on personnel. Your job is to welcome them, and get them settled."

Knox leaned forward slightly, her hands gripping the podium as she emphasized her next point. "Keep in mind, these pilots may not have been trained for your specific type of craft. They're pilots, and at the moment, that's what does matter. Your job is to get them up to speed as rapidly as possible. Simulator time will be scheduled by squadron, as will flight time. Use it wisely, and don't waste a second."

A hand went up near the front of the room. Knox's gaze locked onto it, her expression hardening. "I said I will not be taking questions," she said firmly, and the hand lowered. "We're not opening that can of worms today. Save your questions for later, or better yet, send me a message if you must. I have too much on my plate and too little time. The hangar bays must be cleared and made flightworthy. That is my priority and soon it will become yours too."

Knox paused briefly, letting her words settle. "Replacement flight crew assignments will be coming later today. Be on the lookout for them, for they will be hitting your inboxes. Billeting will change accordingly. Squadrons will be quartered together. Meet your people, and as I said, get them settled, along with yourselves. Work assignments and shift rotations will follow within the next twelve hours. Do not let me catch you or your people shirking. Trust me... you will live to regret it."

She sucked in a breath, straightened, and looked out over the gathered officers. "Make no mistake—we are in a shooting war. No one expected it to come so soon; worse, for the Confederation to be so unprepared. But here we are. We take the cards we've been dealt, and we work with them. This is no pleasure cruise. We must be ready to fight. We don't know where we are going yet or why, but you can be damn certain we'll be going into action, and I think sooner rather than later."

The room fell into a heavy silence, the gravity of Knox's words hitting home. Tabby's mind churned, already thinking through the implications of what lay ahead. This was their reality now—a chaotic scramble to prepare for war, with lives depending on their ability to rise to the occasion.

As if consulting her notes, the CAG paused again, glancing down at her tablet. She shifted her stance, leaning forward on the podium as she looked up, her gaze cutting across the compartment.

"Captains Tabby and Woodward," she called out, "make yourselves known."

Tabby raised her hand. "Here, ma'am." She could feel every eye turning toward her.

"Here," Dev added, lifting his hand in acknowledgment.

Knox's gaze lingered on them both, her expression unreadable as her dark eyes assessed them. After what felt like an eternity, but was only a blink of an eye, she gave a small nod, as if coming to some private conclusion. "Excellent work out there, both of you," she said, her voice carrying an undercurrent of approval. "Especially you, Tabby. Taking out that assault carrier was not only dangerous but downright impressive. It was a good, solid kill."

"Thank you, ma'am," Tabby replied. The sensation of being under scrutiny didn't lessen; if anything, it intensified. She could practically feel the unspoken questions swirling in the minds of her peers.

"Both of you," Knox continued, "stick around. I want a word with you. As for the rest of you, go rest. As I said, I'm going to drive you like a rented mule. Be ready when the orders come. That is all... dismissed."

Chairs creaked as the officers rose in near unison, the room filling with the sound of shifting boots and quiet murmurs.

Several cast glances or nodded toward Dev and Tabby as they passed, their expressions a mix of curiosity and respect.

"Getting into trouble already?" Missy quipped with a grin, glancing back at Tabby and Dev before joining the steady file of squadron leaders streaming toward the exit. Moments later, the last officer disappeared through the hatch. It hissed shut behind them, leaving the compartment eerily silent. The sudden absence of chatter and movement made the room feel larger, the quiet almost oppressive.

"This can't be good," Dev murmured under his breath, his tone light but carrying an undercurrent of apprehension as they made their way toward Knox.

"I know," Tabby replied softly, unease creeping into her voice. She adjusted the collar of her flight suit as if trying to shrug off the tension. With each step, a faint prick of adrenaline heightened her senses. Whatever Knox wanted, Tabby was certain it wouldn't be a casual chat.

With a grimace, Knox had climbed down off the platform and now stood waiting for them. There was no warmth in her expression, only the hard-edged determination of someone who had little time to waste and a tough job to do.

"Both of you proved yourselves out there," Knox said, her voice suddenly heavy with a weariness that lined her sharp features. The exhaustion in her eyes was unmistakable, and Tabby could see that the CAG was running on fumes. "I'm going to pay you back in kind—reward success with more responsibility and a greater workload. In short, I am going to pile it on and then some."

Tabby barely resisted the urge to groan.

Knox's gaze sharpened, scanning them both with almost clinical precision. "I need two senior assistants," she continued, her tone making it clear this wasn't a request. "And both of you are now it. Thank you for volunteering."

Tabby felt a knot form in her stomach. She understood now

why Knox had called them out during the briefing. It wasn't just to acknowledge their achievements—it was to establish credibility in the eyes of their peers. Knox had chosen them as her enforcers, a move as tactical as it was ruthless. In that moment, Tabby realized the CAG was one cutthroat bitch.

"You're going to help me bring order to the chaos that's been dropped on my lap," Knox said, her words biting like cold steel. "When you speak to the other leaders, you will do so with my voice. If you take any pushback, you come and see me. I will break heads. Is that understood?"

"Yes, ma'am," Dev said, his reply crisp.

"Aye, aye, ma'am," Tabby echoed.

"You'll need to manage these new responsibilities alongside your squadron workloads—for now. The XO assures me I'll be assigned adequate assistants soon, but until then..." She paused, her eyes narrowing as she studied them for a long, pointed moment. "Both of your squadrons were the last to touch down. Have either of you gotten any sleep since coming aboard?"

"No, ma'am," Tabby admitted.

"Not a wink," Dev added.

Knox gave a curt nod. "All right. You have eight hours. Get what rest you can—sleep, eat, do whatever you need to recharge. After that, report to my office for assignments." She turned and pointed to a hatch to the left of the platform with the podium. "The space wing command center is in there, through that hatch, my office too. Questions can wait until then. Dismissed."

Both came to attention and turned to go.

"Tabby," Knox called after her. "Wait a moment, please."

"Ma'am?" Tabby stopped and turned back, her expression neutral, wondering what more the CAG wanted. Knox waited for Dev to clear the compartment before speaking again.

"I saw the footage," Knox began. "What happened when your squadron jumped through the beacon."

Tabby felt a tightening in her chest. She did not want to talk about it now. Her jaw clenched, but she said nothing. What was there to say? They'd died and it was her fault.

"I know what it's like to lose people," Knox continued, her voice softer now, almost kind. "Trust me when I tell you, there was nothing you could have done to change the outcome. The enemy screwed with the beacon. There was no way to know... no way to prepare."

Tabby's chest tightened further. She fought to keep her voice steady. She really did not want to talk about what had happened. "I'm not so sure, ma'am."

"What more could you have done? Tell me. I want to hear it."

Tabby had no answer for that, which pissed her off. Her anger flared white hot, but she dared show none of it.

"That's what I thought." Knox's expression hardened. "We're in a war. Bad things happen to good people. Training increases your odds, but it doesn't guarantee survival."

"Yes, ma'am," Tabby replied automatically, though the words felt hollow.

Knox took a step closer, her limp suddenly very noticeable. There was heat in the CAG's eyes. "Don't 'yes, ma'am' me, Captain. I know you feel like hell. You're blaming yourself... The guilt... it burns. I know the feelings all too well. But what happened wasn't your fault. That kind of thinking will destroy you, eat you up from the inside out, and I can't afford to lose someone of your caliber. I will say this again. It was *not* your fault."

She wanted to believe Knox... but at the same time she felt so guilty, so angry, so responsible. The CAG's gaze was unrelenting as it bored into her, and for a moment, Tabby felt as though the CAG could see straight through to her soul.

"After your people died, you could have broken off and run for open space," Knox said firmly. "But you didn't. You remained in the combat zone. You rallied what was left of your squadron, brought them together, and you went after that assault carrier. That took guts, grit, and heart. I can respect that. I *need* that version of Tabby. This ship *needs* her. Do you understand me? You are still needed."

"Yes, ma'am," Tabby said again, though her voice was quieter. "I understand."

Knox's voice hardened further, her exhaustion barely masking the steel beneath it. "I know you're replaying every moment in your head, wondering what you could have done differently. I've been in your place. Take it from one who knows. I will say it again, you are not at fault. What happened could have happened to anyone, including me. It's time to move on."

Tabby stood there, feeling the emotion well up from inside. The rage flared. How dare this woman tell her to move on! Her people did not deserve that. It was an effort to keep it from surfacing.

"I understand what you are going through." Knox's voice softened again, though her words remained direct. "You've been knocked down, Tabby. The question is, will you get back up? Can you?"

Tabby did not immediately respond. She blinked. She *had* been knocked down.

"Can you get back up?" Knox pressed.

"I'm already up," Tabby said, though the conviction in her voice felt fragile, like it might shatter under scrutiny.

Knox nodded, her expression unreadable. "I need you to stand strong, girl, strong and tall. There's work to be done. The commodore will be taking us into another fight, another battle soon enough, and if I am any judge, before we're fully combat ready. Grieve later, not now. That's all I am saying. Focus on your job. Help me get the space wing ready for what's to come, what they will face out there in the dark."

Tabby swallowed hard, the lump in her throat suddenly

refusing to budge. She felt another hot surge of anger toward Knox. "Grieve later? Is that an order, ma'am?"

"If it needs to be," Knox replied. "And here's another: you are spent. Medicate and knock yourself out. Get some sleep. I need you fresh when you report for duty. That's not a suggestion—that's an order."

"Yes, ma'am," Tabby said, her voice steadier now as she forced the anger back down from where it had come.

"Dismissed," Knox said firmly, and with that, the CAG turned away and limped to the hatch that led to space wing command and her office.

The anger and rage subsided some. Feeling like a wrung-out dishrag, Tabby made her own way out of the compartment in the opposite direction. She stopped just beyond the hatch and sucked in a deep shuddering breath, her hands curled into fists at her sides. Her vision blurred for a moment, and she blinked hard, refusing to let the tears come.

Losing her people was agony.

Still, Tabby knew she had a job to do. The CAG had said as much. There would be replacements, new pilots and crew to welcome and get settled, people she would train to do a difficult job.

Knox's words replayed in her mind. *Stand tall. Stand strong.*

The anger inside her flared again, hot and consuming. It fought against the sadness, the pain of loss. Sucking in a deep breath, she let it out. She straightened her shoulders and lifted her chin. Though it pained her to admit it, Knox was correct. She could not wallow in self-pity. She had a job to do. That had to become her focus.

"Stand tall," Tabby muttered to herself, the words a quiet growl that burned with purpose. "Grieve later."

A passing crewman gave her a curious look, but she ignored him.

"Pick yourself up and stand strong," she added, louder this

time, as though speaking it could make it unshakable. And in that moment, she knew: those would be her watchwords, her personal mantra. *Stand tall. Stand strong.*

Knox was right and Tabby hated her for it. She had been knocked down. But now, Tabby would pick herself up. She had a job to do, and the better she did it, the more of the enemy she'd kill. The anger within burned hot and bright. For now, that was enough.

EIGHT

STROUD

The hatch irised open with a hiss of pressurized air, its segmented panels sliding back into the bulkhead like the petals of a mechanical flower. Once open, Stroud stepped through, followed closely by Sergeant Major Burns, who moved with the practiced ease of a man who'd seen more deployments than he cared to count. A wave of noise greeted them, an uneven chorus of instruction, chatter, and the occasional shouted correction rising and falling like surf against a distant shoreline.

The assembly and training compartment was vast, stretching nearly the length of a city block. Overhead lights bathed everything below in a harsh, sterile glare, too white and too bright, the kind that made shadows vanish and left faces looking wan and drawn.

This was part of marine country, the heart of the ground force's onboard operations, typically reserved for drills, zero-G exercises, and simulated live-fire training. Its modular design allowed for reconfiguration of the space to suit training needs. Walls could drop down from the ceiling or slide into place from floor tracks, dividing the space into mock terrain, urban zones, along with different and varied environments like ship corridors.

Now, though, the area had been hastily repurposed for simple training. The compartment was filled with civilians, hundreds of them, divided into groups clustered around stations with instructors. These were the volunteers.

Navy corpsmen moved briskly between groups, their uniforms marked by blue armbands and medical kits slung across their shoulders. Marine instructors, voices hoarse from repetition, demonstrated how to apply tourniquets, dress wounds, and transport casualties under difficult conditions. Medical personnel demonstrated how to administer injections, among other more complex tasks, and answered questions with clipped efficiency. As each group rotated from station to station, it was all organized chaos, a flurry of motion, gestures, and barked commands that threatened to overwhelm but somehow maintained a rhythm and organization of its own.

Having halted just inside the threshold, Stroud simply stood there, his eyes methodically scanning the compartment. He took it all in, the faces drawn tight with concentration, the nervous and unsure hands at work. These were ordinary men and women, their clothes still bearing the hallmarks of civilian life. They'd soon be issued uniforms, ship suits. Yet now they were being hastily armed, not with weapons, but with knowledge that might mean the difference between saving a life or losing one when the alarms sounded, and the worst happened.

Without conscious thought, Stroud's hand drifted to his sidearm, fingers resting lightly on the grip holstered at his hip. The motion was automatic, reflexive, an old habit. Beside him, Burns remained silent, arms loosely folded across his chest in a deceptively relaxed posture. His stance was that of a man used to waiting, to watching, shoulders squared, feet set just so. His eyes scanned the compartment with quiet intensity, clearly noting not only the layout and movement, but also the people:

likely assessing who was focused, who was floundering, who might crack under pressure. Burns didn't need to speak; he rarely did in moments like this. His presence was enough. He was the kind of man who could walk through a storm and come out dry, and everyone around him knew it.

The hatch behind them slid shut with a low mechanical whine, sealing off the corridor. As it clicked back into place, Stroud started forward. Burns followed. Voices overlapped in dozens of different conversations, some sharp and commanding, others tentative or confused as they made a comment or asked a question and received an answer from an instructor.

Close by, a group of trainees knelt in a half-circle around a collection of simulated casualties, mannequins with simulated wounds, embedded injury indicators, and data strips for medical scanner feedback. This wasn't CPR or bandaging.

It was triage.

A marine staff sergeant, wearing a medical badge, moved through the group with studied confidence. She was young, maybe mid-twenties, her voice clipped and precise despite the clear exhaustion that tugged at the corners of her eyes. Her fatigues were crisp, still neat despite what had to have been a long day. She wore a tactical vest, and a belt loaded with color-coded triage tags—red, yellow, green, black—and a thick black marker used to scrawl time stamps or injury status directly on limbs or foreheads.

"Red—critical... life-threatening injuries that can still be treated. Red is an individual that can be saved. You move them first, or they die," she called out, holding up a tag for emphasis as she paced before the group. "Yellow—serious, but stable for now. They can wait some. Treat them as soon as resources allow. Black—no pulse, no breathing, or injuries so severe that even with treatment, survival is unlikely. If they're that far gone, nothing we or the surgeons do will change the situation. You simply tag them and move on to the next casualty." She swept the group with a sharp look. "This isn't about saving everyone. We can't do that. It's about saving as many as possible in an orderly and proficient manner. You've all got at least some medical experience. That's why you are in this group. Don't freeze. You do what you can, with what you've got, in the time you have. Seconds matter." Her voice dropped a fraction, serious and direct. "Triage means sorting. We identify who needs help the most, who can wait, and who can't be helped. I can promise you... you won't like it. You don't have to like it. That's normal. But you do the job as trained, or more people die."

Stroud had seen triage before—real triage, on bloody battlefields and in shipboard med bays. Hell, he'd been triaged once himself. He knew what it meant when it was done right... life.

One of the volunteers caught his attention. A woman, crouched beside a mannequin, her hands gently checking the pulse at the synthetic neck. She wore civilian fatigues, a plain gray jumpsuit with a red medical sash looped across her chest. There was something about her.

Familiar.

She was too familiar. Where had he seen her before?

Her eyes lifted, as though sensing his gaze and interest. Their eyes met and for a moment everything else fell away, including the background noise. Her expression shifted subtly to surprise, recognition, and something deeper.

She stood, brushing her hands on her thighs. "Colonel Stroud."

The group fell into an uneasy pause. The volunteers looked between the woman and the officer in command of the marine contingent aboard *Surprise*. Even the sergeant faltered for a beat, noticing him and Burns for the first time and stepping forward out of habit. Stroud raised a hand, halting her in her tracks.

"My apologies for interrupting, Sergeant. Just a moment,

please." He turned fully to face the woman, narrowing his eyes slightly as he studied her. "Do I know you?"

Her smile was faint, tired, and worn at the edges... but there was a quiet warmth to it, something steady and real beneath the exhaustion. "You probably don't remember me," she said, her voice low, eyes locking onto his beneath the harsh overhead lights of the compartment. They suddenly shimmered faintly, moisture pooling despite her effort to remain composed. "I am Kelly. We never really met, at least formally. Back on the loading dock... the boarding port at Midway Station... my daughter." She paused, swallowing hard clearing her throat. "There was a man. He was station security. He grabbed her." She cleared her throat again, the words coming thick with emotion. "He held a gun to Michelle's head. You... you and the sergeant major stopped him."

The words struck like a jolt to the chest, unlocking his memory in a flood of images. The echo of shouts in the loading bay, the moment when everything narrowed to one singular focus. The rogue security officer, uniform in disarray, sweat slick on his brow, the man's drug-addled eyes, wide and erratic. He had been cornered, frantic... a girl clutched before him like a shield, eyes wild with terror as he pressed the pistol muzzle to her temple. He had been surrounded by armed marines with no way out and was threatening to kill her.

There had been no time to hesitate. Stroud had acted on instinct... years of training compressed into mere moments. He'd closed the distance, distracting the man, and struck when the opportunity had presented itself, a clean, full-force blow to the jaw... All of it came rushing back to him. He remembered the sharp ache in his hand, the way the knuckles had throbbed for hours after. Unconsciously, Stroud flexed his right hand, feeling the ghostly memory of the pain.

"How's your daughter?" he asked, voice rougher than he intended. "I meant to check in on her, but as you can imagine... a lot has gone on since the ship pushed back from Midway."

"She's okay," Kelly said, her voice gentler now. "She was discharged from medical last week. Michelle is in our quarters, drawing again." Her lips twitched upward, the memory of her child's resilience clearly strengthening her words. "She loves to draw. She finds it comforting. One of the crew loaned her a tablet to draw on."

Before he could reply to that, she stepped forward in a rush, her arms reaching. Stroud stiffened, caught off guard by the sudden contact, his body going rigid as her arms wrapped firmly around him. For a moment, he stood frozen, uncertain how to respond. Then, awkwardly, he patted her shoulder before he allowed himself to return the gesture, hugging her back and offering the comfort she sought. It was something... human, something he'd not done in a long time, something he'd not experienced since leaving his daughter behind. It felt good.

It felt right.

"I'm glad she's okay," Stroud said quietly, disengaging and stepping back. His eyes met hers again. "What's your last name?"

"Osca... Kelly Osca," she said softly. "Thank you, Colonel... for saving my little girl. I am so grateful."

"There's no need to thank me," Stroud replied. "I was just doing what needed doing." He glanced at the triage group, then to the sergeant who had paused nearby. Everyone was watching. "Now, don't let me keep you from your training. Sergeant, carry on."

"Yes, sir," the staff sergeant replied, giving a sharp nod. She raised her voice. "Show's over... back to work, people."

The volunteers, momentarily distracted, turned back to their practice. Kelly returned to her mannequin, kneeling once more and picking up her training marker along with her scanning kit. She glanced once at Stroud, nodded her thanks, and then returned to her work.

Stroud lingered, watching her for another beat, eyes distant, his thoughts drifting elsewhere. He turned and continued down the row, his posture heavy with reflection and thoughts on what had happened. Burns fell into step beside him without a word. For several paces, the two men walked in silence, the din of instruction swelling around them like a tide.

"It was good," Stroud said at last, his voice low, "saving that girl... especially on a day when so many couldn't be helped."

"It's what marines do," Burns said, "fight for the innocent, for those who can't defend themselves." He paused, then added with quiet conviction, "And it did feel good to deck that bastard."

Stroud didn't reply, but he didn't need to. The truth of it settled in his chest like a stone warmed by fire, heavy, solid, enduring. They passed another group, arranged in rows and on their knees atop rubber mats. The civilians leaned forward, hunched over CPR mannequins. The dummies were almost absurd in their simplicity—only torsos, no arms, no legs, neutral faces staring blankly at the overhead lights. Their synthetic chests rose and fell beneath the steady rhythm of repeated compressions, a faint mechanical click accompanying each press to confirm proper depth.

"Lock your elbows!" barked the marine instructor, a corporal with sleeves rolled up past the elbow of his fatigues, revealing forearms laced with old scars and inked symbols. He moved between rows like a drill instructor on a parade field, sharp-eyed and quick to correct. "Let your weight do the work. It saves you effort. Thirty compressions, two breaths. I said... thirty compressions and two breaths! You're not trying to be gentle, you're trying to bring someone back from the edge. Big difference because that takes effort."

A woman near the front stopped pumping and hesitated.

Her hands hovered uncertainly above the mannequin's chest, her brow deeply furrowed in concentration as she looked down at it. She was in her mid-thirties, dressed in a civilian jacket, sweat already dotting her forehead, despite the compartment's chill. The tension in her shoulders spoke of anxiety, but also determination... someone desperately trying to get it right.

"Don't stop," the corporal said, dropping into a crouch beside her, his voice lowering. "You need to keep going or the patient dies."

"What if I hurt him?"

"Your patient is dead. You are trying to bring them back. Keep that pressure steady and pump hard, until someone arrives with an AED. If you crack a rib, that's fine, you hear me? Better a broken and fractured rib than a dead patient. You're not going to hurt, you're going to help. Now keep going and put some effort into it."

She met his eyes briefly and nodded once, jaw tightening with resolve. Stroud paused, watching her force past her hesitation, her hands pressing down with renewed effort. The mannequin's chest dipped and popped, making a clicking sound with each thrust, the motion now almost disturbingly lifelike. Around her, others continued the drill, some grimacing with the exertion, or muttering counts under their breath, syncing their movements to an internal cadence.

They continued forward, stepping carefully around a line of stretchers laid out in a straight row along the deck. Civilians in mismatched clothing and hastily issued blue vests bent low under the direction of a Navy corpsman, their faces flushed with effort as they practiced the art of lifting and carrying casualties. They worked in teams of two, gripping the stretcher's reinforced handles, adjusting their posture with clumsy coordination. Others stumbled through simulated and uneven terrain marked by loose crates and strategically placed obstacles.

The corpsman barked out corrections, occasionally repositioning their grips or demonstrating the proper way to lift without straining the back. Weighted mannequins wrapped in blankets lay on the stretchers.

Just beyond that organized chaos, the next group was clustered tightly around a low metal bench, its surface lined with aging but serviceable foam padding that had clearly seen years of use. Here, the lesson was quieter but no less critical: wound care and trauma stabilization. The instructor stood at the center, a gray-haired doctor in a red-marked duty smock that hung loose around his wiry frame.

He didn't raise his voice. Despite the noise of the compartment, he didn't need to. There was something in his tone, measured, precise, a steadiness that cut cleanly through the ambient noise and drew attention like a magnet.

"Tight and high," the doctor said, his fingers moving deftly over a synthetic limb mounted to the bench as he demonstrated what he wanted. The training arm was molded from pale, pliable rubber and stained liberally with vivid red dye, a simulation of arterial bleeding that pulsed through a small embedded pump.

Crimson liquid oozed and flowed from a jagged mock wound, trailing down the foam and onto a metal catch tray beneath. "You want the tourniquet as high on the limb as possible... without getting into the shoulder and pelvis. Arteries, especially severed ones are elastic... so above the wound, always above, never below. You cut off blood supply below the injury and you're wasting time. Might as well shout at the bleeding and hope it stops."

He looped the black strap with an economy of motion born from years of practice and training, pulling it tight in one sharp tug. A practiced twist of the windlass and a quick locking clip... and the flow of artificial blood slowed, then ceased entirely. The demonstration was clean, clinical, final.

"Time matters," he continued, glancing up at the semicircle

of trainees gathered around him. "Write the time of application directly on the patient's forehead with the marker in your medical kit, not their chest, and certainly not on their hand. Their forehead is the one place the surgeons absolutely cannot miss. Doesn't matter if it looks messy. What matters is that they know how long that limb's been starved of blood. We might be able to save the patient, but if we don't know the ticking clock, we can easily lose the arm, understand? Knowing helps the triage team as well."

The civilians surrounding him nodded, some furiously scribbling notes into tablets or old-fashioned notebooks. Others turned to synthetic limbs of their own, fumbling to mirror the motion, hands working with uncertainty.

For a time, Burns and Stroud watched the class. As they worked, for every trainee who had the technique down, there were two more struggling, tourniquets hanging awkwardly or twisted out of alignment. But the doctor didn't scold or correct with irritation. He simply moved among them, calm and methodical, his expression gentle as he guided one pair of trembling and unsure hands after another. Mistakes at this stage were only to be expected.

"They'll learn," Burns muttered beside Stroud, his voice low but certain, like a man stating a weather forecast he knew would come true.

Stroud gave a short grunt of agreement, his eyes fixed on a nearby cluster. A teenage boy, no older than seventeen, was hunched over a training limb, his hands visibly trembling as he fought to secure the tourniquet. The strap bit into the synthetic flesh with a twitch of tension, the boy's lips moving in silent repetition of the doctor's instructions, clearly mentally repeating each step. It wasn't perfect—far from it.

"This might even manage to save a life or two, maybe more than a few if we're fortunate," Stroud commented to Burns. He didn't look away from the boy until the task was finished. Then they moved on, weaving through the compartment's improvised layout. Colored tape, laid in overlapping grids and chevrons, divided the floor into training lanes, bright yellows for triage, blue for transport, and red for trauma zones.

"Every single person here volunteered for this," Burns said. "We've got just under four hundred screened so far, cleared, and assigned to casualty care and support alone. Not too bad, all things considered." Burns's eyes swept the compartment. "Give us another forty-eight hours and we'll have more, and at least half of these will have been completely run through this training loop."

"They know what's coming?" Stroud asked, looking over at Burns. "What'll be expected of them once we're in another ship-to-ship engagement?"

"I'd say they know well enough," Burns replied. "We've made it plain, this isn't shelter-in-place duty. There will be no hiding below decks for them, being guarded by security detachments and handing out blankets to the other civies. They'll be near the action... triage zones, casualty hubs, evac corridors... the sections of the ship that will be the first to take damage. When the hull buckles and smoke rolls in, along with the fire and radiation, they'll be the ones helping to pull people out of hell itself. If things go sideways, they'll be dragging stretchers through fire, smoke, and shattered corridors. We've even shown them the training videos of what they will potentially face. A few backed out after that, but most stayed."

"Good." Stroud's jaw flexed, the muscle there tightening "We're going into battle soon enough. I have a feeling we will need their assistance."

"As do I, sir," Burns said, his voice quiet, a somber echo beneath the ever-present din of the room. "And time is not on our side."

They passed yet another team in the midst of a hands-on evacuation drill. The object was simple at first glance: extract a wounded individual from a damaged area of the ship. In practice, it was anything but. Obstacles had been placed strategically: collapsed struts, broken conduits, various crates standing in for scattered debris. The marked path was uneven, narrow, and cluttered.

Two civilian women, both in their late twenties by the look of them, struggled to carry a weighted training dummy strapped onto a collapsible stretcher. One made a misstep, catching her foot on a foam beam meant to simulate a fallen girder. She stumbled, tripping, and nearly falling, but caught herself at the last moment. Through sheer will alone, the two kept the stretcher upright, though it was far from a smooth ride for their patient, the dummy.

"They'll get better," Burns said as they continued to watch.

Stroud gave him a glance, skeptical. "You think they'll hold up when everything goes to shit?"

"I think most will," Burns said with a shrug. "There will be some who will panic and scream their heads off, becoming part of the problem instead of the solution. That's just how people are wired. We train 'em best we can and hope it all sticks. It's not like we're forging marines out here, putting them through weeks of field conditioning and drills until they sweat blood, piss bullets, and can handle most any situation with a cool head. At best, these people might get two weeks of training before we see combat again. You and I both know that's not enough."

"It will have to be."

"Aye, sir, it will have to be." Burns waved a hand toward the nearest group of trainees, a mix of tired faces and furrowed brows bent over bandages and splints. "This? This is just extra sets of hands, ones we are going to need soon enough. You and I both know truth in that."

Stroud gave a quiet nod and turned away. They walked on, their footfalls merging with the low drone of voices, the clatter of gear, and the occasional sharp bark of instruction. Each step carried them past more volunteers, men and women hunched in concentration, brows furrowed as they learned how to save lives in places where chaos would be the only constant.

Stroud's gaze shifted as they passed another training lane. A pair of older women, one with silver-streaked hair tied back in a rough bun, the other with short, cropped hair, were practicing how to move a casualty using nothing more than a sling and a short length of cord. The dummy between them was awkward and intentionally heavy. They moved with care, grunting as they coordinated their movements to avoid further injury. They talked to each other as they worked, faces tight with effort but filled with resolve.

"I never thought I'd see this, at least not on a warship," Stroud said finally, the words emerging like a breath held too long. "Civvies training like this..." He shook his head, his tone carrying something caught between disbelief and reluctant respect. "It's us who are supposed to be helping and protecting them..."

Burns gave a low grunt, the sound more than agreement. "It's not about uniforms anymore, Colonel, not on *Surprise*," he said. "It's simple survival. Every pair of hands counts, helps us edge toward mission success, whether they know which end of a rifle to hold or not."

They continued toward the compartment's main entrance, weaving through knots of volunteers and instructors still engaged in training. The murmur of effort and focus surrounded them again, a low and constant thrum filled with tension and determination. There was something rare in that atmosphere, something unmistakably human... people doing something hard, something outside their comfort zone because they understood it mattered and there would be a real need. There was grit in the way they moved, an urgency in every step, every gesture, that came from knowing the cost of failure, and also what was to come.

At the hatch, they paused. Stroud took one last look over his shoulder, his eyes sweeping the compartment. Ordinary civilians... now, something more, reaching beyond themselves. He found it inspiring.

"Damage control training is next," Burns said.

Stroud gave a short nod, bringing his thoughts back into the moment. "That's on Deck Two. Let's walk and not take the tram. I could use the exercise."

"You are the boss."

They stepped into the corridor beyond, the hatch shutting behind them with a low hiss. The passageway, one of the *Surprise*'s main arteries, was alive with movement. Marine personnel, along with a few civilian volunteers, streamed past, moving in both directions.

"The next group's mostly ex-construction," Burns continued as they walked, turning to the right and following the corridor. "They're all civilian maintenance and construction teams from Midway Station, mainly contractors. A few even worked the orbital yards in the Core. Some did tours with salvage ops. That background should give them a leg-up. They'll take to damage control quicker than most. At least, I think they should."

"How many have we managed to clear for training?" Stroud asked, his tone distracted. "How many have been screened?"

"So far... I'd say around two hundred," Burns said. "We're prioritizing them above others, but it still takes time. There are a lot of people that need checking. We should have another three hundred cleared by tomorrow and ready to begin training."

Movement caught the corner of Stroud's eye, a figure brushing past on the far side of the corridor, to his left. He was lean, dressed in a pale-blue utility jumpsuit with the yellow stripe of main engineering. He moved with purpose, but not confidence, not the easy rhythm of someone who belonged here in marine country, far from main engineering or secondary maintenance.

Something about this man didn't fit. He seemed out of place, and it rubbed Stroud immediately wrong. His eyes flicked to the colonel, just for an instant, then snapped hastily away a moment after their gazes met. Sweat beaded on his brow despite the cool, climate-controlled air. Turning his gaze down to the deck, his pace quickened as he passed.

Stroud felt it immediately, deep in his gut. A subtle tension coiled in his core. Something was not right about the tech. He slowed, coming to a halt. Burns kept going, taking another two steps, before noticing the change and stopping himself.

"Colonel?" Burns asked, casting a sidelong glance. "What is it?"

Looking back the way they'd just come, Stroud jutted his chin. "That tech. The one in blue. See him?"

Burns turned just in time to catch a glimpse of the man rounding a bend in the corridor, moving at a brisk pace that had become almost a jog. "The engineer? What of him?"

Stroud was already in motion, moving back the way they'd come and after the tech. "Let's find out where he's going."

"What's wrong with him?" Burns asked curiously, already adjusting his stride, falling into step once more beside his colonel.

Stroud's jaw clenched. His eyes stayed locked on the bend ahead where the man had just disappeared. "I don't know. Something's off. I want to talk to him."

"All right," Burns said.

"Come on, let's catch up." The two marines picked up the pace, shifting into a light jog. Marines coming from the opposite direction moved aside quickly, surprised expressions flickering across their faces to see their colonel and sergeant major moving at such a pace.

The corridor curved to the right, a design meant to mitigate explosive force in the event of a catastrophic event. As they rounded the bend, Stroud's eyes searched, found, and locked onto the fleeing technician again. He was ahead, but still visible, weaving through foot traffic with increasing urgency. He shot a look back over his shoulder, spotted them, and broke into a flat-out run.

Stroud's voice snapped down the corridor like a whipcrack. "You there! Stop! I said stop! Stop that man!"

The man whirled mid-stride, hand darting under his jacket.

"Gun!" Burns shouted, lunging. He slammed into Stroud, knocking him aside just as the weapon barked, incredibly loud in the corridor. The angry buzz of a bolt round ripped past them, the air humming with the residual heat of its passage. A split-second later, an impact echoed behind with a dull thud as the round hammered into a bulkhead.

Like an explosion, panic detonated through the corridor. Marines scattered, dropping flat to the deck or diving toward recessed doorways and support struts. The man fired again, a wild, desperate shot that scorched the air as it passed, hissing loudly.

In a fluid motion, Stroud dropped to one knee, his hand drawing his sidearm in a near blur. The weight of the pistol settled into his grip like a memory returning, an old friend. In the blink of an eye, it was up. He aimed and pulled the trigger. The pistol bucked in his hand. He fired again, a second shot. Burns, braced against the corridor wall, had his own pistol out. He fired a pair of shots in rapid succession.

The technician staggered as the bolt rounds hit, his body jerking violently, arms flailing, eyes wide with pain and sudden confusion. He collapsed backward and to the deck, landing hard, the pistol flying from his grip and skittering across the deck. His legs gave a violent spasm and then he lay still. Silence suddenly reigned in the corridor.

Smoke curled from the blackened holes in his jumpsuit's chest where the rounds had struck home. Blood began to pool rapidly beneath him, slick and dark against the polished corridor plating. Stroud rose smoothly, weapon still leveled and trained on the target. He advanced carefully, ready to fire again if necessary, if the man so much as stirred. His weapon held ready, Burns flanked him, scanning the area for secondary threats. They stepped over to the body. The corridor was nearly silent now, except for the distant echoes of muffled shouts of alarm from down the passageway.

Burns knelt beside the technician. Reaching out, he checked quickly for a pulse. After a moment, he shook his head. "Clean hits. Center mass." He looked up. "Good shooting, sir."

Stroud didn't respond at first. His eyes were locked on the corpse, jaw tight, shoulders tense, pulse pounding. The man was at least in his thirties. He looked ordinary and unremarkable... too ordinary, and yet, he'd still stood out to Stroud as not fitting in.

Why?

In death, like the mannequins in the training compartment, his eyes stared blank and lifeless up at the ceiling. No CPR or medical care would bring him back. The lights overhead gleamed off the blood as it spread in jagged streaks across the deck.

Something about this wasn't right...

This wasn't someone simply hiding contraband from the screening teams, a drug dealer. This wasn't a smuggler. His gut told him so.

Stroud's gaze went to the fallen pistol lying a few feet away. It was an MS-219, a snub-nosed standard-issue pistol, one that threw explosive bolts. The weapon was used almost exclusively by the Navy. His gaze returned to the dead man. This felt like something more sinister. Burns looked up at him, and their eyes met. An unspoken understanding passed between them like a signal. Stroud turned, glancing around at the nearest marines in the corridor. They'd climbed back to their feet and, wide-eyed, stood watching.

"Clear the area!" Stroud barked. "Now!"

Within moments, Burns and Stroud were alone.

"Sergeant Major," Stroud said, holstering his weapon. "Call security and a forensics team. I want this bastard searched, scanned, and identified. I want to know everything... who he is, where he's been on the ship, and who he's spoken to. I want his quarters searched, and I want to know how the hell he got a bolt pistol..."

"You think this is an infiltrator?" Burns asked quietly, turning his gaze back to the dead man. "You believe him to be the enemy?"

"I do."

NINE

GARRETT

Garrett entered the conference room that sat just off the bridge. With no chairs in sight, the room emphasized function over comfort—a deliberate choice he'd made long ago to streamline meetings, not to mention speeding them up. People tended to talk less when they had to stand for long periods. The bare bulkhead walls were interrupted only by recessed displays, which glowed faintly, cycling through system diagnostics and HTD data.

"Attention on deck!" Shaw's voice rang out, sharp and authoritative.

The captains came to attention, conversations dying midsentence. Garrett's gaze swept across the compartment, taking stock of the senior officers now under his command, those who commanded the starships attached to his task force. Toward the back on the left side, Tina and Jason, who'd been deep in conversation like the rest, straightened into positions of attention, their expressions carefully neutral as they turned to him.

"At ease," Garrett said, moving around and to the head of the table at the far end of the space. The assembled officers relaxed. Shaw moved to Garrett's right, his tablet in hand, his face set in a mask of tightly controlled anger as he tapped upon it. Garrett caught the flicker of frustration in his second officer's eyes, a telltale sign that Shaw's patience had been tested. That was not a good sign, but it was also not the time to pull him aside and ask what had happened. He would do that later when they were alone.

Positioned directly opposite Garrett, on the other end of the table, was Norwood. Garrett had always disliked the man. He supposed the feeling was mutual. Norwood exuded his usual air of self-importance, his sharp gaze hinting at barely concealed irritation, likely at having been summoned all the way from his ship. Or perhaps it had just been that Garrett had put him off and not yet addressed the man's concerns when it came to seniority among his peers.

Garrett allowed the room time to settle, giving the officers a moment to claim their places at the table's edge. He glanced once more at Shaw, who finished tapping on his tablet, then directed an icy glare toward Norwood. Whatever had transpired between them was evident in Shaw's taut expression, but Garrett decided to let it ride. He'd find out what had occurred later. Garrett was here to lead, to set the tone, and to address the very real challenges ahead and get everyone working together as a team.

"Thank you all for coming," Garrett began. He let his gaze drift across the room, pausing just long enough to meet each captain's eyes. "We have a lot to cover, so let's keep this focused and efficient. If you have something to say, make it count. I would like to—"

"I do have something to say," Norwood interrupted, his tone sharp and impatient. "Why did you keep us waiting? And why the damned blood test just to meet with you? We've been treated like common criminals."

Garrett's jaw tightened. Norwood's natural arrogance had always been an irritant, but in this moment, it was particularly grating. The captain's posture was as rigid as his tone, his thin frame held unnaturally straight, as if a steel rod ran the length of his spine. Everything about him screamed control, from his impeccably pressed uniform—each crease razor-sharp—to his silver hair, combed and styled with a near surgical correctness.

His features, sharp and angular, only added to the effect. A narrow nose, high cheekbones, and a jawline that looked chiseled from marble lent him an air of austerity, but the faint sneer tugging at the corners of his mouth made it clear he felt no respect for the proceedings—or for Garrett. His cold and cutting eyes scanned the room as though he were appraising subjects in *his* court. It was a posture Garrett recognized immediately, one meant to impose authority and demand deference.

"I would know why we were subjected to such treatment," Norwood demanded, "and why, pray tell, you waited so long to call us together, to hold this very necessary meeting?"

"Let me make something abundantly clear: this is *my* ship, *my* task force, and *I* make the decisions on when we meet."

The captains around the table shifted uncomfortably, their eyes darting between Garrett and Norwood. Garrett felt the anger welling up within him, burning away the remnants of his dwindling patience. He understood the challenge for what it was—open defiance. But why? What was Norwood hoping to gain? Irritating and insulting one's superior was not a good way to guarantee advancement, let alone foster a working relationship.

"You did not answer my question," Norwood said. "Why were we kept waiting? I really want to know." His gaze swept the room theatrically, as if inviting others to share in his indignation. No one moved to join him.

Garrett's eyes narrowed. "We are on my schedule, Captain, not yours."

"I don't care whose schedule you think you're on,"

Norwood snapped, his frustration spilling over and his voice rising.

At Garrett's side, Shaw stiffened, his hand curling tightly around the tablet he still held, as if resisting the urge to intervene. Garrett exhaled slowly. He had underestimated Norwood's ambition. Of course, the man would seize on the chaos and uncertainty of what had happened to make a power play. Garrett could feel every gaze in the compartment, assessing, judging... they were all on him, clearly wondering how he would react. How many others here shared Norwood's resentment?

The question lingered in his mind as he locked eyes with Norwood, the other captain's expression filled with righteous indignation. Garrett realized he had a choice—shut this down now, decisively, or risk allowing doubt to fester among the assembled officers. He could not allow the latter for it would undermine his authority. Fine, Garrett thought, if Norwood wanted to play, he'd play.

"Captain," Garrett said, his voice calm but edged with steel, "I am well aware of your seniority in grade and the game you are trying to play here. Let me remind you of something crucial. Seniority does not equate to authority. This is my task force, my ship, and my command. I make the decisions. You are here because I allow it, and Fleet assigned you to my task force. Do you understand me?"

Norwood blinked, caught off guard by the sudden force behind Garrett's words. He appeared to hesitate. It was almost as if the man had not expected a challenge from a superior over blatant disrespect. How odd? The silence in the room was suddenly profound. Norwood genuinely looked taken aback.

Garrett's voice dropped, quieter but no less commanding. "If you have an issue with my leadership, Captain, you are free to file a formal complaint through proper channels when we return to Confederation space. But until then, you will show me the respect my position demands."

Norwood bit his lower lip for a moment, looking around the conference table. His gaze returned to Garrett, and with it, his expression hardened. His cheeks colored. Garrett knew without a doubt a fight was coming.

"Are you really aware of my true seniority in grade? I was to be promoted to rear admiral, commanding a battlecruiser squadron. Next week was to be my swearing-in ceremony."

Garrett held very still. He had not known that. In the confusion, it must have been overlooked by Yenga. The other captains around the table shared looks with one another.

"We should take a vote to see who commands this expedition," Norwood said, his gaze sweeping the table again, with calculated confidence. "I nominate myself as the most senior and qualified officer present. I have the experience to lead along with Fleet's trust. My promotion is indicative of that."

Garrett blinked, surprised by the sheer audacity of the man. A murmur of discomfort rippled through the assembled officers. Garrett could feel their gazes shifting between him and the challenger. Deep within, like a rising tide, anger surged, threatening to overtake him. But Garrett clamped down on it, forcing himself to remain composed and in control.

"Captain Norwood, this is not a democracy. I am the commodore and therefore senior, no matter when you were to be promoted or what command you were to be assigned. You are still captain of a starship under my command. That is the end of the discussion."

Norwood's lips curled into a sneer. "You are a *job* captain. A finisher. Every officer at this table has more experience in command of a commissioned starship than you. You cannot deny it."

There it was, the moniker of jobbing coming back to bite. Being attached to Construction Command, even ranked as a captain, meant little to line officers like Norwood. Garrett understood it was something not easily dismissed or overlooked. He would always be looked down upon by such men as inferior.

The hatch hissed open. Garrett almost blinked in surprise as Sergeant Major Burns stepped in with quiet purpose, his face grave and presence like a looming storm. Norwood, with his back to the hatch, was unaware of the sergeant major's presence. Garrett glanced over at Shaw, who gave him a nod. He suddenly realized his second officer had anticipated this confrontation. Shaw must have realized what was coming moments before Garrett had arrived. By then, it had been too late to do more.

"You are a failed officer," Norwood pressed, his voice rising as he looked at his fellow captains, clearly seeking to drum up support. "A man who couldn't even command a proper starship until this one was handed to him in a moment of crisis. He doesn't deserve to lead us. He does not have the command experience!" Norwood turned his gaze back to Garrett. "You are unfit. It is time for you to admit that sad fact and step aside."

The officers around the table once more shifted uncomfortably, some exchanging wary and concerned glances. Garrett could feel the tension radiating from them. Norwood was on very dangerous ground.

"Elias," Jason said to Norwood, breaking the silence, "that's enough. We all saw what the commodore did during the battle at Midway. None of us would have made it out were it not for him."

Garrett's jaw tightened, his anger blossoming dangerously close to the surface. The last thing he needed was someone fighting his battles for him, especially a friend. That smacked of weakness. He would... *could* not allow his authority to be undermined—not here, not now, not ever.

Before Garrett could speak, Norwood turned on Jason with a dismissive wave of his hand. "He got lucky, nothing more. Any one of us could have done the same with a ship like this." He paused. "I say we put it to a vote, choose our leader… someone we all respect."

"There will be no vote," Garrett said firmly, his voice cutting through the compartment like a blade. "That talk ends now. Fleet put me in command of this mission, and that is final. Whether you believe it or not, I am the most qualified person to lead."

"I, for one, will not serve under you," Norwood spat back, his words dripping with open disdain and venom. He made a show of glancing around the table, as if rallying allies. "And there are others here who feel the same." His gaze snapped back to Garrett, and he jabbed a thin, accusatory finger toward him. "You are not qualified to command even a garbage scow. Had you the least bit of skill, Fleet would have long ago given you your own ship. Surely, you can see the obvious. In a time of war, you are not competent to lead."

Shaw shifted beside Garrett, and opened his mouth, ready to speak, but Garrett raised a hand to silence him. "I will handle this."

"I would like to see that," Norwood sneered. "So, *job captain*, what will you do if we refuse to follow you?"

"Captain Norwood," Garrett said forcing himself to speak calmy to Norwood, though steel laced his tone. "You have crossed a line. I will give you one last opportunity to step back."

"I think not," Norwood said haughtily, straightening his thin frame. "The only acceptable course of action is for you to step aside and hand over command to someone more qualified, someone these captains can respect. You cannot command the task force without us. Surely that is plain, even to you."

Garrett let out a slow, resigned breath, the understanding of what he must now do settling over him. Norwood had forced his hand the moment he opened his mouth. There was simply no turning back. To do so was to surrender everything. The only option was to attack.

"If I refuse your demands, you will not follow my orders?" Garrett asked calmly, though he felt anything but. "Do I have that correct?"

"You do have it correct," Norwood said with finality, turning his chin up to Garrett and looking down the bridge of his nose. "I will never follow a job captain into battle. To do so would be suicidal."

A wave of sadness washed over Garrett, momentarily dulling the anger burning within him. He gave a nod. "Very well, then."

Norwood's face twisted into a triumphant sneer. He slapped the table with a flat palm. "You see reason after all? I didn't think you would. Now, let us take a vote on who will lead." He turned to another captain. "Rens, you said you'd nominate me and back my claim should it come to this... well, now is the time."

"Once more, you are mistaken, sir," Garrett said quietly, his calm tone drawing Norwood's attention like a tether snapping tight. "Captain Norwood, effective immediately, you are relieved of command."

"How dare you—" Norwood hissed.

"Sergeant Major Burns," Garrett barked.

"Sir," Burns replied crisply as he stepped up to the table, next to Norwood. The captain stiffened, almost jumping at the sergeant major's sudden appearance.

"Kindly take Captain Norwood into custody," Garrett ordered.

"You want me to place him under arrest, sir?" Burns asked plainly, glancing over at the captain in question.

"That is correct," Garrett affirmed, his gaze locking on Norwood like a steel vice.

Norwood's head snapped between the sergeant major and

Garrett, his face a mask of incredulity. His sputtering words burst forth, loud and indignant. "Arrest? Whatever are you talking about? We are here to decide who leads."

"You clearly misjudged the situation, sir, and I think that's stating things rather kindly. Fleet decides who leads, not you," Burns said and then looked at Garrett. "What charges do you prefer entered into the log, sir?"

"Disobedience of orders, insubordination, and refusal to obey lawful commands. And that's just the start." Garrett shifted his attention. "Captain Norwood, you will be confined until we return to Confederation space, where I can hand you over to the appropriate authorities for court-martial. I will let the prosecutor and convening authority decide if they should add conduct unbecoming an officer to the list"—Garrett glanced briefly to Rens, who had gone ashen—"also conspiracy and attempted mutiny."

Rens visibly swallowed.

"How dare you! Have you gone mad?" Norwood's voice cracked with disbelief, his indignation rising. "You are nothing more than a jumped-up job captain!"

"I believe the title you're looking for is commodore," Shaw interjected coolly, just as the hatch hissed open again, revealing two marines, both carrying sidearms secured to their hips. They stepped into the compartment.

Norwood looked around at the marines and then back at Garrett, his face turning a livid shade of red. His mouth worked for a long moment.

"You bastard," Norwood snarled, his voice trembling with fury. "Do you know who my mentors are? Do you even know the fire you're playing with?"

Garrett didn't flinch. He already knew where this was headed.

"Admiral Omaga and Admiral Isabel will hear of this,"

Norwood declared, his chest puffing out as though the names alone could shield him from the consequences of his actions.

"Admiral Omaga is a long way from here at the moment," Garrett said plainly, "and sadly, Isabel is likely dead. I think I will take my chances."

"You are making a grave mistake," Norwood warned.

"It is you who have made the mistake," Garrett replied. "And now you are wasting my time. Sergeant Major, as distasteful as it is, kindly carry out your duty."

"Aye, aye, sir." Burns moved with purpose, his imposing frame closing the distance between him and Norwood in a heartbeat. "If you would come with me, sir."

Norwood's eyes darted around the compartment, searching desperately for support. "Are you going to let him get away with this?" he demanded of the other officers. "We talked about this!"

A woman to Garrett's left spoke. "I only listened. I do my duty as is expected, and I follow orders of my immediate superior. I won't throw away my career for the likes of you, Norwood. You were always a pompous fool."

Norwood's cheeks flushed a deep crimson as he glared at his peers. "Cowards, the lot of you," he hissed, then turned back to Garrett. "You fool, you will get us all killed through incompetence, and you don't even realize it."

"Sir," Burns interjected as he took hold of the captain's upper arm, "we can do this the hard way or the easy way. The choice is yours. I know my preference... but you might prefer something more, shall we say... dignified."

Norwood turned a withering gaze on Burns, his expression that of a superior staring down an impertinent subordinate. Burns remained unfazed, his posture rigid and unyielding as he gestured to the marines waiting by the hatch. Norwood stared at them, then shot one final venomous look at the officers around the table. His lips pressed into a line, and without another word, he shook off Burns's grip and straightened his uniform.

Turning, he marched toward the hatch. The two marines stepped aside and moved into positions to flank him. As the hatch slid open, Norwood paused and turned back to Garrett, his voice an unhappy hiss. "You'll regret this."

Garrett met his gaze. "I already do."

Norwood turned away and stepped through the hatch, the two marines trailing close behind. Burns followed, but halted at the threshold and lingered briefly, casting a final look around the room at the other officers, before addressing Garrett. "Sir, do you wish me to remain?"

"No," Garrett replied, his voice hard and clipped. "I don't believe there will be any further need for your services. Thank you, sergeant major."

"You are welcome, sir," Burns said with a crisp nod. "I'll see Captain Norwood settled in appropriate quarters and report back when it is done."

"Carry on, Sergeant Major," Garrett said.

Burns exited, the hatch sliding closed behind him with a soft hiss. Silence descended. The gathered officers stood awkwardly, their gazes shifting uneasily between one another. Garrett remained silent for a moment longer as he gathered his thoughts.

"I trust we are done with such unpleasantness," Garrett said. He looked down for a heartbeat and then back up. "Fleet gave me a job to do, and I intend to do it with or without your help. If anyone has similar thoughts on my fitness, now is the time to make your feelings known. I will relieve you, but there will be no rancor, no other consequences, and no court-martial. Speak up if you do not wish or feel you are unable to serve under my command."

The room fell silent again, a heavy pause stretching long enough to ensure the point was clear. No one spoke. Garrett gave a single, measured nod, the subtle shift in his demeanor signaling it was time to move forward and get to the purpose of the meeting.

"There are certain things you do not know," Garrett began. "For starters, the enemy has had access to Confederation space for some time. Fleet only recently became aware of this fact. In short, we have been infiltrated."

"The Haier Barber chain," one of the officers interjected. It was Rens, the same man who'd apparently supported Norwood.

"That could be it," Garrett said, inclining his head slightly. "Then again, there may be another point where the enemy has gained access to our star systems. Fleet and the Intelligence Directorate are still investigating. Secondly—and this is crucial —the enemy we fought at Midway was human. At least, some of them were."

"Human?" Jason asked, his expression marked by disbelief. His reaction mirrored that of several others who exchanged unsettled glances before turning their full attention back to Garrett.

"We took prisoners when they attempted to take my ship," Garrett continued. "Fleet believes they are using captured humans—their descendants—not only as soldiers but as spies, deep-cover agents, and saboteurs. They may be enslaved or simply brainwashed."

"That's why you had us tested." Jason snapped his fingers, the realization clearly dawning in his tone. "They've seeded the Confederation with human spies. I am guessing you're tracing genetic lines. The story about contraband and drugs is just a cover."

"It's a cover story all right," Garrett confirmed, "but not entirely untrue. Shortly before we pushed back at Midway, we discovered Bloom aboard. Using the contraband as a blind serves dual purposes: screening for genetic ties to captured populations, and identifying illicit substances. The critical take-away is this: there is a fifth column operating within Confederation space, potentially even aboard this ship—or yours. At this point, we just don't know for certain." Garrett paused to allow them to digest that. "This is a recent development. We need to identify and neutralize any such threats. Your cooperation in this matter is not only appreciated but required. Every single person must be tested—my people and yours. There can be no exceptions. I am certain you can now see why."

There were several nods. Garrett continued before anyone could speak. "I will be sending you a detailed report outlining everything we currently know. You are not to share this information with anyone without my express permission. Officially, we are conducting a drug and contraband sweep. That's all anyone else needs to know until we are ready to act... to round up any enemy agents we discover. I would prefer to do it all at once. There's less risk that way."

"That's scary shit, sir," Rens said, his voice carrying a faint tremor.

"And you are?" Garrett asked, though he already knew the man's name from earlier.

"Captain Marco Rens of the *Dante*, sir."

The *Dante* was one of Garrett's battlecruisers, and Rens was a man in his mid-forties, with a stocky build that gave him an air of solidity. His square jaw and neatly trimmed beard added to his no-nonsense appearance, though there was a guarded look in his gray eyes that hinted at a man accustomed to watching and waiting before making his move. His uniform was pristine, the creases sharp, suggesting a disciplined nature, but the way he shifted uneasily under Garrett's gaze betrayed a lingering uncertainty. Rens seemed like a man who preferred the safety of established protocols over the chaos of unexpected events, someone more comfortable following than challenging authority.

"Do you share Captain Norwood's opinion of my status as commodore?" Garrett asked plainly, his tone sharp and direct.

"No, sir, I do not," Rens replied, his voice edged with tension. It was clear he knew he was not on good footing. "I will follow your orders to the utmost."

"Then we will leave it at that," Garrett said, giving a curt nod to dismiss the matter.

"Thank you, sir," Rens said, his tone filled with relief.

Garrett turned his attention to the others in the room. "Let's go around the room before we continue," he said, gesturing to the assembled officers. "I already know Captains Martin and Grimes. They were in my academy class." He looked to the officer directly to his left and raised an eyebrow at her. The message was clear.

"Sir, I am Kim Collier, commanding the *Ernest Renan*."

Another battlecruiser. Collier was tall, with close-cropped black hair that framed an angular face.

Garrett's gaze traveled to the next officer.

"Nelson Terrence, sir, Fast Frigate *Yamahiko*."

Terrence was lean, with weathered skin and a slightly crooked nose, his brown eyes quick and alert. His short, sandy hair was kept neat and styled. He gave a firm nod. "It is an honor to be assigned to this mission."

That meant the rest were destroyer captains.

"Aisha Karim, the *Fontaine*."

Karim had a smooth, dark complexion with an honest, but serious face. Her braided hair was tied back neatly, and her strong jawline added to her aura of natural authority. "I am also pleased to be here. The alternative was to remain behind in Midway, and I did not find that appealing."

"I can imagine," Garrett said and looked to the next.

"Liam O'Connell, sir, the *Seminole*."

O'Connell was broad-shouldered and stocky, with ruddy cheeks and a thick auburn beard streaked with gray, though he was beginning to bald. His hazel eyes betrayed what seemed like an easygoing nature despite his gruff looking exterior. "My ship stands ready, sir."

Garrett gave a nod and looked to the next officer.

"Nia Abebe, sir, the *Bear*."

Abebe was tall and lithe, her deep brown skin almost glowing under the soft lighting of the room. Her tightly coiled hair was kept short, and intense dark eyes conveyed a quiet, steady resolve, not to mention intelligence.

"Mei-Ling Zhang, sir, the *Apache*."

Zhang was petite, with jet-black hair tied into a sleek bun. Her porcelain skin and high cheekbones gave her an elegant appearance, while her eyes missed nothing.

"Kaoru Tanaka, the *Kern*, sir."

Tanaka was of average height but had an imposing presence. He had a no-nonsense manner about him. His neatly combed salt-and-pepper hair added a scholarly air to his otherwise disciplined military bearing. Tanaka swept his gaze around the table, then returned it to Garrett. "The *Kern* is standing by to carry out your orders, sir."

"I appreciate that, Captain," Garrett said, and he did.

"Diego Torres, sir, the *Fulmine*."

Torres had a rugged handsomeness, with olive skin, and short, dark curls. A faint scar ran along his left cheek, giving an edge to his otherwise charming smile and deep brown eyes.

Each captain was a distinct piece in the puzzle Garrett would need to fit together to ensure the task force's success. And now, he was down a captain. He'd have to find a replacement for Norwood. Hopefully, the man's executive officer was up to the job, for it would help to have someone familiar with the *Palestro* to operate her.

"First, let me say it is a pleasure to meet you all and have you under my command," Garrett began, his voice firm. "The road ahead of us will not be an easy one. Fleet has assigned us a mission that is both challenging and critical to the war effort. Before we can proceed to our ultimate objective, there is something we must accomplish first, something critical to our mission's success."

"And what is that, sir?" Torres asked.

Garrett nodded to Shaw, who tapped a series of commands into his tablet. A moment later, a three-dimensional hologram flickered to life above the table. It displayed a sleek, elongated device with an intricate design of interlocking components, glowing faintly blue as it rotated slowly in the air.

The captains leaned in, their expressions curious.

"This is a newly developed piece of technology," Garrett continued. "Fleet only recently approved its use after successfully testing the device in the Davros System. Make no mistake, this is a game changer. Next to the Mothership, it is the most significant strategic advancement we've had in decades, and it will help turn the tide in the war." Garrett paused. "More importantly, we are going to put it to good use."

"What is it?" Tanaka asked.

"This," Garrett said, gesturing toward the hologram, "is a jump point disruptor, and we are going to save Third Fleet with it."

TEN

STROUD

"By the blackened and wretched sun," Stroud muttered, his voice low but charged with fury as he gazed through the one-way glass. The harsh lighting in the cell made the scene on the other side feel even more surreal. His fists clenched at his sides, a storm of emotions roiling beneath the surface. "Fuck me."

Beside him, Burns stood motionless, his expression grim and brooding, also deeply unhappy.

Inside the cell, the prisoner lay slumped in a chair, his head tilted unnaturally to one side. Blood trickled from his ears and nose, dark against the pale hue of his lifeless skin. Even though the dead man was a prisoner and the enemy, this was now potentially a crime scene.

A medical and forensic team of three worked around the deceased, collecting data and information. One was running a scanner over the body, imaging it. The speakers were off, so even though the team on the other side of the glass spoke, no words reached Stroud and Burns.

The overhead lights illuminated every gruesome detail. Off to the side, the interrogation team, two women, stood in tense silence, their postures betraying their unease as they watched.

"What the hell did they do to him?" Stroud asked, his tone edged with disbelief. He wanted to pound on the glass in frustration. He had lost a valuable intelligence source, one that might have given the Confederation real insight on the enemy.

Burns shook his head slowly, his face like carved granite. "Nothing out of the ordinary. They injected him with truth serum... really, they followed standard procedure. He died shortly after."

"Well, it sure as hell wasn't standard this time, was it?" Stroud snapped angrily, gesturing toward the body. The sterile, clinical setting of the cell only seemed to amplify the horror of the scene.

Burns exhaled heavily. "I think it's tied to the implants. I reviewed the security footage. They secured him to the chair, administered the serum, and then"—he hesitated, his jaw tightening—"he started convulsing, violently. They called medical immediately, but within forty seconds, he was gone. No pulse, no brain activity... Stone dead, sir."

Stroud's gaze lingered on the corpse, his mind racing. "I was really hoping we could get something useful out of him, actionable even."

"My money's on the implants," Burns said. "Care to make a wager, sir?"

"Tamper-proof soldiers," Stroud said, his voice heavy with disgust. "Is that what you are saying?"

Burns nodded. "That's my read on it. These implants... they're not just advanced biotech—they're fail-safes. You try to dig into a person's brain, interrogate them, extract information, the implants suicide the host. I don't know how it works yet, but I bet when Neelan and his people perform an autopsy, that will be confirmed. Somehow, the implants knew what the truth serum represented and finished him."

"That's cold-blooded," Stroud muttered.

"Very cold-blooded, sir," Burns echoed grimly. "Almost like

the kamikaze pilots of the Second World War, where the wheels of the aircraft fell off after they got into the air. Basically, there was no coming back."

Stroud rubbed at his eyes, feeling the fatigue of the day. Reporting the prisoner's death to the commodore was one thing—explaining the unexpected situation in his brig and how it had happened was another. He cast a weary glance at Burns.

"Sergeant Major," Stroud began, his voice tinged with irritation, as another matter came to mind, "can you explain why the captain of the *Palestro* is currently occupying one of my cells just down the corridor? He's requested to see me."

Burns let out a heavy breath, crossing his arms over his chest. As if gathering his thoughts, he did not speak immediately. "There is no other way to say it, sir, but the captain of the *Palestro* is an asshole, a real dyed-in-the-wool major asshole. They don't get any worse than that, at least in my humble opinion."

Stroud raised an eyebrow. "That's an officer in the Confederation Navy you're talking about."

"I know it, sir. Doesn't make it any less true, though."

Stroud stared at him for a moment before letting out a resigned sigh. "Go on, explain. What happened? I want to hear it all."

Burns shifted his weight from one foot to another and glanced down at the deck a moment before meeting Stroud's gaze. "He challenged the commodore."

Stroud blinked, momentarily stunned by the revelation. "He did what? Are you serious? He challenged Commodore Garrett?"

"Captain Norwood questioned the commodore's right to command the task force," Burns said, his tone flat but laced with disdain. "He thought he was better suited than someone who had been a mere job captain. It was rather stunning to hear."

"You've got to be kidding me," Stroud muttered. He shook his head. "Tell me this is a jest."

"I wish I could, sir." Burns scowled. "The man outright defied Commodore Garrett, refused to take and obey his orders. You know how some captains get. They think they're untouchable—like gods walking among mere mortals, their shit immune to the stench that follows the rest of us around. Norwood is one of those bastards... ah excuse me, sir, err... one of those gentlemen whose shit doesn't stink. But it did today and he got what was coming..."

Stroud pinched the bridge of his nose, his annoyance building. "What the hell was he thinking?"

"I'm not sure he was thinking at all, sir," Burns said with a shake of his head. "Apparently, he was to be promoted to admiral. He thought that gave him the right to challenge the commodore in front of every captain in the task force. I was there. It was a stupid thing for him to do and didn't end well for him. That's why he's in the brig."

Stroud's tone grew sharper. "I really don't believe this..."

"Believe, sir."

"How bad was it... really?"

"I've got the recordings. They've been entered into the official record. They're... well, quite damning if you ask me, but I'm just a dumb grunt and not part of the judge advocate general's corps." Burns hesitated, then added, "Would you like me to send them to your tablet?"

Stroud let out a long, unhappy breath. Feeling terrible frustration, he rubbed his jaw and then nodded. "Do it. I will take a look at the recording as soon as I am back in my office."

"You won't like it, sir," Burns said.

"I am certain I will not."

"Norwood believed that others, such as Captain Rens, would have his back. That they thought alike on the matter," Burns said.

"Bloody hell," Stroud said.

"When push came to shove, none of the other captains stood by him, though." Burns pulled his tablet from his belt. He began working the control surface.

The *Palestro*'s captain had overstepped in a way that could ripple through the entire task force. Stroud couldn't decide whether to be angrier at Norwood for his arrogance or at the situation for adding yet another complication to an already difficult and frustrating day.

"Done," Burns said, lowering his tablet and reattaching it to his belt. "The recording is in your box, sir. If I had to guess, I think he mistook our commodore for being"—Burns gave a sick chuckle—"weak."

Stroud's sharp gaze flicked to the sergeant major at the use of the word *our*. He approved, for Garrett was someone to follow. "That was not only poor judgment on his part, but a mistake."

"A big one, sir," Burns agreed. "Colossal as they come."

"It really happened in front of the other ship captains?" Stroud asked, still not quite believing what the man had done.

"Yes, sir," Burns confirmed. "The entire task force command structure was in the conference room, you know the one, right off the bridge. The captain er... commodore uses it all the time. Norwood didn't just question the commodore's authority—he challenged it outright, called for a vote on who would lead. By the way, you might be interested to know, he proposed himself as the most qualified candidate."

Stroud exhaled heavily. "This is worse than I thought."

"I can't disagree with that." Burns hesitated briefly, then added, "Sir, after reviewing the recording, you'll also want to have a word with the *Palestro*'s marine commander, Captain Murphy. Technically, while docked to *Surprise*, he falls under your authority. He called me with questions."

"What did you say?"

"Only that his captain had been arrested," Burns said. "I referred him to you."

"How long ago was this?" Stroud asked.

"Ten minutes before you met me here," Burns said.

Stroud nodded grimly. "I'll handle it before the day's out. Let him know I will be reaching out to him."

"A face-to-face might be better, sir. You'll need to show him the recording as well," Burns suggested. "That way, there's no ambiguity, no question on the egregiousness of the offense. From what I've heard, the crew of the *Palestro* isn't happy with the situation, maybe even feeling disagreeable. The sooner that gets nipped in the bud, the better."

Stroud could well imagine their unhappiness, for crews usually became attached to their captains, unless they were real bastards. "This is a mess."

"The dead prisoner or the captain of the *Palestro* being a damned idiot, sir?"

"Both," Stroud replied tersely. He rubbed the back of his neck, the tension there mirroring the storm in his mind. He gestured toward the lifeless prisoner in the cell. "I want to know exactly what killed him before we even think about questioning any of the other prisoners, let alone waking them up. We need to better understand what we are dealing with here..."

"Yes, sir." Burns turned his gaze back to the cell, his sharp eyes scanning the scene where the medical team worked in grim silence around the still body. "Do you want to speak to the interrogation unit?"

Stroud considered for a moment, his jaw tightening as he weighed the options. After several seconds of consideration, he shook his head. "No, not yet. Let's hear from medical first, confirm what we're dealing with before we complicate things further."

"Yes, sir."

Rubbing the back of his neck again, he ran his gaze across

the cell. Something on the floor caught his attention. He'd not seen it before. Stroud stepped closer to the glass, his eyes narrowing as he focused on a spot just to the left of the bunk.

"Hold on, Burns, look at the floor."

"What is it, sir?" Burns asked, stepping forward to peer through the glass.

"There's writing there," Stroud said, pointing. "On the floor, see it?"

Burns leaned closer, his eyes following Stroud's gesture. "I see it now. Red writing... by god, it looks like it's drawn in blood."

Stroud's gaze flicked back to the prisoner. The bandage that had once covered a wound on his temple was gone, leaving the dried and clotted traces of what was likely the source of the writing material. After a moment, he spotted the discarded bandage on the bed. He peered closer at the crude, hastily scrawled markings on the floor.

"It's not just writing," Burns said after a moment. "That looks like the pendant we took from him—there's something else too, some sort of a design. Ever seen anything like it, sir?"

"No." Stroud frowned, studying the shapes. There was a crude depiction of the pendant and, sure enough, as Burns said, another symbol he didn't immediately recognize, along with a strange scrawl that seemed to be writing of some kind. It looked like the man had also drawn a sun and then written something next to it. The lines of text were deliberate, purposeful and in some alien script.

"Make sure it's imaged and analyzed," Stroud said firmly, stepping back and away from the window. It all meant nothing to him. "Send it to the intelligence unit, and also flag it for CIC to look at. Commander Senica spoke to me. She wants to see anything out of the ordinary when it comes to the enemy and the prisoners we took."

"The new third officer?" Burns asked.

Stroud gave a nod.

"What do you think of her, sir?"

"She's intelligence branch of Fleet, or was," Stroud said. "Seems to have her head screwed on right. Get everything we have to her, anything we draw from this mess."

"I'll see to it personally, sir," Burns replied. He hesitated for a beat, then added, "And what about Norwood?"

"I'll review the recording of what went down between him and the commodore. As I said, I will speak to Murphy. Either way, Norwood's a prisoner until we return to Confederation space. He speaks to no one other than the guard or legal representation, if he requests a representative from the JAG Corps."

"An attorney won't do him much good out here," Burns said. "He's staying in the brig for the duration, unless the commodore orders otherwise."

"That's right," Stroud admitted.

"And if any of his crew—say, his second—want to see him?" Burns asked, his tone careful. "How do you want that handled?"

"Everything goes through me," Stroud said firmly. "Any communication he has with his former crew, if I allow it, will be fully monitored and recorded, according to the uniformed code of military justice. We do everything by the book. He can rot in that cell until someone takes him off our hands."

Burns nodded. "Understood. Speaking about his accommodation, what comforts of home are we offering him?"

"A tablet for entertainment and any personal items he requests from his ship—within reason, of course. Beyond that, he stays in the brig. His rank warrants no special treatment. Make sure the guards understand that point."

"Yes, sir."

"Have we learned anything about the man who pulled the gun on us?" Stroud asked.

Burns shook his head. "He's a black hole, other than he was logged coming aboard. I don't think he ever stayed in the quarters assigned to him. Upon closer examination, his tag doesn't match his biometrics, and he did not show up in the database, genetic-wise, of captured populations."

"Not good," Stroud said, feeling terribly unhappy.

"I don't think so either. He's either organized crime or..."

Stroud shifted his gaze back to the cell, where the medical and forensic team worked over and around the prisoner's body. He frowned, his thoughts momentarily clouded by the strange circumstances surrounding the death. Then he shook himself. There was nothing more he could do here.

"I need to get back to work. I'll report the prisoner's death to the commodore."

"And where will you be after that, sir?"

"With the new leadership we've promoted," Stroud said. "I'm already late for that meeting. Organizing an entire marine expeditionary unit from scratch is far more work than I ever expected, let alone anticipated."

"Like a stroll in the park, sir?"

Stroud gave a grunt of amusement. "I wish. But then again, anything worth doing right is never easy."

"No, sir, it most certainly is not."

ELEVEN

TABBY

With a grunt of effort, Tabby maneuvered the wheeled pallet into place, its wheels squeaking slightly as it rolled. With another hard shove, she pushed it firmly against the bulkhead wall of the massive hangar bay. Then she tabbed the lock button on the wheels, holding it in place.

Around her, the hangar echoed with the sounds of labor—voices calling out orders, shouts from one person to another. There was the clank of metal on metal, the sound of hammering, along with the heavy hum of machinery at work. Powerful engines occasionally ramped up or cycled in test. The acrid tang of lubricant, mixed with the ever-present smell of propellant was strong on the air.

Nearby, four marines worked in unison to shove another heavily loaded pallet toward the same wall. The pallet was stacked high with sealed crates bearing medical insignias.

For hours, Tabby and the people assigned to her had been working to unload the automated supply transports that had arrived in a haphazard manner from Midway Station. Whatever could be hastily loaded onto the transports and taken aboard had been. The frantic effort had left no time for personnel to properly handle everything upon arrival, and they'd been unceremoniously abandoned where they'd landed, cluttering the hangar deck.

The CAG had been on Tabby's ass—and everyone else's—to get the deck cleared up and serviceable for operations. She'd been calling almost hourly for updates.

A sharp siren blared, followed by the rhythmic pulse of warning lights. Tabby turned instinctively, watching as a massive overhead crane groaned to life. It reached down, connected, and lifted the now-empty supply transport they'd just unloaded, the automated craft's reflective hull gleaming under the overhead lighting as it ascended toward the yawning hatch above.

Beyond the hatch and the launch tube, the void of space awaited. Like hundreds of others before it, this transport would be jettisoned and abandoned to free up valuable space aboard *Surprise*. It would be forever consigned to the depths of deep space, drifting for all eternity.

Tabby glanced around the hangar, taking stock of the progress they'd made over the past two days, which had been a great deal. Much of the clutter of supplies and equipment had been hauled away. Dozens of small craft had been moved to designated cradles along the walls or maintenance bays—what ground crew called garages.

The deck, once an impassable maze of piled supplies, equipment, and craft, was now mostly open. It was beginning to feel close to being operational, and Tabby could see the light at the end of the tunnel. Within a few hours, the work would be complete, and Bay Two would open for business and be ready for combat operations.

She adjusted the sleeves of her flight suit and turned to the marines, who had just locked the pallet in place. Everyone was dirty and tired. This was not easy work. "All right, that's one more down. Let's keep this up. We only have ten more to go from that transport. We're almost there."

A chorus of acknowledgments followed, their voices tinged with exhaustion but also determination. The siren sounded again, signaling the crane's return.

"Ma'am, someone's coming," one of the nearby marines, Lance Corporal Kelley, said, nodding toward an approaching officer before turning away to answer one of his squadmates.

Tabby straightened and turned her gaze to the figure crossing the hangar deck, making a beeline for her. It was Husky—Lieutenant Cooper—her executive officer. He was one of the survivors of her squadron.

Doing her best to forget what had happened, Tabby had thrown herself into her work. The sight of Husky brought it all back. Reality smacked her again: eight out of thirty-six had survived. A lump of grief and anger tightened in her chest, but she pushed it back down. There was no time for that now, to dwell on the dead.

The CAG's words rang in her mind. *Grieve later.*

"Mom." Husky greeted her with a crooked grin, using the nickname the squadron had given her as he came up.

Hearing that made the feelings suddenly worse but she managed to clamp down upon them. She could not afford feelings, not now, not for a long time. She had a job to do and she meant to do it.

"Husky," she replied, straightening further and attempting to brush the grime from her hands. A short while before, one of the motorized sleds had sprung a hydraulic leak and she'd fixed it, but not before getting the pink fluid all over her hands, arms, and legs. She glanced down at her flight suit, streaked with dirt and lubricant, not to mention the hydraulic fluid. She felt every bit as grimy and dirty as she looked. Every part of her body ached too. "What's up?"

"We've been assigned seven new pilots," Husky began. "All

aviators with fighter backgrounds... so seven fighters, with one torpedo bomber, and two assault boats. That's the new makeup of our squadron, at least according to the CAG's orders."

"I know. We'll be getting the craft for them later today. It could be worse—we could've been assigned shuttle pilots to fill our empty slots instead, like some of the other squadrons."

"Yeah, it could be worse," Husky said. "Of the seven fighters we're getting, only four are operational and ready for immediate use. The rest are still crated up and need to be assembled."

Tabby gave a weary nod. She was not surprised by that. "It'll take a week or two, tops. We will have to lend a hand to help get the job done too."

"I was afraid of that." Husky gave a sour nod. She knew he did not much enjoy manual labor.

"Did you see our new additions settled?" Tabby asked.

"I did," Husky said with a nod. "We have our own squadron area now." He paused, his sharp gaze appraising her. "I haven't seen you much over the last two days. I know CAG's been keeping you busy, but will you be coming to speak with them, the newbies, I mean? It would be good for all of them to see you... morale-wise. Some were hit pretty hard by our losses."

Tabby hesitated for a moment. She could imagine how broken up her people were. She felt responsibility pressing down on her like the packed crates lining the hangar walls, waiting to be taken away to stores. Not only did the old hands need her, but the replacements would as well. They would all look to her for guidance, to provide the path forward.

Would she fail them too? Tabby pushed that thought roughly aside.

"Yes," she said finally, doing her best to keep her voice firm. "I'll speak to them. They need to know where we stand and what's expected. I will speak to everyone. We must go on." She hesitated a moment, hardening her heart. She didn't want to ignore these feelings, but she knew she had to. There was simply no other choice, and Tabby wasn't a quitter. She was a fighter. "We *must* stand strong."

Husky gave a curt nod, a hint of approval in his expression. "Good. They'll appreciate hearing that from you."

Tabby glanced toward the remaining pallets that they'd unloaded a short time before and her busy marines, more than two dozen of them, not to mention everyone else in the bay, hundreds of personnel. They were all her responsibility. CAG had put her in charge of clearing and organizing Hangar Bay Two. Dev had the headache of handling Hangar Bay Three. She had no idea who was responsible for bays one and four.

Tabby moved to a small crate along the bulkhead wall where she'd left a soiled towel and a half-finished cup of coffee, long since gone cold. She picked up the towel, wiping her hands free of the dirt and grime that clung stubbornly to her skin. The coffee caught her eye, tempting, but she decided against it. She'd already drunk enough to fill a bathtub.

"I'll be done in a couple of hours," she said, glancing back at Husky. "I'll make time to meet them before I hit the rack."

"Good." Husky nodded. His expression softened slightly. "Oh, and I saw Chen in medical."

Tabby stopped wiping her hands and turned toward him. "How's he doing?"

"He's up and about," Husky replied, leaning casually against a nearby pallet. "They're still not sure what scrambled his brains during the beacon jump or what it did to him, but they said he'll recover. His biometrics look good. He's being held overnight for observation and will be discharged come morning. Light duty only for at least the next week."

"That's some good news at least," Tabby said, her voice tinged with relief. She'd been worried about Chen but hadn't had the time to check on him. The CAG had kept her too busy. "Thanks for the update."

"No problem," Husky said.

Tabby continued wiping her hands, feeling the grit and grime slowly give way to the microfibers and fabric of the towel. "Our boats are going to need significant work. Make sure you prep the squadron for maintenance and repair. It's time for everyone to get their hands dirty. We can start on them tomorrow, make it a team effort and ensure our birds are as ready as possible for what's to come."

"I will pass along that good news."

"Did you get the garage numbers we were assigned? I sent them to your tablet. They should be in your inbox."

"I did," Husky confirmed. "I even went and took a look."

Tabby raised an eyebrow. "And?"

"They're not bad, actually," he said with a shrug. "Plenty of space to work, and the tools look up-to-date. Most of what we need is there and on hand. Some of the equipment's still boxed and crated, but we can work with that."

Tabby glanced at the marines pushing and guiding pallets stacked high with supplies toward the bulkhead walls. Other teams were removing pallets and taking them to stores. She ran her gaze around once more and gave a satisfied nod. The hangar was beginning to look more organized, but there was still much to do. "We've got our work cut out for us, Husky."

"As always," he said. "But we'll get it done."

"We have no choice but to get it done," Tabby said. "Everyone needs to pull in one direction. We're going into combat and we must be ready for that. Understand me?"

"I do," Husky said.

A shuttle moved past them, its bulk supported by a wheeled dolly system attached to the landing struts. A bot was towing the shuttle steadily forward, its mechanical treads clinking faintly against the hangar's deck plating. Trailing behind it was a group of five, all in flight suits. The motion caught Tabby's eye, and she turned her attention toward them.

A frown creased her brow as she realized something was off.

Cursing softly under her breath, she took a step away from Husky and called out sharply. "Lieutenant Tibbits!"

One of the men in the group glanced over his shoulder. After a moment of searching, his gaze settled on her. "Ma'am? How can I help?"

"Cradle 55-A is aft, *not* forward," Tabby shouted, her voice carrying over the ambient noise of the bustling hangar. "You're heading the wrong way."

Tibbits stopped in his tracks, confusion flickering across his face. He looked back the way they'd come, and then turned toward her, clearly uncertain. "Are you sure, ma'am?"

Tabby planted her hands on her hips. "Of course I'm sure. You have a tablet, along with a map I provided, one showing the locations of every cradle in this hangar bay. I suggest you use it. And if you can't read a map, Lieutenant, find someone who can."

Tibbits's face flushed crimson. "Ah... yes, ma'am," he stammered, fumbling for the tablet clipped to his utility belt. He hastily activated it and began poring over the display, muttering as he oriented himself. Meanwhile the bot continued to tow the shuttle away from the group, which hadn't stopped when he had. No one had thought to give it an order to halt.

Shaking her head in exasperation, Tabby turned back to Husky. "Sorry about that."

Husky smirked, his arms crossed as he straightened. "You've got a way with people, you really do."

"Don't start," Tabby warned, though a faint smile tugged at her lips. She glanced back at Tibbits and his group as they suddenly realized the shuttle was getting away. They began running after it.

"I'd better get going." Husky shifted his weight as though preparing to leave, but something in his posture made Tabby pause. He hesitated, his eyes flicking to a nearby group of marines pushing another pallet out of the way. There was a sudden unease about Husky, something that didn't fit his usual demeanor.

"What is it?" Tabby asked.

Husky glanced around again, his hesitation growing. Finally, he took a step closer and leaned in, lowering his voice so that it barely carried over the clamor of the hangar. "They tested me and the others in the squadron—a blood test."

Tabby arched an eyebrow. "They tested me too. Said they were looking for illicit substances, something about finding drugs aboard. I even saw them sweeping for contraband with a dog and sniffers earlier."

"That's what the marines told me as well." Husky's voice dropped further, and he cast another cautious glance around the bustling hangar. The marines nearby were preoccupied with their tasks, the background noise of machinery and chatter a natural shield. "But I don't buy it."

Tabby's interest sharpened. "You think they're looking for something else?"

Husky gave a slow nod. "I do. I heard a rumor. They got prisoners after the battle. And they're human."

Tabby felt a cold chill race down her spine. She had heard whispers of the same from a marine earlier that day—claims of a dead enemy, one of the boarders... human, with the woman swearing it was true. Tabby had dismissed it as typical scuttlebutt, but it seemed all the marines were convinced. The idea of humans fighting for the enemy, turning against their own, was deeply unsettling.

"I don't know what to make of it," she admitted after a moment. "But if that's true..." Her words trailed off, her unease plain and unspoken between them.

"They're hunting for something," Husky pressed, his tone firm. "And it's not drugs. Did you notice the security details posted at every entrance to the hangar bays?"

Tabby frowned, recalling the heavily armed marines

stationed by each access point. At the time, she had assumed it was just heightened security, nothing unusual after Midway. But now, with Husky's words echoing in her ears, the pieces began to fit together in a way that made her skin crawl.

"I did," she admitted, her voice quiet. "You think it's connected?"

Husky met her gaze, his expression grim. "I'm certain of it. Whatever's going on, it's bigger than they're letting on. Maybe some of the enemy weren't killed during the boarding action... They might be among us... hiding out."

Tabby gave a slight nod, her gaze shifting toward the hangar's entrances where marines were stationed. The sheer number of armed guards screening everyone who entered or exited the hangar seemed a tad excessive. Not only were personnel being checked identification-wise, but their belongings were being searched and scanned with a thoroughness that went beyond standard procedure.

"Have you been down to the magazines?" Husky asked, his voice lowered. "Have you been down there?"

Tabby shook her head, curious. "No, I haven't. Why?"

"I went to put in a replenishment request for our birds. The protection there is... well, it's"—he paused, searching for the right word—"excessive. Tabby, it all seems like overkill to me."

"Basic security," a new voice interjected. Tabby turned to find Lieutenant Marcus Peters approaching, his boots clicking softly against the deck. The marine lieutenant and his squad had been working with her for the last two days. It was clear he had overheard the last part of their conversation.

"Husky, this is Peters," Tabby said, gesturing between the two men. "He's been helping us get the hangar squared away. Peters, this is Lieutenant Cooper, my executive officer."

"Pleasure to meet you," Husky said, extending a hand.

"Good to meet you as well," Peters replied, shaking it firmly.

"Why all the extra security?" Husky asked bluntly. "You

can't walk ten meters without hitting a checkpoint or seeing armed marines."

"Commodore's orders," Peters answered matter-of-factly. "We took on a lot of personnel at Midway, including civilians. It's a natural precaution." He flashed a smile, one Tabby thought was meant to be disarming. She found it anything but. "Plus, there was the enemy's attempt to take *Surprise*. If something like that happens again, we'll have ready reaction teams stationed throughout the ship, and it's a big ship. We've even started running counter-boarding drills. We will be better prepared should it happen again."

"We're in deep space," Husky countered. "No immediate threats, right? So, why the tight security net? It's as if you boys are intentionally locking the ship down."

As if it didn't much matter to him, Peters gave a nonchalant shrug as he looked away at a pair of naval ratings moving by. He turned back to Husky. "A lot of what we do in the military doesn't make sense on the surface, even when you dig a little. But orders are orders. My job is to carry them out, nothing more, nothing less."

Tabby allowed herself a small smirk at that. "Out of everything I've heard today, that makes the most sense to me."

Peters chuckled lightly and turned to her. "Ma'am, I'd like to request some time to take my team to grab chow. They've been at this nonstop for six hours."

Tabby glanced over at the marines, who were still moving supplies with dogged efficiency. She decided they'd earned a break.

"All right, Peters. Take your people to the mess. I need to check in with the CAG anyway and give her an update on our progress. She prefers those updates to be in person."

"Thank you, ma'am. We will be back in forty minutes." Peters gave a sharp nod to Husky, and then headed off.

Husky watched the marine lieutenant go before turning

back to Tabby, his brow furrowed in thought. "What do you think about all this security? Is it really just about the civilians, the boarding action, and standard military nonsense?"

Tabby folded her arms, leaning back against the nearest crate. "It's hard to say. I just don't know."

"My gut tells me it's more than he said and is letting on," Husky muttered, his tone laced with suspicion. He looked directly at Tabby. "Mark my words, something else is going on. Something is wrong, seriously wrong, something they are not telling anyone." He glanced around the bay. "I think some of the enemy escaped after the fight and are hiding in plain sight."

"Whatever it is, we still have jobs to do," Tabby replied, her voice firm. "It's someone else's headache. Now, get to it, and keep those rumors to yourself. The last thing I need is grief from the CAG because my executive officer is causing a stir. She's hard enough as it is. Trust me, you don't want to get on her bad side."

"All right. I will see you later." Husky gave a final scowl at the nearest marines before turning and heading back the way he'd come. Tabby watched him go, then let her gaze sweep across the hangar bay. Lieutenant Peters had formed his platoon into a tight double column and had begun leading them toward the closest exit. It was then she noticed something odd; she'd not picked up on it before. Every marine she had been working with was armed.

She looked around, scanning. Sidearms hung from the hips of every marine in sight. Even Peters wore a holstered pistol. She frowned. In all her years of service, she had never seen an entire marine contingent aboard a ship armed, especially while performing routine duties like basic manual labor. Until Husky had mentioned the heightened security, she hadn't thought much of it. But now, the sight struck her as significant.

What *was* going on here?

Then again, she reminded herself, the Confederation was

now in a shooting war. Maybe this was just the new reality... Be prepared for the unexpected?

A sharp tone sounded in her ear, signaling an incoming call. She connected to it using her implants.

"Tabby here," she said.

"This is Knox," came the reply. The CAG's no-nonsense voice was unmistakable. "Do you have a moment? Now that Bay Two is nearly clear, I've got another job for you, one you are just going to love."

"I was about to head your way, ma'am," Tabby replied, keeping a groan from her voice. "I'll be there in ten."

"Good. I'll be in my office waiting," Knox said before disconnecting.

Tabby glanced around the hangar once more, taking in the almost cleared bay and the marines working throughout. She tossed her soiled towel aside, grabbed her now-cold coffee, and began making her way to the CAG's office. Whatever Knox wanted, she had a feeling it wouldn't be a simple request, and it would come as an order.

Putting the thoughts of the armed marines aside, Tabby glanced around at the bay again and almost grinned. "She's simply rewarding success with more work."

TWELVE
GARRETT

"Before we begin, sir, I've reviewed the footage," Commander Sabel said, her accent thick and unmistakably Russian in heritage. Her English was fluent, though it carried the distinctive cadence of someone who'd learned it later in life, most likely in her teens.

Seated across from Garrett in his office, she exuded composure, but he could see the subtle tension in her posture, the slight twitch of her fingers as they rested on her lap. Sabel was in her early thirties, with a wiry frame that bordered on being gaunt. Her sharp, attractive features—high cheekbones, a straight nose, and piercing blue eyes—hinted at an inner steel. Her shoulder-length brown hair was tightly tied back, though a few strands had escaped, softening an otherwise severe appearance.

"And?" Garrett prompted, leaning back in his chair as he regarded her.

"I do not approve of his actions," she said evenly, though the discomfort in her voice was evident. "Captain Norwood is clearly in the wrong. You need not concern yourself. I do not have a problem serving under your command, sir. I will not be questioning your orders."

Garrett studied her closely. Words were one thing, actions were another. Sabel's service record was impeccable. She'd graduated near the top of her academy class and had received glowing performance reviews in every post she'd held, including those under Norwood. Her rapid rise through the ranks suggested she'd caught the attention of someone influential, a person who was quietly guiding her career, choosing choice assignments for her, like *Palestro*. But the question remained—after what had happened with her CO, could he trust her?

"I cautioned him... but he did not listen," Sabel continued when Garrett didn't respond.

Garrett leaned forward, his elbows resting on the desk as he pointed a finger at her. "So, you knew what he was planning?"

"No, sir," she replied quickly, her voice steady, gaze unwavering. "I had hoped he would listen to reason. Apparently, he did not and decided to push the issue with you." She expelled an unhappy breath. "Sir, Captain Norwood at one point believed he was in the running to command this ship, that Fleet would select him when it was completed."

Garrett raised an eyebrow, surprised. That was news to him, but it sure explained a great deal. He wondered who had told the man that. Isabel? Omaga? At this point, it no longer mattered.

"He'd been studying the specifications of *Surprise* for months. Instead, he got word of his promotion to admiral and command of a battlecruiser squadron..." She paused, as if thinking. "That was just two weeks ago."

"I see," Garrett said.

After a moment, she ventured, "May I ask a question, sir?"

Garrett nodded.

"Do you intend to remove me from my current assignment.

If so"—she cleared her throat, and looked briefly away—"I—I would understand."

"I'm still deciding," he said in a measured tone as he continued to scrutinize her.

Sabel straightened in her chair, a faint glimmer of vulnerability and worry breaking through her otherwise stoic demeanor. "*Palestro* is my ship, sir. I've become attached to her and the crew. I've spent two years of my life on her. She is my home. I can and will follow your orders, as well as those of whoever you install to command. I ask that you give me a chance to prove myself."

Garrett nodded slowly, weighing her words. He could see the faint flicker of pain in her eyes at the thought of being reassigned, the desperate hope to remain aboard the ship. He understood that feeling all too well. Finally, he leaned back in his chair.

"You can stay."

Sabel's shoulders slumped slightly in relief, though she quickly straightened again. "Thank you, sir." She hesitated, then asked, "Who will you tap to command?"

Garrett leaned forward again, folding his hands on the desk. He resisted a grin. "Actually, I was thinking of you."

Sabel blinked, clearly taken aback. "Me?"

"Yes," Garrett replied. "You know the ship and her crew better than anyone. You've been aboard for two years, and very soon I'll be taking *Surprise*—and *Palestro*—back into battle. I don't have the time, let me say that again, I don't have the time to bring in someone new. Someone who doesn't know the ship as well as you, let alone her crew. In another year or two, you would have likely gotten your own ship. And nobody, in the short-term, can prepare *Palestro* for combat better than you. So, what do you say? Do you think you can handle the job, skippering a battlecruiser?"

Instead of answering immediately, Sabel sat in silence, her expression pensive. Her gaze drifted to the desk for several seconds before she finally nodded and looked back up at him, meeting his gaze, her resolve clear. "I can do it, sir. I will do it."

Garrett studied her closely. That she hadn't answered immediately reinforced his belief in her capabilities—she wasn't impulsive, and she understood the grave responsibility that would come to rest upon her shoulders.

"The job is yours, then," Garrett said firmly.

A chime sounded, interrupting the moment. Garrett accepted the call. "What is it?"

"Captains Martin and Grimes are here to see you, sir," Keeli's voice came through, filling the office. "They are your next appointment. They've been waiting for about twenty minutes."

Garrett glanced at the clock displayed on his console. He was running ten minutes late, hence the call—another sign the day was moving faster than he could manage. There was never enough time for all that needed doing. That was his new reality as commodore.

"Send them in as soon as Commander Sabel leaves."

"Yes, sir."

The call ended with a quiet beep.

Garrett returned his attention to Sabel. "Commander, I need to take this meeting. Please step onto the bridge and see Commander Shaw. He has a brief ready for you. Then come back. I will answer any questions you might have. At that time, we will also discuss my expectations for you and *Palestro* in greater detail."

"Yes, sir," Sabel said, standing with a measured movement. Garrett stood as well, leaning forward to offer his hand.

"Congratulations, skipper," he said, his tone laced with sincerity.

She extended her hand, gripping his firmly. "I wish it was under different circumstances, sir."

"So do I," Garrett said.

Sabel gave a curt nod, turned, and exited the office. The hatch slid shut behind her, then opened again a moment later to admit Tina and Jason. Tina led, her stride purposeful. She looked irritated, as though she'd rather be anywhere else. Jason followed, his demeanor slightly more relaxed, but there was an edge to his presence as well.

Garrett sighed inwardly. This was going to be painful—no way around it. She was furious, and with good reason. He'd killed her mentor—his first captain, Marlowe—and kept that truth buried. Fleet had encouraged it, for they'd eagerly swept it under the rug. He'd told himself it was to protect her, to spare her the pain, but deep down he knew it had also been cowardice. She'd told him as much when she'd learned the truth. And now, it stood like a wall between them. Their relationship—already complicated—teetered on the edge of something fragile, and possibly irreparable.

"Was that Norwood's second?" Jason asked, his tone casual, though his eyes carried a glimmer of curiosity.

"It was," Garrett replied evenly, gesturing toward the chairs across from him. "Sit, please. I've given her command of *Palestro*. I believe she is up to the challenge."

"I see," Jason said, lowering himself into a chair. He exchanged a brief look with Tina as she settled into the other seat. "Norwood was out of line. There's no question about that."

Garrett stifled a yawn. He'd managed snippets of sleep here and there over the last three days, but the exhaustion still gnawed at the edges of his focus. He was loathe to stim again, but he might have to, for the endless tasks and meetings before him left little room for rest.

"Yes, he was," Garrett agreed.

"But the man was to be promoted to admiral," Jason said. "Surely that counts for something."

"Not in my book," Garrett said. "He was placed under my command, and that's the end of it."

"Are you going to let him out of the brig?" Tina asked bluntly.

"No, I have no intention of doing so," Garrett said firmly. "He stays there until I can hand him over to the appropriate authorities."

Both Jason and Tina exchanged another look—one filled with subtle unease. Their dissatisfaction was almost physical, but Garrett hardened his resolve. He understood their perspective, but they needed to understand his as well. This wasn't a one-way street.

"On your own vessels, would either of you have brooked a challenge to your authority, your command, from a subordinate?" Garrett asked. "One who was openly defiant?"

Jason held his hands up in a small gesture of concession. "I wouldn't have tolerated it."

Tina, however, didn't respond. She shifted in her chair, the discomfort evident in her posture.

"Norwood challenged my authority—plain and simple," Garrett continued. "I can't have that. Not now, not ever. I have been given a difficult mission. My job is already hard enough without the people under my command questioning orders, whether they were to be promoted or not. Fleet placed me in command of this mission and me alone... not him. I don't care if he was to be promoted. It never happened, and he was placed under my command. You both need to understand," Garrett tapped the desk with his finger, "that this kind of behavior is not only unacceptable, it cannot and will not be tolerated."

Jason gave a slow nod, his expression thoughtful. "I do understand that," he said after a moment, "but since he's been in the brig for some time now, perhaps he's had a chance to reconsider his stance, a change in heart?"

Garrett stilled, his gaze locking onto Jason. Did he even realize what he was asking?

"A lifetime of service thrown away in an instant of poor judgment," Tina said, her voice quieter, almost contemplative.

Garrett had a sudden, unbidden flash of memory—*a wrecked bridge, Captain Marlowe, wild-eyed and injured, raising her weapon.* She had just shot the helmsman and was about to shoot him. He'd been a heartbeat away from putting her down. The moment felt like a lifetime ago, but its power pressed on him as if it were yesterday.

"Norwood made his own bed, not me," Garrett said. "He must live with his actions. That's the end of it."

"You're ending his career," Tina shot back, her voice low and biting. "Someone who has served with distinction and honor for decades."

"He ended his own career," Garrett countered sharply, locking eyes with her. "The fault rests with him. I resent the implication that this is somehow my fault."

Tina's gaze narrowed, and there was an edge to her voice when she spoke next. "For the first time, I think I am really seeing the man who shot his captain."

The words landed like a blow, and Garrett stiffened, sucking in a breath.

"Tina," Jason interjected, his tone laden with reproach. "That's uncalled for."

"Is it?" Tina turned her glare on Jason, her expression unyielding. The silence stretched, heavy and uncomfortable.

Garrett leaned forward, his voice hardening. "I am what I am. And for the mission I've been given, I must be single-minded in purpose—ruthless. There can be no other way. We are *done* speaking on this matter."

"Are we?" Tina asked.

"We are, Captain," Garrett said firmly as he stared back at her. "Do not test me."

"Will you relieve me too?"

"If I must," Garrett admitted, hating the words and himself as they came out.

Tina straightened in her chair, her posture rigid, her eyes growing colder than before. Though he refused to let it show, Garrett felt a pang of sadness deep in his chest. These were two of his oldest friends. Or they had been. He'd lost Tina, that much was plain, but not Jason—at least he hoped not.

Still, he could no longer afford such sentiment, not now. In this moment, he wasn't their friend—he was their commander. And someday soon, he would send them into battle. The weight of that truth pressed on him hard, but he forced it down, locking it away. As commodore, sentiment was a luxury he could no longer afford, nor tolerate. That was the true price of command, and Garrett was learning that lesson the hard way.

"You both wanted to see me?" Garrett asked, his tone direct, businesslike, though he already suspected this had more to do with Norwood than anything else. "How can I help?"

"I need propellant," Tina said, her voice clipped. "We're below fifty percent. We were scheduled for a refill, but—"

"Speak to Shaw," Garrett interrupted smoothly. "Bring all future matters of that nature to him. He'll ensure you get what we can spare—perhaps top you off to eighty percent. *Dante* and *Kern* are running low too. We must ration until we find a gas giant and can manufacture more. Will eighty percent suffice?"

Tina hesitated for a moment, her jaw tightening as if weighing whether to push and press further. "It will."

"Good," Garrett said. He glanced between them. "Is there anything else?"

"No," Tina said after a moment, then glanced at Jason. "Not from me." She rose, her gaze fixing back on Garrett with an edge of unspoken disapproval, anger, and disgust. "That's all I wanted. With your permission, sir, I'll speak to Shaw and return to my ship." The word *sir* was sharp, nearly venomous.

Garrett nodded, his expression impassive. Without another word, Tina turned and left the office, the hatch sliding shut behind her with a quiet finality.

"That is one angry woman," Jason said.

"I know," Garrett replied.

Jason gave a sad nod. "She will come around."

Garrett wasn't so sure. "Do you need propellant too?"

"No, but I could use some extra personnel," Jason said. "When we pushed back from Midway, I left nearly a hundred stationside. We're a little short-handed."

"Speak to Shaw," Garrett said. "He will do what he can."

"I will." Jason hesitated. "You might want to reconsider Norwood, ask him to change his position. He's a stuck-up ass, sure, and I've never much liked him, but he's a good captain, solid as they come. He knows his trade well, and Fleet thinks he has promise otherwise they'd not have considered him for promotion."

"If I reconsider now, it demonstrates weakness," Garrett explained, shaking his head. "No. He's relieved for the duration of this mission. I cannot give ground on this, not an inch. To do so would thoroughly undermine my authority and invite second-guessing. I will not have that. Fleet can decide his fate afterward. If they want to rehabilitate him, even if they want to reprimand me, that will be their decision. It certainly will not be mine."

"The other captains asked us both to come speak with you... on account of our close ties, our shared history."

Garrett stilled. He did not like the idea of his captains talking behind his back, especially about Norwood, but he knew that was an inevitability.

"Norwood is not getting a second chance," Garrett said

firmly, the finality in his voice leaving no room for argument, "not from me."

"I figured as much before I walked in here," Jason admitted, his expression softening slightly. "Still, it's a pity."

"It is," Garrett agreed, his voice quieter now. "I don't feel good about it, but personal feelings have nothing to do with my decisions anymore."

"I suppose not," Jason said, folding his hands in his lap.

"Level with me, do you think there will be trouble from the other captains of the task force?" Garrett asked, studying his old friend closely.

"No," Jason replied after a moment, his tone thoughtful. "At least not for now. If you screw up—make the wrong call—there might be. They saw what you did at Midway, how you handled the ship. After what you shared about the disruptor, the enemy and Third Fleet... they're on board."

Careful not to show it, Garrett felt a wave of relief wash over him.

He stood, crossing to the recessed cabinet built into the bulkhead beside his desk. He selected two glasses. They had a clean look and were solid. He generally drank his diminishing supply of whiskey and bourbon out of them. He grabbed a half-finished bottle of bourbon and returned, placing them on the desk, then sat back down. "Care to join me in a drink?"

Jason's lips curled into a faint smile. "I thought you would never ask."

Garrett poured a precise measure into each glass, a finger each, and slid one across to Jason, who caught it deftly. Lifting it to his nose, Jason inhaled deeply. "Surely this isn't simulated?"

"Kraken Tell Dawn, straight from Old Methosa, the real deal."

Jason raised an appreciative eyebrow. "That must've cost you an arm and a leg."

"It was a gift from Gray," Garrett admitted, lifting his own glass and taking a whiff.

"Admiral Gray?" Jason asked, a note of surprise in his voice.

"The one and only." Garrett held his glass up, the amber liquid catching the light. "To *Surprise*. Without her, we'd both be dead."

"To *Surprise*," Jason echoed, clinking his glass against Garrett's before taking a measured sip. He closed his eyes briefly, plainly savoring the smoothness. "That's remarkable."

"It is," Garrett agreed, his tone tinged with appreciation, "quite good."

Jason lowered his glass and stared at it for a long moment, his expression darkening. "Jim... I checked the logs, and Julia didn't make it. Her ship was destroyed in the fighting at one of the beacons. An enemy dreadnaught jumped in almost on top of her. *Cerberus* barely scratched their shields before her main reactor was hit and went critical. No escape pods were observed."

Garrett had already known—he had checked for himself—but hearing it aloud from Jason struck a deep, painful chord in his heart. He felt the power of the loss settle, conjuring an image of Julia's radiant smile during their last dinner at Little Hill. She had been so eager to join Third Fleet, so full of life... Now... she, along with so many others, was gone.

"And Eric?" Garrett asked quietly. He'd been unable to find any information on him.

Jason shook his head. "As far as I know, he was still stationside when everything went to hell. I have to assume he's dead."

"Yeah..." Garrett nodded slowly and took another sip of the bourbon. Two of his oldest friends were gone, and one who had survived loathed him with a burning hot passion. It was a bitter truth to swallow.

Jason broke the silence. He cleared his throat and sat up straighter. "Besides going to Dows, what's this mission

Command gave you? What's the ultimate objective? What did they ask you to do?"

Garrett's gaze hardened as he set his glass down. "I'm not ready to talk about it yet."

Jason leaned forward, curiosity etched into his features. "It's important, isn't it?"

"Very," Garrett admitted. "Fleet thinks so, and I agree. But..."

Jason pressed gently, his tone softening. "It's just us here, you and me. Who am I going to tell?"

Garrett trusted his friend implicitly, but the fewer people who knew the mission's ultimate objective, the better. Especially with the looming threat of enemy infiltration hanging over their heads. Someone had already hacked the security system once, and they did not yet know how it had been done. Garrett couldn't afford any additional risks, the word getting spread around too much. Besides, he needed time to refine a plan, one that wouldn't just succeed but would also give them a fighting chance of surviving, of escaping after the job was done. That way, the captains of his task force would not think him mad.

"Not yet," Garrett said firmly. "Soon, though."

He drank the last of his bourbon, savoring the lingering warmth. Jason drained his own glass, setting it down with a pleased sigh.

"I don't envy you, Jim," Jason said. "But truth be told, I think Yenga chose the right man. You proved that at Midway."

"Thank you," Garrett said quietly.

The buzzer sounded, sharp and urgent. It was the bridge alert, only used when there was trouble. Garrett sat up, his focus narrowing instantly, and accepted the call.

"Sir," Keeli's voice came through, "Colonel Stroud is on the line. He says it's critical to the safety of the ship. Should I put him through?"

"Do it," Garrett said.

A tone sounded as Keeli dropped off and Stroud was connected.

"Colonel," Garrett began, "what's the situation?"

"Sir," Stroud said, his words brisk and filling the office, "as you know, we've identified seven individuals so far with genetic markers linking them to lost colony worlds."

Jason straightened at that, his eyes sharpening.

"I read the report this morning, Colonel," Garrett said. "They were civilians we took aboard. We're going to round them all up at once. I assume there are more we have yet to uncover?"

"I believe so too, sir," Stroud replied. "But this isn't about that. As you're aware, those that we've identified have been nano-tagged. We have been tracking their movements closely. Five of the seven left the civilian area of the ship where they had been quartered and are currently congregated near Reactor Two, quite close."

The words hit Garrett like a hammer.

"Reactor Two?" That was one of the ship's primary power systems. If it was sabotaged or—worse—caused to go critical, the resulting detonation would be catastrophic. It would end their mission very quickly.

"Correct, sir," Stroud confirmed. "They entered a nonsecure storage compartment about three hundred meters from the reactor. Shortly after, the security system and net in that area went down."

"It was brought down."

"Yes, sir, it was."

Garrett felt ice slide down his spine. "I assume you've already taken appropriate steps to protect the reactor?"

"I have, sir," Stroud said. "I've got a standing force stationed around it, guarding all possible access points. They've been alerted to the situation, and I've deployed reserve teams that are closing in on the enemy's position as we speak. The deck has also been saturated with nanite probes. Even with the security system down, we're monitoring everything that happens there. As of now, the targets are still in the storage compartment."

"Do we know what they're doing in there?" Garrett asked, his mind parsing possibilities.

"We do, sir," Stroud's tone darkened. "They're arming themselves, with pistols. Our surveillance indicates they have access to an explosive of some kind... We're unclear on the type. I wanted to inform you before we engage."

"Will you be storming the compartment?" Garrett asked.

"No, sir," Stroud said firmly. "I'd prefer to draw them out into the open where we can neutralize the threat efficiently, essentially let them come to us and hit them at a point of our choosing. That puts my boys and girls at less risk. Do I have your authorization to proceed?"

Garrett's gaze flicked to Jason, whose jaw was tight. "Do what you deem necessary to protect the ship."

"Thank you, sir."

"Stroud, I want to watch it go down," Garrett added.

"I'll ensure the feed is routed to the bridge."

Garrett paused, a new thought striking him. "Colonel, make certain the rest of your teams across the ship are on high alert. There may be other groups preparing to strike."

"I've already issued that alert, sir," Stroud said.

"Good," Garrett replied. "Carry on, then."

Garrett terminated the call and leaned back in his chair, exhaling deeply. The enemy wasn't just out there; they were aboard. The thought of that alone was chilling in the extreme.

"The sooner the screenings are complete, the better," Jason commented, his voice low. "It's unsettling knowing we have enemy agents on board."

"Agreed." Garrett opened a drawer and retrieved a pistol wrapped in its holster, placing it on the desk. Jason's gaze drifted to the weapon.

Garrett stood, clipped the sidearm to his thigh, and locked eyes with his old friend. "I suggest you and your key personnel go about armed from now on."

Jason gave a somber nod.

"Care to watch the action with me?" Garrett asked.

Jason rose to his feet. "I would."

Without another word, Garrett strode toward the hatch, his mind already on what was about to go down.

THIRTEEN

GARRETT

Shaw was not at his station when Garrett stepped onto the bridge. He and Sabel were likely in the conference room. Brent, standing near the entrance, gave him a casual glance as he passed, but said nothing.

Garrett paused to survey the bridge. His new station was complete and functional. The repairs to the damaged hatch were still ongoing. The work was loud and noisy. Part of the bulkhead around where the new hatch would be installed had been opened to access interior components. Four marines stood by the entrance, scanning each individual's ID tag who sought access. The bridge crew worked quietly at their stations, clearly doing their best to ignore the noise and continual distraction.

Lieutenant Gunter Krebs sat at the tactical station, his expression focused as he worked through some issue. He was a solid choice for Tyabni's replacement—reliable and sharp. Krebs had been the man's immediate backup, but Garrett couldn't help but feel a pang of loss that surfaced at the thought of his former tactical officer. His absence left a void Garrett felt acutely, for the man had been truly exceptional.

"Keeli," Garrett called, drawing her attention. "Stroud is

sending several feeds to the bridge. Kindly route them to the admiral's station."

"Yes, sir," came Keeli's prompt reply.

Without another word, Garrett turned and headed for the admiral's bridge, Jason close behind. Brent followed them and once on the bridge, he took up a position by the hatch and to the side of it.

As expected, no one was present on the admiral's bridge. Garrett moved to the central display table, its glossy surface catching the light. He reached out, activating it with a thought sent through his implants. The table came alive, projecting a series of feeds in the air above its surface. The holograms flickered for a moment before stabilizing.

"Let's see what we're dealing with," Garrett murmured, his voice low as he focused on the unfolding situation. Jason stepped up beside him.

Placing both hands on the table's edge, Garrett leaned forward. Each feed was from the helmet camera of an individual marine, identified by name, rank, and positional tags, displayed in the corner of each video. Alongside the live feeds, a small two-dimensional map hovered, showing the ship's layout in the section where they were operating.

Garrett studied the map for a long moment, orienting himself. He quickly found the storage compartment. A cluster of five ominous red dots glowed inside, clearly marking the enemy's location. Also, around it, farther out, he could see the positions of friendly forces tagged in green. The enemy was completely surrounded.

Another feed, from an overhead drone, provided an aerial view of a corridor near the storage compartment. Half a dozen marines in light armor stood poised, weapons held close. The tension in their body language was plain but they looked ready for action.

"When you told us about the threat, I couldn't believe it.

Not at first," Jason admitted quietly, his tone carrying an edge of unease as he watched the feeds with an almost morbid fascination. "I mean... come on... really?"

"I understand," Garrett replied without turning away. "I had difficulty accepting it myself, even after the fight on the bridge. The idea that our enemy might be human... it's hard to wrap your head around."

"Your latest brief said they might be fanatics. Religious even?"

"We're beginning to think so," Garrett said. "One of the prisoners we had in custody hinted at it, but we're still piecing things together. Whatever their ideology, it's deeply ingrained—possible brainwashing."

Jason glanced at him. "You said '*had*'. What happened to the prisoner?"

Garrett straightened. "He died during interrogation. His implants triggered a fail-safe, releasing a neurotoxin medical's never seen before. He suffered seizures, then cardiac arrest. We're working on ways to understand and deactivate these implants in the others we have in custody. If we're able to do that, we might be able to get some real answers."

Jason exhaled, shaking his head. "Cold-blooded doesn't even begin to describe it. Can you imagine if the Confederation required that of its soldiers?"

"No, I cannot," Garrett said grimly. And, truthfully, he couldn't.

Jason pointed at the screen. "They're moving... the enemy."

Garrett's gaze snapped back to the holographic display. The five red dots, previously stationary, had left the storage compartment and were now out in the corridor. They moved in tight formation, deliberate, and purposeful, heading in a beeline toward Reactor Two.

A knot of tension coiled in Garrett's stomach.

"Okay, listen up, people. The enemy's on the move. They're

armed and wearing light body armor," a voice announced over the comm, emanating from a concealed speaker embedded in the table. "When ordered, Assault Team One will move to contact and engage with extreme prejudice. All other units, hold your positions, unless otherwise ordered. I repeat, hold. We are not engaging from multiple directions. I don't need a blue-on-blue incident." The speaker paused briefly. "The enemy is about to enter the ambush zone—a portion of the corridor with no hatches on either side and no cover. Stand by..."

"This is Stroud." The colonel's voice cut through. "Our latest scan confirms the enemy is carrying an explosive device. We believe it to be a compression warhead, estimated yield: one megaton."

"Holy shit," Jason whispered.

Gripping the table, Garrett felt a cold sliver of dread trace its way down his spine. One megaton. That wasn't just catastrophic—if detonated close to the reactor, it meant annihilation.

"This is a critical threat," Stroud continued. "Prisoners will *not* be taken. I say again, prisoners will *not* be taken. Maximum force is authorized. Neutralize the threat."

The marines remained poised and steady, holding just before an intersection in the corridor. From the map, Garrett saw they were out of sight as the enemy advanced toward them.

"This is bad," Jason muttered, his voice hollow. "They're not just infiltrators. This is a suicide mission. They detonate that device and take out the reactor, there's no way they survive. Everyone dies. They really *are* fanatics."

Feeling grim, Garrett nodded silently. He wanted to look away from the screens but forced himself to watch. These moments demanded his personal attention, for his people were going into battle. Lives hung in the balance, and as commodore, the ship's safety rested squarely on his shoulders as did every soul aboard.

Garrett's knuckles whitened as he gripped the edge of the table further, his eyes glued closely to the feeds. The red dots moved closer to the ambush point, an area that was marked in a red flashing bracket. Then they entered it.

This was the moment.

Either his marines would succeed, or the ship—and everyone on it—might not survive the next few minutes.

"Team One... go, go, go!"

Instantly, the marines advanced, their rifles raised and ready for action. Garrett felt an almost surreal detachment as he watched the scene unfold through their helmet cams. The clarity of the footage, paired with the steady cadence of the marine's breathing, made it unnervingly real.

No, it was all too real.

Fixating on the lead marine's feed, a Lieutenant Garcia, Garrett tracked their advance as they approached the intersection. His eyes darted to the two-dimensional map on the display table, where green icons representing Team One crept closer to the red blips of the enemy. His gaze snapped back to the feed just as the lead marine, rapidly followed by the others in his team, rounded the corner.

The perspective of the feed shifted abruptly as Garcia, next to the bulkhead wall, dropped to a knee, rifle aimed downrange. The enemy was in view—five figures clad in mismatched, lightly armored suits.

The red blips on the map faltered, and in the video, Garrett saw why: the enemy had frozen, their body language broadcasting a mix of shock and confusion at the sudden appearance of the armed marines, who had appeared as if out of nowhere. Their hesitation lasted less than a heartbeat—but it was a heartbeat too long.

Garcia fired, the sharp bark of his rifle deafening in the

confined space. The rest of Team One unleashed a torrent of fire, their coordinated violence overwhelming and immediate. The enemy barely had time to react. Garrett saw one reach for a weapon before being hit and crumpling to the deck, another flinched back and collapsed as rounds tore through his armor, shredding it like paper.

The fight, if it could be called that, was over in seconds. Save for the faint echo of gunfire, the corridor fell silent.

Still watching through Garcia's cam, Garrett's attention locked on the aftermath. The enemy lay sprawled across the floor like discarded dolls, blood pooling beneath them and spreading outward in dark, glossy patches.

"Advance," Garcia growled, and with that, the marines of Team One moved carefully forward, rifles aimed at the downed figures, scanning for threats and signs of life. Garcia pointed his rifle at each figure as he came upon them, clearly doing a visual scan before moving on. He didn't pause until he reached the last figure at the rear of the group.

Shot in the chest and leg, she was still alive. The young woman gasped raggedly, clutching at her chest with a hand. Thick oily blood seeped through her fingers. She couldn't have been more than twenty-five. Her face was pretty—almost deli-cate—red hair pulled back in a tight bun. Her wide, terrified, and shocked eyes were fixed on Garcia, before darting to a brief-case that had fallen just out of her reach.

Garrett's breath caught as he saw her hand twitch toward the case. It was a slow, desperate movement, but the intent was clear. Garcia didn't hesitate. His rifle rose, the barrel leveled directly at her face. She froze, her fingers hovering a dozen centimeters from the briefcase. Her eyes locked onto the muzzle of the weapon pointed at her. The moment stretched, unbear-ably tense. The only noise was her labored and ragged breath-ing. It came with a horrid sucking sound.

"Don't even think about it," Garcia growled.

"The Conclave is the only way," the woman rasped, her voice strained by pain. Blood streaked her lips and teeth. Her eyes went from fear to a mix of defiance and desperation, possibly even religious zeal. Garrett did not know which. "The tide is coming. You are blind to what's ahead." The helmet cam caught every detail of her twisted expression, her words spat like venom. Garrett read real hate in her eyes. "The Conclave is everything. The Confederation is nothing. Tell your commodore to surrender this ship. Nothing can withstand the tide... not him, not you... not this monstrous ship."

"I'm just a marine, ma'am," Garcia said, his tone flat but edged with disdain. "I eat crayons for breakfast, lunch, and dinner. But I've got two words for your Conclave: fuck and you."

Her lips curled into a feral snarl, her eyes filling with rage. Then, with a grunt, she lunged for the briefcase. Garcia's rifle barked once, the report deafening in the narrow corridor. The explosive round struck the side of her head, obliterating her skull in a single, brutal instant. Blood and gray matter sprayed across the bulkhead and deck, her body convulsing once before falling limp. Her outstretched hand stopped just short of the briefcase, the scene seemingly frozen in grotesque stillness.

Garcia exhaled slowly, lowering his rifle. "Enemy neutralized," he reported calmly. "I believe we have the device. Send the EOD team up."

Garrett and Jason watched as two marines hurried into the frame, handheld scanners at the ready.

"Daniels," Garcia pointed to the briefcase. "Scan that thing."

Without a word, he scanned the briefcase while the other began methodically sweeping the lifeless bodies.

"This is the device," Daniels confirmed, pointing at the briefcase. "It's hot, looks like it's improvised, not one of ours."

He hesitated and glanced over at Garcia. "I really don't want to open this."

Garrett activated his comm channel via his implants. "Colonel Stroud."

"Sir," Stroud's voice came through immediately.

"I want that weapon ejected from the ship," Garrett ordered. "No attempts to disarm it, don't open the bloody thing. It could be booby-trapped."

"Yes, sir," Stroud replied without hesitation. "I had the same thought."

The orders were relayed. Daniels acknowledged them. After a brief visual inspection, he backed away, and a spider bot trundled into view. EOD and the marine Corps emblem were stenciled on its side. Garrett had never much like spider bots as he had an aversion to their eight-legged biological cousins. Most people didn't like them either, but they were efficient machines in a wide range of tasks.

The bot's mechanical limbs clinked softly against the deck as it moved close. A mechanical arm reached down and carefully gripped the briefcase and then lifted it into the air.

Nothing happened.

Garrett released a breath he'd not realized he'd been holding. The device had not detonated. Without pause, the bot began a swift retreat, the techs following closely.

"Colonel," Garrett said. The comm line between them was still open. "Now that we know the enemy has access to compression devices, I want the ship thoroughly swept, radiological, biological, chemical... the works. Start with the storage compartment they were in and expand outward. Involve Commander Senica. Anything you need, resource-wise, she will give you. Any problems, report them directly to me."

"I understand, sir. We'll get on it immediately," Stroud replied.

Satisfied, Garrett cut the connection. He exchanged a glance with Jason, who shook his head slowly.

"That was too close," Jason said, his voice low.

Garrett didn't reply. His gaze had returned to the feeds. How many more of the enemy were aboard his ship? And what damage could they do before Stroud's marines caught and took them down?

"How did they smuggle a warhead aboard without the security system noticing?" Jason asked, his tone heavy with disbelief.

"They clearly hacked the system," Garrett said sourly. The thought of the ship's security net being compromised by the enemy churned his stomach. *Surprise* was supposed to be an impenetrable bastion, yet the enemy had managed to breach her defenses. How deep did that breach go?

On the screen, Sergeant Major Burns appeared in the frame, walking among the bodies. His expression was etched with disgust, his eyes lingering on each of the fallen for several moments, as if committing the dead to memory, before moving on. When he reached the young woman's lifeless form, he stopped briefly, then turned away, his jaw tight.

"Bring up the body bags and stretchers," Burns ordered to someone out of view. "I want these pieces of shit brought to medical for a full examination."

"With your permission, sir," Jason said, breaking the silence on the admiral's bridge and drawing Garrett's attention, "I'll return to my ship immediately and have it swept from stem to stern."

Garrett nodded. "That's a good idea. I'll issue the same directive to the rest of the task force. Go and get it done. Report what you find."

Jason didn't wait for further acknowledgment. He turned on his heel and left, his pace brisk. Garrett shifted his attention back to the feeds, watching as the marines worked methodically to secure the scene. They stripped weapons from the enemy and began thoroughly searching the bodies, removing any items they found and setting them aside. Once each body was cleared, it was bagged up and moved onto a stretcher, before being carried away. The process was grim, clinical, and efficient.

A chime sounded, interrupting the silence. It was an incoming call.

"Garrett here," he said, activating the channel.

"The device has been placed in an escape pod and ejected from the ship, sir," Stroud's voice came through. "It's now at a safe distance. The pod will be detonated shortly. The bridge has already been notified."

"Good work, Colonel," Garrett said. "And pass that along to your people. They did well."

"I will, and thank you, sir," Stroud replied.

"Colonel?" Garrett's tone shifted, growing harder.

"Sir?"

"Move on the rest of the suspected agents—and any others you discover as the testing continues," Garrett said firmly. "You don't need to check in with me first. Take them out immediately. It's clear leaving them be until we've tested everyone is too great a risk."

"Aye, aye, sir, I understand," Stroud acknowledged without hesitation. "I will keep you informed of our progress."

"Thank you." Garrett cut the connection, his mind dwelling on what had just transpired. They had narrowly averted a catastrophe, but the threat was far from over. The screening process could not be completed fast enough, yet he knew that even when it was done, he might not be able to rest easily.

Garrett turned away. He had duties to attend to, a task force to run, and—ultimately—an attack to plan.

Stroud, Burns, and Major Ramirez stood off to the side, as they watched Neelan and Pascal work around the patient. The man lying on the bed was one of the prisoners they had captured during the boarding attempt. A grenade blast had incapacitated him, inflicting significant trauma to his right side that still bore visible traces despite the efforts of medical intervention.

Except for the medical bed upon which he lay, the cell was spartan, as was typical aboard *Surprise*. The walls were smooth and sterile, an off-white that seemed to absorb the harsh overhead lighting rather than reflect it. A faint hum of machinery underscored the stillness, broken only by the occasional soft beeping from the prisoner's biometric monitors.

Though his wrists and ankles were shackled to the reinforced bedframe, the prisoner's injuries made him seem less a threat and more a pitiful figure. Still, Stroud knew better than to underestimate the enemy, no matter his condition. Experience had taught him that.

The man—barely more than a boy by Stroud's reckoning—looked no older than eighteen. Short brown hair framed a face that could only be described as pleasant, almost disarmingly so.

There was a softness in his features that seemed at odds with the idea of him as a combatant. Yet his uniform had told another story. It had identified him as Corporal Watson. He now wore a medical gown.

The fact that the enemy spoke English disturbed Stroud. That they were human at all made the situation even more unnerving. It was a twist of the knife, a reminder that this was no longer just a war against unknowable aliens but against their own kind.

Neelan and Pascal moved about the patient with handheld scanners, passing the devices over every inch of the prisoner's body. The scanners emitted faint whirrs, beeps, and occasional bursts of light, which danced across the prisoner's still form. Periodically, the doctor and scientist exchanged brief, muted words, their voices pitched low, the tone clinical, businesslike. Whatever they were finding—or not finding—seemed to keep their focus razor-sharp.

Stroud's gaze shifted momentarily to Burns, who stood with arms crossed, his expression unreadable, but his eyes tracking their every movement. Beside him, Ramirez seemed equally grim, his hand resting casually on the sidearm holstered at his hip. Stroud could sense their collective unease, for it mirrored his own. This entire situation, from the nature of the enemy to the peculiarities of this prisoner, set his instincts on edge.

The hatch hissed open and Lieutenant Commander Senica strode in. She moved with the quiet authority of someone accustomed to command. Her gaze swept the room before settling on the unconscious prisoner and lingered there for a long moment. With a curt nod to Stroud, she stepped closer to the restrained figure.

"So, this is the face of the enemy," Senica said, her tone flat, though the faint edge in her voice betrayed her unease.

"Corporal Watson," Stroud confirmed, his voice equally grim.

"They even use our rank structure," Senica remarked, a faint frown forming as she shook her head. "I find that disturbing."

"You're not alone in that," Stroud admitted, his own gaze locked on the figure before them. The young man on the bed looked deceptively innocent—too ordinary to be the enemy. That only made it worse. "Among the dead we found men with the ranks of private, sergeants, lieutenants, and captains next to their nameplates and on their shoulders, very much like our own military. There was even one general. He was older, at least by ten years, than most of those who boarded the ship."

"I heard you took down four more infiltrators this morning," Senica said, stepping back to them.

"They didn't go quietly," Burns replied with a grimace. "To say they're fanatical is the understatement of the century. One of my men is in surgery... a knife wound. Give it two more days and we should be done screening everyone. Hopefully, that will be the end of it."

"With the number we've uncovered aboard, I'd wager the problem is much larger than Fleet or ID suspects," Senica said. "It is clear our enemy has had years to infiltrate the Confederation. And we didn't even know it." She turned her gaze back to the prisoner, her expression hardening. "What's the count now—twelve?"

"Thirteen, as of a half-hour ago," Burns corrected, his voice clipped.

"None of our service members have tested positive, though," Ramirez added. The major, with his slightly disheveled uniform and the shadows under his eyes, looked every bit as tired as Stroud felt. He had been burning the candle at both ends, not only supervising, but actively working to speed up the screening and testing process. "Only the civilians so far. That's a positive, at least."

"Agreed, a small miracle," Stroud said. "The military's background screening process seems to be working in our favor. It has to be incredibly difficult to plant agents when every detail of a recruit's history is scrutinized."

"Now... illicit substances are another matter," Ramirez said. "We're finding entirely too many addicts and regular users."

Senica arched an eyebrow. "How bad is it?"

"About six percent of those we've screened have tested positive for minor, illicit drugs," Ramirez replied, his voice heavy with frustration. "Slightly less than one percent... the hard stuff —marines and Fleet personnel are included, even an officer or two."

"Some are using some really dangerous shit, worse than Bloom," Burns added sourly.

"Anyone who's into the worst of the worst has been taken into custody," Stroud said. "They're currently being held in the brig."

"The commodore will have to decide what to do with them." Senica turned her sharp gaze back to the prisoner. "How is it going here?"

"We've been waiting for them to finish up," Stroud replied. "It has been taking some time."

"Doctor, did the procedure work?" Ramirez asked.

Pascal looked up from his scanner, his expression sour, as though the question itself annoyed him. "Of course it worked. We're just confirming none of the implants are still powered, let alone having any residual energy within. So far, they're all nonfunctional... which is to be expected."

The irritation in Pascal's tone was strong. It was as if Ramirez had directly questioned the man's competence. Stroud, watching the scientist, felt his usual disdain bubble up. Pascal had been a thorn in his side since coming aboard *Surprise*. From the moment he'd arrived, he'd complained incessantly, first to Garrett, then Shaw, and finally to him—about accommodations, the substandard lab facilities, the food, and just about anything else he could find fault with. Stroud had taken a dislike to the civilian almost immediately, and months of exposure had done nothing to soften his opinion. Brilliant as Pascal might be, his attitude made him a pain in the ass to everyone around him, including his fellow scientists, who for the most part loathed the man with a passion.

"Doctor Neelan," Stroud asked, doing his best to hide his irritation and bypassing Pascal, "what is your opinion on the matter? I would like to hear it."

Unlike Pascal, Stroud respected Neelan. The ship's head doctor was brusque and could be just as irritable, irascible even, but he had a clear dedication to his work and the people he treated... He cared. To Stroud, personality aside, that counted for everything, especially when it came to a medical doctor.

Neelan straightened, his attention shifting to the colonel as if he'd momentarily forgotten the marines were present. "I believe it worked."

"Excellent." Stroud clapped his hands together, a sharp sound in the confined space. "Then let's wake him and get this show moving."

"I'm hesitant to do that," Neelan said, frowning. "Especially after what happened to the last prisoner. My job is to heal, Colonel, not to harm."

"We understand," Burns interjected. "None of us want to harm him unnecessarily, but this is a necessity. We need to find out more about them, the enemy. Right now, we know very little. Doctor, counteract the sedative and wake him."

Neelan let out a slow breath, still clearly reluctant, but he moved to comply. At the small table beside the bed, he adjusted the IV drip, shutting it off. He picked up a syringe filled with a pale-yellow liquid, and without hesitation, he administered the contents into the IV line. Afterward, he stepped back, folding his arms as he watched the prisoner intently and waited.

"The electromagnetic pulse," Pascal said, rubbing his hands

together, "clearly disabled the implants. The question remains—can he live without them?"

"I've been wondering the same thing," Neelan admitted, his scowl deepening as he studied the prisoner.

Stroud suppressed a flicker of irritation. This was the first he'd heard of such a possibility, and the uncertainty only added to his unease. Still, the outcome—whatever it was—would provide valuable insight into their enemy.

The prisoner began to stir, his fingers twitching as his arms tugged feebly against the restraints. His chest rose and fell in shallow breaths. Moments later, his eyelids fluttered, and he blinked up at the ceiling, confusion clouding his features.

For a long moment, he simply lay there, his breathing ragged but steady. After a minute or so, his awareness seemed to sharpen. He turned his head slowly, his gaze sweeping the room. Stroud watched as the prisoner's eyes flicked from one face to another, pausing on each with a mixture of bewilderment and growing wariness.

"Where am I?" the prisoner croaked, his voice hoarse and barely audible. Stroud caught the words despite the faintness.

Neelan picked up his handheld scanner, the device emitting a soft hum as he passed it over the prisoner's chest and head. He studied the results displayed on the small screen, then glanced over at Stroud. "His vitals look good, Colonel. I think we're in business."

The prisoner groaned and pulled more forcefully against the restraints holding him down. The metal frame of the bed rattled under his efforts as he jerked at them hard.

"Where am I?" Watson demanded, his voice growing louder and edged with frustration, not to mention confusion.

Stroud took a step closer to the bed, locking eyes with the man. "You're aboard the Confederation Starship *Surprise*. You, Corporal Watson, are our prisoner."

"Prisoner?" Watson's face twisted with incredulity. He

tugged harder against the restraints, his muscles straining. "I should be dead."

"You're very much alive," Neelan interjected, his tone clinical. "Though your implants have been disabled."

The words brought Watson up short. His movements stilled as his head turned toward the doctor. Confusion clouded his features, his brows knitting together. "Implants? What are you talking about? What implants?"

"Interesting," Senica murmured under her breath, her eyes narrowing. "How very fascinating."

Watson's gaze darted back to Stroud, a flash of anger creeping into his expression. "What implants?" he repeated, his voice rising. "You're making no sense. Speak plainly!"

Stroud studied the man, searching for any sign of deception. The bewilderment etched on Watson's face didn't seem feigned, and that troubled him. Could the soldier truly be unaware of the implants that had been integrated into his body? How was that even possible?

"You don't know?" Stroud asked.

"I don't know what the hell you're talking about!" Watson snapped back. His hands curled into fists as he yanked against the restraints again, the bed frame rattling and shaking in protest. "Explain this! What implants? What did you do to me?"

Stroud raised a hand toward Neelan, halting the doctor as he was about to speak and likely answer the question. He shook his head firmly, and Neelan closed his mouth, understanding the silent command.

Before anyone else could speak, the prisoner's eyes went wide with a sudden, wild panic. He tried to sit up, straining almost impossibly hard against the restraints that kept him pinned to the bed. His head whipped around, scanning the room frantically.

"The gods... their voices... they're gone. They are *gone!*"

Raw with disbelief, Watson's words came out in a gasping whisper. His struggles intensified as he thrashed violently against the bindings. "I cannot feel the gods. I cannot touch them. I cannot hear them!" His voice cracked with the anguish of loss. "Their love is gone! What have you done with them?"

Senica stepped closer, her eyes narrowing as she studied him. Her tone was clinical, detached. "I find this simply fascinating."

"I cannot hear them!" Watson screamed, the sound tearing through the room. His face contorted with raw pain, his words now a tortured yell. "I cannot hear them! I cannot hear the voices!" He twisted and jerked at the restraints, shaking the bed violently. "What have you done with the gods? What have you done with my gods?"

"What voices?" Stroud asked. "What voices are you hearing? Who is talking to you?"

"You've taken them from me!" Watson's gaze locked onto Stroud, burning with fury and despair. "It is, as was foretold! You are truly evil, a wicked people! You have taken the gods from me. Bastards!"

The rage dissolved into deep, wrenching sobs. He muttered incoherently between gasps, tears streaming down his face as he seemed to break under the weight of his anguish.

Stroud maintained a calm, measured tone. "Doctor, I believe we've heard enough. Sedate him."

Neelan didn't hesitate. He reached for another syringe, quickly drawing its contents and injecting it into the prisoner's IV line. As the sedative took effect, the prisoner's sobs slowed, his body losing its tension. The drip was adjusted once more, and Watson's eyelids fluttered closed as his breathing evened out. A heavy exhale marked the moment unconsciousness claimed him again.

The room fell silent except for the faint hum of medical

equipment. Stroud straightened, his gaze shifting from the now-still prisoner to Senica. "What do you think?"

"I think this explains a great deal."

"The voices, the gods," Ramirez said. "What did he mean by that? What's he talking about?"

Stroud shifted his gaze back to Watson and stared down at the sedated prisoner, a storm of thoughts brewing beneath his composed exterior. Thinking on the man's implants, he suspected he already knew, though the possibility chilled him to his core. The prisoner's words had unearthed memories of some of humanity's darkest struggles, the kind whispered about in training halls and only half-believed by the younger generations.

"Are there implants in his head?" Stroud asked.

"Yes, there are three implants in his head," Neelan said, turning his gaze back to the prisoner with a speculative expression.

"Do you know what they do yet?" Stroud asked. "Do you have an idea?"

Neelan shook his head. He bit his lip as he considered the question a moment more. "I suppose an advanced implant could be designed to stimulate the auditory cortex to create the sensation of hearing voices, while higher-level integration with the prefrontal cortex could make those voices seem internal and perhaps even interactive, as if someone or something... is... talking to him. Though in this case, I'd lean heavily toward something... something internal."

"That sounds awfully familiar," Burns said. "Like a nightmare from the past."

"Artificial general intelligence," Pascal said quietly, his voice carrying a mix of awe and unease. His gaze was fixed on the unconscious Watson, his expression shifting between professional curiosity and something close to primal fear. "His gods... I suspect they aren't divine. They are artificial constructs. When we killed the implants, that's who he lost connection with... the voices... his gods... the ones giving him his marching orders."

With those words, the room fell into a heavy silence. Burns and Ramirez exchanged uneasy glances, their discomfort plain.

"That is quite possible." Neelan conceded, his gaze still on the prisoner. "Which implants exactly are doing it? The processing power alone would have to be immense, not to mention storage for such a thing... keep in mind this is far beyond our level of technology and speculation at this..." Paling, he looked up at Pascal. "What if it's external, and he's just receiving the voices?"

"We don't know anything for certain yet," Stroud said evenly. "But if this is what it looks like, we're staring down a nightmare humanity thought it had buried for good."

"That's what it sounds like, though, isn't it?" Burns said. "An artificial intelligence, commanding these people? Guiding them, telling them what to bloody do?"

"It's worse than that," Pascal said, his tone grim. "If what he said is true, they don't just follow it—they worship the intelligence or intelligences."

Burns shifted uncomfortably. "You mean like some kind of... cult?"

"More than a cult, a religion," Pascal replied. "A civilization built around reverence for a machine-based being, fanatical, completely devoted. You heard him. They see us not as enemies but as blasphemers—wicked, evil."

"Hence the fanaticism," Burns said. The room's atmosphere grew heavier with each word, the implications dawning on everyone. "What do we do with this, Colonel?"

"Let's get him to the interrogation unit. I want this man wrung dry. With no implants, they should be able to drug him and question him thoroughly. I want to know everything he knows and then some. One way or another, we need to confirm our suspicions."

"Yes, sir," Burns said. "I will get him transferred immediately to an interrogation cell."

"Doctor," Stroud said, turning to Neelan, "now that we know the procedure works, I want you to start on the next prisoner, one you deem capable of answering questions. We need answers, and Watson may not give us everything that we need."

Neelan cleared his throat, reluctant but resolute. "I'll prep the next subject, but I won't lie, Colonel. If these implants connect them to their gods, disabling them might not just cut their communication—it could destabilize them mentally, leading to some level of psychosis." He hesitated a moment and glanced back at the prisoner. "I... I hope it's not really AI."

"I understand the risks involved, but we need the information in their heads. We don't have a choice. Get it done."

Neelan gave a nod.

Stroud turned to Pascal. "I want a deeper analysis on these implants and how they work, what they do."

"I'd like to involve Dr. Reid—one of my physicists," Pascal said. "She has a specialization... ah... extensive knowledge when it comes to artificial intelligence and its historical impacts. If this is what we think it is, she could prove invaluable in studying not only the implants... but it... them, whatever we want to call it."

"Bring her in, then," Stroud said after a moment's thought, "discreetly. We cannot have the knowledge of this spreading."

The colonel cast one last look at Watson, lying motionless on the bed, his face serene. He hoped the man's gods were not AI. After a moment, he shook himself. No one had moved. Everyone, seemingly lost in their own thoughts, was staring at the sedated prisoner.

"Let's get moving, people."

FIFTEEN

GARRETT

Garrett stood on the admiral's bridge before the table, surrounded by the lines of unfinished panels and exposed conduits that were becoming all too familiar to him. He knew at some point it would be finished and fully functional, but it still bothered his professional eye.

Shaw stood at his side. Before them were Doctors Pascal and Reid, both clad in the standard-issue lab attire adapted for shipboard use: a skintight ship suit with a white jacket and patches identifying them as science division. A hologram of the jump point disruptor rotated slowly above the table.

"Captain," Pascal began, his tone brisk and precise, "I—"

"It's commodore now, Doctor," Shaw interjected smoothly, his voice carrying a strong note of correction.

Pascal's brows furrowed, clearly annoyed by the interruption. "That's right. My mistake." He redirected his attention to Garrett, his irritation already dissipating as he launched back into his report. "Commodore, we've made significant progress on constructing the device. I have an entire team of ten of my people working on the project. The first should be completed within a day, and the second a few days after that. Its architecture is quite unique, particularly when it comes to generating the precise magnetic fields required to maintain separation of the materials, some of which are quite exotic."

Garrett gave a slow nod. "That's good news, Doctor."

Things were moving faster than he had dared to hope, at least on this front. The screening and testing for enemy agents seemed to be dragging. Now that dozens had been arrested for illicit drug use, people were actively avoiding the testing teams and had to be hunted down and found. Though rumors were flying about the ship concerning terrorists and drugs, the infiltrators did not seem to be aware yet that they were the focus. Garrett wondered how long that would last.

Pascal allowed himself a small, satisfied smile. "Yes, we think so too. As you're likely aware, we've requisitioned resources—some of which were difficult to obtain. It required the cannibalization of several torpedoes and shipkiller missiles. On top of that, engineering had to part with rare elements typically used for reactor stabilization and gravitic drive components."

"I'm well aware," Garrett said, his voice neutral but firm. He was wondering where this was going and why Pascal and Reid had requested a meeting.

"Good, good," Pascal continued, his words gathering momentum. "But we've encountered a problem."

"What kind of problem?" Garrett asked.

Before he could say more, Shaw turned a sharp gaze toward Pascal. "You've mentioned nothing about this to me."

Reid spoke up. "It has to do with the technical specifications provided by Admiral Gray. Commodore, were there any additional details concerning the mechanism's operation that you left out?"

Pascal looked over at Reid and snapped his fingers. "Exactly. We are constructing the device based solely on the schematics we received. But we don't have a comprehensive understanding of how it interacts with a jump point. Right now, we're working on faith, as it were. It would be incredibly helpful to know more about the device's underlying principles. We have some theories, but nothing concrete."

Garrett met their gazes evenly. "What you have... well, that's all we were given—just the specifications and the directive to launch it directly at the gravitational wake of the jump point."

Reid bit her lip and shifted her weight slightly, a contemplative look in her brilliant blue eyes. For a physicist, she wasn't at all what Garrett had expected. Her fit runner's build and confident bearing stood out against the stereotype of an absent-minded scientist. Her snow-blonde hair framed an attractively sharp face that betrayed the gears turning in her mind as she processed information.

Reid looked back up at him, her blue eyes locking onto his with an intensity that made Garrett feel as though she was peeling back layers to scrutinize his very thoughts.

"You do realize, Commodore," she said, "that once we're finished and the device is built, there's a significant chance it may not work at all. There's no apparent trigger mechanism—none that we've been able to identify. The payload is simply a mixture of elements, most of which are kept isolated by magnetic containment fields. That was the trickiest part to get correct."

Garrett stiffened. The possibility that the device might not work hadn't crossed his mind, and now suddenly, that prospect loomed large. He turned to Shaw, who met his gaze with a shrug.

"No trigger?" Garrett asked looking at Pascal for confirmation.

"No," Pascal said, shaking his head emphatically. "We've analyzed it from every conceivable angle. Our best hypothesis is that the unique conditions of a jump point—the gravitational flux, what you erroneously call the wake and subsequent energy distortion—could cause the magnetic fields of the disruptor to collapse. That, in turn, might serve as the trigger. But..." He trailed off, his hands gesturing in frustration.

"You just don't know," Garrett said, finishing the thought for him.

"Exactly." Pascal's irritation was strong. He slapped a palm lightly down on the table. "And I detest working with unknowns, especially with something of this magnitude."

"I suppose we are just going to have to trust Fleet on this one," Shaw said.

"I never trust," Pascal said.

"What do you mean?" Garrett asked.

"We might want—well, I recommend testing the device first," Pascal suggested. "See if it actually works before relying on it in a critical moment."

"How exactly would we do that?" Shaw asked, his eyebrows arching. "We're in the middle of deep space, and there's no jump point anywhere nearby."

"We find one and test it," Reid said simply, as if it were the most obvious solution.

Garrett crossed his arms, his brow furrowing. "Meaning to delay the mission further... and take *Surprise* to a star system with jump points? That's what you're proposing?"

"Yes," Pascal confirmed, his expression unflinching. "It is the only way to be certain. We are currently constructing two devices. We use one in a test."

"I don't believe we have the time to do that," Garrett said, shaking his head. He hadn't told either of them the true urgency of their first stop or its secondary significance, saving Third Fleet. And with each day's delay, Garrett was feeling mounting pressure to move, to get there before it was too late. "We'd have to locate an unsettled system, then search for a jump point. That takes time we don't have. What if we encounter the enemy while conducting this test or some other hostile force?" He let the question hang, watching Pascal and Reid exchange a glance. "No," he continued, his tone firm and shaking his head, "this is very likely going to be an in-the-field test. When we deploy it, it *must* work."

Pascal scowled at Garrett. "I'm not comfortable with that. Testing something so critical under live conditions—without knowing it will work—is reckless, foolish even."

"I'm not comfortable with it either," Garrett said, his tone softening slightly. "But we have somewhere to go, somewhere the device may be needed immediately. Every passing day and delay in departing for that destination increases the risk of failure."

"I see," Pascal said after a long pause. "Sooner rather than later, then."

"That's right," Garrett affirmed.

Pascal's eyes narrowed, and he wagged a finger at Garrett. "You must understand, Commodore, that if we're wrong—if Fleet made a mistake—this device might not work at all. In fact, as we said earlier, there's a chance it could do absolutely nothing."

He didn't like hearing it, but it was a truth Garrett couldn't ignore. "Then I guess we'll just have to find out when the time comes."

"Commodore," Reid said, "you must understand—neither of us ever envisioned something like this. It's beyond anything we've encountered or even conceived of. The design is extraordinarily advanced, and we're not entirely sure where Fleet got the idea in the first place. Some of the techniques involved are groundbreaking—potentially hinting at an entirely new branch of astrophysics. We've done our best to follow the instructions and are fairly certain we've constructed the device correctly. But truthfully, we still don't understand how it works. At best, we have theories, but there are a lot of unanswered questions."

"I understand all too well," Garrett said, keeping his voice steady. "Admiral Gray assures me that if you build it as directed, it will work. Fleet has already tested it successfully. We have to trust in that."

Reid's lips tightened slightly, and Pascal let out a heavy breath, his frustration evident.

"All right," Pascal said finally. "I don't like it, but I'll admit—it will be fascinating to see what happens. It should do... *something*."

Garrett nodded, glancing at the holographic display hovering over the table. The intricate design of the device, with its magnetic containment fields and layered compartments, was both awe-inspiring and unsettling. The unknowns surrounding it gnawed at the edges of his mind, but he couldn't afford to let doubt take hold.

"Something," Garrett echoed quietly. His gaze hardened. "Let's hope that 'something' is exactly what we need."

"Agreed," Shaw said.

Garrett regarded Pascal for a moment before shifting his focus to Reid. "I understand you've been reviewing the interrogations of the prisoners."

"We both have, Commodore," Reid said. "With the deactivation of their implants, the results have been... enlightening, and the studying of the implants, more so."

"And what conclusions have you drawn?" Garrett asked, his gaze narrowing slightly as he studied their expressions.

Reid hesitated, a flicker of discomfort crossing her face. She glanced at Pascal before answering, as if seeking affirmation before continuing. Pascal gave a nod, and Reid turned back to Garrett. "Have you received the report from Commander Senica?"

"I have," Garrett said, his voice steady, "and I've read through it, but I'd like to hear your thoughts as well."

Reid shifted on her feet, exhaling slowly as though steeling herself. "It's... potentially the worst-case scenario," she admitted, her tone grim.

Even though Senica's preliminary report made it plain, Garrett did not want to hear that.

"The enemy appears to be ruled—or perhaps controlled—by what they perceive as gods... digital in origin," Pascal added. "That is our current thinking."

"It's not rock solid," Reid added, "but we are becoming increasingly certain."

"Digital gods?" Shaw's head snapped toward Garrett, his sharp tone betraying his surprise. Clearly, this was new to him. Garrett had received the initial report from Senica earlier that morning, but Shaw had clearly not gotten to it yet.

"You need to read Senica's report," Garrett said to him.

"I will as soon as we are done here," Shaw said and then hesitated, looking back at Pascal and Reid. "We're talking about artificial intelligence here, right?"

"It seems that way," Reid said.

"Humanity fought a three-century war to rid ourselves of artificial general intelligence," Shaw said. "As a species, it almost broke us."

"And now we find the enemy seems to be ruled or guided by them," Pascal continued, shaking his head. "If this theory holds, each prisoner might have an AI residing in their implants—or at least the shade of one."

"A shade?" Garrett's gaze sharpened as he leaned forward, his hands resting on the edge of the table. "That wasn't in Senica's report. Explain yourself, Doctor."

"It is just a thought." Pascal adjusted his stance, his expression serious. "I've examined the implants closely. Doctor Neelan has contributed as well, but my expertise lies in the design and function of neural connectors, so I have some basic understanding of advanced implant devices and how they work." He hesitated briefly, as if organizing his thoughts. "None of the prisoners are aware of the implants embedded in their bodies, which suggests an extraordinary level of technological sophistication. They may have been installed at birth or at some later time. We just do not know."

Garrett nodded grimly, already familiar with that troubling detail.

"I haven't had the opportunity to fully dismantle and examine these devices yet, especially the ones embedded in the head, but I've conducted detailed imaging and molecular scans," Pascal said, gesturing with his hands as though outlining the devices he was speaking about. "From these scans, I can infer their potential functions. At least I believe I can. They are exceptionally advanced—beyond our current technological capabilities. However, based on their structure and capacity, I don't believe they could house a full-fledged intelligence... in that they don't have the latent storage capacity. At least I don't think they do. That's where the term 'shade' comes in. Think of it as a limited intelligence—a sub-mind, if you will."

"A sub-mind," Garrett repeated, testing the term on his tongue. "Designed to monitor the host?"

"Exactly," Reid interjected. "A full intelligence would require a substantial level of storage capacity. A sub-mind, much less. Theoretically, it would be able to interact with the individual, offering limited guidance or perhaps even exerting subtle control. It could shape their thoughts, decisions, or perceptions, maybe even act as a conscience of sorts. Or it could simply be a monitor. The fact that several of the hosts expressed they hear the gods themselves and talk back to them, lends this theory credence."

"I see." Garrett exchanged a deeply unsettled glance with Shaw. The thought of even a fragment of artificial intelligence guiding or influencing humans was a specter out of nightmares—a reminder of humanity's darkest chapters, when thoughts had been actively regulated.

"Think of it like a personal controller," Pascal said, his tone measured but brimming with excitement and uneasy fascination. "In our history with the Masters, such devices existed, though they were limited in their distribution. The Masters controlled humanity through manipulation, propaganda... those sorts of psychological means, turning one sect or group upon another, fostering division, hatred, with the goal of keeping humanity from uniting. This is somewhat different. Since the hosts are unaware of their implants, we don't know if all humans—or what they call their Union—have them or if they are specific to soldiers and infiltrators. It could be that these implants are installed at birth, or perhaps they are only issued to a select few. Right now, with so little information, there's no way to tell."

"So, they're slaves," Shaw said bluntly, his voice edged with disgust. "That's what they really are..."

"If our theory is correct, yes, unknowing slaves," Reid added, her expression grim. "Their gods speak directly to them. Imagine how that would shape one's psyche."

Garrett felt his jaw tighten. The more he learned about this enemy, the less he liked it. They were fighting people who genuinely believed the Confederation was evil, people whose every action might be guided by something beyond understanding. It wasn't just war; it was ideological domination at an almost unfathomable level.

"It is possible," Pascal said, placing a hand on the table, "though I emphasize this is highly theoretical and unproven, that the implants are quantumly connected. If that's the case, the storage for such a true digital intelligence might not even reside in this physical universe, but another."

Shaw let out a low whistle. "So, even if they don't have an AI in their head, one could be speaking to them constantly?"

"That is possible, though I think it's unlikely," Pascal admitted. "From what we've observed, the implants don't seem like a conduit. Still, the idea of quantum entanglement for storage or real-time communication across incredibly vast distances is something we must consider, until it can be ruled out."

"Wait a moment." What Pascal had just said rang a warning bell with Garrett. "Long-range communication? So, you're suggesting that someone on this ship could be in direct, real-time communication with the enemy somewhere else, say in one of their home star systems. Is that correct?"

"It is a possibility, though one I think unlikely," Pascal said.

Garrett just shook his head. There was so much they did not know.

"Regardless," Pascal said, "this is a profound opportunity—a chance to study something we thought eradicated from our species' history. It's a doorway to a deeper understanding of current and future threats, and of our own past."

"That is a dangerous door to open, Doctor. It will be difficult to close," Garrett countered.

"I recognize that. However, much of what the Confederation knows about AI is, of course, highly classified," Pascal continued, glancing at Reid with an almost envious expression. "Only a handful of individuals, like Dr. Reid, have access to some of that knowledge."

Garrett's eyes shifted and then lingered on Reid for a moment longer. Her expertise in artificial intelligence made her presence more than coincidental. Was this why she had been assigned to *Surprise*? Had the Confederation already known or suspected the Push was AI-driven? The unanswered questions gnawed at him, and he hated being left in the dark.

"He is right, Commodore," Reid said, her tone deliberate. "This may be an opportunity to learn something useful."

"Useful?" Shaw snapped. "I think it would be better to just kill them before they become an even greater menace. Artificial Intelligence is nothing to mess with. Once loose, it can cause all sorts of havoc. It's one of the reasons why *Surprise*'s systems are segregated and firewalled off from one another."

"I understand that." Reid arched an eyebrow, remaining composed. "However, there may be an opportunity here to speak with one."

"Speak with one?" Shaw leaned forward, placing both hands upon the table, incredulous as he gazed at her. "Why would you want to do that?"

"Because we've never had any meaningful dialogue with the enemy," Reid explained. "We don't truly know what they want."

"Yes, we do," Shaw countered. "They want humanity's destruction."

"That may not be entirely correct," Reid said patiently. "We now know they haven't killed everyone they've conquered. The prisoners we've taken are living proof of that."

"So, it may simply be subjugation that they want," Garrett interjected. "Or removing the threat the Confederation represents to their order of things... this Union?"

"That may be more accurate," Reid conceded. "However, there could be an opportunity to explore peace if we open a dialogue, at least the possibility."

"Humanity created artificial general intelligence once," Shaw said bitterly. "It was a plague, just like this alien AI seems to be. The Push is proof of that."

"That's true," Reid acknowledged. "But that's why this is an opportunity—a chance to study, understand, and prepare for what we're facing." She turned her full attention back to Garrett, her gaze intense. "The more you understand your enemy, Commodore, the better equipped you are to fight it. Is that not true?"

Garrett weighed her words carefully. He saw Shaw's skepticism etched in every tense line of his face, but Reid's point carried its own merit. Knowledge had always been humanity's greatest weapon.

"All right," Garrett said finally. "It's something to think on. But for now, let's move on." He glanced at Reid. "Senica's reports mention the infiltrators had a different set of implants than the soldiers who stormed the ship, smaller, less invasive. Did you get a chance to examine those?"

Reid nodded. "We've begun a preliminary analysis. They appear more advanced than those given to the soldiers—dedicated to specific functions—"

"Like what?" Shaw interrupted.

"We don't know yet, but they might assist the host in such activities as hacking or systems infiltration," Pascal said.

Garrett shared another look with Shaw. He knew what the commander was thinking... *Surprise*'s security net.

"They're specialists," Shaw said grimly.

"That is quite possible," Reid confirmed.

"Ultimately, their purpose and function are still a mystery," Pascal cautioned, "but I believe we've identified and can disable the suicide implant. That would allow us to study the host with most of the implants intact and functional. It could tell us a great deal."

Garrett nodded, considering the implications, especially when it came to an AI residing inside the prisoner.

"We have more work to do, but we're making progress." Reid hesitated for a moment, biting her lower lip as her gaze dropped briefly to the deck before returning to Garrett. "I think it might be worth trying to engage with one of the prisoners whose implants haven't been fully deactivated. Attempting to communicate with the artificial intelligence within—if there is one—could provide valuable insights. Of course, we may be misjudging and dealing with something entirely different. There's no way to tell for sure. But even the attempt would tell us a great deal."

Garrett turned to Shaw. "What do you think?"

After a moment's thought, Shaw gave a small shrug. "I don't like it, sir, but what the hell... it may be worth a roll of the dice. We may learn something useful."

"If there is an AI in there... in the implants, can it escape?" Garrett asked. "Something like that happened during the Great War."

"I don't think so," Reid replied. Her confidence wavered just enough to be noticeable, though she quickly reinforced her statement. "Especially if it's just a sub-mind or shade. A full AI would need a direct connection to the ship's systems, her mainframe—an access point—and we can ensure it doesn't have one."

Garrett considered her words, then gave a sharp nod. "Very well. We'll make it happen. Have the interrogation unit proceed with the attempt. If you wish to try to talk to it personally, I have no issue with that."

Reid's eyes lit up with determination and excitement. "Thank you, Commodore."

"Anything else?" Garrett asked, looking between Reid and Pascal.

"No," Pascal said, shaking his head.

"Then we're done here," Garrett said. "Thank you both for your work."

"You're welcome, Commodore," Reid replied, her voice steady but carrying a hint of anticipation.

As Garrett stepped away, he couldn't shake the weight of what potentially lay ahead... if they were right. The thought of engaging with an AI—even one diminished to a *shade* or *sub-mind* as they called it—was unnerving. But knowledge was power, and in this war, power was something they desperately needed.

Shaw fell into step behind him as they made their way to

the main bridge, with Reid and Pascal trailing close. Brent brought up the rear.

Garrett swept his gaze across the bridge, taking everything in as he moved toward his station. The engineering team working on the hatch was making visible and real progress. They would be done in a few hours.

At his station, Garrett paused to study the HTD on the main screen. *Surprise* was holding position in deep space. The feed showed a perimeter of small craft flying combat patrol. Nothing else was out there...

He was about to assume command, when he turned back to Reid and Pascal, who had yet to depart. "Doctors, inform me if you learn anything significant."

Reid nodded, her posture upright and professional as she stepped closer. "I plan to write a full report for your review, Commodore, on everything we learn," she said, her blue eyes briefly shifting to a group of newly arrived engineering techs. The team, clad in yellow suits and hard hats, maneuvered a sled loaded with equipment toward the bridge hatch. The marines stepped aside to let them pass. Her gaze flicked back to him. "I'll make sure to send it to your attention."

"I look forward to reading it," Garrett replied and turned toward the command station. Shaw was already seated, bringing up data on his display.

"Hey, who are you?" one of the engineering techs working on the hatch asked.

"We were told to bring this equipment to the bridge, that you needed it," a tech with the sled replied. "I just do as I'm told."

"The job's almost done. We don't need any of that crap—" The chief's voice cut off abruptly. "Where are you going?"

Garrett felt a sudden chill wash over him. Turning, time seemed to stop. From the back of the bridge, the three newly arrived techs were staring directly at him. Their expressions betrayed a predatory intensity. The one in the lead broke the moment by starting forward, and with that movement, time seemed to snap back into motion. Hand reaching into a pocket, he advanced with purpose, closing rapidly on Garrett, while the one on the left reached into a toolkit he was carrying. Out of the corner of his eye, Garrett saw Brent reacting, turning, his rifle coming up... but so slowly.

Garrett's hand dropped instinctively to his sidearm, taking hold of the grip and yanking the weapon free of the holster. In a blur, the man with the toolkit pulled a snub-nosed weapon out and brought it to bear.

Garrett's heart stilled.

Reid stood between the two of them. Like a deer in headlights, she seemed frozen in shock at what was happening. Without thinking, Garrett lunged forward, closing the distance in a flash, shoving and knocking her roughly aside. She let go a scream as she went down and hit the deck.

A sharp crack rang out as Brent fired his rifle. Struck from behind, the man with the pistol staggered forward a step. The weapon in his hand discharged, a single round hammering into the deck at Garrett's feet and ricocheting off. He dropped the toolkit, tools clattering everywhere as Brent fired again, hitting him squarely in the back, and like a puppet with its strings cut, he collapsed in a heap.

The one closest, who was still moving toward Garrett, now had a pistol out and was bringing it up, aiming to kill. Garrett dove, throwing himself hastily to the side as the pistol barked loudly. The angry buzz of a round whipped past his head, so close, he swore he could feel the wind of its passage. The pistol barked again.

Another miss.

Landing hard on the deck next to Reid, Garrett raised his own pistol, aimed, and pulled the trigger, all in one instant. The gun bucked in his hand, the shot striking the second assailant square in the shoulder, spinning him around to face Brent. Before Garrett could take another shot, Brent fired again, the rifle stuttering twice, throwing the man backward and to the deck. Without hesitation, Brent shifted his aim, and the rifle stuttered again, dropping the third assailant, just as he was beginning to take aim at Garrett with a sub-machine gun.

Looking around, Garrett saw no more attackers. He let go a relieved breath, and still clutching his pistol, allowed his gun hand to drop to the deck. It had all begun and ended in the blink of an eye, and it had been close... too close for comfort.

Silence followed, a profound stillness, broken only by the faint hum of the ship's systems and Reid's unsteady breathing close at hand. Brent moved forward, his weapon trained on the fallen assailants. As he approached them, he shot three more times, putting a round in the head of each man. The last one twitched violently, then lay still. Someone on the bridge cried out. It was followed by a retching sound.

"Stay down," Brent growled at Garrett, his eyes sweeping the bridge and then out and into the corridor, past the construction work, scanning for additional threats. After a moment, he relaxed a tad, lowering his rifle slightly. His voice carried a sharp edge as he turned to the marines who now had their weapons up and ready. "Stop standing around with your thumbs up your asses. Get that sled off the bridge and call for EOD to check it. I want the sled moved to an emergency pod for ejection and disposal if needed. Also get more marines up here. And you"—his glare fixed on the nearest, a sergeant—"you idiots are supposed to screen everyone, and you just let them waltz onto the bridge? What the fuck were you thinking? No one, and I mean no one, comes through without a full check and search. That includes the fucking engineering techs working on the bridge hatch. Is that clear?"

"Yes, sir," the marine sergeant replied, turning to his team. A string of orders followed as the marines moved to secure the access point. One marine began pushing the sled toward the exit, his voice steady as he called in a request for EOD support and reinforcement.

Still lying on the deck, Garrett's eyes followed the sled as it was moved away. A knot of tension sat on his chest. Was it possible the sled contained a compression warhead? Almost instantly, he shook the thought away.

No, if the enemy had one, they would have simply detonated it in the corridor and killed them all. The bridge crew and Garrett, their target, would not have stood a chance. The sled had served as nothing more than a decoy—a clever ruse to bolster their cover as a repair crew—and it had worked all too well.

His attention shifted to the three attackers sprawled on the deck, their lifeless forms bent at unnatural angles. Blood pooled beneath them, glistening under the bridge lights. The smell of it was so strong that Garrett could taste iron on his tongue.

Pistol still in hand he turned his gaze to Doctor Reid. She was lying where he had pushed her, trembling slightly, her breath shallow and ragged. Her wide eyes were fixed on him, reflecting a mix of shock and disbelief.

"You... you saved me."

"Are you okay?" Garrett asked, his voice steady despite the adrenaline still raging through his system.

"I am fine," Reid replied gruffly, though her tone betrayed a lingering shakiness. "I am alive... thank you."

Brent stepped back and extended a hand, helping Garrett to his feet. "Good reaction time there, boss," he said gruffly. He turned his gaze to the man Garrett had hit. "And a nice shot under duress. It likely saved your life."

Garrett ignored the comment. Holstering his weapon, he reached out a hand to Reid, pulling her up and to her feet. The pull was a bit too firm, and for a brief heartbeat, she was pressed tightly against him, her eyes searching his face for a protracted moment. She smelled faintly of lavender. Garrett felt an unexpected stirring deep within, but he quickly suppressed it and stepped back, brushing the moment aside as he surveyed the bridge.

Wide-eyed and shaking, Pascal was crouched behind Garrett's station. When he saw Garrett looking his way, he flushed a crimson color and stood. The rest of the bridge crew remained frozen at their posts, their faces pale, clearly shocked by the violence that had erupted in their midst. It had happened so unexpectedly and fast, they had not really had a chance to react. Only Shaw stood steady, sidearm in hand. The construction techs had taken cover behind consoles and equipment, whatever shelter they could find.

Reid gasped and brought a hand to her mouth as she gazed upon the dead.

"Don't look," Garrett said.

She shook her head and took a step closer, gazing down at the nearest. He reached out a hand to restrain her, but she shook him off. She seemed suddenly fascinated. "That's all right. I can handle it. This is not the first time I've seen the dead, especially the enemy. I've been in the morgue, examining their bodies. I... I was just taken aback is all."

Garrett gave a nod of understanding. He glanced around. There were too many people on the bridge. He needed to restore order and control.

"Clear the bridge," Garrett ordered sharply, his voice sounding harsh to his own ears. He was appalled at what had just happened, and was becoming terribly angry with every passing moment. "Everyone who isn't essential bridge personnel, out... *now*." He turned to Reid and Pascal, his tone firm, though he softened it a tad. "That includes you too. I need you both back on the job. There is too much at stake."

"Of... of course," Pascal said, his voice shaky, his hands trembling. He took Reid's arm and began to lead her away. At first, she resisted, looking from the dead to Garrett. "Dr. Reid, come, please..."

Almost reluctantly, she gave in, following after Pascal. The techs didn't need to be told twice. They headed toward the exit in a rush. Garrett noted reinforcements were arriving as marines were coming up the corridor, boots pounding on the decking. Garrett watched as Reid followed Pascal, her posture tense. From out in the corridor, she glanced back at him and for a moment their eyes met.

Then she was gone, swallowed up by dozens of marines rushing past and onto the bridge. The unexpected stirring for Reid lingered, but he pushed it aside, as a surge of anger boiled up at what had just occurred and how close the enemy had come to killing him.

"Wanna bet these bastards came from the civilians brought aboard?" Brent muttered darkly.

"The sooner the screening is completed, the better," Shaw said, holstering his pistol.

Garrett's eyes narrowed as he took in the dead. There was no hiding or concealing this... not anymore. Soon the entire ship would know the enemy was among them. Garrett noted all three attackers wore engineering ID badges. His anger flared anew.

If these infiltrators were civilians, they should have been confined to their designated sections of the ship. How had they gotten the badges? How had they managed to bypass the checkpoints and security to get all the way to the bridge? His thoughts went to the conversation with Pascal and Reid. Hacking... infiltration implants or an AI? Or was it just lax security? Garrett did not know, but he intended to find out.

"Keeli," Garrett said curtly, "call Colonel Stroud to the bridge. I need to speak with him. I want to know how these bastards got past our checkpoints and onto to the bridge armed."

Turning, he pointed. "Sergeant, ensure every single person

entering my bridge is thoroughly searched and scanned. No exceptions. Is that understood?"

"Yes, sir," the sergeant replied quickly. "I apologize—"

"I don't want apologies," Garrett snapped. "Just make sure the job's done right."

"Yes, sir."

Without another word, Garrett strode toward his quarters, his mind racing with questions. He paused and looked back. "Shaw, see that this mess is cleaned up. You have the bridge."

"Aye, aye, sir," Shaw replied. "I have command."

SIXTEEN

TABBY

Ducking low, Tabby was mindful of the tight clearance overhead as she navigated her way forward over the top of *Max*'s hull toward the bow fronting. Her gaze was fixed on the spider bot skittering just ahead, which she controlled and directed through her tablet.

The ceiling, hanging low, was studded with conduits and lighting strips, all hazards for the unwary. Carrying a reader that doubled as a portable scanner and hunched low, Sanchez moved behind her, equally cautious against knocking her head against something... Her eyes flicking between the ceiling and the bot.

The spider bot carried a section of armored plating. The piece spanned three meters in length and half a meter in thickness. It was an impressive slab of engineered resilience and would shortly become part of *Max*'s protective shell. The plating gleamed dully under the overhead lights, its matte finish bearing subtle patterns that hinted at the intricate layers embedded beneath the surface.

Designed to withstand the punishing realities of space combat, the plate had been made from a tungsten-carbide-ceramic composite. The material gave it an incredible hardness and resistance to high-energy impacts, while the ceramic elements layered throughout absorbed and dissipated the energy of weapons like lasers and masers.

Embedded within the plate were carbon nanotubes—microscopic structures that reinforced its overall strength and durability, ensuring it could endure tremendous stresses. The outermost layer was sacrificial and designed to burn away or vaporize under concentrated energy strikes, dissipating the force outward before it could penetrate deeper into the hull and reach the crew.

This wasn't merely armor plating; it was the culmination of countless advances in material science and warfare. Yet, for all its sophistication, it did not make *Max* invulnerable, not by a long shot. Hit hard enough, the armor would fail, which was why they were replacing several sections.

"This garage isn't half bad," Sanchez commented, her voice echoing faintly in the enclosed space as she carefully stepped over a sensor blister. "It's a little tight, but *Max* fits, and it's warmer in here, much better than *Neptune*. I nearly froze to death every night aboard that carrier. Heck, I had to requisition a second blanket."

"Don't remind me. That was one cold ship." Suppressing a yawn, Tabby shifted her gaze around the confined bay where *Max* had been tucked neatly away for maintenance. The heavy, reinforced hatches that led to the wider hangar were closed, sealing them off from Hangar Bay Two.

Tabby had cranked the heat up earlier, bringing the temperature to a cozy warmth. She'd been surprised at how insulated the garage was... though that was now a double-edged sword, for the warmth was making her sleepy. "At least the heating elements work."

"My cabin's not too bad either," Sanchez said. "It's surprisingly roomy. But I share it with Smith from Husky's boat, and she's all right. It's paradise compared to the squad bay on *Neptune*. You know... a girl could get spoiled on this ship."

"I know what you mean." Tabby nodded wearily as she yawned. She needed some rack time and did not want to stim, not again. She'd done that too much of late and had paid the price with intense headaches, like she'd drunk too much.

She glanced around once more as the bot continued forward, its many legs clunking against the armor as it moved. Floor to ceiling lockers lined the bulkhead walls of the garage. They were meant to house the tools and equipment essential for maintaining a craft like *Max*, but Tabby had quickly discovered, after they'd moved *Max* in, that most of them were empty.

The Mothership had been pressed into service before she could be fully outfitted, leaving much of the equipment required virtually nonexistent and hard to get. Husky's earlier survey had not been thorough enough, and she had been unhappy to find out how many essentials the Nighthawks were lacking.

They didn't have it as bad as some. Entire squadrons had been left without proper gear, forcing crews to share what few tools were available or wait on the overburdened manufacturing plants and printers to churn out what was needed.

Under ideal conditions, on a normal carrier, if they'd had a proper ground crew, *Max* would already have been reskinned and polished, looking as good as new. Instead, the battered assault boat carried the scars of battle for all to see.

"*Surprise* isn't too bad," Tabby agreed, her tone grudgingly optimistic, as the spider bot trundled up to the exposed section of the pressure hull. The machine halted. Tabby keyed in a series of commands and checked her tablet as the bot began to follow the instructions.

She moved forward another half-meter to see better. While it worked, she ran her hand across the edges of the hull, feeling the chill still lingering in the metal, despite the warmth of the garage.

The bot hummed softly as it adjusted the plate, carefully lowering it toward the exposed section of *Max*'s hull. Its mechanical arms adjusted the heavy piece as it came down, making the job look almost easy. A moment later, the plate clicked into place with an audible snap, fitting seamlessly against the inner structure. Tabby keyed in the next set of commands she'd preprogrammed, and the bot emitted a soft whirring as it began bonding the plate, its built-in tools emitting brief flashes of light as it fused the material to the hull and the adjacent pieces of armor.

This was the tenth plate they'd replaced, the result of a direct hit from a maser-driven point defense system, likely from the carrier they'd attacked and destroyed. The strike had burned through the outer layers of the armor and left the pressure hull dangerously exposed, but in the end, the armor had done its job and saved them. Despite the tediousness of the process, each replacement plate brought *Max* one step closer to operational readiness.

Tabby glanced over at Sanchez, who held the reader, studying it, the display casting a faint blue glow on her face. "How's it looking?"

Her boots thunking against the hull, Sanchez moved closer to the bot. She passed the scanner over the freshly bonded plates, then over the one the machine was still working on.

"Looks good," she said after a moment. "I think this is the last one."

"It is," Tabby confirmed.

"That took longer than I'd expected," Sanchez remarked, stifling a yawn herself.

"You know why that is, don't you?"

Sanchez shook her head. "Why?"

Tabby gave a grunt of amusement. "Because we're not the

ones usually doing the work. That's why it took longer. I'm sure a handful of regular maintainers could have had this wrapped up much quicker, then broken for tea, crumpets, and coffee."

"You have a point there, ma'am." Sanchez smirked, holding up the scanner as if making a toast. "Though I'll never admit it aloud, I've got a whole new appreciation for our maintainers."

Tabby silently agreed, running her gaze over the hull surrounding them. The older plates around the replacements bore the scars of combat—pitted, scorched, and gouged in places. They looked rough and mismatched, awful to the untrained eye when compared with the newer armor, but detailed scans had confirmed their structural integrity, so there had been no immediate need to have them replaced.

"Ma'am," Sanchez stepped back from the bot as it continued its bonding work, sealing the new plate in place. She looked over at Tabby. Her expression was cautious, her tone lower than usual. "Did you hear about yesterday's attack on the bridge? Apparently, the commodore was almost killed. He was the target."

Tabby turned to meet Sanchez's gaze. "I did. I was planning on calling a squadron meeting to address it. CAG gave a briefing earlier this morning."

"She did?"

Tabby gave a nod.

"I heard there are enemies on the ship... infiltrators," Sanchez said, her voice tight with concern. "Is that true?"

Tabby's thoughts turned to her conversation with Husky a couple days before. He had been alarmingly accurate and had picked up that something was wrong.

"That's why they were testing... collecting blood samples," Sanchez continued, "wasn't it? They were hunting for the enemy, hiding among us. The marines are all armed, and they mean business. I always thought the bastards were hydrogen breathers... that's the only part that doesn't make sense to me.

How can aliens hide among us? Unless the rumors are true about humans boarding the ship..."

"It's all true."

Reader dropping to her side, Sanchez froze.

"The enemy that tried to take the ship is human," Tabby continued. "They've apparently had access to Confederation space for some time. There's no other way to say it... they've infiltrated us... using the direct descendants of those captured during previous Pushes. Think of them as brainwashed fanatics. They look like us, act like us, but they aren't us anymore. I'm told they prefer death to capture."

Sanchez inhaled sharply, processing the revelation. "That's not good."

"No it's not. The blood test, well, it identifies them. And when it comes to that, there's some good news."

"What's that?"

"I was told they're expecting to finish screening everyone aboard sometime today. Once that's done, they'll have weeded out the enemy. With luck, that will be the end of it."

Sanchez let out a slow, shaky breath. "It's hard to imagine, humans turning on their own kind, even if they are brainwashed," she said, her tone carrying equal parts disbelief and unease.

"Very." Tabby glanced back toward the bot as it was coming close to finishing its work, the quiet hum of its tools the only sound in the bay. Tabby decided to change the subject. "How'd the system checks go? Did the diagnostic finish?"

Almost shaking herself from her thoughts, Sanchez glanced at her handheld reader. She studied it for a long moment before answering. "The general diagnostic is complete. Nearly everything checks out. There's a minor fault with atmospherics in life support." She tapped on the device for a moment. "It looks like one of the scrubbers needs some love. Likely a clogged filter. The subsystem diagnostic check is next. Chen's working on that. He's also repaired the comm link to our implants and that looks good too. That beacon jump up range to Midway burned out the interface." She paused, and sucked in a breath. "I hope we never have to go through something like that again. It left me with a splitting headache that lasted for more than a day."

"Agreed," Tabby said. "I don't think I will ever look at a beacon the same way." She paused, studying the bot for a moment, before shifting her attention back to Sanchez. "How's Chen doing? Tell me, how is he really doing? What don't I know?"

Tabby knew he was inside the boat, combing through *Max*'s internal systems, making repairs where needed. It was his first full day back on duty, and though she trusted his skills, she couldn't shake her concern, her worry for him. When she'd seen him, pale and reserved, he just hadn't seemed right. His gaze alone had been distant.

Sanchez hesitated, lowering her voice as her eyes swept around them to make sure the coast was clear—that Chen had not joined them. "He seems all right," she said carefully, but there was a shadow of doubt in her tone. "I think the experience shook him up something bad."

"That's only to be expected." Tabby's brow furrowed. "We got lucky."

"We did," Sanchez agreed. "But he's been too quiet since he got back from medical, and that's unlike him. You know how he is when he's off duty, the life of the party."

Tabby nodded slowly, for she'd noticed it too. He was withdrawn, sullen.

"We *all* almost died, ma'am," Sanchez said, her voice barely above a whisper. She glanced at her reader again, as if it could somehow offer reassurance. "Truth to tell, I'm worried about him."

"Me too," Tabby admitted, and then made up her mind on how she wanted to approach the issue. "Do me a favor. Go check on Chen. For the next few days, make sure he's not alone for too long. After what he's been through, he needs company right now, friends more than anything else. I will speak with Husky tonight. When you're not around or available, he'll see that someone's close at hand."

"What about a shrink, ma'am?" Sanchez asked. "Have you considered that? It might help for him to have someone to talk to, you know... someone trained for that sort of thing."

Tabby almost grimaced at the suggestion. It was generally best to avoid the shrinks, the psychologists, and therapists, for one could easily end a career if they thought you unstable, and that was often subjective... sometimes even random. At the same time, Tabby knew they were there to help... and sometimes could do wonders.

"I thought about that and asked around," Tabby said after a long moment. "Unfortunately, there are very few aboard, and they're all booked for weeks."

"All right, I will check on him, regular like. If he wants to talk, I'll let him."

"Thank you," Tabby said. "Go now, if you would. I don't want him alone for too long, and it's been a few hours..."

Sanchez looked toward the bot, which had finished its work and was waiting for new commands. "Are you sure you are good here?"

"I will be fine," Tabby assured her. "Besides, the job's done. All I need to do is return the bot."

"Right, then." With a nod, Sanchez turned for the ladder, which was located toward the thruster pods at the aft end of the boat. She stopped herself and looked back. "Oh, I almost forgot, our replenishment arrived about thirty minutes ago."

"The ordnance we ordered?" Tabby asked, straightening.

Sanchez nodded. "A full restock of PDS rounds and missiles... no torpedoes, though. Apparently, those are being rationed for the bombers only. Husky said the armorer told him their stocks are low. They've got plans to manufacture more, but... there are other things currently taking priority, like parts..."

A shortage of torpedoes was a critical concern, but there was little they could do about it. At least now they had something to shoot with. "Shipkillers and PDS rounds will do."

"When will we begin the loadout, ma'am?" Sanchez asked.

"When would you like to start that fun task?"

"I am thinking this afternoon, just after lunch," Tabby said.

"It'll take several hours at least."

"Yes, I suppose it will," Tabby said, her exhaustion creeping up again like an unwanted guest. It was time for some coffee.

"I am so looking forward to that, I can't express the amount of joy it fills me with just thinking about reloading *Max*," Sanchez said wryly. "It's kinda like going to the dentist with a toothache... that's always fun, so why shouldn't replenishment be..."

Tabby gave a soft chuckle, and with that, Sanchez made her way aft and to the ladder. A moment later, Tabby was alone. Turning back to the bot, she typed a command into her tablet and the machine responded with a beep, before scuttling away, its segmented legs clinking softly. It would be waiting when she climbed down. Then she'd have to walk it all the way back to its recharging cradle in the main hangar bay.

Her gaze wandered over *Max*'s hull, the once-pristine surface bearing the marks of battle. In another life, just weeks earlier, she might have felt minor frustration and irritation at how the boat looked, compared to others on station that were shipshape and Bristol fashion. But now, it spoke to resilience—a symbol of what *Max* had been through... what they had all endured and overcome. The scars gave her craft an almost defiant air, like a boxer's injured pride after a hard-won fight.

Her thoughts turned to her squadron. Over the past few days, the CAG had kept her not only running from one fire to another, but juggling between tasks and jobs, leaving her precious little time to connect with her team, let alone manage them. Husky had stepped up, but it was not the same. She hated it. Her people needed her, and she had to find a way to make sure they became a cohesive force—a team—before the next engagement, which was surely on the near horizon.

The main hangar bays were now clear and fully operational. She'd been told *Surprise* could currently launch more than three hundred small craft, the entire complement that were currently flightworthy and operational. It was a powerful space wing, impressive to be sure, since the average Fleet carrier typically carried only around eighty.

Knox had told her that between fighters, interceptors, torpedo bombers, and assault boats, *Surprise* had more than six hundred small craft, and that didn't even account for the marine assault transport wing. The only problem was almost half were not ready. When all were operational, it would be a force to be reckoned with.

With the bays clear, Tabby had fought with Knox for time with her squadron. After a conversation that bordered on being tense, Knox had finally relented, giving in some. Tabby had won a tactical victory, and, albeit grudgingly on the CAG's part, she'd been given a break of three days to spend exclusively with the Nighthawks. It wasn't much, but Tabby would take it. Today was day one, and everyone was busy working and maintaining the squadron's craft.

A double ping in her ear pulled her from her thoughts. She accessed the message through her implants. The voice was automated, flat and emotionless.

"This is an action notice from the CAG. Prep for combat within forty-eight hours. Make sure your squadron is prepared, and your spacecraft are armed and ready. That is all."

The message repeated itself.

"Not yet." She stilled, her breath escaping in a soft exhale.

Forty-eight hours... not nearly enough time to make much, if any, of an impact other than make sure their birds were ready. Tabby lightly hammered her fist against the boat's armor. She closed her eyes and sucked in a deep breath before letting it out. After a moment, she opened her eyes and unclenched her fist. "It is what it is. War waits on no one."

Through her implants, she opened a comm channel.

"Husky here," came the prompt response.

"Get everyone together," Tabby said firmly. "We just received an action notice. We will meet in our briefing room in an hour. We have a lot to do with very little time."

"I'm on it, Mom," Husky replied without hesitation.

Tabby closed the connection. A ping from her tablet drew her attention. She glanced down at it. There was a message from Knox. It was marked priority. Almost reluctantly, and fearing what it contained, Tabby opened the message.

CONGRATULATIONS, YOU ARE NOW ONE OF MY SEVEN WING COMMANDERS—KNOX.

"Wing commander?" Tabby exclaimed aloud, her exhaustion suddenly forgotten as her mind raced. That meant, at the minimum, she would be leading several squadrons into battle, likely attack craft. Tabby closed her eyes. Now, she was responsible for even more people.

"Fucking Knox."

Thinking of the mounting tasks ahead and all that needed doing, Tabby made her way to the ladder and started down it. Her mind churned. There was so much left undone, and her squadron—her squadron—was nowhere near ready. They were a patchwork group of strangers thrust together by circumstance. And yet, they had one critical advantage, one thing in common: they were trained pilots and crew. That alone was a foundation she could build upon. If they could fly, they could fight, and if they could fight, they could kill the enemy.

The days of milk runs—simple, routine missions, trainings,

where the biggest challenge was staying awake and alert—felt like a distant memory, almost another life. She paused at the base of the ladder, gripping the cold metal rung tightly, her thoughts lingering on the enemy. They weren't just faceless foes —this enemy was human, brainwashed, and fanatical. That made the fight ahead even more personal.

War wasn't fair; it never had been. Tabby knew that all too well. She'd learned that lesson the hard way. Fairness didn't save lives or win battles. Fairness didn't ensure the survival of her squadron or the civilians who depended on them. It didn't protect the future of the Confederation. What did, was grit, determination, and the willingness to make impossible choices, to soldier on. War demanded everything one could give. Tabby now understood that. She accepted it, even if it left a bitter taste in her mouth.

What lay ahead wouldn't be easy—she had no doubt of that —but she would do everything in her power to ensure her people were as ready as they could be. There was simply no other choice. And when the time came to fight, Tabby intended to kill as many of the enemy as she could and keep on killing. They'd earned it.

SEVENTEEN

GARRETT

"With the infiltration threat neutralized and the devices constructed, we are now free to head to the Dows System." Garrett's voice was steady as he gestured toward the hologram hovering over the conference table. The display projected a detailed map of their target star system, its strategic positions highlighted in red.

Particularly prominent was the Beleris jump point. Garrett scanned the captains gathered around the table as he continued. Flanking him, Senica and Shaw were present as well. "As has been outlined, the basic plan is simple and straightforward, and so too are our options, given what we find when we arrive. If I'm right—and if we're in time—we'll be saving lives. That, and we will be able to get the assets we need to complete our ultimate mission."

He had spent the last hour laying out the details of the operational plan, outlining contingencies, and answering questions as they came. It was a plan crafted with heavy input from Shaw and Senica during an exhausting series of late-night sessions over the last week.

Around the table, the captains of the task force stood in

silence. Garrett had given them a lot to think on. Their expressions ranged from grim to outright displeasure, perhaps even distaste. Garrett noted the tightly pressed lips of Tina, the slight shake of Torres's head. None of them were happy with the options he had presented, the possibilities of what they might have to do, and he didn't blame them, for if he was correct, they could be going into a difficult fight.

"And if you are not right, sir?" Abebe asked, her tone careful but edged with doubt.

"We will adjust accordingly," Garrett replied evenly.

"As outlined in the presentation," Senica interjected, "we have several options available to us. Those depend on what we find on reaching the observation point. Worst-case scenario—if the enemy has fully breached the defenses around the Beleris jump point and gained control of large tracts of the system—we simply withdraw. If that means giving up on Third Fleet, then we will... but, I don't believe that will be necessary."

Garrett turned his gaze back to the holographic display, keeping his expression unreadable as the room settled back into a tense silence. The captains knew as well as he, the success of the mission hinged on what they found when they arrived.

"I've sent the plan, along with the contingencies we discussed, to your personal tablets," Garrett said. "Review it carefully. Think it through. If you have suggestions for improvement or tweaks, I want to hear them." He paused, scanning the room. "Preliminary thoughts? Additional questions? Now is the time to speak your mind."

The room remained silent for a long moment, the captains exchanging brief glances but saying nothing.

"I have a question that doesn't pertain to the plan, sir," Collier said.

"Go ahead."

"It's about the infiltrators." Collier's gaze shifted to Senica.

"What about them?" Senica asked.

"Your brief earlier indicated they are highly religious. Are we certain of that?"

"We're fairly certain they are," Senica replied to Collier. "We've interrogated six individuals thus far, all with their implants rendered nonfunctional. Each expressed unwavering devotion to what they call the *Conclave* and the *Union*. They also mentioned a star system where their gods supposedly reside, a holy place. It's apparently a lifegoal of every believer to make a pilgrimage there, whether human or not. As near as we can gather, few ever manage to make that journey, and those that do are considered especially blessed."

"The Conclave being their gods, and the Union their state, correct?" Collier asked. "I believe that's what you had said."

"That is our current understanding," Senica affirmed.

"And you believe these so-called gods are intelligent beings that are artificial in nature, constructed, like those humanity fought centuries ago," Torres interjected, "the voices they claim to hear?"

"At this point, it is a distinct possibility," Senica said. "However, it's important to note... we are not completely certain and still have many unanswered questions. If these gods are indeed AI, we don't know if they reside within the implants, operate externally, or are something else entirely. What we do know is that deactivating the implants has profound effects on the prisoners' mental state."

Torres sucked in a breath. "I see."

"And keep in mind, much of what we're gathering, intelligence-wise, is from interrogations conducted while the prisoners are under the influence of mind-altering drugs. We're not always getting the most coherent answers. As for the suicide implants, our first attempt to deactivate one resulted in the subject's death. We had hoped to speak with the suspected intelligence within."

That statement caused a ripple of unease around the table.

"How exactly did the subject die?" Torres asked.

"After the suicide implant was deactivated, essentially rendered into a nonfunctional state," Senica explained, her tone clinical, "the interrogation began without drugs. Within a few seconds, the implant reactivated, releasing a neurotoxin that killed him instantly. As best we can determine, the damage we inflicted on the implant was somehow repaired, allowing it to function as intended."

"So, something within him recognized the tampering and responded accordingly?" Torres pressed. "It killed him?"

"That seems probable," Senica confirmed. "It aligns with our current thinking."

"Do we know if their ships are controlled by AI?" Collier asked. "Have any of those questioned even hinted at such a thing?"

"We don't have concrete information on that," Senica replied, "but it is a possibility we must consider."

"Biologics, whether knowingly or not, functioning as slaves..." Rens shook his head. "It raises the stakes of this war in new ways."

"How so?" Jason asked.

"We may ultimately find ourselves fighting to liberate a people," Rens said, "an enslaved people."

Garrett had not thought of that possibility. It was something to seriously think on and consider. But now was not the time or place to have such a debate. Garrett had to keep the focus on the mission at hand. "Are there any further questions... specifically concerning the plan we are about to undertake?"

"The enemy has a back door to our space, possibly more than one," Torres said, looking around the table as he spoke. "It only makes sense they'd eventually try to deal with Third Fleet. I am not sure what we will find when we get there, but I am betting there will be the potential for a fight."

"The enemy's focus might simply be containment," O'Connell interjected. "We have to consider that possibility. Their goal may be to bottle Third Fleet up, deal with it later."

"That's possible," Shaw conceded with a curt nod, "but in our estimation, unlikely."

"Yes, we think it very unlikely," Senica said, speaking up.

"I doubt the enemy will be there at all, attacking into Dows," Tina said abruptly, her voice breaking through the speculative atmosphere. It was the first time she'd spoken during the entire meeting, and her tone carried a note of heavy skepticism. Every eye in the conference room shifted to her.

Garrett could read the anger radiating in her eyes as she continued, her gaze moving from Senica to Garrett and then the rest of the conference room. "Why force their way through a heavily defended jump point when they don't have to? We've spent years preparing that system for an active defense and those just beyond it. If they've infiltrated the Confederation, they know what's waiting for them, don't they? Dows is a fortress—Javelin Station is the largest and most powerful battle station we've ever built. We've also stationed a powerful fleet there with one of our best admirals. The news services... Confederation Propaganda... they talk about Dows all the time and the defenses we've prepared. There's no way the enemy could miss the significance of what we've done there. It would be madness for them to make a frontal assault through the Beleris jump point and fight their way tooth and nail across the system to overcome Javelin. The cost of that would be unthinkable."

"We can only hope that's the case," Garrett said, drawing every eye back to him. "If it is, our task will be much easier. We jump in, deliver the technical specifications for the disruptor, offload any extraneous personnel, refit properly from Javelin's depots, take on any personnel we require, along with a few more powerful ships, and then proceed to our main objective and hit it hard."

"And what is that, sir?" Sabel asked, her tone careful but

pressing. "Our ultimate objective... What is the target? Where are we going after Dows?"

"For the moment, that will remain confidential," Garrett replied evenly. "I am afraid that at Dows, some of the ships in the task force will be left behind in favor of heavier units, ones that will better ensure success of the mission. As such, we are on a need-to-know basis."

"I don't like that," Tina said, after a pause adding, "*sir*."

Garrett resisted the urge to scowl. Around the table, the captains exchanged glances. It was clear that Tina wasn't the only one unhappy with the lack of information.

"You don't have to like it, Captain," Senica said, her voice cutting through the room like a blade. Her tone was icy, devoid of any warmth. "It's basic operational security. When the time comes for you to know, if that time comes, it will be revealed."

Garrett glanced at Senica, taken aback. She was staring directly at Tina, her gaze unflinching and hard. Had the two women crossed paths before? Was there history between them? Or was Senica simply responding to Tina's barely veiled hostility?

Sensing the need to defuse the tension, Garrett raised a hand to his third officer, signaling her to stand down. Casting him a sidelong glance, she nodded curtly.

"At this point, our target is on a need-to-know basis," Garrett said. "What we must focus on is what we are about to attempt. Assume we are going into action. The enemy might already be fighting Third Fleet for control of the system. Then again, they may not be. We won't know until we arrive. Make your ships ready for departure and deployment, but more importantly, prepare for combat... expect it. The first transition will occur in less than twelve hours. I look forward to hearing your thoughts on the plan after you have had a chance to digest it. That is all—dismissed."

The officers straightened to attention briefly before

filing out one by one. There was no talking. Garrett had given them a lot to think about. Tina lingered near the end of the line, her expression a stony mask as her gaze flicked first to Senica and then to Garrett. When she finally turned to leave, following the others, Garrett called after her.

"Tina," he said firmly, "remain a moment."

She froze, her posture rigid, and stepped aside to wait as the last of the captains departed. Garrett turned to Shaw and Senica, dismissing them with a subtle nod. "Excuse us. What I have to say to Captain Martin is of a private nature."

"Yes, sir," Shaw replied, already moving toward the bridge. Senica hesitated for a moment, glancing between Garrett and Tina, before following. Her expression was unreadable, though Garrett caught a flicker of tension as she glanced back at Tina before the hatch slid shut.

"How can I help you, *Commodore?*" Tina asked, her voice hard and deliberate, the emphasis on his title unmistakable.

"If the enemy is not at Dows when we arrive," Garrett began, meeting her gaze unflinchingly, "I will arrange for your transfer as soon as we reach Javelin Station."

Her eyes narrowed, a dangerous edge flashing in them. "You'd take my ship from me, like you did Norwood?"

"That's not what I'm saying," Garrett replied. "I'm certain there will be other frigates available. I'll ensure one is assigned to replace *Valkyrie* in the task force. You would effectively be assigned to Third Fleet after that."

"I see." Tina's expression softened slightly, though her eyes remained guarded. She glanced down at the deck, her hands flexing at her sides, before looking back up. "Given our history, that might be for the best."

"I think so too." Garrett softened his tone as he continued. "I regret what's happened between us, the hard feelings. I should never have kept the truth from you."

"No, you shouldn't have," Tina shot back, her voice cutting. "You knew I'd be hurt, and that's why you said nothing."

"I did know," Garrett admitted, his voice weighted with sudden weariness. "You were close to Marlowe. It's why I kept it to myself, especially after Fleet decided to have everything swept under the rug. Me included."

"That was a coward's path," Tina said, her tone laced with bitterness. "Marlowe was more than a mentor—she was like a mother to me, the one I never had. And you... you shot her down. How could you do it?"

Garrett remained silent for a long moment, gathering his thoughts. When he spoke, his voice was steady. "She was wrong, Tina. If I hadn't acted, women, children, civilians all—would've been lost. I couldn't let that happen. Marlowe was injured, not thinking clearly. She wanted vengeance at any cost, even if it was against the innocent. I... I just couldn't allow it."

Tina's expression wavered, her gaze turning inward as though grappling with what he'd just said. Hoping he'd finally gotten through, Garrett took a cautious step closer, his hand reaching out, but she stepped back, shaking her head.

"Don't," she said, her voice trembling with emotion. "Don't touch me."

Stung by her rejection, Garrett withdrew. They stood in silence together for several heartbeats, neither speaking.

"Very well," he said quietly, his tone resigned. "I promise you this: I won't hide the truth from you again."

Her posture stiff, Tina swallowed hard. "There was a time," she said softly, her voice barely audible, "when I thought I loved you. Back at the academy... I was young, foolish. Now..." She shook her head, leaving the thought unfinished.

Garrett felt a deep pang of sadness. He reached out again, hesitated, then let his hand fall back to his side.

"We're done here," he said at last, his voice growing firm. "If I can, I'll see to it that another ship replaces *Valkyrie*."

"Thank you," Tina murmured, her voice barely above a whisper. She turned toward the hatch but stopped as it slid open, revealing the bridge beyond. She looked back at him, her expression indecipherable. "You expect the enemy to be there, don't you? Be honest with me."

"I do, and it is a real possibility. We've been here in the deep dark for nearly two weeks—long enough for word of the assault on Midway to reach Third Fleet HQ in Dows, but not long enough for Bryer to really react to the attack, to marshal his forces and respond with strength and real power. If they haven't done so already, I expect the enemy to attack soon. They won't delay long. Third Fleet is too strong, too well-supplied to ignore. They need to tie it down, and they'll strike hard to do it."

"But that'll cost them, buckets in blood," Tina said, taking a hesitant step back into the room. The hatch hissed shut behind her.

"Tell me... when has the enemy ever cared about casualties?" Garrett asked, his voice dropping. "They know they have our backs to the wall. They're close to reaching the Core. They'll throw everything they have at us to make sure this Push ends on their terms, one which sees the Confederation effectively crushed and broken. Maybe this Push or the next... the survivors will be serving and worshiping new masters."

Tina nodded slowly, her gaze lingering on him. "That thought is frightening."

"It is."

"All right." She looked about to turn away but hesitated. "Senica..."

"What about her?"

"I didn't realize she was aboard, that she's your third officer. Last time I saw her, she was an intelligence operative."

"She was assigned to *Surprise* at the last minute, right before we left Midway," Garrett explained. "I take it you have history with her?"

"It's not the good kind, if that's what you are asking. Watch her closely, Garrett. She can't be trusted. She's a wolf in sheep's clothing."

Garrett's brow furrowed, but he gave a small nod. "I'll keep that in mind. Make sure your people are ready for what's ahead. I believe we're going into the fight of our lives." Garrett paused. "And take care of yourself, Tina."

"I will, Commodore," Tina said, her tone devoid of the earlier venom. She turned and stepped through the hatch. It slid shut behind her, leaving Garrett alone in the conference room.

For a long moment, Garrett stared at the closed hatch and felt a tremendous sense of loss. He had the sudden feeling he'd never see her again, at least in this life. With a heavy breath, he returned to the table. The holographic display of the Dows System flickered faintly in the air, the Beleris jump point glowing an ominous red. It drew his attention. Resting his hands on the edge of the table, Garrett leaned forward and stared at it.

What would they find waiting for them?

Garrett sat at the small round table tucked into the far corner of his office, deliberately avoiding his desk where he so often felt shackled by duty. The subtle strains of a violin concerto drifted through the compartment, the music emanating from speakers embedded in the walls. Dimmed to evening mode, the lighting cast a warm amber glow that softened the cold, utilitarian lines of metal and composites, giving the space a surprisingly human warmth.

He took a sip from a glass of water, the chilled surface beading with condensation that pooled into a perfect ring beside a datapad he'd been using. With a flick of his fingers, one report slid aside, replaced by the next, a series of department readiness summaries compiled and forwarded by his executive officer.

Garrett's eyes scanned through the meticulous notes from engineering, tactical, life support, and flight operations. The verdict was consistent across the board: most departments were operating at only seventy to eighty percent readiness. *Surprise* was hamstrung by staffing shortages, not having a complete and trained crew. It wasn't disastrous, but it was far from optimal. Though over the last few days, with intense training, they had made progress toward this issue. It was the reason to go to Dows, to pick up trained crew, people who were specialists in their jobs... people he'd need to pull off the impossible.

Navy personnel brought aboard at Midway during the chaotic evacuation had been hastily assigned to vacant billets wherever they might prove useful. The new crew hailed from a patchwork of ships, each with its own command style and operational rhythm. Some hadn't set foot aboard a vessel in years, if ever, having spent their careers stationside buried in administrative roles.

The truth was unavoidable: despite the hasty training they'd been put through, not everyone would be ready in time if it came to a real knockdown drag-out fight. That was the reality with which he was faced. He had to go into battle with what he had on hand. There was simply no alternative.

He skimmed the final lines of the summary, then pushed the file aside with quiet finality and tapped into the next report: *CIVILIAN VOLUNTEER READINESS*. The file took longer to load, the system cross-referencing data scattered across medical, logistics, and the auxiliary command systems. Over the last few days, more than two thousand civilians had been run through a series of crash-course training programs.

Garrett leaned back slightly, rubbing the line of his jaw as he scanned the report. The courses had been focused and practical: damage control, basic triage, emergency medical care, and casualty evacuation. On paper, the programs were solid, as thorough as circumstances allowed. But the reality was harsh. These weren't seasoned spacers or hardened marines. They were civilian technicians, administrative clerks, cargo loaders, ordinary people pulled from safe, structured lives and thrust into roles meant for trained professionals.

Still, when it came to battle, someone had to crawl into fire-scorched compartments to drag out the injured. Someone had to keep the wounded breathing long enough for medics, doctors or, if they were lucky, one of the ship's few available surgeons to treat them. That grim necessity didn't care who wore a uniform or what training they lacked, just that the job was done.

He exhaled, a long breath that barely disturbed the quiet air of his office. The rim of his glass chimed faintly as he set it back beside the datapad. Garrett stared at the readiness summary a moment longer. Then, with a flick, he dismissed it.

Leaning forward, he laced his fingers and rested his elbows along the edge of the table, posture tight despite the relaxed setting. From the speakers, the music swelled, a surge of strings rising into a mournful crescendo that filled the room with borrowed emotion. It was an old Terran composition, Mozart perhaps, or Bach... he wasn't sure anymore, and it didn't matter. What mattered was that it filled the silence, smoothed the edges of tension. It helped him relax some.

His gaze drifted toward the wall-mounted display, and the real-time tactical overlay. Icons marked *Surprise*'s position, surrounded by nothing but the yawning black of the deep dark. Around the Mothership there was little traffic, only a single combat space patrol of interceptors and a handful of training and test flights arcing through their assigned zones like distant flares in the gloom.

To the right, a second screen displayed their mission objective. The Dows System blinked steadily in the upper-right, a lone marker pulsing like a heartbeat on a lifeless chart. Its presence felt distant, almost abstract, but Garrett couldn't shake the weight of it pressing at the edges of his thoughts.

He didn't like going in blind. Jumping into an unknown system without fresh and up-to-date intel, what was happening there. It felt like threading a needle with a blindfold on. He had plans to correct that to some degree upon arrival in the system, but they had no reliable data on current conditions in Dows. That worry was keeping him up at night.

Garrett leaned back again, the chair giving a quiet, familiar creak. One hand came up to rub at his temple, his fingers tracing the tight line of a tension headache that never quite left him these days. He wasn't getting enough sleep. The fatigue was always there now, a persistent ache woven into the fabric of his being, draped across his shoulders like a lead-lined coat. He wore it as naturally as his uniform, as if he no longer noticed its burden. But rest would have to wait. He couldn't afford the luxury... not yet. There was just too much that needed doing.

He pulled up the next report in his queue, concerning security. Before he could delve deeply into it, before his eyes had even adjusted to the new file's layout, a soft buzz from the intercom cut through the background music, gently interrupting the melancholic strings. He tapped the small, recessed control embedded in the tabletop.

"Garrett."

Shaw's voice came through. "Sir, Doctor Reid is here. She's requested a few minutes of your time. She said it's personal in nature. I figured you were still up and would not mind."

He glanced at the time in the corner of the holo-display. It was late, though not too late for a quick meeting. Curiosity sparked in the back of his mind. Whatever had brought her here and to the bridge at this hour, it was enough to step outside normal protocol.

"Send her in," he said, brushing his fingertips across the surface of the tablet to clear it.

The connection cut with a soft click, and moments later, the door to his office hissed open. Doctor Bethany Reid stepped inside, holding a small rectangular package in both hands. Garrett pulled himself to his feet as she hesitated just past the threshold, her eyes sweeping the compartment in a quick, assessing glance before settling on him. She looked worn down, like everyone else aboard, but the intelligence behind her gaze remained sharp.

She wore a pale gray jacket over her shipboard uniform, sleeves rolled neatly to her elbows. Her blonde hair was pulled back in a loose braid, strands escaping at her temples.

"Doctor," Garrett said. "Come in."

"Thank you, Commodore. I hope I'm not interrupting anything important." Her voice was soft but carried a quiet steadiness. There was a hint of hesitation, nerves maybe, or something harder to name in her manner. She seemed somewhat ill at ease.

"I've just been reviewing standard reports. I was trying to get a little ahead on my administrative duties before calling it a night. In a few hours we jump to Dows." He gestured toward the round table and the extra chair. "Please. Have a seat."

She stepped forward and sat down, gently placing the package on the table. "I wanted to give you this... a thank you."

Garrett sat in the opposite chair. "A thank you?" He arched an eyebrow, looking from the package to her. "You didn't need to—"

"But I wanted to," she said quickly, cutting him off. Then, more quietly, "You saved my life. I believe that deserves my gratitude."

He studied her for a moment, letting the silence settle between them, then reached forward and unfastened the lid. Inside, nestled in padded lining, lay a bottle of champagne, real champagne, not the synthetic stuff that was easily available. The weathered foil at the neck and the faded, hand-printed label marked it as something rare. The bottle was the kind of luxury you didn't normally stumble across on a space station.

He gave a low whistle as he looked up. "This isn't something you pick up at the PX."

A faint smile curved her lips, tinged with sadness. "I've been saving it. I was going to open it when we made a breakthrough, some noteworthy discovery in deep space that actually mattered to humanity. But with the war back on and sooner than expected... I don't think that moment's coming anytime soon."

Garrett set the bottle back into its padded cradle and gently closed the lid with both hands, his touch careful, respectful. He slid it across the table toward her, the gesture slow and deliberate. "I appreciate the gesture, Doctor, truly, but I cannot accept this... Save it for something special."

Her gaze met his without hesitation. "You can and you will accept this gift," she said firmly. "Please... there's no telling what will happen when we reach Dows." Her voice caught just slightly. "The other day on the bridge... I would not be here without you..."

She trailed off, leaving the words unfinished, but they didn't need to be spoken. The power of that moment, the fear, the uncertainty, the razor-thin line between survival and loss, stood quietly between them. The music continued in the background, strings whispering a mournful tune that wrapped around the silence like a shawl. After a long pause, Garrett gave a slow, thoughtful nod. "All right," he said, giving in, his voice low. "Thank you for the considerate gift."

Glancing down at the box, she smiled again, this time weakly. He ran his hand over the smooth top of the box, fingertips tracing the grain of the packaging, then looked back at her, the edge of a wiy smile of his own forming. Her eyes seemed deep in the low lighting as she looked back at him.

"Well," he said, "seems a shame to let it go to waste, especially since I'm officially off duty. Would you care to share a glass with me?"

"Now? Open it now?" Reid blinked, clearly surprised.

"Why not? As you said, we don't know what's going to

happen in the coming days. Why take the chance of letting it go to waste? So, Doctor, would you do me the honor of sharing a glass with me, perhaps even finishing the bottle? We can celebrate our mutual survival... together."

"Yes. I'd like that," she said, then smiled, a real one this time, unguarded and warm. It softened the lines of fatigue in her face and brought a subtle brightness to the room that the lighting never could. Garrett found himself watching her smile longer than he meant to.

He stood, crossing to the recessed cabinet built into the bulkhead beside his desk. Inside were a few personal effects and a small bar shelf. He selected two glasses, unadorned, functional, but with a quiet elegance to them.

Returning to the table, he sat and carefully worked the foil from the bottle's neck. The cork released with a soft pop, and a faint tendril of cold vapor curled up into the air, quickly fading.

Garrett poured with a steady hand. The champagne frothed in the glasses, bubbles rising in a lively rush before settling into a gentle, persistent fizz. He handed her a glass and raised his own, the rim catching the warm amber light.

Reid raised her glass, her expression shifting, the smile fading into something quieter, more wistful. "To survival and a time after the war... when all of this is just a story we tell our children, and their children after them. To peace and to the nightmare that is the Push finally ending."

Garrett met her eyes, the flickering light from the table's ambient glow catching faint reflections in the champagne's surface. He thought on the ultimate mission and gave a firm nod. "I'll drink to that."

They touched glasses with a quiet, crystalline clink that rang briefly in the silence, a small, delicate sound. Each took a sip. The champagne was cool and crisp on the tongue, dry but refined, its flavor holding up remarkably well despite years spent traveling across half a dozen or more star systems. It tasted like something rare, a reminder of what the galaxy could still offer beyond simple survival and existence.

The moment lingered, fragile and fleeting. For just a few heartbeats, the war felt far away, as did Garrett's crushing responsibilities. The room was calm, the hum of the ship and the soft strains of music the only reminders of the world beyond.

He poured them each a second glass, the champagne catching the soft overhead light as it frothed and settled. As the bubbles rose lazily, Reid glanced down, watching them swirl, then looked up at him.

"I grew up on Arlannis," she said, brushing a loose strand of hair behind her ear. "It's in the Core, third planet in the Solari Veil Star System. Beautiful place, if you like rain and mist and mountains that disappear regularly into the clouds. My family still lives there, my mother, father, and my younger sister. I haven't seen them in years. We exchange the occasional holo-message but not much more. It never seems enough."

Garrett listened, silent, his attention focused on her. Not just out of courtesy, but because there was something in her voice, a softness, a weight.

"I went into science thinking maybe I could help end this war," she continued, her hands cupped around the glass. "Not just write reports on theoretical stuff, but to really help. Maybe I'd build something, create something that changes the equation... something that keeps families like mine from living under a Sword of Damocles... waiting for the day when the sky opens up, and the enemy rains fire down."

Garrett gave a slow nod.

She gave a quiet laugh, a touch of self-deprecation in it. "To someone in uniform trained to fight and defend us civilians on the front lines, I'm sure that sounds naive."

Garrett shook his head slowly. "Not at all. That's why many of us serve, to protect the people we love, the families we left behind... to stand as a shield between them and the enemy.

That's why I wear the uniform. That's what I've dedicated my life to."

Doctor Reid looked at him, a faint smile rising on her lips. It lingered, touched by something unspoken, and in that small silence, the war felt distant again, diminished. Garrett thought he could get lost in a moment like this, in eyes like hers.

By god, she is beautiful!

He felt a stirring within, a hunger. She was serving on his ship, though she was a civilian, and she wasn't in his direct command structure. That was a fine line, and Garrett knew it. But at that moment, he didn't care, especially with what Fleet wanted him ultimately to do.

She took another sip, then held her glass in both hands, turning it slowly. There was a quiet nervousness there. Overhead, the amber glow cast warm light across her hair, catching the gold tones in soft highlights. Garrett simply watched her for a moment, this brilliant, composed woman, letting down her guard.

He leaned back in his chair, his own glass resting against the table's edge. "Arlannis," he said thoughtfully. "I've never been there. But I've heard the mountains are something else, something to see."

"They are," she said, her voice gaining confidence, warming again. "Tall, jagged ridgelines of blue-gray stone. Cloud forests climb right up the slopes, all the way to the peaks. We used to hike them when I was a kid. My dad always insisted we get outside, no matter how miserable the weather, and experience nature. At the time, I hated it. I was much more at home with my books, my studies. Now... I miss it. We had all the gear," she added with a soft smile, "especially for when the weather was awful. I didn't appreciate it at the time, but now I sure do."

Garrett chuckled. "Character-building."

"Exactly," she said, grinning now. She gave a nervous laugh.

"Though back then, I was pretty sure he was just trying to get us all killed on some mud-slick trail."

He nodded, letting the moment linger. He reached again for the bottle and topped off both their glasses, setting it aside with the same care as before.

"What about you?" she asked, her voice soft, hesitating only slightly. "Where did you grow up?"

Garrett considered the question for a moment, eyes drifting toward the far wall before settling back on her. "Nowhere as special as you," he said finally, his tone even. He didn't feel like dredging up old and unhappy memories. "I've spent the last few decades ship- or station-bound. For a very long time, I've had no place I could call a real home. I've just been moving from ship to ship, job to job. It has become my life..."

Reid tilted her head, studying him. "That sounds... lonely."

He gave a small shrug, the kind that was neither agreement nor denial. "You get used to it. In a way, it has its own rewards. There are no attachments, nothing to lose... just the work, which I love."

She didn't press. She'd clearly heard the edge in his voice, recognized the subtle warning that marked the boundary of something unspoken. Instead, she eased back a little, her tone softening once more. Reid swirled the last of the champagne, watching the bubbles rise and vanish.

"I get it, you know," she said, almost to herself. "What you said about never really having a home. I have not had one for a long time either."

She looked up, her eyes meeting his, and something unguarded passed between them.

"I've spent most of the last decade buried in a government research facility. It was secure, controlled, boring, and isolated. Months would go by without stepping outside. Half the time, I'd forget what the sky even looked like." She gave a faint, self-deprecating laugh. "It was supposed to be a prestigious assignment, cutting-edge research, all the resources I could ever want. But after a while, it just felt like... like being buried alive... being a prisoner, one under guard too... and my coworkers were far from exciting. Most didn't have what you could name a personality or even proper manners." Her voice grew quieter. "That's why I volunteered for this... to get away, to feel like I was actually doing something and making a real and material difference. So, I guess we've both got something in common... been floating out there, never quite settling down." She looked up at him, meeting his gaze.

Garrett didn't speak. He just nodded, slow and silent. He understood, more than he cared to admit. She finished her drink in a single pull and set the glass down gently, her fingers lingering on the rim for a moment.

"I should go," she said, rising abruptly. "I'm sure you've got more work to do, and I'm taking up your valuable time."

He rose as she did, the motion automatic, born of habit and courtesy. He didn't want her to leave. Not yet. He was surprised by how much he found himself enjoying her company, the quiet warmth of her presence, the soft scent of her perfume in the air between them. The room, dimly lit and filled with gentle music, suddenly felt colder at the thought of her absence, of her leaving.

They stood facing each other, caught in an uncertain pause. Eyes met. Neither moved. The silence stretched, awkward and heavy with things unsaid. Then, almost abruptly, she turned. She took a single step toward the door and hesitated. She looked back at him, the flicker of indecision plain in her eyes as she bit her lip. And before Garrett could speak, before he could find the right words to stop her, to ask her to stay longer, she took a step closer, leaned in and kissed him. It was soft and quick, more spark than flame, but there was a passion behind it, a terrible desire and longing, that caught him completely off guard.

His thoughts scattered as she pulled back just as fast, cheeks flushed, breath shallow. "I'm sorry," she whispered, voice cracking with emotion. "I shouldn't have—I..."

She turned away, already halfway to the door when Garrett moved on instinct and without real thought. He stepped forward after her, his hand reaching out. He caught her arm, firm but not rough, stopping her mid-step.

"Bethany," he said, his voice low.

She turned toward him, lips parted, eyes wide with something like fear, fright that she'd overstepped, or maybe hope.

"Don't go."

The moment held, frozen on the edge of something deeper. He didn't try to explain. He didn't say another word. He just pulled her toward him. The second kiss came fast, urgent and consuming. It wasn't gentle. It was fire and tension at the same time, a silent pressure breaking loose all at once. She melted into it, into him, her hands pressing to his chest as though anchoring herself, while his arms wrapped around her like he never wanted to let go.

For one fleeting, perfect moment, everything else vanished. The war, the ship, the burden of command... the upcoming jump to Dows, the ever-present shadow of the enemy.

All of it faded away.

There was only this, this moment, raw and real, shared between two people who had forgotten what it meant to feel human, who had given up everything for a life of service.

Garrett pulled back just enough to look at her when they came up for air, breathing hard, his forehead nearly touching hers. Bethany's eyes searched his, lips still parted, cheeks flushed with emotion. There were questions in her gaze, unspoken things hanging between them, but no resistance, no retreat. She wanted this as much as he did.

Garrett reached for her hand, fingers threading with hers, and took a slow step backward, toward the rear of the office, leading her along, where a narrow door stood half-shadowed in the soft light. It led to his cabin. He didn't speak. He didn't ask. He simply gave her the choice.

Bethany allowed herself to be pulled along and followed without hesitation. The music played on, soft and mournful behind them, fading into the quiet as the cabin hatch whispered shut.

NINETEEN

GARRETT

"Transition complete," Lieutenant Heller announced. Eyes fixed on the data cascading onto his screen, his fingers darted across the interface as he worked to pull up additional information.

The bridge was unnervingly silent. The soft hum of the air handlers and the beeps from various control panels only accentuated the stillness, the atmosphere taut with anticipation. If a pin had dropped, Garrett would have heard it.

"Wormhole has closed," Heller reported. "We are no longer in the deep dark. We've arrived at the designated coordinates, sixteen light hours out from the Dows Star System." He partially turned, looking at Garrett. "Everything looks spot-on, sir."

The location had been chosen with great care. Positioned well above the ecliptic plane, *Surprise* had a commanding vantage point of the entire star system. The high inclination minimized interference from planetary bodies and allowed for a clear line of sight to key areas of potential engagement. From here, optical and passive sensors could sweep over nearly everything, rapidly giving them a picture of what was occurring in-system.

More critically, the ship's position was carefully chosen to remain far enough from the Dows star to avoid detection by sensors, or at least minimize it. Even the subtle distortions caused by the warping of the space-time layers during their arrival were negligible, producing neither the intensity nor the type of energy commonly monitored by standard detection systems.

"McKay, begin charging the gripper drive," Garrett ordered, turning to the bridge engineering tech.

"Aye, aye, sir," McKay responded briskly. "Twelve hours and counting on the clock till we will be able to activate the drive."

Garrett shifted his focus to Cassidy, the ship's sensor officer, who was hunched over her station. The soft glow of her console highlighted her intense expression as she worked the controls, analyzing incoming streams of data, clearly trying to make sense of what she was receiving.

"Lieutenant Cassidy, report," Garrett prompted.

Cassidy didn't look up as she continued to manipulate the interface. "No objects or immediate threats detected within range, sir. Optical sensors are gathering long-range data on the star system. We're too far out to link into the defense network. I am feeding everything to CIC for analysis. They have an entire team on it."

He had expected nothing different. Garrett's gaze momentarily drifted to the HTD. The screen displayed an empty expanse around his ship, confirming Cassidy's report. He activated a comm channel.

"CIC here," came Senica's voice.

"Commander, what are you seeing?" Garrett asked.

"A great deal, sir. We're analyzing the incoming data

streams, trying to make sense of it all," Senica replied. "Keep in mind, given our current position, everything we're receiving is approximately sixteen hours old. We should have a preliminary assessment for you shortly. Give us a few minutes."

"All right," Garrett said, terminating the channel. Around his ship, the HTD showed a serene void; beyond dust and a few roaming asteroids, there was not much of anything.

"Shaw, stand everyone but key personnel down. We're not going anywhere for at least the next twelve hours. Might as well have them get some rest."

"Aye, aye, sir," Shaw acknowledged as he turned to his station, working to relay the stand-down orders.

Garrett shifted his focus, opening a comm channel to his chief engineer. One of the side screens at his station flickered to life, displaying Tam's face. The faint remnants of bruising along his cheekbone were still visible, though they had faded considerably over the past two weeks. The improvement was notable, and Garrett felt a flicker of relief at seeing his engineer in better shape.

"Captain," Tam greeted, then quickly corrected himself, "Excuse me, Commodore. How can I help?"

"How's the gripper drive holding up?" Garrett asked.

Tam's lips curled into a faint smile, his voice carrying a note of pride. "No faults to report, sir. The drive is functioning flawlessly."

"Like a well-oiled machine?"

"Precisely, sir," Tam said.

"And the main battery?"

"Should function as designed, sir."

"And the gravity drive?" Garrett inquired.

"Operating within expected parameters," Tam replied with confidence. "The coils are spinning. We can get underway on your orders. All systems are green across the board."

"Excellent," Garrett said. "We won't be using the gravitic drive until we jump deeper into the system. Anything else I should know?"

Tam gave a slight shake of his head. "We're ready for action in all respects, at least on engineering's side, sir. I can't speak for anyone else."

"Very good, Chief," Garrett said, offering a slight nod. "Thank you."

"You are welcome, sir."

He terminated the connection, the screen going dark. Pulling up the detailed map of the Dows System, Garrett rubbed his jaw thoughtfully. The star system was dominated by six planets, each with their own moons of varying sizes and compositions, and three expansive asteroid belts. The interplay of planetary orbits and belts painted a dynamic, intricate picture, a sort of slow-motion cosmic ballet.

The Beleris jump point drew his focus. It was the entryway into Dows, the direct link to the nearest enemy-held star system, one that had fallen during the last Push and where the enemy had stopped their advance.

Twelve massive asteroid fortresses stood guard around the jump point. Dragged from the belts and carefully positioned, they'd been reinforced with layers of armor, shielding, and point defense systems. Each fortress was a marvel of engineering. Turret clusters capable of firing powerful masers, high-caliber railguns, and long-range missiles dotted their surfaces, giving the fortresses the ability to rain devastation on anything attempting to breach the jump point.

Strategically placed minefields further enhanced the defenses around each fortress. The mines were equipped with advanced proximity triggers and cloaking fields to render them nearly invisible until the moment of contact. The entire setup was designed to grind the enemy down, inflicting maximum casualties and destruction before they could even hope to advance into the system. Garrett rubbed his jaw as he regarded the defenses. Just getting past them would be an incredibly tough job.

The only other jump point was located on the far side of the system. It led to Sora. This system connected Dows ultimately, through several more star systems, to Midway and the rest of the Confederation, or at least it had. Javelin Station dominated the area, a behemoth of a battle station sitting a mere one million kilometers off the Sora jump point.

Encased in thick ablative armor and protected by overlapping energy shields, the station housed a staggering array of offensive and defensive systems. Orbital platforms and a network of smaller asteroid forts reinforced its already powerful defenses, creating a deadly kill zone around the Sora jump point. Any enemy wishing to move deeper into Confederation space would have to deal with Javelin first, and that would be no easy feat. Everything was designed to be very costly.

The station also served as a logistical hub, with vast docking bays capable of housing and servicing entire squadrons of warships. Garrett knew that Third Fleet's flagship, *Indomitable*, a massive super dreadnaught, was one among several stationed here in this system, along with battleships, cruisers, destroyers, and frigates, and thousands of smaller support craft. The best the Confederation had to offer was on the front line... or what had been the front line two weeks ago.

Garrett leaned forward, scrutinizing the orbital patterns of the system's planets and moons. The innermost planet, a scorched, barren rock, orbited close to the star, providing little strategic value. However, the third planet, Calydra, a gas giant, served as a critical fuel source. Large harvesters and refineries floated within its upper atmosphere, extracting hydrogen and other gases with the purpose of supplying the fleet with maneuvering propellent, key reactor materials, and much more.

The asteroid belts provided raw material for the system's

industrial and logistical needs. Mobile platforms and automated factories operated within these belts, ensuring a steady flow of resources to the massive factories and printers located at Javelin.

The other planets, former colony worlds, had been abandoned, the populations relocated. They now only served in an agricultural capacity, to feed the fleet or for rest and relaxation... shore leave. Every piece of infrastructure, every ship, every station in the Dows System served one purpose: to cater to the fleet's needs and stop, or at the very least delay, the enemy from advancing farther into Confederation space.

Everything he saw spoke of strength and Confederation power. Yet, Garrett couldn't shake the unease gnawing at him. He knew no fortress was impregnable. The enemy was cunning, relentless, and had a disturbing knack for exploiting human weaknesses, as well as a willingness to sacrifice their own people in large numbers to achieve an objective.

His next move hinged entirely on what the passive sensors and optical systems revealed. He could feel the tension mounting within at the delay, the lack of information, not knowing what was happening in-system. He forced himself to maintain a calm and composed demeanor. His crew depended on his strength... on the certainty he projected in the face of the unknown.

A soft ping broke the tense silence on the bridge, drawing his attention to the comms. It was Senica. Garrett immediately opened the connection.

"Sir, it's begun."

"It has?" Garrett felt his heart plummet.

"Yes, sir. We've detected large-scale energy discharges near the Beleris jump point and somewhat beyond. Active fighting is clearly underway. We are still processing what the optical sensors are reading, but the data is coming through, and it's plain as day. I'm integrating everything into the HTD. The more time that passes, the more accurate the picture will become."

A monitor to Garrett's right flared to life, the HTD filling the screen with a detailed layout of the Beleris jump point and its surroundings. He leaned forward, his jaw tightening as information rapidly began populating across the display in real time. Data tags lit up like a swarm of fireflies, each representing ships, and weapons' discharges.

A massive debris field marked the place where the original defensive line had been overwhelmed. Garrett had never seen anything like it. An amazing amount of wreckage littered the area around the Beleris jump point, what were clearly the remnants of the once-mighty network of asteroid forts.

Mixed in among the debris were the shattered and broken remains of dozens upon dozens of capital-sized starship hulls... the enemy's initial assault wave. Garrett's chest tightened as he absorbed the implications of what he was taking in, what he was seeing. The scale of destruction alone was hard to comprehend.

"They already have a foothold," he muttered, his tone heavy with resignation.

"Yes, sir, they do," Senica said, "and it fits squarely with one of the contingencies we planned for."

Garrett shared a look with Shaw, who had been listening in and studying the HTD at his own station. His executive officer gave a shake of his head and returned his attention to the screen. Garrett did the same.

Large numbers of enemy ships had entered the system and were moving outward from the jump point, while even more were arriving with every passing minute. And where the fighting was currently occurring between Fleet units and the enemy, farther out from the jump point, energy signatures flickered and flared—registering intense maser strikes and bursts of missiles detonating.

Garrett zoomed out to take in a wider view of the system. The fighting seemed mostly to be confined to an area around three to four million klicks from the jump point, but it was moving beyond that. Still, the enemy had broken through the first line of defense and out into the system. That was not ideal, but Garrett would work with the cards he'd been dealt.

How far had they gotten? That was the real question.

"Senica," Garrett said, "I don't see fighting throughout the star system, like in Midway."

"We don't either, sir," Senica said. "It appears as if the enemy has yet to exploit the beacon network... or they may not be able to, at least in Dows."

"How is that possible?" Shaw asked. "Surely, if they could do it in Midway, they should be able to pull it off here."

"Maybe not," Senica countered, "the codes to access the beacons are different than those at Midway. They may not have been able to hack or steal them beforehand."

"That is certainly a possibility," Garrett conceded. "Senica, what about the other jump point?"

"Nothing there, at least no enemy," Senica replied from CIC. "We can see Javelin plain enough along with a handful of larger ships, mainly dreadnaughts standing off the station, but that's about all... at least that we can discern from this distance. Given additional time we will undoubtedly identify and uncover more, but since we're not tied into the tactical feed, at this distance, all we have is what the optical and passive sensors are picking up."

"I understand," Garrett said.

"It's not much to go on," Senica continued. "We have pinpointed where the bulk of Third Fleet is concentrating. At least we think we have. Fleet units across the system are burning for this point. I have marked it on the HTD for you. I have also designated the rally location as Alpha Zulu."

Garrett looked and saw the point in space that had been

tagged. It was between Beleris and Sora, roughly fifteen million kilometers from the jump point, and clearly had been selected with the intention of giving battle and pushing the enemy back out of the star system.

"So, that's where the main battle will take place," Garrett said.

"I think so, sir. There is no telling how many fleet units are already there, in position and waiting. They are undoubtedly operating on reduced emissions. Now, whether they can manage to defeat the enemy on their own, I have no way of knowing. We'll keep monitoring and piecing things together, sir, but the picture we're seeing so far... it's not a good one. The enemy is inside the system, and they're here in force. If I had to hazard a guess, I'd say the enemy's assault has been going on for less than twenty-four hours, maybe a little longer, and it's important to remember what we're seeing right now is sixteen hours old."

Garrett nodded, his mind churning with the implications. "Thank you, Senica," he said before terminating the connection.

Garrett leaned forward in his chair, his eyes scanning the HTD. The minutes seemed to crawl as fresh data trickled in, each update painting an increasingly dire portrait as more and more enemy ships were identified and tagged, along with new arrivals flashing into existence as they jumped into the system from Beleris. A very large force was headed directly toward the point now labeled Alpha Zulu. Already, CIC had identified forty major enemy combatants, capital ships all, in that force, which they had designated Tango One—an intimidating mix of dreadnaughts, battleships, and carriers, along with a swarm of smaller vessels acting as escorts and strike elements.

There were several red flashing tags representing enemy ships clustered near the Beleris jump point, Tango Bravo. They seemed to have positioned themselves strategically around it. Garrett studied these for a long moment. There were two dreadnaughts, a battleship, and five cruisers. Whether they were damaged, or a reserve force, he could not tell.

It seemed to Garrett the enemy attack had come as a surprise. Otherwise, a substantial force would have been sitting on and around the Beleris jump point in a layered defense pattern, waiting and backing up the now-destroyed forts. There would be more wreckage otherwise... but... he just didn't know. The reality was, as Senica had said, the bulk of Third was likely in the process of concentrating at Alpha Zulu and, he suspected, other points deeper in the system. Those would be for ships that could not make it to Alpha Zulu in time.

Surprise's sensors just couldn't see it all yet, the true tactical picture. But what he was seeing, Garrett did not much like. This was almost a worst-case scenario.

Shaw looked over at Garrett. "What are we going to do?"

"I don't see that we have a choice," Garrett said firmly.

"There's always a choice," Shaw replied, his tone quieter but edged with insistence. "You know that as well as I, and sir, it looks like things are nearly too far gone. Third Fleet is in a bad position." Shaw paused, looking at Garrett meaningfully. "You don't think we have a choice, though, do you?"

"Not this time." Garrett gestured at the glowing screen before him. "And, it's not too late. We can still shut that jump point down, cut off the enemy in-system, and keep the bastards from reinforcing further. It will give Third a chance to potentially recover and punch back, to hold the system. By killing the jump point connection to enemy space, we can give them some breathing room, what they need to counterattack and save the system."

Shaw leaned closer, lowering his voice so only Garrett could hear. "We have the primary mission to think on. You've been given broad latitude to carry out your orders, but the target system is still our ultimate priority."

"I know." Garrett matched Shaw's tone, his voice a near

whisper. "But, Third Fleet needs our help, and we can make a real difference. Do you doubt that?"

"No," Shaw admitted after a moment, "I don't doubt it. But to help, we now need to put *Surprise* at serious risk, and that endangers the overall mission. We'd have to come in relatively close to the jump point, at least several million kilometers out, just to effectively deploy the disruptor as planned given this contingency. A longer jump increases the risks of potentially missing with the main battery. We know a short-range shot can work, and it is fairly easy to calculate, but we've never attempted a long-range one, ten to fifteen million kilometers or for that matter even farther out." He gestured to the tactical display before him, his concern evident. "Worse, once we jump in, we can't use the gripper drive for another twelve hours while the system resets and recharges. Between now and the time we jump in, more enemy units will have arrived. We could... no, *will* be jumping into a hornet's nest."

"You're right," Garrett admitted. "The invasion of the system has only just begun. We can save lives here and preserve assets the Confederation desperately needs—ships, trained personnel—for a time when we can really push back, when we'll have more Motherships to strike at the enemy, to take the fight directly to them. Dows is not yet a lost cause, not by a long shot. The bulk of Third Fleet hasn't even gotten in on the fight yet. The proof of that is the lack of additional wreckage around the jump point and the ships burning hard for Alpha Zulu. Besides, we don't have a choice in the matter. We need more trained personnel and a larger strike package, task force wise, to accomplish the mission that's been given to us."

Shaw studied Garrett's face, then turned back to the tactical display. "You've made up your mind, then?"

Garrett nodded, his resolve hardening. "I have. We're going in."

Shaw let out a slow breath, his focus shifting to the HTD,

He studied it for a long moment, then looked back over at Garrett and let go a resigned breath. "You know, sir... we've come all this way. It would be a shame to leave the party early."

"Yes, it would," Garrett agreed.

"Let's show the enemy just what *Surprise* can do and get some payback for Midway."

"XO, that's my thinking exactly."

TWENTY

TABBY

"Transition complete. We are in the Dows System. Oscar Flight, prepare to launch... acknowledge, over," echoed through the comm in her helmet. Tabby's heart thudded against her ribs, hammering away, a mix of adrenaline and resolve surging through her at the thought of what was to come, a true and hot combat launch. As if sensing her and the boat's readiness to go, the restraints across her chest and waist tightened automatically, locking her securely into her seat.

"Oscar Flight ready." Her voice was calm and firm as she transmitted back. She knew her entire squadron was listening in, and it wouldn't do to let them sense the turmoil she felt inside.

Confined within her suit, and amplified by the enclosed space, the rhythmic sound of her own breathing filled her ears. Ahead, on a side screen, the lights in the launch tube repeatedly flashed red. In an instant, they switched to green. A moment later, the magnetic catapult engaged, hurling the assault boat forward with raw, unrelenting force.

The jolt was instant and breathtaking, slamming her back into the molded contours of her seat. This was a combat accelerated launch, what pilots called a hot launch, and there was nothing else like it.

Tabby's eyes remained fixed on the forward camera feed, which captured the dizzying speed as *Max* hurtled down the launch tube. The lights lining the tunnel blurred into streaks, flashing past with mesmerizing rapidity. Then, in a heartbeat, they were gone, replaced by the infinite black of open space.

The assault boat cleared the *Surprise*'s gravity field in a flash, inertial dampeners kicking in and working to compensate, taking over now that they were clear of the ship. The crushing weight receded, allowing her lungs to expand fully once again. A brief sensation of weightlessness teased at the edge of her awareness before the gravitic systems reasserted themselves, and she was pulled down into her seat.

The HTD in front of her flickered to life, casting a ghostly blue glow throughout the cockpit. Data flooded the screen, populating rapidly. Contacts materialized in layers, identifying friendly craft, marking trajectories and designations. The sheer number of tags was staggering. Dozens upon dozens of small craft were being launched in synchronized waves, several every ten seconds, each catapulted rapidly away from the Mothership seemingly in all directions, and they kept on coming.

"We are free and clear to navigate, ma'am," Chen's voice broke through. "Gravitic drive stands ready."

Tabby hesitated briefly, allowing *Max* to drift further from the *Surprise*'s gravity well and wake. Then, her fingers moved over the controls, bringing the boat's gravitic drives online and up to twenty percent power. The propulsion system came to life with a deep, resonant thrum, a sound that seemed to settle in the pit of her chest. It was the sound of raw, unbridled power, controlled and ready for action.

Simultaneously, she engaged the warp bubble generator, a complex system designed to manipulate space-time itself. The bubble expanded outward, encompassing *Max* and a thin layer of surrounding space. The sensation was subtle, a barely perceptible shift, but she felt it just the same.

Once the bubble was up and in place, she keyed in another command. *Max* surged forward, transitioning from a modest ten gravities to a blistering fifty. Tabby's body pressed lightly into her restraints, the inertial dampeners working overtime to adjust for the sudden and dramatic acceleration.

Her eyes flicked between the forward display showing the plotted course and the HTD. The space around her was alive with motion as craft worked to join and form with their respective squadrons. She spotted her own people who were moving to take up position upon her lead. Tabby performed a quick headcount: two assault boats, one torpedo bomber, and six fighters.

A pang of frustration tugged at her. Several craft had been grounded due to technical issues or were simply incomplete and not yet fully assembled, leaving her squadron light. There was no helping that. For now, these nine were all she had. But they were good machines, piloted and operated by competent people.

It would have to be enough.

"Mama's little ducks," she murmured, her lips quirking into a half-smile. She hardly knew most of them, but their lives were her responsibility. She toggled her comms. "Oscar Flight, fall in on my wing. Keep it close and tight. Let's show the others how the Nighthawks do it."

She waited till they were in formation, then switching channels, she sent orders to the larger formation. "Wing One, all squadrons, form up on the Nighthawks. Let's get this done."

Her gaze flicked briefly to the HTD. The display showed six other squadrons trailing along the same plotted course as they moved into position, their formations tight and disciplined. Beyond them, dozens of additional squadrons were maneuvering and slotting in with their respective wings. Some veered off, mainly fighters and interceptors, to establish a protective screen around the Mothership, while two other attack wings were also making for open space.

Tabby's attention shifted, catching sight of the starships that had been hard-mated to *Surprise*. Now detached and under their own power, the massive vessels were gracefully maneuvering away, creating distance from the Mothership as they prepared for the engagement to come. Their sheer scale was awe-inspiring, their enormous hulls illuminated faintly by the distant light of Dows's star.

In her years of service, Tabby had seen orbital stations smaller than the *Surprise*. Yet, watching these colossal starships move independently against the vast blackness of space, she felt an unshakable sense of awe. It was something entirely unprecedented in the annals of warfare. The weight of the moment was not lost on her. This was history being written in real time, and she was a part of it.

Surprise's gravity drive flared to life, the energy expended exploding on the HTD like a torch on a pitch-black night. The mammoth ship began an aggressive turn to port, her motion fluid yet undeniably powerful, almost graceful.

The HTD squawked, pulling Tabby's attention back to the display. Sensor data began flooding in, painting a vivid picture of the surrounding space. The Mothership's tactical feed had lit up with critical information. Their entry into the Dows System placed them over four million kilometers from the Beleris jump point, and it was marked as being under hostile control. The HTD's threat board showed dozens of enemy starships clustered around the jump point. They were sitting there, as if waiting for something... but what?

The icons represented an array of vessels—destroyers, frigates, heavily armed battlecruisers, an enormous carrier, and two hulking dreadnaughts. Intermixed with these were hundreds of smaller craft, likely fighters, interceptors, and bombers, flitting about like a swarm of locusts.

The enemy formation was parked just beyond a massive field of wreckage that ringed the jump point and seemed to be expanding outward.

What could have caused that?

Tabby sucked in a breath as understanding dawned. A battle had unfolded there...

For a long, sobering moment, Tabby found herself staring at the aftermath of the fight, thinking on the carnage, the cost in lives. The wreckage—starships and forts—told a grim story of desperate resistance and a devastating tactical defeat.

Her gaze shifted back to her own wing, their icons glowing steadily on the display. How many of them would survive the day? How many would return home... how many would be consigned to the cold embrace of space for all eternity?

The HTD flashed, drawing her attention once more. An enemy battleship had materialized at the jump point. Almost instantly, the battleship's shields flared to life, a faint halo of energy enveloping the vessel. Moments later, her gravity drive engaged, flaring brilliantly. The massive warship began to move ponderously forward, picking up speed as she went, cutting a path through the wreckage... shoving everything in her way aside.

Tabby zoomed out on the HTD, expanding the view. Beyond the jump point, deeper into the system, the situation was dire. Between ten and twenty million kilometers away, the display revealed clusters of enemy vessels—dozens upon dozens of them actively in motion. They had come together in what looked like three distinct battlegroups. All three were burning away from the jump point. For the moment, they were no threat as they were moving in the opposite direction.

One of the battlegroups was even locked in active combat with a small Confederation force. The defenders—a battlecruiser, destroyer, and frigate—were clearly retreating, falling back toward the prepared defensive lines closer to the heart of the system. Tabby could only imagine the hammering they were taking.

But where was the bulk of Third Fleet? She continued studying the HTD and then she saw it, a massive scrum fifteen million kilometers away around a position marked as Alpha Zulu. Two large fleets, one Confederation, one enemy were engaged in a long-range missile fight, with Fleet maintaining range and pulling back toward the planet Calydra. The data on the fight was incomplete and sparse.

Tabby's knowledge of the Dows System was limited to what she had gleaned from briefings and propaganda, once even pilots talking at a bar who had been here. The star system was supposed to be a fortress, with a large mobile fleet, a bastion of unyielding strength. Yet, as she scanned the wreckage around the jump point, it was clear that the reality was far from the boasts of invincibility. Her gaze went back to the fleet fight. The enemy outnumbered the friendly forces considerably.

Frustration settled over her as she noticed gaps in the data on the HTD. Much of the star system remained a blank slate. The absence of information told her that *Surprise*, and by extension her own craft, was not yet integrated into the system defense network. The tactical picture *Max* was receiving was incomplete, reliant solely on their own sensors and the limited data feeds provided by the Mothership.

That told her the rest of the Third was out there somewhere...

"Coming up on the initial point, ma'am," Sanchez reported, her voice ringing a little too sharply in Tabby's helmet.

Wincing, Tabby dialed down the volume. She turned her attention back to the HTD, where their plotted course and the squadrons attached to her wing glowed a steady dull green. The vector showed they were on course, each ship locked into its role, like pieces on a chessboard.

"Listen up, boys and girls, we're almost at the IP," Tabby sent to her wing. "As soon as we reach it, go dark until I say otherwise—absolutely no comm traffic, even point to point. We'll coast at fifty gravities as silent as possible. Make sure your station-keeping systems are engaged, and all emissions are kept to an absolute minimum. Now, report readiness to your squadron leaders."

The comm channel briefly filled with acknowledgments as her own pilots checked in. Then everything went quiet. The silence that followed was heavier than any words might have been. She focused on the plot again, watching the countdown to the initial point tick closer.

A shrill alert from the HTD pierced the tense quiet, drawing her gaze. The enemy was reacting. Multiple ships near the jump point had fired up their gravitic drives and were turning toward them. They'd clearly spotted the massive ship and were increasing power and coming onto a course to intercept. Their intent was clear. They were coming for *Surprise*.

A pinging tone sounded in the cockpit.

They were at the IP.

"Set for stealth running," Tabby ordered, as she killed the alarm.

"Aye, ma'am," Chen responded. "Powering down systems, heat sinks engaged, stealth field coming online... We're going stone cold."

Tabby felt the subtle shift as *Max's* systems transitioned. The deep thrum of the gravitic coils began to fade, the vibrations steadily diminishing as their rotational speed dropped to a bare minimum. Around her, the lights dimmed to a faint glow, and several non-essential systems powered down. The reactor's output fell to minimal levels as well, barely enough to keep life support and critical systems powered and operational. She glanced at *Max*'s health board, relieved to see everything shifting smoothly into low-power mode. There were no anomalies, no faults.

Tabby checked the HTD again. Low-powered point to point laser links had been established by the station-keeping systems. It immediately told her the entire formation was still in place. More importantly, the wing was dropping into stealth mode, and no one had fallen out.

"We are stealthed," Chen confirmed a moment later.

"Very good," Tabby replied. With a quick command, she reintroduced atmosphere back into the cabin. A few moments later, a faint hiss reached her ears as oxygen filled the space. Cracking open her faceplate, she drew in a deep breath of the cool, metallic-scented air and leaned back against her seat, letting the momentary relief steady her nerves from launch.

Her gaze flicked back to the plot. They were now roughly forty minutes from the first waypoint and a planned course change. The Mothership was steadily accelerating away from the Beleris jump point. The enemy's speed had increased too as they moved to pursue. *Surprise*'s task force was forming a protective screen while interceptors swarmed around her like a hive of bees defending their queen.

Meanwhile, Tabby's wing was still coasting off into the blackness of space, leaving their mother behind. Tabby's gaze went back to the HTD. It painted a picture that was clear to her experienced eyes. The chessboard was set. The other wings that had headed off in opposite directions were now gone, vanished from the HTD.

The moves were being made.

And now, the game had begun.

TWENTY-ONE

GARRETT

"All vessels are away," Shaw reported. "The task force is moving into formation to cover us. Interceptors are still launching. CAG reports the attack squadrons have already engaged stealth mode and are away. They are now ghosts in the dark. The distance is so great, there's a good chance the enemy did not spot them as they slipped away."

"We can only hope," Garrett said, acknowledging the report.

"Sir, we are onto our new bearing," Heller said.

"Thank you, helm. Increase speed to 10 g."

"Aye, aye, sir. Increasing speed from 5 g. to 10 g.," Lieutenant Heller replied. A low hum resonated through the deck plating as the ship's gravitic drive responded, a faint vibration accompanying the boost in acceleration.

"Guns," Garrett said, turning toward Krebs at the tactical station. "Do you have a firing solution for the gripper cannon, yet?"

"I'm still working on it, sir," Krebs answered. "As soon as I finalize the solution, CIC will double-check my calculations. I believe we want the package to hit the target cleanly."

"Yes, we do," Garrett affirmed. "We only get one shot at this and need to make it count."

"Yes, sir."

Garrett's attention shifted to Keeli at communications. "Keeli, any luck tying us into the system's communications network?"

"No, sir," Keeli replied, frustration creeping into her tone. "We're locked out."

"Even with the latest authentication codes?" Garrett asked, arching a brow as he glanced over at Shaw.

"The system doesn't recognize us, sir," Shaw interjected, "and our codes might not be their latest, at least when it comes to Third Fleet."

"I suppose not," Garrett said. "Still, I imagine our presence hasn't gone unnoticed. The news is likely working its way up the chain of command as we speak."

"We are a little hard to miss," Shaw quipped.

"Yes, we are," Garrett agreed.

"What do you suppose the enemy thinks of us?" Shaw asked.

"I'd love to know." Garrett spared Shaw a grin. Then, shaking off the thought, he refocused. "Keeli, prepare an encoded and encrypted message for Javelin. I'll record it at my station and send it to you for transmission."

"Yes, sir," Keeli said. "Ready when you are."

Garrett worked his console. A flashing indicator lit up on his main monitor, signaling the recording was live. He straightened. "This is Commodore Garrett of the Special Missions Group. I am in command of the Confederation Mothership *Surprise* and its accompanying task force. We are preparing to engage the enemy and intend to alter the current dynamics on the field. Kindly tie us into the Tactical Flow Channel, System Tactical Net, and FTL Communications Chain to facilitate coordination. Garrett out."

Terminating the recording, Garrett forwarded the message to Keeli with a tap of his controls.

"I've got it, sir," Keeli said. After a brief pause, she added, "Message sent. It should reach Javelin Station in approximately twenty-two minutes, possibly sooner if a comm platform intercepts and relays the transmission via FTL."

"Thank you," Garrett replied. "Cassidy, do you have a count on the enemy moving to intercept?"

"Thirty-two ships, including small craft, burning our way, sir," Cassidy reported.

Garrett's gaze shifted to the HTD. He rubbed his jaw, feeling the stubble as his eyes locked onto the pursuing enemy, which was in the process of coming together in what looked like a spherical formation. He knew the limitations *Surprise* currently faced: the ship couldn't exceed 10 g. without compromising the stability needed to use the gripper cannon's wormhole. Even worse, their course could not deviate until the weapon fired; the complex calculations required for the cannon to function left no room for error. Even if they were a fraction of a degree off, the exit wormhole would appear in the wrong place and they'd miss the target.

The enemy, though still out of general engagement range, was closing the gap steadily. Garrett mentally calculated the timing. They had at least three hours, possibly a bit longer, before the enemy entered extreme range... that was if they kept their current speed, which he did not intend to maintain for longer than was required.

At some point, though, regardless of what he did, he would be in range of the enemy, and that's when the shooting would start. Garrett was under no illusions. His task force would undoubtedly take a beating. That said, he'd anticipated this scenario, and when the time came, had plans in place to strike back a hard blow.

"Commander Senica," Garrett said, opening a channel. Her

image appeared on one of his side screens. She seemed calm and collected, under control. He could hear voices behind her as her team worked.

"Sir?"

"What do we have burning toward us?" Garrett asked. "Do you have a breakdown on ship types yet?"

"Yes, sir, I do," Senica replied, her tone brisk. "We've identified thirty-two vessels... at this range, our confidence on ship type is high. Two are dreadnaughts, five are battleships, and the remainder are smaller combatants—frigates, destroyers, and corvettes. One of the battleships may be a battlecruiser. She's lagging behind the others, and we're still working to get more information on her. Some of the other ships closing on us are in the way. Regardless, the enemy's acceleration profile suggests a coordinated approach, likely with the intention of ultimately coming together into a cohesive formation to maximize overlapping point defense fields against any incoming fire we might throw their way."

Garrett gave a slight nod, digesting the information. "What else?"

"There are several ships that haven't turned to pursue and engage," Senica continued. "They're holding position near the jump point—a carrier, two battleships, and six smaller vessels. It is likely they're damaged and are undergoing emergency repairs. One of the ships, the carrier, is venting atmosphere, what appears to be a heavy hydrogen-oxygen mixture."

"Hydrogen breathers," Shaw said. "Not human, then."

"Correct," Senica said. "That's my personal assessment."

"No assault carriers in the group headed our way?" Garrett asked. "I want to avoid being boarded again."

"None detected, sir," Senica confirmed. She hesitated briefly before adding, "I don't believe any of those ships have significant troop-carrying capacity. At our current velocity, the enemy will enter engagement range in roughly three and a half hours. The sooner we go to maximum acceleration the better, sir, as it will draw things out and give us time to recharge the main battery."

"I'll ensure we don't take longer than needed," Garrett said, his voice firm. "Once the package is delivered, we'll adjust accordingly. What about numbers on the main fleet fight?"

"We're still analyzing that, sir," Senica said. "Since we're not tied into the system network, we don't have a complete picture. It appears the enemy has the strength of at least a battle fleet task force. It looks like Third is facing ten to twenty dreadnaughts, at least twenty-five battleships, thirty battle cruisers, and large numbers of supporting vessels, cruisers, destroyers, frigates... say fifty plus. There are even more enemy assets enroute."

Shaw let out a whistle. "Third's in trouble."

"At Alpha Zulu, they are," Senica said. "From what we are able to observe, what's on the field is only forty percent of Fleet's strength in-system, at least according to the Order of Battle in our records. We don't have a good count yet on how many friendly ships are destroyed or hidden in some way from our sensors."

Garrett rubbed his jaw, thinking on that for a moment. "Thank you for the report. Don't let me keep you, Commander. Carry on."

Senica nodded, and her image vanished as the connection was cut. Without missing a beat, Garrett opened a channel to Colonel Stroud. The marine commander's face filled one of his monitors, his features calm and controlled.

"How can I help you, sir?" Stroud asked.

"I expect to be engaged within the next three to four hours," Garrett said.

Stroud nodded, his expression a hard one. "Understood, sir. Do you anticipate a boarding action?"

"No, not this time," Garrett replied. "We will undoubtedly

take damage, and…" He hesitated briefly, glancing toward Shaw, who was listening. Their eyes met, and a grim unspoken understanding passed between them. "There's a good chance it will be bad. We're facing more on the field than was anticipated."

"I understand, sir. I'll ensure my marines are ready to assist with damage control and casualty care," Stroud affirmed without hesitation. His tone carried the confidence of a seasoned commander who had weathered crises before. "Don't worry about us. We will do our part."

"Colonel," Garrett added, "I want you to reinforce the sentries posted around critical areas and infrastructure of the ship."

"That's already been taken care of, sir," Stroud said. "I've reinforced the guard on all sensitive areas. If there are any infiltrators still lurking among us, or if they've made further attempts to manipulate the security system to cover their tracks, we'll be ready."

Garrett felt a flicker of unease at the thought. The security breach was a serious issue—one they hadn't yet resolved. How extensive it was, he had no idea. But with a battle looming, it wasn't something he could afford to address right now. Priorities had to be set, and his focus needed to remain squarely on the fight ahead.

He gave a curt nod, his expression resolute. "Thank you, Colonel. Keep me updated."

"Yes, sir," Stroud replied.

Garrett terminated the call, the screen going dark as his mind returned to the tactical situation at hand.

"Sir." Krebs's excitement was plain. "Solution is plotted, set, and confirmed for the gripper cannon. CIC concurs it is a good and true solution. Railgun is online and charged. We are ready to fire on your orders."

Instantly, everything on the bridge stilled. All eyes turned toward Garrett. It was as if everyone was suddenly holding their breath.

The time had come.

Would the weapon even work? He adjusted the view, zooming in to focus on the jump point and locked it in. The enemy ships that were sitting off it were still there. They hadn't moved. A carrier flashed into existence. It was larger than most Garrett had seen.

"Everything appears good, sir," Shaw said. "I concur. We are ready to shoot."

"Fire," Garrett ordered.

"Firing."

A rapid surge of energy coursed through the ship, not just visible on the consoles but... it was tangible in the air. Garrett felt a faint prickle run across his exposed skin, more of a tingle than anything else. The small hairs on his arms and the back of his neck stood on end. The lights on the bridge dimmed momentarily, casting everything in an eerie, ghostly half-light.

Several alarms blared their warnings, their harsh tones cutting through the tension as the ship's systems reacted to the event. Outside, space itself seemed to ripple and distort as immense forces focused on a single point and bent the fabric of reality. Yet, the cacophony of alerts and warnings was fleeting, silenced almost as quickly as it began when the surge dissipated.

Like the first time the main gun had been used, the entire sequence was breathtakingly fast—a transient event that lasted barely a fraction of a second... too rapid to register what had occurred. Yet, in that sliver of time, the event horizon of a minia-ture wormhole materialized, twisting space-time to carve an almost instantaneous path across the void.

The disruptor, encased in a missile warhead, was already in motion before the wormhole fully stabilized. The railgun, with its staggering acceleration of fifty thousand gravities, launched the payload toward its destination with incredible force.

Faster than an eye could blink, the disruptor entered the wormhole. Four million kilometers away, the wormhole's exit point yawned open, releasing the device, before collapsing back into nonexistence. A millisecond later, the disruptor reached the gravitational wake of the jump point and then vanished.

Nothing happened. Silence reigned on the bridge. Gripping the armrests of his chair, Garrett stared at the HTD, willing something to happen... anything. But nothing did...

His heart sank.

"It didn't work," Shaw breathed.

"Sir," Cassidy said, looking around. "I am getting some very strange readings from the jump point."

At that moment, Garrett saw the jump point convulse, releasing a blinding pulse of radiation. That burst, along with the gravity wave that followed in its wake, raced outward through the surrounding space, distorting the HTD's display in a flickering cascade of chaotic data. A moment later, the HTD stabilized and cleared.

The enemy carrier, which had emerged mere seconds before at the jump point, was caught in the midst of not only the radiation burst but the gravitational upheaval. Her hull buckled and fractured... then was torn apart in a brutal display of raw power.

The jump point heaved again, expelling an even larger burst of radiation that surged like a tidal wave of energy. The enemy vessels positioned around it were struck hard. Unable to withstand the overwhelming gamma rays and electromagnetic fury thrown their way, shields collapsed almost instantly under the onslaught. The radiation was so intense Garrett didn't need detailed sensor readings to understand the grim reality of what had just occurred—the crews had been cooked alive in a mere instant.

As if the radiation wasn't catastrophic enough, the debris field from the earlier fight at the jump point followed. The violent gravitational shockwave slammed into the enemy ships, the wreckage acting like shrapnel. Swamped by the maelstrom of destruction they were obliterated in moments.

On the bridge, Shaw broke the silence. "I'd say it worked."

There was an almost collective sigh of relief from the crew as Garrett leaned back in his chair, his gaze fixed on the HTD, watching as the jump point continued to spew random bursts of radiation outward into space. He shook his head. No one in their right mind would move a ship close to it, not now, for to do so would mean instant death.

"It worked," Shaw repeated.

"I'd say so," Garrett agreed. He straightened in his chair and shifted the HTD to the force closing on them. "Guns, begin charging the main battery again."

"On it, sir. Six hours and counting," Krebs confirmed.

"Helm," Garrett continued. "Increase speed to 50 g. Inform engineering I'll want to start working on 75 g. as soon as we stabilize at 50."

"Aye, aye, sir," Heller acknowledged. "Increasing speed to 50 g."

Shaw leaned closer, his voice lowered so only Garrett could hear. "You do realize that when the main gun's energy reservoir and power banks are recharged, we won't be able to fire at those speeds?"

"I know," Garrett replied, his gaze still fixed on the HTD. He expanded the view to encompass both the jump point, which was continuing to behave erratically, and the enemy. "We'll have to decelerate when the time comes. But let's see how things play out first."

Shaw gave a nod, his expression contemplative as he turned back to his station. The quiet of the bridge was broken by the tone of an incoming call. Garrett tapped his console, and Commander Senica's face appeared on one of his side screens.

"Sir," Senica began, "based on the energy readings we're

receiving, I'd say the jump point is currently non-functional. It's throwing off massive waves of broad-spectrum radiation. I'd like permission to share the sensor data with Pascal, Reid, and their team. There's the potential to learn something valuable from this."

"Make it happen," Garrett said tersely. At the mention of Bethany, his thoughts went to their last encounter in his cabin, how it had ended, in his bed, the press of her body against his... He felt a strong pull of want for more. He forced such thoughts away. He had a job to do and a battle to fight. Personal feelings could wait... That was, if they survived what was to come.

Garrett's gaze returned to the HTD. He pulled back the view and studied the system. His jaw tightened, and he resisted the urge to scowl.

Where was the rest of Third Fleet?

He did not want to finish that thought... but he knew they might not even be in the system. Bryer might have taken them to Midway to strike at the enemy. If that was true, that meant the admiral had gotten word that the Push was on, starting at Midway. But why had he not reinforced the defense at Beleris, strengthened it? The lack of information was a reminder of their isolation, being locked out of the system nets. Garrett found it incredibly frustrating.

He had so many questions.

"We're on our own for the time being," Senica said, "and are in for a stern chase."

"Indeed," Garrett said. "Carry on, Commander." He terminated the connection, the screen going dark.

Turning back to the plot, Garrett rubbed his jaw, his expression tightening as he contemplated the challenges ahead. His mind churned through the countless variables and scenarios he had meticulously prepared for. Despite his careful planning, the force pursuing them was stronger than he had anticipated.

His gaze drifted to the countdown timer displayed on his console, each second ticking away with maddening slowness. Six hours. Six long hours until the main gun was ready to fire again. Until then, they would have to endure—hold, fight tooth and nail, and weather the coming storm.

Garrett's fingers curled into a fist before relaxing, his focus sharpening. When the moment came and the weapon was ready, *Surprise* would unleash its full fury, revealing her devastating power. Garrett would show them *Surprise*'s true bite.

TWENTY-TWO
STROUD

Stroud paused and scanned the auditorium—marine officers ranked captain and above. More than one hundred were present, and he had been addressing them for the last ten minutes. It was standing room only at the back and to the sides.

This was the leadership of his command, his cobbled-together expeditionary unit. Each officer present had received directives tailored to their respective assignments. They would translate his commands and leadership into action, and, ultimately, the success or failure of the mission.

To his right, Burns and Ramirez stood at parade rest on the stage with him. They were silent, grim, and represented both his right and left hands. He relied heavily upon them to help get things done. That was what it meant to be part of a team, something Stroud was working to instill in his new command.

He did not personally know most of those present. That was concerning. Almost all of them were new, with the exception of his own battalion, and those officers were now spread thin across the entire expeditionary unit, helping to get it stood up. Most of the officers and crew picked up at Midway had never trained or worked together. But they needed to now. There was no alternative.

The last two weeks had been a whirlwind of activity that had flown by in a near blur. Between assembling a cohesive command structure from scratch and rooting out the infiltrators, Stroud felt like he'd been running a marathon with no finish line in sight, let alone sleep. They'd accomplished a great deal, but the road ahead was still steep and treacherous, and there was a long way to go.

"Most in this auditorium don't know me," Stroud continued. It was time to wrap this up and send them on their way. "But... we are all of the Corps, all marines, and marines lead by example. What are we?"

"Marines!" The reply thundered back.

Stroud gave a pleased nod. "That's right. We're marines, and as officers, I expect you to set the standard. No matter what happens or how bad things get over the coming hours, you must keep your head. You must lead. Do that and the rank and file will follow." Stroud paused as he regarded his officers. "We will be in engagement range in the next few hours. There is no doubt there will be a fight, ship against ship, and it will not be easy. Our role will be one of support. You know what to do, and I expect you to do it."

"What are we?" Burns roared.

"Marines!" Those assembled roared.

"Damn straight. Look to your duty." Stroud paused to suck in a breath. "That is all."

"Dismissed!" Burns barked, his voice sharp and authoritative.

Chairs scraped against the floor as the officers rose in unison. Conversation filled the air as the officers began filing out of the auditorium. The compartment buzzed with an undercurrent of tension, excitement, and purpose, a near physical energy that accompanied men and women preparing for battle.

Burns took a step closer. "A pretty speech, sir. It brought a tear to my eye."

Stroud found himself scowling as he looked over at the sergeant major. Ramirez appeared thoroughly amused by the comment.

"Excuse me, sir." A captain had approached the stage and was looking up at him.

Stroud gazed down upon the woman. Half of her face was burned, scarred. Her eyes were a pale gray, and they had a far-off look to them, one that only combat veterans recognized.

Her nameplate said: MIXON. He recalled her and the picture that had come with her service jacket. She was one of the officers picked up at Midway. She appeared younger in person, fit, and hard. If Stroud recalled, she'd served on Covero, a hellhole of a world, one of the few places that had rejected Confederation authority. Not only had she served, but she'd done so with distinction and been decorated accordingly. He knew he was fortunate to have her.

Clearly interested in what was coming, Burns took a step closer.

"Captain Mixon," Stroud said. "How is your recon company?"

She blinked, clearly surprised that he knew she commanded a recon unit. Her company was one of the few that had arrived intact and not in pieces.

"My company's ready for what is to come, sir."

"I expect so. How can I help you, Captain?"

"Sir," Mixon began, "we're posted to main engineering for security purposes. I have two Fleet medics attached."

"And what of them?" Burns asked.

"Main engineering is in one of the most fortified places on the ship, part of the armored citadel. It is unlikely to see casualties. I am offering my medics up to sections of the ship that are more vulnerable, where they can do some good. If an enemy weapon penetrates the defenses and main engineering takes a hit... well, sir, we have bigger problems at that point than just two medics."

Stroud gave a slow nod as he considered her. "That's not a bad idea." He looked over at Burns. "What do you think, Sergeant Major? Do you see any issues detaching them?"

"I think it's a bloody good idea," Burns said. "We should consider doing the same for other units like Mixon's."

"It makes sense to me," Ramirez piped in, stepping up. "I wish I had thought of it."

"I will have the orders cut," Stroud said to Mixon. "Anything else, Captain?"

"No, sir."

"Thank you, carry on."

"Yes, sir." Mixon turned and left.

Stroud watched her leave, then looked over at Ramirez. "You will see to that?"

"I will, sir."

As the last few officers reached the exit, including Mixon, a tone echoed through the ship's intercom system, the 1MC, halting everyone in mid-step. The compartment fell silent.

"This is the commodore speaking," Garrett's voice came. "We have entered the Dows System. The enemy got here before us. There is active fighting going on between them and Third Fleet." Garrett paused. "A short while ago, we employed an experimental device with the express purpose of disrupting the Beleris jump point. I am pleased to report the device worked as expected. The jump point is currently unusable and will remain in that state for some time. We have effectively severed the connection between this system and enemy-occupied space."

Garrett paused, apparently to allow the significance of that statement to sink in. Even Stroud felt a glimmer of hope and relief at the news, though it was tempered by the knowledge of the fight ahead, what they would soon face.

"We are unfortunately in a position where Fleet is unable to render us immediate assistance. That means we have to look to ourselves for we will soon be engaged by an enemy force. To the civilians we've taken aboard, please remain where you are. Shelter in place. Do not panic. Stay calm. The Mothership is the most powerful vessel the Confederation has ever constructed. She has teeth and a serious bite. We also have an entire task force in support, not to mention our interceptor screen. To the crew, see to your duties, and *Surprise* will carry us through. Stand by for action. That is all."

The tone sounded again, and the intercom fell silent.

"Bloody hell." Burns let out a low growl, his voice rough and unfiltered. "This is going to be a shit show. He just said so."

"Why, Sergeant Major," Stroud said with a faint smirk, "I already thought it was one. In fact, I seem to recall you declaring it."

Burns crossed his arms, his face darkening. "It's gonna get worse," he said flatly. "Mark my words, sir, it's gonna get bloody worse."

The last of the officers had slipped out as soon as the commodore had signed off, leaving the auditorium eerily quiet. Only Stroud, Burns, and Ramirez remained. They were alone... something rare of late. Stroud knew it wouldn't last. Moments of quiet like this were fleeting, and he intended to make the most of it before duty inevitably intervened. With so many under his command, interruptions were only to be expected.

"All right... before the shit hits the fan, I want to make sure we're on the same page for what is to come. Ramirez and I will be in headquarters at the start, coordinating damage control efforts, responding to assistance calls, and overseeing internal security." He gestured toward Burns. "The sergeant major will be on the move with his teams, providing reinforcement and guidance where it's needed most and ensuring our people stay sharp and focused. Everyone clear on their roles so far?"

Burns gave a firm nod. "Crystal clear, sir."

"I'm with you, sir," Ramirez said.

"Good. We've positioned security details around all critical areas of the ship," Stroud continued, his voice echoing slightly in the empty auditorium. "The captain doesn't anticipate another boarding attempt, but that doesn't mean we can let our guard down. Our focus in that regard will shift to internal threats—potential infiltrators or fifth column operatives we might have overlooked or missed during the sweeps. If there are any left, they might take advantage of the chaos and strike."

"I think we got everyone, sir," Ramirez said. "We've scanned and tested all tagged personnel. Anyone not having an identity tag would stand out. The internal sensors would have found them. But either way, the civilians are locked down and secure."

"We must still remain vigilant," Stroud said.

"Yes, sir," Ramirez said, "and we will be."

"All right," Stroud said, his thoughts shifting gears. "Damage control parties have been stationed ship-wide. They're equipped with everything they need—fire suppression gear, breaching tools, medical kits. Casualty care supplies are stockpiled throughout the ship where they'll be most effective and easily accessible. The senior officers know their assignments. So, I ask—are we missing anything?"

A silence settled over them, the kind that seemed to stretch. Ramirez's brow furrowed, but he said nothing.

"Just the unexpected, sir." Burns, standing with his arms loosely crossed, finally broke the quiet. "We're heading into combat, and last time... well, we got lucky with the boarding action. This time might be different. We just don't know what might occur."

"Luck's a fickle thing, Sergeant Major," Stroud said. "Let's make damn sure we don't rely on it." His words hung in the air like a storm cloud, and for a moment, the three men stood once more in silence. Stroud let go an explosive breath and stopped pacing, leaning against the podium. He scanned the now empty auditorium. "I feel like we're missing something."

"We're not, sir," Burns said.

"How can you be so certain?" Stroud asked.

"Because you can't prepare for every scenario, everything that could happen," Burns said. "That's an impossibility. We're marines, we're trained to react and adapt."

Stroud gave a slow nod as he considered and absorbed the sergeant major's words. "Thank you for reminding me."

"That's my job, sir," Burns said. "That and mothering you."

Stroud gave an amused grunt. Looking between them, he sobered and turned his gaze upon Ramirez. "Speaking of security and the civilians, has there been any progress on solving the network issue or at least figuring out what was done, how security was compromised?"

Ramirez shifted his weight, his boots scuffing faintly against the deck of the stage. "We've still not been able to nail down how they breached the system, how exactly it was done. All infiltrators went down fighting—none survived. That left us without the ability to interrogate and seek direct answers." He blew out a long breath. "So far, we've found no backdoors, no lingering traces of malicious code, a whole lot of nothing."

"We might have to wipe the entire system clean and reload it from scratch," Burns said. "Rebuild it from the ground up. Brent's people were talking about doing just that when I met with them last."

"What a bitch that will be," Ramirez muttered, shooting a sidelong glance at Burns.

The sergeant major shrugged. "Anything worth doing usually is a pain in the ass, sir. I figured you'd know that by now, especially being a marine and all."

"Someone's getting eloquent," Ramirez said.

"Am I, sir?" Burns asked with a straight face. "I thought I was just sharing my hard-earned wisdom is all, gathered over a long and storied career."

"Storied career?" Ramirez smirked. "Why, Sergeant Major, I'm not quite sure what you mean. Care to elaborate? I would love to hear more of your wisdom and how it applies to the current situation... not to mention that long and storied career."

"Well, since you asked, I would be honored to—" Burns started, but Stroud raised a hand, cutting him off.

"We will worry about it later, after what is to come. Now, let's get to work before the shooting starts."

TWENTY-THREE
GARRETT

"Helm, what is our current speed?" Garrett's eyes were on the HTD. The enemy was still doggedly closing on them. They were perhaps a little more than forty minutes from an effective engagement window.

"Fifty-eight gravities and still accelerating, sir," Heller replied.

"Thank you."

"Sir," Keeli interjected, turning slightly from her console to meet Garrett's gaze. "I now have access to the system nets, tying the TFC into the HTD. They received our message. I have the acknowledgment. FTL comms are live as well."

"That's encouraging," Shaw remarked, glancing toward Garrett. "It took them long enough."

"It did." Garrett shifted his focus back to the HTD as it began updating in real time with Third Fleet's data and analysis. The previously sparse display pulsed with a fresh sea of icons, tags, and annotations. Lines of data scrolled across the edges of the projection, detailing ship movements, engagement zones, estimated enemy ship types, intentions, and much more, including the running fleet fight on Alpha Zulu.

Garrett zoomed out, scrolling across the display to gain a broader understanding of the tactical situation throughout Dows. The display lit up with overlapping layers of information. It took him several moments to begin to make sense of it all. A call from Senica chimed, interrupting his study. Garrett accepted it.

"Sir," Senica said, "the fight is not going well."

"I can see that."

"Yes, sir," Senica confirmed. "They are outnumbered and taking a beating. The weight of missile fire is heavily in the enemy's favor. We've also identified a secondary force, a rendezvous just beyond Alpha Zulu at Calydra. It's for those ships that were clearly unable to make the initial rendezvous."

"Calydra... the gas giant?" Garrett asked.

"Yes, sir. The force at Alpha Zulu is falling back on the defenses at Calydra."

Manipulating the HTD, Garrett brought Calydra into view. A powerful series of fortresses ringed the gas giant. By his estimates, Bryer's force, what was left of it, would reach the Calydra engagement window in less than ten hours. The question was, how many of the admiral's ships would survive that long? Likely, not enough to make a material difference to the gas giant's fixed defenses.

His eyes tracked to the friendly forces in motion, each coming from various locations throughout the system and heading toward the defensive zone around the planet. Pushing hard, all were at maximum military power. One of those was *Indomitable*. She and her escorts were more than eleven hours out. As the flagship, *Indomitable* was likely where Admiral Bryer had stationed himself. His jaw tightened as he scanned the data, checking tags. Despite Fleet's apparent coordination, something was off and not quite right. Garrett scrolled over the system, searching for more of Third Fleet. Even with the sensor feeds now fully integrated, the number of ships seemed woefully insufficient, lacking even.

"Where's the rest of Third Fleet?" Shaw asked. "I don't see them on the HTD."

"I don't know," Garrett admitted.

"They're not here, sir," Senica said. "Much of what's on the list is simply not in Dows. The jump beacon network is also currently offline and marked as nonfunctional. However, there are indications that some of the beacons were recently used by friendly forces before being deactivated again, likely by *Indomitable*'s group. Without using the network, they would not have been able to cross the system so quickly."

Shaw blew out an unhappy breath. "Selecting Alpha Zulu as a point to rally now looks like a mistake. Bryer is going to lose much of its strength before they can reach the safety of Calydra's defenses and reinforcement." Shaw looked Garrett's way. "They must have received word of the attack at Midway. That's the only explanation... otherwise, why deactivate the beacons, or at least selectively shut them down?"

Feeling a sinking sensation in the pit of his stomach, Garrett could not help but agree. Coming here might have been a mistake. Third Fleet had a slim advantage, but when it was all over, they wouldn't have much left.

"I guess Bryer wasted no time and sent the bulk of his forces down the system chain to meet the enemy head-on, or at least reinforce the defenses there," Shaw said after a moment.

"They may have even gone for Midway, leaving only this force behind," Senica added. "Bryer might not have thought the enemy would attack into the teeth of his defenses. I mean, why bother when they already have an access point near Midway, one that was virtually unguarded?"

"Clearly what was left behind wasn't prepared for an attack," Shaw said. "They just weren't ready, otherwise they'd have been sitting off Beleris, reinforcing the forts."

Garrett's thoughts churned as he thought matters through. With the Beleris jump point disabled, it wasn't all bad. Cut off from reinforcement, it was clear the enemy no longer had the firepower to sweep across the entirety of the system, sowing destruction wherever they wanted. They certainly did not have the strength to overwhelm Javelin Station. That much was plain, but they might be able to destroy the critical infrastructure around the gas giant. And if they did, that alone would hurt Bryer, hindering his efforts at refueling his ships with propellant. And the enemy had the strength to do it too, even wreck or seriously damage the bulk of what was left of Third Fleet in the system. But he could not see them completely defeating Bryer, not now.

"Senica, how many friendlies are headed to Calydra's relief?" Garrett's gaze shifted to the enemy fleet. A number of units were burning behind it. They had entered the system after the bulk of the enemy had begun moving for Alpha Zulu. All were out of weapons range. He counted at least forty vessels of varying types, mostly battleships and cruisers.

"Seventy-four majors, along with about sixty smaller vessels," Senica answered. "There are already fifty combatants there, mostly frigates and light cruisers. The bulk of the rest should arrive within an eleven-to-fourteen-hour window."

"After the enemy reaches the engagement window," Shaw said.

"That's correct."

"With the jump point disabled, if I were in the enemy commander's position," Garrett said, half to himself and thinking aloud, "I'd have pulled back... brought all of my forces together, regrouped, and concentrated my available firepower. Only then would I make a move with everything I had on hand. But that's not what the enemy is doing, is it?"

"No, it's not," Shaw said grimly, leaning over his station to examine the same data. "They might think they have an opportunity at Calydra, to strike there before Third's firepower in the system can fully concentrate."

"That might be it." Still, the enemy's actions gnawed at Garrett. They were attacking into the teeth of some of Dows's most powerful fixed defenses and would not come away unscathed. Sure, they could batter Bryer terribly and likely ultimately overwhelm Calydra's defenses and wreck the industrial infrastructure around the planet, which was now clearly the goal, but then they would have a fight with the Fleet units that were, even now, burning toward the gas giant. Fleet would grow stronger, while they weakened.

Everything Fleet had left in the system seemed to be headed there or rallying in a position where they could rapidly group up and then burn for the planet. The enemy's strategy was more than reckless... it was senseless. The sheer volume of losses they were accepting to achieve the goal of hurting Third Fleet, the apparent disregard for self-preservation, suggested...

What?

"Beyond keeping Third Fleet on the wrong foot, this makes no sense," Shaw said. "It really doesn't. There has to be something we're not seeing..."

"Tactically, I agree," Senica said. "It's as if the enemy has decided to take out what they can before they're overwhelmed and destroyed."

The thought hit Garrett like a cold blade. He straightened. "What if they just don't care about losses?"

"What do you mean?" Shaw asked.

"Perhaps they don't think like we do. If they're ruled and governed by an artificial intelligence, maybe the cost in biological lives means nothing to whoever is calling the shots," Garrett said.

Shaw's brow furrowed as he considered Garrett's words. "You think it's an AI pulling the strings? That it's willing to throw everything at us just to achieve... what, destruction, a weakening of our forces here in Dows?"

"Maybe it's not about winning in the traditional sense," Garrett said. "If it's an AI, it could view everything—ships, biologics, resources—as simply game pieces on a board... sacrificial pawns to achieve a broader goal, the ultimate breaking of the Confederation."

"If you are correct, everything is expendable, then," Shaw said.

"I could see that," Senica said.

Garrett's gaze darkened as he stared at the HTD. If that was the enemy's logic, it would make them far more dangerous than he'd initially imagined. A commander who cared little for casualties was one who wouldn't stop until they were destroyed and annihilated—or had broken everything standing in their path. And for all he knew, the biologics manning the enemy ships, like those they had captured and interrogated, were fanatical believers who thought their sacrifice a righteous thing, something that brought them closer to their gods...

That certainly explained the Push and the horrendous losses the enemy repeatedly endured just to shove their way forward. Garrett leaned back in his chair, stretching out his back, for it had grown stiff. Another thought hit him. Fleet... Yenga... had they already come to this conclusion?

The mission to Indigo, the planned strike there, might be more important than he'd originally considered... critical even to getting the enemy thinking about their own losses, the casualty rates they were taking. Another thought struck Garrett like a lightning bolt. How much did the Confederation really know about the enemy? How much had they concealed from their own people? There was just so much he did not know...

"Sir," Keeli called from her station, swiveling to face him. "I have an incoming call from Admiral Bryer."

"Fighting Joe," Shaw remarked, raising an eyebrow as he glanced at Garrett. "You're running with the big dogs now, sir."

"I'll take it in my office," Garrett said, rising from his station. "Shaw, you have the bridge. Senica, I will get back with you later."

"Yes, sir," Senica said, and the channel went dead.

"I have command, sir," Shaw replied.

Garrett strode toward his office. Brent waited by the hatch with a casual air, though his eyes betrayed a readiness that never left him. The man didn't speak, merely offered a slight nod as Garrett approached.

The hatch hissed open, and Garrett stepped inside. A moment later, it slid shut behind him with a hiss and a muted thud, sealing him in the quiet, controlled environment of his private domain. Admiral Bryer's image was already projected on the far wall and waiting, the holographic display as sharp and clear as if the man himself were standing there in person.

Garrett had seen the admiral in vids, but this was the first time in virtual person. He stepped into view, taking in the visage of one of Fleet's most celebrated figures. Bryer's face was a map of hard lines and angles, his cheeks and chin appearing as if they'd been hewn from granite. His steel-gray hair was cropped short, a contrast to the almost inky-blackness of his penetrating eyes. Those eyes seemed to weigh and measure everything they saw. Garrett was certain this man did not suffer fools lightly.

At the same time, Garrett could read the stress and pressure the admiral was under. He could only imagine the hard decisions the man had made over the last few hours.

"Admiral," Garrett greeted.

"Commodore Garrett," Bryer replied, his voice deep. "I must admit, your arrival was unexpected. Not unwelcome, but certainly not anticipated—particularly with what you've done to the jump point. Speaking of which, what exactly did you do? My people are still scratching their heads over it."

Garrett allowed himself a brief smile. "We have a jump point disruptor, sir."

Bryer scowled at that. "I've never heard of such a thing."

"It's a new development. I will be sending you the technical specifications shortly so you can begin constructing more such devices. The disruptor renders the jump point unusable for roughly two weeks. Consider it a gift from Admiral Gray."

"That would have been helpful sooner, but you won't see me looking a gift horse in the mouth, not now." Bryer's eyes narrowed as they studied Garrett through the projection. "Is that why you came—to deliver this piece of technology? Will you now jump away?" He paused, glancing off screen. "Though from the deployment of the task force you brought, that does not seem to be your plan..."

"It's not," Garrett admitted. "If I could, I would be away, long before the enemy enters effective firing range. We need time to recharge the gripper drive—about nine hours from now."

"You'll be engaged well before then," Bryer said bluntly, his tone devoid of sugar-coating. "And you, sir, are outnumbered."

"I'm aware of that," Garrett replied, meeting Bryer's gaze. "It seems we have something in common, sir."

"It does," Bryer said, "doesn't it?"

"There's no doubt about it... We're going to take beating before this is all said and done. I calculated that the risk of coming here was worth it."

"So, you weren't ordered to Dows," Bryer said, his tone shifting as realization dawned, "not to relieve us."

"No, Admiral, I wasn't," Garrett replied evenly. "Our assignment was a different mission—one critical to the war effort. That said, my orders left room for some discretion. Once I learned about the disruptor, I saw an opportunity to make a difference here, especially if the enemy moved against Dows to pin you down. Besides, my crew is cobbled together—whoever we could get aboard before we were forced to leave Midway. I'm short on trained spacers, and my strike wing is far from full strength. You, Admiral, have everything I need—seasoned personnel, strike and support squadrons... capital ships, battle-ships, and dreadnaughts that can better ensure my mission succeeds, a strike that will hurt the enemy."

"I see," Bryer murmured, eyes narrowing slightly as he processed the implications. "I can help with that—and I will. But first, we need to deal with the enemy in-system."

"We do," Garrett agreed. "Judging by the deactivated beacons, you got word the Push was on?"

"I received a dispatch the day before yesterday," Bryer replied. "Once I heard about the beacons at Midway, I had them all deactivated the moment the enemy burst through the Beleris jump point." He paused. "I understand it was bad at Midway."

"It certainly was not good. The losses are... devastating, but with the disruptor, we will have a chance to stop the Push and recover."

Bryer gave a slow nod. "I can see that. These disruptors might even stop the war."

"Not if the enemy develops the gripper drive or something like it," Garrett said. "They saw us leave Midway via a worm-hole which we created. It's only logical to surmise they will begin working on how we managed it."

"The war will continue, then." Bryer blew out a tired breath.

"Sir," Garrett said, "where is the rest of your fleet?"

"Don't you worry about that. I have more than enough on hand to do what needs doing." Bryer's tone hardened. "That said, the enemy has begun advancing up from Midway and is moving in our direction. Without jump beacons to speed their advance, they are at least two to three months out."

"We have a second disruptor constructed," Garrett said. "It was meant as a contingency in case the first failed or something unexpected happened with the deployment. We will hand it over just as soon as we are able."

"That would be most welcome," Bryer said. "But... first you need to deal with the enemy force closing on you."

"I do," Garrett admitted. "Sir, I'll transmit the disruptor plans to you shortly, along with my orders and those concerning the Special Missions Group."

Bryer's eyes locked on Garrett. "Which you're a part of?"

"I am, sir," Garrett confirmed and then wondered how Bryer would take the next part. "I'm answerable only to Admiral Gray."

"I see. I'll respect that. Do what you need to do, and I will do the same. Now, Commodore, I have a battle to fight. We'll speak again when this is all over."

"Yes, sir," Garrett replied.

The admiral appeared ready to end the call, his hand moving toward his controls, but he hesitated. His dark eyes softened, if only for a moment. "Thank you for coming here, Garrett. My people and I owe you a debt, one I fear we can never adequately repay."

Before Garrett could respond, the admiral terminated the call and the projection blinked out, leaving the office in silence. He stood there for a beat, the weight of the exchange settling over him. Then, with a purposeful stride, he turned and made his way back to the bridge. Like Bryer, Garrett had work to do—and a battle of his own to fight.

Garrett sipped his coffee, his face betraying none of the tension roiling inside. The liquid had gone tepid long ago, but he barely noticed. His attention was fixed on the HTD, the swirling icons and dynamic overlays capturing every detail of the impending engagement. Steadily, relentlessly, the enemy had been closing the gap over the past three and a half hours, even as *Surprise* and the task force pushed their gravitic drives to their limits. Despite their efforts, the shooting was about to begin.

"Guns." Garrett tore his gaze from the HTD and glanced toward Krebs, seated at his station. "Is the first volley set?"

"Yes, sir," Krebs replied. "Targets locked as ordered. We stand ready."

"And the task force?" Garrett asked, his gaze shifting back to the HTD, where the positions of his accompanying ships were marked in bright, familiar colors. He had deployed them around *Surprise* in a sort of fan shape. "They've confirmed and understand what is to be done?"

"Yes, sir," Krebs confirmed. "All missiles have been reprogrammed. They will not ignite their gravitic drives, but will coast after launch and maintain station-keeping until so commanded."

"Very good," Garrett said, leaning toward the display. Thinking about what was coming, he hesitated a moment more. "All ships, launch the first volley."

"Launching," Krebs announced. The bridge fell into a hushed silence. A pause stretched as the data on the display updated. "Two hundred twenty shipkillers launched from *Surprise*. Two hundred ten from the task force. All missiles have gone doggo... silent running, no emissions."

On the display, a dense cluster of green markers representing the wave of missiles just launched appeared. Unlike a standard missile launch, which would announce itself with the flare of drive signatures and emissions, these weapons were simply coasting toward the enemy, silent, dark... relying solely on inertia and station-keeping propellant-driven thrusters to stay oriented, at least for the moment.

Garrett's plan was rooted in deception and timing. He knew that trickery would be critical if he hoped to inflict meaningful damage on the enemy force bearing down on them and give himself an edge. For a moment, Garrett allowed himself a flicker of hope. This gambit could work.

It had to work.

"This is an interesting tactic," Shaw said, turning from his station to glance at Garrett. "Where did you come up with it?"

"Back at the academy. I read about a three-ship engagement, a destroyer that used something similar against a pair of pirate cruisers," Garrett replied, his tone even as his eyes remained fixed on the HTD.

"I've not heard of that," Shaw said, a note of curiosity in his voice. "Where and when did it happen?"

"Back during the imperial period.... the Yarra system, I think, but I could be wrong about that."

Shaw's brows lifted in surprise as he studied Garrett.

"You're using a tactic that hasn't been employed in over five centuries?"

"The circumstances are similar enough," Garrett said. "That destroyer could only launch four missiles at a time, though, while the cruisers could each manage six. The captain needed an edge, something unconventional. He was being chased, and well, he got creative."

Shaw's gaze returned to the HTD, his expression thoughtful. "That's an awfully long time for a tactic to be shelved. Did it work?"

"No, not really," Garrett admitted. "The enemy scanners picked up the missiles long before they could ignite their drives. Point defense took most of them out before they hit."

Shaw tilted his head, his skepticism evident. "Then why do you think it'll work now?"

"I don't know that it will," Garrett said frankly. "But this time, the conditions are different. We are farther away, and our missiles are stealthier than those of yesteryear. Back then, battles—outside the Push—were on a much smaller scale. Engagement ranges were smaller too. The tactics were... more creative, more reliant on cunning, maneuver, and positioning than they are today."

Shaw mulled that over for a moment before nodding, his attention shifting back to his station. "I guess we'll see how it all shakes out, then."

Garrett didn't reply; his attention was riveted to the HTD. Everything was progressing as planned, at least for the moment. He was shaping the battlefield, setting the stage for the confrontation to unfold on his terms. In warfare, it was often the smallest details that turned the tide, and Garrett was counting on the edge this tactic could bring him.

"Cuno," Garrett said without looking up. "How long until we're in engagement range?"

"Estimated... ten minutes, twenty seconds," Krebs responded.

"As soon as the second volley is ready across the task force," Garrett continued, "flush the tubes again. Same parameters as before."

"Aye, sir," Krebs replied. "Do you want a third volley after that?"

"No, I believe two will be sufficient," Garrett said firmly. "We'll engage openly when the enemy enters extreme range. I intend to give them something to fix their attention."

"Yes, sir."

A few seconds later, Krebs reported, "Four hundred thirty good launches. All missiles have gone doggo."

"So..." Shaw glanced over at Garrett. "If you don't think this tactic will work, why do it? Why try it?"

"I didn't say that it wouldn't work," Garrett said, his gaze fixed on the HTD. The second wave of missiles was marked clearly on the display, moving steadily toward the enemy fleet. So far, everything was unfolding as planned. "We have an advantage they don't realize. They think they hold the initiative because they're pursuing us, chasing us away from the jump point. But the reality is, the advantage is ours. The initiative lies with us."

Shaw leaned forward, studying the HTD intently. After a moment, he sucked in a breath. "It doesn't matter if they see the launches or not. They're chasing us, fully committed to the pursuit. Once the missiles go live, just beyond their PDS range, it will be too late. They're going to take hits."

"Exactly," Garrett said, nodding. "We've already put eight hundred and sixty missiles into space, far beyond our normal and effective engagement range... but our missiles aren't burning away. They've not even lit their drives yet, and the enemy is speeding right at them. They will bring themselves into range and do some of the work for us. We are effectively getting two extra volleys in before the shooting even begins."

"That's evil," Shaw said after a long moment, a hint of admiration in his tone. "Truly and utterly evil."

"Perspective," Garrett responded smoothly, then looked around. "Mr. Keegan?"

"Sir?"

"Raise shield from current level to full power," Garrett ordered.

"Aye, sir, raising shields to full power," Keegan confirmed.

"Cassidy," Garrett said, "spin up the point defenses and ready the electronic warfare suite."

"Point defenses spinning up, EW systems powering on," Cassidy replied, her eyes locked on the readouts in front of her.

Glancing around the bridge, Garrett studied his people. He could sense the mounting tension in the air, but they were all quietly working at their stations, doing their jobs as they'd been trained. Satisfied, Garrett turned his focus back to the HTD, his gaze scanning the intricate overlay of tactical data. The task force was holding formation in a protective circle around *Surprise*, each ship maintaining a precise distance of no more than six hundred kilometers.

Farther out, and running slightly behind the task force, the fighter and interceptor screen, two hundred strong, maintained their own formations, positioned to intercept and thin out any incoming missiles. It was a layered defense, one Garrett hoped would work.

He shifted the view to the enemy fleet. Their formation was a perfect sphere, with heavier ships concentrated in the center and protected. The lighter classes had been spread across the flanks of the sphere. It was a textbook arrangement—one well-documented and preferred by their enemy—but its limitations were glaring, at least to Garrett. The sphere hindered the firing arcs of ships on the back side and center of the sphere, a flaw Garrett intended to exploit.

Draining the last of his coffee, Garrett set the empty cup back in its holder. His hand moved reflexively to the back of his neck, massaging away the tension that had built up over the last few hours. His thoughts swirled as he contemplated what was to come. The stakes were monumental, and the odds looked stacked against him. But Garrett wasn't above cheating. And that was just what he'd done.

Still, in a moment like this, he couldn't help but question his own decisions. Dropping into the system to aid Third Fleet had been a gamble from the start, one that risked not only his ship but the broader mission he'd been assigned.

Had he made the wrong move? Would it come back to bite him?

Though his gut insisted it had been the right call, the thought, like a hungry dog with a bone, gnawed at him. Would his actions ultimately cost the Confederation everything?

Garrett knew he was testing the very limits of the Mothership concept. Already, he'd demonstrated *Surprise*'s power at Midway and her versatility by dropping into the Dows System, disabling the jump point, and giving Admiral Bryer the tools to hold the enemy at bay.

The real test lay ahead—a battle that would push them to their limits. Garrett was leading *Surprise* and her task force into a standup fight against a superior enemy force. To survive, to win, he would have to rely on every shred of ingenuity and resolve he possessed. He understood the gravity of the risk. It was immense, but necessary. Without risk, there could be no victory.

"A commander who fears risking what he loves," Garrett murmured to himself, "is already doomed to lose."

"What was that, sir?" Shaw asked. "I did not hear you."

Not realizing he had spoken, Garrett looked over at Shaw.

"Missile launch," Krebs announced.

Garrett's gaze snapped back to the HTD, his heart skipping a beat. That had come earlier than expected. His mind raced as he processed the implications—it meant the enemy's missile range was greater than Fleet intelligence had anticipated, and slightly more than their own. The Union had improved their technology since the last Push. There could be no doubt about it.

"Six minutes, twenty-two seconds until impact," Krebs added.

"Cassidy," Garrett called out, "stand ready."

"Aye, aye, sir," Cassidy replied. "Standing by to engage PDS and EW."

"How long until we're in range?" Shaw asked.

"Thirty-five seconds, sir," Krebs responded, his eyes glued to his screen.

"Let me know the moment they cross into our engagement envelope," Garrett instructed, his gaze fixed on the HTD.

"And so it begins," Shaw murmured to himself.

Garrett could feel the weight of the moment settling over the bridge like a shroud. The understanding that the enemy was actively trying to kill you was not a good feeling.

Garrett's eyes narrowed on the HTD, which displayed the rapidly approaching enemy volley. As it closed, the data tag flashed an ominous red.

"Do we have an estimate on how many are in that volley?" Garrett asked. "What's their weight?"

"At least seven hundred," Cassidy replied grimly, her voice barely above a whisper. A moment of silence followed, the power of her words sinking into everyone on the bridge. Garrett even felt a sliver of dread settle in his stomach.

"Very good," Garrett said after a moment, his tone firm, projecting the calm his crew needed. "Cassidy, take this as a personal challenge. I want you to get them all."

Cassidy gave a tight, determined nod. "I'll do my best, sir."

"Losers do their best," Garrett said, his tone suddenly rock hard as he looked over at her. "And you are not a loser. Understand me?"

Cassidy swallowed. Her eyes narrowed as she met his gaze. "Understood, sir, I will take them out."

"Excellent. That's the attitude. That's what I want to hear."

"We're in range, sir," Krebs reported, breaking the tension.

"Fire all missiles," Garrett ordered, his fist coming down on the armrest of his chair with a solid thud.

"Flushing tubes," Krebs confirmed.

On the HTD, Garrett watched as his task force responded. Hundreds of green tags flared to life, representing missiles rocketing away from their ships. Accelerating off magnetic rails, they ignited their gravity drives once clear of the ships and thew themselves downrange at the enemy.

"Good launches across the board," Krebs reported, a note of satisfaction in his voice. "No hang-ups or misfires."

"That won't last," Shaw muttered, his eyes fixed on the tactical display, clearly following the incoming volley. "Recommend we boost energy shielding beyond maximum tolerances."

"Permission granted," Garrett replied without hesitation.

"Keegan, give me one hundred ten percent power to the shields," Shaw ordered.

"Aye, sir," Keegan responded. "Boosting shields to one hundred ten percent."

The lights on the bridge dimmed momentarily as power was diverted to the shield emitters. Garrett leaned forward, his eyes never leaving the HTD. The battle had begun, and every decision he made from this moment on would determine whether they survived the onslaught—or became another collection of wreckage floating throughout eternity in the darkness of space.

The tactical display was an intricate dance of data and projections. His missiles streaked away toward the enemy fleet, their green tags lighting up the void like a swarm of fireflies, while the red tags of incoming enemy missiles steadily closed the distance.

"Electronic warfare active across the task force," Cassidy reported.

"Thank you," Garrett replied, his tone calm, though a knot tightened in his stomach as the missiles crept ever closer on the plot.

"Sir," Krebs said, "it appears the entire enemy volley is aimed squarely at us."

Garrett gave a curt nod, suppressing the unease that threatened to creep into his thoughts. That the enemy would test the strength and power of the Mothership wasn't unexpected, but it didn't make the reality any easier to swallow. He watched as the HTD began to reflect the effects of their electronic warfare systems. Spoofed by the countermeasures, one missile veered wildly off course. Another followed, then several more in rapid succession. Yet, despite their efforts, the weight and power of the enemy broadside pressed inexorably closer, a tidal wave of destruction aimed squarely at *Surprise*.

"The enemy has launched a second volley," Krebs reported.

Garrett's jaw tightened.

"Reload complete. Missiles up. Same targeting package, sir?" Krebs asked.

"Yes, fire," Garrett ordered, his tone sharp and decisive.

"Firing," Krebs confirmed. A heartbeat later, he added, "Four hundred and thirty-eight good launches. Two missiles held up in the tubes. Repair teams have been notified."

The HTD flared again as another volley of green tags surged outward, accelerating toward the enemy with silent, lethal intent.

"Point defense firing. Enemy missiles on final approach," Cassidy called out.

Garrett's gaze sharpened as the HTD transformed into a

chaotic scene. His task force's point defense systems lit up the void, streams of energy fire, mixed with kinetic rounds criss-crossing the space between them and the incoming threat. While staying clear of the PDS fields of fire, the interceptors joined the fight, unleashing their own volleys against the enemy missiles, targeting and picking off all they could. Among them were the growlers, specialized electronic warfare craft, each working to confuse and spoof incoming missiles.

It was a silent symphony of destruction, the coordinated firepower of *Surprise* and her escorts creating a web of defense. On the display, enemy missiles, one by one, began to blink out, their paths abruptly terminated by direct hits or countermeasures. But the sheer weight of the volley continued to bear down on them, and Garrett knew with chilling certainty that not every one would be stopped. He glanced over at Cassidy. Working the controls, her head was bent over her station. Some would inevitably get through. There was no avoiding it.

His fingers curled tightly around the armrests of his chair, his knuckles whitening. This was the test, the true crucible. Could they endure? Or would they break.

Dozens of enemy missiles began to vanish from the plot, their markers blinking out as if they had never existed. Then hundreds disappeared, erased by the sheer weight of counterfire being spat outward, as the missiles screamed in the last thousand kilometers. Garrett sat rigidly in his command chair... watching... waiting...

The task force filled the void with a deadly hailstorm of kinetic rounds. Maser beams and laser batteries slashed through space, their discharges momentarily illuminating the tactical display. Electronic warfare systems continued their unseen battle, spoofing enemy guidance systems and tricking individual missiles, driving them off course. Yet, despite their best efforts, the enemy volley pressed on, steadily closing the distance, until it finally merged with *Surprise*'s tag on the HTD.

Garrett barely had time to brace himself before the ship rocked violently under the impact of multiple detonations. His restraints engaged automatically, snapping tight to hold him securely in place. The deck beneath him shuddered with each hit, a bone-deep vibration that seemed to ripple through the very structure of the ship. *Surprise* groaned in protest. Overhead, the lights flickered once, then steadied.

"Shields are holding," Keegan reported. "We had bleed through, sir, but they're holding at sixty percent."

"Damage is unknown," McKay reported. "Several subsystems are rebooting. Major systems seem unaffected."

Garrett's gaze snapped to the status board, scanning it quickly. Several systems were marked in amber, indicating damage, but all were still operational. None were in the red. There had been no failures... yet. He let out a long breath, the power of the moment easing slightly. The ship's armor had handled the bleed through of energy from the missiles exploding against their shields.

"How many hits did we take?" Shaw asked.

"At least a dozen, sir," Keegan replied.

"Enemy point defense fire detected," Krebs announced, his tone sharp. "Our missiles are on final approach."

Garrett's gaze went to the HTD, the tactical display was alive with shifting and continually updating data. The enemy's point defense systems were in full operation, lighting up the screen with bursts of energy as masers and lasers targeted his missiles. Electronic warfare signatures flared, spoofing and scattering incoming ordnance. Dozens of green tags representing his missiles began to wink out, one after another, erased by the enemy's countermeasures.

Garrett leaned forward, watching intently. His volley continued to streak toward their targets, individual missiles weaving and dodging through the deadly gauntlet of PDS fire. More tags disappeared and vanished from the plot, but enough remained. Then they reached their destination. The display lit up with brilliant flashes of energy as warheads detonated against energy shields and defensive screens, the impacts rippling across the plot like miniature supernovas.

"Good hits," Krebs announced excitedly, a note of satisfaction creeping into his voice. "Good hits."

Unlike his counterpart, Garrett had chosen not to target the heaviest ships, or for that matter a single vessel. Instead, he had focused his fire on the smaller, faster ships—frigates and destroyers... the escorts... the enemy's screen.

His strategy now paid off in spades. One of the destroyers took multiple hits in rapid succession. Her shields failed almost instantly, and moments later, a catastrophic reactor breach split the ship in two with a massive explosion that flared brightly on the HTD. The debris scattered outward, impacting and damaging two other vessels.

Another ship, a frigate, seemed to falter, her gravity drive visibly destabilized and flaring wildly on the plot. Losing steerage, she collided with a nearby destroyer. The two ships briefly merged on the HTD. Then both vanished in a blinding flash of mutual annihilation.

"Three ships destroyed," Krebs reported, his voice even but carrying a note of grim satisfaction. "Ten others hit, four of them are dropping out of formation."

Garrett exhaled sharply. He'd just reduced the enemy's numbers by seven in a single salvo. It wasn't enough to shift the balance entirely, but it was a start. At the same time, Garrett recognized a critical advantage his task force's point defense systems and electronic warfare suites were superior. It was either that or the Confederation's missile technology was more advanced. Perhaps it was a combination of both.

Another key factor played in his favor: the enemy's formation was working against them, their rigid spherical structure limiting their ability to provide better overlapping defensive protection against his volleys.

"Missile launch!" Krebs reported, his voice cutting through the tense atmosphere. "Six hundred plus inbound."

Garrett's eyes immediately snapped to the HTD, tracking the incoming wave. The red data tags representing enemy missiles swarmed the display like a deadly stormfront. They moved with terrifying speed, accelerating rapidly toward his task force. His gaze shifted from this new wave to the one the enemy had fired moments before. That volley was even now closing to contact and approaching PDS range.

"EW active," Cassidy said, her voice steady as she worked the controls. The task force's electronic warfare systems sprang into action, flooding space with countermeasures designed to spoof, scramble, and misdirect the enemy's munitions.

Garrett's gut tightened as he watched the approaching volley. His hands gripped the armrests of his command chair, his knuckles white against the dark material. The HTD displayed a sea of red closing the gap, relentless and unyielding. He let out a slow breath and physically relaxed, forcing himself to project calm despite the storm brewing both on the display and within himself.

It was going to be a long day.

TWENTY-FIVE
STROUD

The ship rocked again, shuddering with a deep, resonant groan that rumbled like a quake through the corridor. Then it shook more violently. Stroud was thrown hard against the bulkhead, his shoulder slamming into the unforgiving panel. He barely managed to keep his footing as the deck beneath him seemed to lurch and twist.

Another hit.

Surprise was taking a real beating. There could be no doubt about that.

"Are you all right, sir?" a marine asked, his voice tinged with concern. The young man, a corporal, was kneeling beside an unconscious crewmember. A medical kit at his side, he had been working to stabilize her before transport to medical, which Stroud knew was currently overwhelmed with casualties.

A little dazed, the colonel blinked, clearing the haze from his vision as his focus sharpened on his surroundings. The corridor stretched out before him, a chaotic, almost surreal scene of destruction and desperation. Smoke swirled under the dim emergency lighting, obscuring the details but not the grim reality. Marines and crewmembers rushed about, their movements frantic as they tended to the wounded, carried stretchers, or hauled rescue and repair equipment to where it was needed. Stroud noticed several civilians among them. Many still wore their civilian clothing, only with a service vest. These were the volunteers who'd been rushed through a hasty training program... Burns's extra hands. Seeing them in action was a victory in itself. They were working to save lives, humanity at its finest.

The air was thick with the acrid stench of burnt metal, melted plastics, and smoke, mingled with the faint, coppery tang of blood. As Stroud took it all in, the sergeant major's words echoed in his mind: *This is a shit show.* He shook his head, a bitter smirk tugging at the corners of his lips. Of course it was a shit show. Every engagement he'd ever been in had become one, and this was no different—chaos and calamity wrapped in an illusion of control.

The smoke made his eyes water and burned his throat. He coughed, hacking for a moment. The smoke twisted and curled near the ceiling, creating ghostly shapes that shifted with each vibration and shudder of the ship.

Along the corridor, several panels had been blown out or torn loose from their moorings, exposing snarls of wiring that sparked intermittently and spoke of live leads. The deck was strewn with debris—twisted metal shards, fragments of broken consoles, and personal effects scattered from nearby compartments.

"Sir, are you all right?" the corporal asked again.

"I'm fine," Stroud responded, rubbing his shoulder free of the discomfort. He straightened, shaking off the lingering ache from the impact. "Don't worry about me. Focus on the wounded, son."

The marine nodded and returned his attention to the unconscious woman, his gloved hands quickly and efficiently applying a pressure dressing to the gash running down her side. Blood had pooled on the deck under her body, dark and glossy.

Stroud's gaze shifted to the source of the smoke—a compartment just ahead. Edges scorched and blackened, the automatic hatch doors had been forced open and stood ajar. Thick dark clouds of smoke billowed outward, accompanied by the acrid stench of melted insulation and scorched metal.

Firefighting hoses snaked into the compartment, their surfaces slick with condensation from the foam being pumped through them. The faint hiss of suppressant being sprayed mingled with the muffled sounds of groaning bulkheads and distant screams and calls for help.

He stepped toward the compartment, his boots crunching on debris. Peering inside, he saw a team of civilians in firefighting gear moving methodically through the smoke-filled space. They were being directed by a marine sergeant. Their reflective visors glinted under the dim light as they sprayed the last stubborn embers, coating every surface with the fire-retardant foam. The compartment was a wreck—consoles reduced to slag, chairs melted into unrecognizable shapes, and the walls scorched black. Unmoving and burned, a body lay on the floor. He did not need to check to know the person was dead.

"Looks like you're getting it under control," Stroud called out as one of the men holding a line looked back at him in question.

"Just about, sir. This one's been stubborn, but we've got it now."

Stroud gave a curt nod, his mind already racing ahead. This was just one corridor and one compartment. How many others across the ship looked the same—or were worse? Along the aft quarter of the ship, he knew of multiple decks where fire had been reported.

Moving into the middle of the corridor and coughing, Stroud stepped away from the compartment and the smoke. He turned back toward the wounded crewwoman and corporal, studying them for a long moment. He shook his head and wondered how much more of a beating *Surprise* could take.

"Sir, you should really be wearing a breather."

Stroud turned to find a staff sergeant standing beside him. He was holding out a spare breather. The man's face, though partially obscured by his own breather, radiated a quiet urgency.

"There are toxins in the air... bad shit..." the sergeant said, motioning with the device.

Behind him, two marines hurried past, their boots thudding against the deck. The sergeant turned to watch them pass. They carried a stretcher between them, its occupant barely recognizable and moaning pitifully. The burned figure was a mess of charred fabric and blistered skin, the extent of the injuries enough to make Stroud's stomach tighten in horror.

"The breather, sir," the sergeant turned back to him.

Stroud took the offered breather and examined it for a moment before pulling it over his head. The device was utilitarian, designed for function over comfort. It formed a tight seal around his face, covering his mouth, nose, and eyes with a smooth, transparent shield. As he adjusted the straps, he could hear the soft hiss of the filter engaging, purging the worst of the smoke and toxins from the air he was breathing.

The relief was almost immediate. The acrid sting in his throat and lungs eased, replaced by the sterile, faintly metallic taste of purified air. His vision, previously blurred and burning from the smoke induced tears, was now unobstructed, the built-in augmented lenses of the breather cutting automatically through much of the haze.

Stroud turned to thank the sergeant, but the man was already gone. The stretcher-bearers had disappeared into the smoke, their patient hanging precariously between life and death.

The ship groaned again as something rumbled under his feet, dully vibrating the deck. A secondary explosion somewhere off in the distance? The battle wasn't just outside the hull —it was here, in these corridors. It was why he had left headquarters to help. He had felt useless there. Stroud needed to be doing something, anything...

The colonel surveyed the corridor with a grim expression. This section had been hit hard. The acrid tang of burnt wiring and scorched metal lingered even through his breather. He could taste it on his tongue. Radiation alarms were blaring intermittently, their shrill tones warning of exposure, though the levels hadn't yet reached a lethal threshold. Later, he'd have to take medication to counter the effects of what he was absorbing.

Marines moved through the chaos, their faces set with a mix of determination and exhaustion. Their uniforms stained with blood and soot, some carried stretchers with injured crew. Others crouched or knelt on the deck, administering first aid to the wounded who had been dragged from damaged compartments. The dead—silent witnesses to the brutality of war—had been moved to the sides of the corridor and out of the way.

This was the cost of war, but Stroud's heart still ached at such sights. At the same time as he surveyed everything, the scene before him was one of confusion, not order. That was only to be expected given the damage that had occurred here. Stroud opened a secure connection to Ramirez, who was still in headquarters, coordinating damage control efforts.

"Colonel," came Ramirez's steady voice.

"Major," Stroud said, his voice muffled by his breather, "ensure all control points are secure. No matter the situation, everyone passing through must be checked for weapons or explosive devices. No exceptions. We must maintain security on vital sections of the ship."

"Yes, sir," Ramirez replied promptly. "I'll relay and reinforce those orders immediately." There was a slight pause before he added, "Sir, with the damage we've taken across multiple decks and the rising number of casualties, maintaining those checks is becoming increasingly difficult. You know how things are…"

"We need to bring order to the chaos," Stroud said simply. "Our people protecting critical infrastructure must remain calm and disciplined, especially our security detachments. Reinforce that message with the teams. Is that understood?"

"Yes, sir," Ramirez affirmed. "I'll see to it."

Stroud terminated the connection and turned his attention back to the corridor. Heavy black smoke billowed from a compartment about forty meters aft, creating an ominous cloud that poured into the passageway like a living thing. Seeing no hoses dragged into the compartment, he started for it. The radiation alarms grew louder as he approached. The smoke in the corridor became thicker. The augmented lenses of his breather began to struggle to pierce it.

As he moved closer, his boots crunching on the debris scattered across the deck, the heat grew. Peering into the compartment, he could see nothing but a swirling void of smoke and shadow, along with a deep orange glow toward the back.

Stroud activated his comm, targeting those nearest. "I need a damage control team at my position immediately. We've got an active fire"—he paused and looked at the identification plaque just to the right of the hatch—"compartment seven-four-alpha."

The ship groaned again, as if protesting her wounds. Stroud stepped back from the compartment. His gaze fixed on the deep, ugly orange glow pulsing ominously from within the compartment, reflecting off the blackened edges of the hatchway and casting flickering shadows that danced along the corridor walls. The acrid stench of burning polymers and charred wiring was noticeable even through his breather. He knew that wasn't a good sign.

Stroud's eyes scanned his surroundings quickly, falling on a coiled fire suppression hose mounted along the wall to his right. When fire and smoke had been detected, it had automatically deployed. Without hesitation, he moved to it, unlatching and unlocking the reel. The mechanism creaked in protest, the sound harsh against the backdrop of alarms and muffled shouts. Stroud began pulling the hose free, each tug met with resistance as the heavy line uncoiled reluctantly.

The heat emanating from the compartment grew more intense. It washed over him in oppressive waves as he dragged the hose into the smoke-filled compartment. Dragging the line and tugging heavily at it, Stroud moved steadily toward the sullen glow lighting up the black smoke.

He was not wearing firefighting gear but his standard fatigues. Sweat beaded on his forehead beneath the breather and began to sting at his eyes. The heat was so intense, it was almost unbearable, but Stroud still pressed forward, tugging repeatedly at the stubborn line.

A marine appeared, gripping the hose firmly just behind him, helping to not only hold, but move it forward. Without a word, they worked in tandem, dragging the cumbersome line closer to the fire. The heat was powerful now, like standing too close to an open furnace.

Judging he was close enough or perhaps was as near as he should get, Stroud stopped and activated the sprayer with a sharp twist of the valve. The hose hissed and puffed as it swelled with pressurized foam, the added weight making it harder to manage. A moment later, the fire suppression foam erupted from the nozzle in a thick, white plume, spraying into the glowing maw of the fire. The foam clung to surfaces, instantly smothering the flames and sending up bursts of steam as it met the searing heat.

Several civilians rushed in. They grabbed hold of the hose, reinforcing Stroud and the marine, adding their strength to the fight. Stroud kept the nozzle steady, directing a torrent of white foam into the inferno. The searing orange glow gradually dimmed, overtaken by the muted light of rising steam and swirling chemical mist.

His arms burned with fatigue, the pressure of the hose unrelenting as the battle against the flames stretched on. Stroud gritted his teeth, his muscles straining with every movement. He didn't let up, nor did those with him. Together, they held the heavy line, extinguishing the last stubborn pockets of fire until there was nothing left to consume.

At last, the compartment fell into an uneasy silence, broken only by the hiss of cooling metal and the faint, steady spray of foam as Stroud sprayed everything again. The oppressive heat slowly began to dissipate, replaced by a heavy, humid atmosphere thick with smoke and vapor.

Stroud, his chest heaving, reached down and twisted the valve shut. The hose sagged as he set it down with a clatter that echoed off the warped and blackened bulkheads.

He wiped sweat from his brow, blinking through the smoke as he surveyed the wreckage around him. The compartment, once a vital part of the ship, was now reduced to a mangled ruin —twisted beams, scorched plating, and debris scattered across the deck. The fire was out, but the damage was devastating. Stroud exhaled slowly, his breath a mix of exhaustion and grim satisfaction. The fight to save the ship wasn't over, but they had won this battle.

He turned toward those who'd helped him extinguish the fire. There were four of them, all in firefighting gear. They stood silent, watching him, clearly waiting for orders.

"What are you staring at?" Stroud growled, his voice hoarse. "Get moving. Find another fire to put out or someone else to pull from the flames. Make yourselves bloody useful."

They snapped to action without hesitation, grabbing their equipment and disappearing through the smoke-filled hatchway. Their heavy boots thunked against the deck as they left, the sound fading quickly down the corridor.

Stroud was alone again. He could feel the sweat soaking into his uniform, clinging to his skin. The compartment still radiated heat. He took a step toward the hatch but stopped, noticing something odd. Looking down, he saw the melted edges of his boots clinging stubbornly to the deck plating with each step. The heat had softened the soles, making every movement an effort, almost as if he were walking through mud.

Stepping into the corridor, where the temperature was marginally cooler, he turned to look back into the compartment. The smoke swirled and billowed, the dark tendrils illuminated by the emergency lighting overhead. The fire was out, but the battle for the ship raged on. Stroud wiped the sweat from his brow above the breather, his eyes tracking the movement of marines and volunteers rushing past in firefighting gear.

Then, amidst the chaos, he noticed something that didn't belong—a man in an orange jumpsuit. Stroud's eyes narrowed. The main brig was located on this deck, but farther down. How had a prisoner gotten loose? The man was carrying a medical bag. He moved with purpose. Stroud's scowl deepened as he stepped forward toward the prisoner.

The man knelt next to an injured crewman who had been dragged out of a nearby compartment. The crewman's arm bore a jagged, bloody gash. He was unconscious but clearly breathing. Without hesitation, the prisoner pulled a pair of scissors from the bag, cutting away the uniform fabric around the injury. From the same bag, he produced a dressing, which he pressed against the arm. The smart dressing automatically secured itself to the wound with a faint hiss.

"This one's ready for transport," the man called out, his voice calm but commanding. "Stretcher-bearers! I need stretcher-bearers!"

Two civilians appeared almost immediately, hefting a

stretcher between them. They moved quickly to load the injured crewman. As they carried him away, the man in the jumpsuit spotted Stroud. He slowly stood, turned, and raised his bloodstained hands in a gesture of compliance as he met the colonel's hard gaze. Stroud's hand had moved to his pistol.

"Who let you out, Norwood?"

Norwood straightened, his expression for a moment unreadable. "Technically, I let myself out. The hatch to my cell popped open after one of the last hits. The frame was warped. Don't worry, Colonel, the other prisoners are still locked up and secured." He gestured to the medical bag, lying at his feet. "I convinced the sergeant at arms to let me help."

"I see."

"You don't need that sidearm. I've got nowhere to run, and I only want to help..." He glanced around. "And by god, right now, you need every hand you can get."

Stroud's eyes remained locked on the former captain of the *Palestro*, studying every movement, every nuance of his tone. Could the man be trusted?

"I'm not doing anyone any good rotting in that cell. On my honor, I'll help. When this is over, I'll go back willingly."

"On your honor?" Stroud's hand remained on his pistol, his doubt plain.

Norwood stepped closer, slowly, his hands still raised in a nonthreatening manner. "I give you my word... on my honor, Colonel. What remains of it. Let me do something useful... please... I need to help."

Stroud glanced at another wounded crewman being carried off, then at the bloodied prisoner standing before him. He'd clearly been helping others, for the blood was not his own. Norwood's expression was earnest, his words unflinching. Finally, Stroud removed his hand from the pistol grip. "Fine, but I swear, if you try anything—"

"I won't," Norwood interrupted. "Thank you, Colonel."

Without waiting, Norwood grabbed his medical bag and hurried toward a woman who had just slumped against the bulkhead farther down the corridor. Stroud stood there for a moment, watching as Norwood knelt beside the woman.

Her hacking cough echoed faintly over the other sounds of the corridor. Stroud shook his head, half in disbelief. Though the commodore might not approve, there was no room for second-guessing, not now. He'd made his decision. Besides, Norwood was right. They needed every able body they could muster.

Turning away, Stroud surveyed the corridor. The wounded, the dead, those caring for casualties, the firefighting teams—it was a grim, chaotic scene, but there was still work to be done. Stroud adjusted his breather to fit more comfortably and moved forward to help.

TWENTY-SIX

GARRETT

"*Valkyrie* has been hit hard, sir," Shaw reported. "Her shields are down, along with defensive screens. The gravitic drive is fluctuating badly. She's falling out of formation and veering away." Shaw paused and looked over at him. "I'm not sure she's fully under control."

Feeling a stab of fear and worry, Garrett's eyes locked onto the HTD as he pulled up *Valkyrie*'s data tag. Tina's ship was decelerating sharply, falling behind the formation, her gravitic drive sputtering—jagged red spikes appearing on the diagnostic overlay.

The energy fluctuations indicated the frigate's gravitic drive was dangerously close to total failure, each fluctuation pushing the ship toward catastrophe. Her warp bubble was destabilizing as well. Hence the emergency braking. *Valkyrie* was also streaming atmosphere and a lot of it. One of her reactors had gone into emergency shutdown mode. The frigate was in real trouble.

Garrett offered up a silent prayer for Tina and her crew. He knew they would need it. A memory forced itself into his mind, fresh and raw—the *Seminole*. Just moments ago, the destroyer's warp bubble generator had failed after a critical strike, followed by a hit that also damaged her gravitic drive. Without the stabilizing force of either system, the destroyer had been torn apart. Now, all that remained of *Seminole* was a rapidly expanding cloud of ionized gas and mangled debris, flickering with residual energy discharges as the wreckage spun through the void.

Bear's fate had been just as brutal and fast. Her shields had been overwhelmed by more than a dozen direct hits. One of her reactors had almost instantly gone critical. No escape pods. No survivors. Just another drifting grave in the vastness of space.

Garrett's jaw clenched tightly as he surveyed the damage to his task force. *Apache* and *Kern* had been hit hard as well. Both had taken crippling damage and been forced to break formation. They were now limping away from the fight.

"The bastards are steadily picking off our escorts," Garrett muttered under his breath, his jaw tightening as he processed their mounting losses. A short time ago, the enemy had shifted much of their fire, aiming to do what he'd been doing to them for some time now—actively stripping away the protective barrier of smaller vessels. Garrett's own volleys continued to hammer relentlessly at the enemy formation. Explosions rippled across the HTD as, one after another, enemy ships either disintegrated in blinding bursts of energy or were crippled so severely they veered out of formation, their gravitic drives failing.

More than a dozen ships had been taken out in a series of well-timed and coordinated strikes. Destroyers and frigates, which had formed the core of the enemy's screen, had been reduced to fragments of wreckage. Others drifted helplessly, their shattered hulls bleeding atmosphere and energy into space.

Garrett watched impassively as a damaged cruiser faltered,

her gravitic coils clearly cracked, steering lost, before colliding with a tumbling wreck. There was a brilliant flash on the HTD, and the cruiser was gone, one more enemy combatant eliminated.

Despite their numbers and firepower, the enemy's screen was weakening. The battle Garrett was fighting was a grim dance of attrition, with each volley and counter-volley taking its toll on both sides.

"Do you want me to message Captain Martin?" Shaw asked, his tone low, so only the two of them could hear. Garrett looked over sharply at Shaw, who met his gaze with a meaningful look. "I could request a status update?"

Garrett considered it, then shook his head. "No, I am sure Captain Martin has better things to worry about. Let her do what she can to save her ship."

"Yes, sir," Shaw said and turned his attention back to his station. He leaned forward, staring at a monitor for a long moment. "Commander Sabel... the *Palestro* is reporting one of her gravitic coils is damaged and cracked," Shaw said. "They've successfully managed to shut the coil down. They're operating on just one coil now. Sabel's not sure how long they can hold formation as they may lose steering due to damage. *Palestro*'s also lost one of their propellant storage tanks. They've also sustained significant casualties—multiple decks are exposed to space, and they're battling at least two major fires."

Garrett pulled up the status tag for *Palestro*. His jaw tightened as the data filled the HTD. The ship had been battered hard. In the last volley alone she'd taken four direct hits. Her shields were all but gone, flickering at critically low levels, and her structural integrity was clearly faltering. Garrett didn't need the display to visualize what the crew must be going through— fire suppression squads fighting desperate battles against the encroaching flames, damage control teams scrambling to repair systems and patch ruptured compartments, medical personnel overwhelmed with casualties. Yet despite all of this, *Palestro* was still moving in formation, holding the line as best she could.

"Are they requesting permission to break off?" Garrett asked quietly, though he already knew the answer. He had lost too many ships, too many lives, to let go of one of his remaining heavy hitters.

"Not in so many words, sir," Shaw replied, his expression guarded. "But the message strongly implied it."

Garrett rubbed a hand along his jaw, weighing the grim options before him. The *Palestro*'s continued presence in formation was critical. Without her point defense and missile coverage, the already thin defensive screen would unravel even faster. He couldn't allow that.

"Can she still shoot and provide point defense?" Garrett asked, forcing his voice to remain steady.

"I'm confident she can," Shaw answered, though his posture betrayed a hint of unease.

Garrett sat in silence for a long moment, then exhaled slowly and hardened his resolve. "*Palestro* stays in formation until she physically can't hold it anymore. We need her."

Shaw's gaze flicked toward Garrett, his expression tense. "Are you sure, sir? Were I in your shoes, I might consider letting her go."

"I am certain." Garrett's tone left no room for argument. "Inform Commander Sabel. She holds the line."

Shaw gave a stiff nod. "Understood. I'll relay the order."

As Shaw turned back to his console, Garrett could almost picture Sabel on the *Palestro*'s bridge, receiving the message—seeing the order flash across her display and knowing what it meant, what the command represented. She would understand the stakes, just as he did, the necessity. But understanding didn't make the burden any lighter, not for Garrett.

Duty was a merciless taskmaster. He'd just sent *Palestro* and her crew into the grinder, knowing full well that the odds weren't in their favor. He hated that this was the only logical choice. He hated that war demanded sacrifices. In that very moment, Garrett hated having command... and loathed himself most of all.

"Sir, our first volley is in the desired range," Krebs announced, drawing Garrett's attention. "Do you want me to send the trigger signal and light them up?"

Garrett's eyes snapped to the HTD, and he leaned forward in his chair, scrutinizing the two dormant and nearly invisible missile volleys coasting through space like unseen ghosts. The first was dangerously close to the enemy—less than fifty thousand kilometers now—an incredibly short distance in space combat. The second was just behind the first and the latest active volley was a mere forty seconds from impact, closing steadily toward their targets while enduring a relentless storm of enemy point defense fire.

"Missile launch detected!" Krebs called out sharply.

A new cluster of red tags bloomed on the HTD, marking yet another enemy salvo, a swarm of destruction rapidly accelerating toward him. Eyeing it, Garrett felt his stomach tighten. His gaze went to *Palestro*, and with that, he made his decision.

"Guns, it's time to go loud," Garrett said. "Light up both volleys."

"Both, sir?" Krebs hesitated for a fraction of a second, glancing at him.

"Yes, both," Garrett confirmed with a sharp nod. "We're going to hit them with everything we have. The timing on this is almost perfect. Do it!"

"Aye, sir," Krebs responded. "Sending the activation codes now."

Garrett's gaze remained locked on the HTD. Moments later, both coasting missile waves sprang to life, their gravitic drives igniting in unison. The icons on the display shifted from dull green to a vivid, aggressive orange. It was a spectacular sight—over eight hundred missiles between the two volleys, deadly shipkillers all, springing seemingly from the shadows and darkness and burning hard. Garrett imagined the enemy's sensors lighting up, the alarm it would create, the absolute shock...

"Guns," Garrett called over his shoulder, "retarget our next volley. Focus exclusively on the heavies. Let's start hitting them hard."

"On it, sir," Krebs replied without hesitation. "Setting solutions now."

Garrett shifted his attention and looked down at the plotted course of his attack wings. They had long since gone dark. He had no idea if they were where they should be, but... if they had stuck to the plan and were on course, well then, they were close enough. It was time to send them in as well. He opened a comm channel.

"Knox here, Commodore," came the voice of his CAG.

"Our people should be in position about now, right?"

"Yes, sir," Knox replied without hesitation, "right where we want them. If they are not, they should be close enough."

"Well, then, it's time. Send them in."

"Yes, sir," Knox said firmly, and with that, the connection closed with a soft chime.

Garrett leaned back into his chair. His eyes drifted once again to the HTD, its display projecting a vivid image of the battlefield, tracking hundreds of fast-moving icons in real time. The activated missile volleys surged forward like streaks of fire, bearing down on the enemy formation. The tension on the bridge was almost a physical thing—each officer and crewmember glued to their stations, their focus unbroken.

There was nothing more Garrett could do now, at least, not at the moment. He had passed on his orders, and now the pieces were in motion. The outcome of the battle hinged on whether his gambit would succeed or fail. His fingers idly tapped against the armrest of his chair, a subconscious reflection of the storm of thoughts racing through his mind. He had committed everything to this moment.

Garrett exhaled slowly, forcing himself to project a sense of calm, even as uncertainty gnawed at the edges of his resolve.

All he could do now was wait.

TWENTY-SEVEN

TABBY

The HTD emitted a sharp squeal, jolting Tabby's focus and snapping her fully awake. *Max* had been drifting silently through the cold expanse of space for what felt like an eternity, one that had dragged on and on. After settling onto their current course at 10 g., they'd shut down the gravitic drive to maintain stealth and limit detection. Then, they'd simply coasted.

The vast blackness had been eerily calm, the only indicators of life beyond the boat coming from the occasional faint energy discharges picked up by their passive sensors. Those were growing steadily closer, a sign of a raging battle—a storm they were about to dive headlong into.

Tabby had no doubt about that.

Chen and Sanchez stirred as the HTD squealed again, their movements sharp, their attention drawn to the screen where a scrolling message had appeared in glowing text.

"Code Blue," Tabby read aloud.

The attack notice had arrived.

"Seal helmets. Prepare for immediate cabin depressurization," Tabby ordered. She closed her own helmet, the seals clicking into place with a faint hiss. Her gloves followed, locking securely as the suit completed its full environmental seal. A quick glance at Sanchez and Chen confirmed they'd heard her. No words were exchanged.

Tabby worked the controls, keying in the command to depressurize the cabin. A faint hiss filled the cockpit as the air was slowly vented, leaving them in the cold, silent embrace of the vacuum. Her breath and voice suddenly seemed overly loud in her helmet as she activated the comm. "Bring up the gravitic drive, raise shields, and activate sensors. Chen, tie us into the HTD feed from *Surprise*. Prepare to drop stealth mode and go active sensors."

Max rumbled to life, sending a low, bone-deep vibration through the hull as the gravitic drive coils spun up, their whir rising in pitch as they and the boat's reactor surged to full power, ready to throw the small craft into motion. Tabby could feel it—the heartbeat of her boat, thrumming with barely contained energy, as if the machine itself were eager to attack the enemy.

Outside, and close at hand, the void lit up with sudden activity as her wing responded. On the HTD, more than a hundred small craft appeared as their drives flared to life, their once-hidden positions now revealed in a synchronized burst of energy.

Tabby opened the wing channel. "Prepare for immediate attack," she commanded, her tone leaving no room for hesitation.

This was the moment they'd been waiting for—and there was no turning back now, for they'd unzipped their collective flies and would be plainly visible to the enemy.

"Link established with the Mothership," Chen reported. "We have a good handshake. Data populating..."

The HTD flashed as it updated, filling with the latest tactical data, showing her the battlefield. Tabby blinked, her eyes scanning the new information. *Surprise* was nearly two million kilometers off, her position clearly marked along with her escorts. Tabby's stomach dropped as she noted the reduced number of starships with her.

Where had the other escorts gone?

The realization sent a chill through her. They'd been disabled or destroyed. But it was the enemy that demanded her full attention. Less than fifty thousand kilometers away loomed two dozen warships surrounded by a swarm of interceptors and fighters forming a defensive screen. The sheer scale of the threat and what they were about to do sent a surge of adrenaline through her veins, sharpening her focus.

"All squadrons, attack, attack, attack!" Tabby ordered her wing. "I say again, attack! Targets of opportunity! Hit them hard! Kill them all!"

The words were barely out of her mouth before she inputted a course for her squadron and transmitted it. Her commands were met with immediate acknowledgment. She keyed the command to *Max* and then engaged the drive. The emergency acceleration pressed her back into her seat as the assault boat surged from simply coasting along to powered acceleration, ramping up rapidly toward a blistering 50 g.

The HTD flared again in warning, drawing her attention. Volleys of missiles were streaking across space. One wave was outgoing, hurtling toward *Surprise* and her task force. Two more were inbound—more than eight hundred strong, screaming toward the enemy formation.

The outgoing wave posed no threat to her wing, but the incoming volleys were another matter. Their timing and trajectory meant they could intersect with their flight path, a potential hazard depending on the sequence of events unfolding ahead. Her jaw tightened as she pushed the concern aside—there was no room for hesitation now. They were committed. They had to go in, before the enemy reacted, sending their fighters and interceptors at her.

"All Oscars, follow me," Tabby transmitted with a calm determination she certainly did not feel. She highlighted a light cruiser on the HTD, the closest enemy, marking it for the squadron. "Target details sent." She keyed in another set of commands, setting the attack formation for the Nighthawks.

Her squadron reacted accordingly, the fighters fanning out to either side of the two boats and the torpedo bomber, which dropped behind her and Husky a little. The other squadrons set their own preferred formations and began to spread out from each other. Tabby saw the data begin to light up on one of her screens as each squadron leader selected a target to attack.

"Activate EW and PDS," Tabby ordered.

"Activated and ready," Chen replied.

Tabby's attention was drawn to a destroyer limping at the rear of the enemy formation. Her gravitic drive was fluctuating wildly, causing the ship to wobble on the HTD.

As she watched, the vessel began to brake and turn away from the main engagement. She considered changing targets and taking her squadron after the crippled ship but quickly dismissed the thought. The destroyer was disengaging and no longer a credible threat to the task force. Her focus needed to remain on targets that were still in the fight.

Her eyes settled on a light cruiser next. The HTD highlighted critical details: shields weakened, hull integrity compromised, though the full extent of the damage was unclear.

It was a prime target, and one Tabby was eager to take down. No one else from the wing had targeted the ship. She plotted in a new attack vector and double-checked it. The course she'd just plotted and set would take them directly to the cruiser, carving a path through the enemy formation and, if executed correctly, clear out the other side to safety. Her calculations placed their arrival and departure through the enemy formation just ahead of the second wave of missiles—by mere seconds. The margin for error was nonexistent.

"New target set... along with course," Tabby called over the squadron channel. "All interceptors engage enemy attack craft as we pass through their formation. Do not, I repeat, do not break off. We go through them and come out the other side. A second wave of missiles is incoming, and we can't afford to be caught in its path when it arrives. Confirm and acknowledge."

The replies came swiftly, one after another, the clipped responses of seasoned pilots who understood the stakes of what they were about to attempt. Tabby's eyes flicked back to the HTD. From the opposite side of the enemy formation, another attack wing was closing fast, their icons streaking toward the enemy. Moments later, she noticed the third wing converging from yet another angle.

The attack was a coordinated, multipronged assault, including the two missile volleys, all designed to hit the enemy from multiple directions and nearly all at once. For a moment she marveled at the brilliance of the plan, and its simplicity. She knew without a doubt they were about to hurt the enemy. Hard.

"Stay frosty," she called.

Tabby shifted her gaze to the incoming missile volley. Enemy PDS fire was ferocious, an overwhelming wall of kinetic rounds, masers, and laser blasts ripping through space. The sheer volume of firepower was staggering, a chaotic storm of flaring detonations and streaking energy beams. Missiles by the dozens winked out of existence as they were hit and taken out. But no defense was perfect, and some inevitably broke through, homing in on their targets.

Tabby watched it all with a sense of awe and fascination.

Dozens of icons representing enemy ships erupted into flashes of energy as shipkillers reached their targets and warheads detonated, blasts slamming into and against shields or tearing through defensive screens and digging deeply into the hulls of starships in all their fury.

Tabby's eyes flicked across the display, taking in the destruction as they continued to close on the enemy. A destroyer's icon blinked out entirely as one of her reactors went critical, the vessel disintegrating into a spreading cloud of plasma, atmosphere, and debris.

A frigate vanished from the plot an instant later, consumed by the explosion from a direct hit. A light cruiser, her warp bubble destabilized, fragmented violently as temporal distortions ripped through the vessel's structure, tearing her apart from stem to stern.

In the midst of the chaos, a battleship emerged from the carnage, her shields flickering, on the verge of collapse and sputtering weakly as she plowed through the wreckage of the ships before her. Instantly, Tabby knew this was an opportunity. If they could hit the battleship before she could get her shields back up and stabilized, they might be able to do real damage and make a difference.

Her decision was swift. Changing targets, Tabby plotted a new course, and input commands for her squadron. She checked the course to make sure they would clear the enemy formation before the second wave of missiles arrived. Everything looked good.

"New target... battleship," she ordered as she sent the new plot, her voice crisp and steady. "We release missiles first, followed by torpedoes at close range—no less than ten thousand klicks out. Mark and confirm."

One by one, the confirmations came through, terse and professional. Her people were focused, but Tabby knew the danger they were flying into, the maelstrom and lethal gauntlet that would be upon them soon enough.

"Enemy fire has shifted," Chen reported, his voice tense. "They are targeting the incoming attack wings. Very little fire is directed at the second wave of missiles."

Tabby saw it immediately. PDS systems were now focusing on the three separate wings making their attack runs, the red icons of the kinetic rounds and energy beams blazing through the display. The defensive fire was spread out, but that did not make her feel any better. Thousands of projectiles were streaking toward them. Maser and laser bursts lanced out, brilliant and terrifying.

The battleship, clearly determining the incoming threat, shifted all of her considerable defensive fire at the Nighthawks, spitting death outward. Tabby's gut clenched. The enemy's interceptors began to react too.

One of her squadron's fighters vanished from the HTD, obliterated in an instant by a direct hit. Lieutenant Erickson was gone—a newly assigned pilot, one she'd barely had time to meet.

Then another fighter was gone. The plot updated, the icon disappearing as if it had never been there. The reality of war was harsh and random... unforgiving. The final klicks were flashing by as they drew closer... the enemy fire growing more intense with every passing second as they closed to attack range.

Max shook violently, the sudden jolt throwing Tabby forward against the restraints. Her heart skipped a beat as alarms blared in her helmet. They'd been hit. A glancing blow, she realized a heartbeat later. Anything more, and *Max* would have been reduced to scrap, and she'd never have known.

"Shields at forty percent," Chen said, his voice tight. "They're holding!"

The PDS was firing now, automatically targeting incoming ordnance. Tabby could hear the rapid discharges of the batteries. Her eyes remained locked on the HTD, the distance to the enemy battleship steadily ticking down. She tuned out everything else—the blaring alarms, her own breathing in the confines of her helmet. The battleship her sole focus...

"Ready missiles," she commanded.

"Missiles armed and ready, ma'am," Sanchez replied.

The glowing marker for the battleship loomed larger on the display, every second bringing them closer to the critical moment. Then it came—the ten thousand kilometer mark. Close enough for their shipkillers to have a near-guaranteed impact.

"Fire!" Tabby ordered, her voice firm and decisive, sounding harsh in her own ears.

"Firing," Sanchez acknowledged.

Tabby felt the faint shudder as the two shipkiller missiles were released and catapulted forward by the boat's railguns. Once clear, the HTD showed their gravitic drives igniting, brilliant flares of energy propelling the missiles forward at impossible speeds. They streaked toward the target, accelerating to a speed far beyond anything an assault boat like *Max* could achieve.

"Reloading missiles, five minutes fifty seconds," Sanchez added, already preparing for the next volley.

Tabby clenched her teeth. Five minutes was an eternity. More important, they'd be beyond the enemy and out of range by the time the missiles reloaded. But she didn't have time to dwell on it.

"Hit them with masers as we pass," she ordered. "Strafe them hard."

"Masers firing," Sanchez confirmed.

Max seemed to vibrate with a low, resonant hum as the masers discharged. The rapid pulses of energy shot toward the battleship. The sound of the masers recharging between discharges reverberated faintly through the hull, along with those of the PDS batteries. On the HTD, the markers for the maser strikes lit up, peppering the battleship and indicating glancing hits on its already weakened shields. Tabby figured every little bit counted.

The enemy capital ship loomed larger now, her massive bulk cutting a dark silhouette against the distant backdrop of stars. *Max* surged onward, the roar of his gravitic drive pushing them toward their rendezvous with danger and beyond.

Husky's missiles had launched right after hers, streaking toward the battleship nearly alongside the torpedo bomber's payload which released a fraction of a second later. All across the front, the assault boats and bombers from her wing were unleashing their fury upon the enemy. The HTD was an overwhelming kaleidoscope of movement and confusion, with missile tracks, small craft, and enemy defensive fire creating a near-impossible tangle of data.

Tabby forced herself to focus.

Her breath caught as one of her missiles blinked off the HTD, hit by a burst of point defense fire. The other missile struck home, smashing into the battleship's fluctuating shields near midships. The impact sent a ripple across the shield barrier, weakening it further. Then came Husky's payload—two shipkillers slamming home in rapid succession, causing the shield to collapse entirely.

Tabby barely had time to register the breach before the torpedo bomber's weapons closed the deal. Two torpedoes, designed for maximum destruction, streaked into the now-exposed hull of the battleship. Impacting hard, they easily penetrated the thick outer armor and burrowed deep into the pressure hull before detonating.

The first explosion was brutal, but the second was catastrophic.

The battleship fractured down her midline, her structure unable to withstand the sheer force of the internal blast. A heartbeat later, one of her reactors lost containment. The resulting explosion lit everything up, a starburst of destruction that sent waves of debris and radiation scattering outward in all directions.

Max surged past the carnage, catching the tail end of the detonation and blast. The assault boat bucked wildly, its systems struggling to compensate for the shockwave. The hull thumped loudly with direct impacts, and Tabby was slammed back into her seat as the restraints locked tight, holding her in place. Warning alarms blared across the cockpit. The status board lit up with damage reports, a sickening mix of amber and red spreading across critical systems.

"Shields are down," Sanchez reported. "Damage to the lateral quarter. Looks like we got singed bad. Working on getting the emitters back online. Missiles are good... masers are down and offline."

Tabby gritted her teeth and forced herself to stay calm. A quick glance at the HTD confirmed her wing had broken through the enemy formation, leaving a trail of destruction in their wake. The other wings were clear as well. Behind them, half a dozen enemy ships were out of the fight—either obliterated or so heavily damaged they were slowing, breaking away from the main group. She watched the final moments of an enemy destroyer. The ship's warp bubble collapsed, and a second later, it flared brilliantly on the HTD.

Her gaze shifted to her own squadron for the first time since the attack run, and her stomach sank at what she saw. Only one torpedo boat and two fighters remained. Husky was gone... She looked at her wing... and froze... horror overtaking her.

So few... so very few...

There were less than fifty craft remaining. She cleared her throat as a wave of nausea rolled over her, but she forced it down, steadying herself with a deep breath. She had to keep cool, maintain command, set the example. She had to stand tall, stand strong.

From her position in *Max*'s cockpit, Tabby's gaze locked onto the HTD. Her jaw tightened as she watched the second missile wave close in on the ragged enemy formation. It was like waiting for a storm to crash down on a battlefield, the eerie stillness just before the hammer fell.

"Come on... hit them hard," she urged under her breath, her voice barely audible over the low, steady hum of *Max*'s systems.

The enemy ships shifted their attention away from the attack wings and opened up with a desperate point defense fire on the incoming volley, which was on final approach. Maser beams, laser bursts, and kinetic flak rounds lit up the void like strands of burning wire. Missile after missile disappeared from the HTD, consumed by the inferno of enemy fire, but the storm was too vast and too close to stop, and the enemy had shifted fire too late.

Then it happened.

Like a wave crashing powerfully onto a beach, the missiles struck home, and the HTD erupted with blinding markers of detonation. In quick succession, a string of energy blooms dotted the enemy formation. One of the battleships took a direct hit by several missiles, her shields collapsing in a violent discharge of plasma before the next detonation tore deep into her hull. Explosions rippled across the massive ship's length, and a moment later, the icon blinked out of existence, replaced by a navigational hazard marker.

Another enemy ship—a cruiser—staggered violently, listing to starboard in the aftermath of the strike. Her drive signature flickered erratically before the vessel spiraled into the wreckage field created by the destroyed battleship. A moment later, her icon vanished entirely.

"Two gone... no, three," Tabby murmured, her eyes darting to a destroyer limping out of formation, shields down and streaming atmosphere. A late missile found her a heartbeat later. Then she was gone. "That's how you do it."

The restraints eased, and sitting forward in her seat, Tabby considered what she wanted to do next. They still had missiles and could shoot, which meant they could kill the enemy. Tabby sucked in a deep breath and let it go. She knew what she had to do... and yet, she found herself hesitating at the controls.

"We're going back in, aren't we, ma'am?" Sanchez asked.

Tabby looked up. Sanchez and Chen were staring at her.

Through the faceplates of their helmets, she could read the naked worry, fear, and concern in their eyes. Tabby felt the same within her own heart. How they had managed to survive the storm they'd just flown through was anyone's guess. To do it again...

Tabby desired nothing more than to head off into deep space and away from the fight. Then she thought on Husky and the others who'd died... *Surprise* and the rest of the task force, all fighting for their lives, for the Confederation, for humanity.

Heart hardening, Tabby shook herself and keyed in a new course and sent the updated coordinates. She opened comms to the wing. There was no hesitation in her voice when she spoke, no room for doubt. "The job's not done. New course set. Fall in and ready for attack."

TWENTY-EIGHT

GARRETT

The ship rocked violently. A loud crash echoed from his left as a bulkhead panel tore loose from the wall and clattered to the floor. Smoke was in the air, adding to the haze that already lingered after the previous impacts. The acrid stench of burnt electronics and melting metal was strong.

The enemy had switched their focus back to *Surprise*, pouring fire into the Mothership. The task force was now a fractured remnant. *Ajax* and two of the destroyers were all that remained on his screen. All three ships were heavily damaged. Her gravity drive failing, *Palestro* had at last broken off. On the enemy side, the numbers had thinned as well, but the remaining combatants were a real concern: three dreadnaughts, four battleships, and one battlecruiser, all no longer in a recognizable formation.

"With that last volley we've taken significant damage, sir," McKay's voice cut through the haze; his tone was strained. He glanced over to Garrett, his face drawn with the stress of the situation. A cut on his temple bled freely, running down his cheek and onto his uniform.

"I've lost more than half of our point defense cannons on

the aft quarter," Cassidy reported. "Although their volleys are not coming in with as much weight, more missiles are getting through. We just took seven hits."

"I understand," Garrett replied. "How are the shields?"

"Shields on the aft quarter are at less than five percent, defensive screens are even lower, with many in a nonfunctional state," Keegan responded, his eyes flicking between the HTD and the status board at his station. "We can't get them back up as they keep getting battered down. There has been significant bleed through. Our armor is almost gone too. We're starting to take real damage."

Real damage?

In the stress of the moment, Garrett bit back the urge to snap at Keegan. *What does he think they'd already taken?* His gaze shifted to the status board—red lights were blinking across almost every section. The enemy was relentlessly pounding his ship, and they were hurting.

"We're fighting fires across multiple decks," Shaw said. "We're not in a good position. Something has to change and quick."

Garrett turned his attention to the enemy formation displayed on the HTD. The once-cohesive sphere had completely unraveled, ships lagging behind as their damaged systems struggled to maintain acceleration and do their best to close on *Surprise*.

Surprise's attack craft—what few remained—had been pulled back after expending their payloads of missiles and torpedoes. They'd inflicted significant damage, leaving wrecks and crippled ships in their wake, but the cost had been staggering.

Against all odds, his plan had worked brilliantly. The combination of the doggo missiles and the attack wings had been devastating, catching the enemy off guard and striking hard. But the tactical victory had come at a steep and terrible price. Over two-thirds of his assault boats were gone, their brave crews either dead or marooned in space in life pods. His torpedo bombers had fared no better; nearly all had been lost. The fighters, which had provided cover as the attack went in, had been decimated as well. But he had hurt the enemy bad.

"Firing missiles," Krebs announced. "Eighty-two good launches. *Ajax* reports her magazines are expended. They have nothing left to shoot, sir. Their PDS is degraded too. They have no more kinetic rounds."

Garrett felt his jaw tighten at the report.

"Guns," he said, "how long until the gripper cannon is ready?"

"Twelve minutes, thirty-two seconds," Krebs replied.

"I'm not sure we can wait that long." Shaw glanced over at Garrett. His expression was grim, mirroring the tension that hung thick on the bridge.

"She will hold together," Garrett said firmly. "I have faith in her. *Surprise* won't fail us."

But still, Garrett had his doubts. *Surprise* had been built strong, but how much more could she take? His mind raced. The gripper cannon was their ace in the hole, a weapon capable of turning the tide of the fight and finishing it, but twelve minutes might as well have been an eternity under the current onslaught. "Guns, can we fire it early?"

"The gripper cannon? No, sir," Krebs responded quickly. "The main battery requires a full charge to manipulate space-time. I don't understand the science behind it, but that much was made clear. A partial charge will fault the system."

Garrett exhaled sharply, frustration bubbling beneath the surface. He rubbed his jaw again, his eyes fixed on the HTD as his mind worked through his options. His thoughts lingered on what Krebs had said—charge. The word stuck in his head like an itch he couldn't scratch.

"Charge..." he muttered under his breath as if saying it out loud would help.

Shaw turned to him, his brow furrowed. "What was that, sir?"

Garrett blinked, unaware he'd spoken aloud. "What?"

"You said 'charge'," Shaw repeated, his tone laced with curiosity. "What do you mean?"

"That's right, I did," Garrett said, the flicker of an idea forming in his mind. He turned sharply to Krebs. "Guns, are our ship-to-ship maser cannons charged?"

"No, sir," Krebs responded without hesitation. "They're not charged because we're out of effective range."

"Begin charging them now," Garrett ordered, his tone leaving no room for debate.

Krebs hesitated for only a heartbeat. "Aye, sir. Charging the maser batteries now."

Shaw leaned forward, his expression a mix of curiosity and concern. "What are you intending?"

His gaze still locked on the HTD as he finalized his plan, Garrett didn't answer immediately. Then, he turned to Shaw and met the other's gaze. "I'm tired of running." Garrett shifted his focus. "Keegan, what's the status of our forward and side-facing shields?"

Keegan scanned his console quickly. "Forward shields are near one hundred percent, sir. Side-facing shields are holding at around eighty percent, though they've taken some hits."

"And our point defense systems on the forward section?" Garrett asked.

"Fully operational," Cassidy reported. "We're at one hundred percent capability there."

"Very good," Garrett said, leaning forward, almost eager, in his chair. He keyed in a new course, scrutinized it for a long moment, ensuring everything was in place, before sending it to Heller. "Helm, new course. Execute when ready."

Heller's eyes darted to his console. He studied the course for a few seconds, and Garrett saw the exact moment the realization hit him. Heller's face went pale, and his eyes widened in disbelief as he looked back at Garrett. His mouth opened as though to protest, but no sound came out.

Garrett's gaze sharpened. "Do you see any errors with that course, Mr. Heller?"

The helmsman swallowed hard and looked over the plotted course again, then shook his head. "Ah... no, sir. I do not."

"Then kindly execute it," Garrett said, his tone firm. "And do so before those inbound missiles reach us. I don't believe we want them impacting against our aft quarter."

"Yes, sir. Braking now. I'll begin our turn to port once we're below 20 g. It will put less stress on our hull."

Garrett leaned back in his chair, his eyes fixed on the HTD as Heller carried out the order. His mind raced with the implications of the course he'd just plotted. It was bold, risky, and, if he was being honest, borderline reckless. But it was also the best shot they had at survival—and victory.

"Let's see if the enemy is ready for a fight on our terms," Garrett said, his jaw tightening as the ship began to decelerate.

"You're planning on charging them?" Shaw said, his disbelief plain.

"I am," Garrett replied without hesitation. It came out as a near growl. "Their forward-facing shields have taken a beating, and by this point, they're seriously degraded. Just like our aft shields. I will bring us in close and hit them hard with the masers as we pass. It should buy us the time we need."

The ship began to shudder slightly as the gravity drive started braking and slowing their forward momentum. Garrett could feel the subtle tug of inertia as the dampeners strained to compensate against the G-forces exerted by the rapid deceleration. The groan of the hull under stress reverberated faintly through the bridge, a reminder of the strain the *Surprise* was under.

"Shaw, coordinate with the CAG," Garrett ordered. "I want our interceptor screen to position themselves to catch as much of the incoming missile volley as possible. Put them ahead of us and get them moving into the firing line immediately."

Shaw turned to face him, his expression grave. "That will be incredibly dangerous for them."

"Yes, it will," Garrett admitted. His gaze remained locked on the plot, watching as *Surprise* reached 20 g. and began her ponderous turn to face the enemy head-on. "It must be done. We don't have the luxury of holding back. This is an all or nothing moment."

"That will mean certain death for many of those pilots," Shaw said quietly, leaning closer so only Garrett could hear. His tone carried both a warning and a plea. "Is this really what you want?"

"It cannot be helped," Garrett said firmly, his eyes not leaving the HTD. His heart ached at the thought of what he was doing, but he hardened his resolve and forced himself to focus on the bigger picture. Survival and victory depended on these sacrifices.

"PDS firing," Cassidy reported from her station. "Electronic warfare is fully active."

Garrett's gaze flicked to the HTD, where the incoming missile volley now bore down on *Surprise* from the port beam, almost broadside. To his relief, the maneuver had placed mostly undamaged PDS batteries into firing positions, unleashing a storm of defensive fire. Kinetic rounds filled the void between *Surprise* and the oncoming threat, joined by tightly focused beams from maser and laser batteries.

One by one, enemy missiles began disappearing from the plot, their icons winking out as they were neutralized. Despite the intensity of the defense, the ship shook under an impact that managed to break through and detonate against the shields.

"One hit," Keegan reported tersely. "Port shields are down five percent, very little bleed through. Defensive screens are holding."

"And our aft shields?" Garrett asked, his attention shifting momentarily to the rear of the ship.

"Recharging, sir. Currently at ten percent and climbing."

"Very good," Garrett said, his tone betraying no sign of the relief he felt.

Shaw exhaled slowly, glancing between the HTD and Garrett. "I'm beginning to see the logic in your madness, Commodore. But when we close to contact, they'll be able to hit us with their masers too."

"I know," Garrett acknowledged. His jaw tightened as he stared at the enemy formation on the display. "But I'm betting we have a few more masers than they do. And I trust our shields to hold longer than theirs."

Shaw nodded slowly, though his expression remained grim. "I hope you're right."

On the HTD, Garrett watched his interceptor screen adjust to their new orders. The small craft decelerated sharply, their thrusters flaring as they pivoted in near-perfect unison. A moment later, they surged forward, accelerating hard as they aligned themselves with the next incoming wave of missiles. Garrett felt a pang of guilt as he watched the interceptors burn toward the enemy fire, knowing full well the sacrifice he was asking of those pilots. He had no doubt they too understood what they were facing. And still they went willingly...

"Good hits," Krebs called out from the gunnery station, breaking his thoughts. "Scratch one battleship."

Garrett shifted the HTD's focus back to the enemy formation. His latest missile volley had struck home. There was no hint of slowing or a deviation on the enemy's part. Garrett couldn't help but wonder what their commanders were thinking as they saw *Surprise* decelerate and execute her turn, clearly coming about. Did they think it madness? Or did they recognize it as the calculated and desperate gamble it was?

Surprise completed the turn, her massive hull still groaning faintly under the strain of the maneuver. The ship began to move forward, accelerating once more, this time, heading straight for the heart of the enemy formation. Garrett noticed that *Ajax* had mirrored the movement, staying at their side. Shaw must have relayed the new course. *Ajax* was now their last escort... as the two destroyers were lagging behind, both clearly having some difficulty, their gravitic drives fluctuating erratically.

"Keeli, advise *Ajax* to break off," Garrett ordered. "Have them steer clear of what's to come. Have all escorts break off. They can't do much more good out there."

"Aye, sir," Keeli responded.

"Missiles incoming," Krebs reported, tone steady. "Time to impact, two minutes, ten seconds."

"Very good," Garrett acknowledged, his voice calm despite the tension knotting in his chest. "Cassidy, you know what to do."

"I do, sir," came the confident reply.

Keeli turned back to him. "*Ajax* says they're staying by our side, sir."

Frustration flared within Garrett. He glanced down at the HTD. Both destroyers were breaking and turning away, but *Ajax* remained where she was, stubbornly sitting off the forward starboard quarter. "Open a comm channel to her captain at my station."

"Channel open," Keeli replied.

Garrett's screen flickered to life, revealing Jason seated at his station aboard the *Ajax*'s bridge. Smoke hung in the air behind him. There were people calling to one another. It was clear *Ajax* had taken hits. Yet Jason's demeanor was calm and collected.

"We're not going anywhere," Jason said, preempting Garrett before he could speak. "We've still got our ship-to-ship masers, and our energy-based PDS system is mostly operational, especially our forward-facing batteries."

Garrett's jaw tightened. "And if I order you to break off?"

"Didn't you already do that?"

"I did."

Jason grinned at him. "Then you can court-martial me later for disobeying orders. Jim, you need every gun you can get for this pass. Besides, some of their fire might come my way. It'll take a little of the pressure off *Surprise*." He paused and grew grave. "The Mothership means more to the Confederation than my battlecruiser. You and I both know that. Your mission, whatever it is... well I suppose it's more important than... one—*my* ship, isn't it?"

Garrett felt a lump rise in his throat. He didn't respond immediately, struggling to find words that would adequately convey the storm of emotions within him.

"We've got this," Jason said, his voice firm, his conviction absolute.

Garrett gave a small nod, his voice hoarse as he finally spoke. "Good fortune, my friend."

Jason's expression softened ever so slightly. "If not sooner, I'll see you in the next life."

And with that, the connection cut, leaving Garrett staring at a blank screen. For a long moment, he sat there, his heart heavy, before turning his focus back to the HTD. The battle was far from over.

"Speed now at 20 g.," Heller reported, his voice tight, the strain of the moment evident in his tone. "25 g. and climbing."

"Heller," Garrett said. "Hold at 40 g. and be ready for emergency deceleration on my orders—after we pass them."

"Aye, aye, sir," Heller replied. "Will hold at 40 g. until you order otherwise."

"How long until we're in maser range?" Garrett asked, his gaze flicking to the HTD, where the icons of the enemy formation loomed closer.

"Three minutes," Krebs said without looking up from his console. "Missiles away... eighty-two good launches. All of them running hot, true, and normal. Staggered attack pattern engaged."

Garrett rubbed his jaw, the rasp of stubble against his palm grounding him in the moment. He watched as the missile tags surged toward the enemy formation. At the same time, a new wave of red enemy missile tags streaked toward *Surprise*, rapidly closing the distance. They were committed now. There was no turning back.

The silence on the bridge was almost suffocating, broken only by the occasional beep of a console or the faint hum of the ship's systems. *Surprise* had endured the enemy's punishment, but she still stood strong—battered, yes, but with her teeth bared and ready to strike.

"Sir," Shaw said, breaking the silence as he turned toward Garrett. His voice was low, urgent. "Our course brings us dangerously close to the enemy. If one of their ships decides to ram us—especially if it's AI-controlled—at these speeds, well... the impact would be catastrophic. I suggest we adjust course just prior to contact... make it more difficult for the bastards."

The words sent a chill down Garrett's spine. He hadn't considered the possibility of a kamikaze maneuver. The thought of *Surprise*—his ship, his crew—colliding with an enemy dreadnaught at these velocities was a nightmare.

"Helm, did you hear that?" Garrett asked, his voice harder than he intended.

"I did, sir," Heller responded, already working at his station.

"Plot a course adjustment just before contact," Garrett ordered. "Avoid the bastards but keep us on target for the maser strike."

"Aye, sir," Heller said. A moment later, the revised course appeared on Garrett's HTD and plot. There were two adjustments, subtle but precise, a minor veer with each movement that would force the *Surprise* to thread the needle between the enemy ships without compromising their attack run, and hopefully keep the enemy guessing where they'd actually be. With luck, if a ramming attempt was made, there wouldn't be time for the enemy to react to the final course adjustment.

Garrett studied the track, then glanced over at Shaw. His executive officer's eyes were fixed on the display, his expression tense.

"What do you think?" Garrett asked.

After a moment, Shaw nodded. "I believe we are good."

"Heller, execute when ready," Garrett said.

"Aye, aye, sir," Heller replied. His hands hovered over the controls for a heartbeat before he entered the command. "Executing."

On the HTD, *Surprise*'s icon moved slightly, her path and course shifting just enough to mitigate the risk of a catastrophic collision while keeping them on a trajectory to deliver a devastating blow. The next course adjustment would be more extreme and at the last moment before they passed the enemy. Every second brought them closer and closer to finding out if his gamble would pay off—or if it would cost them everything.

Garrett's eyes remained glued to the HTD as the latest wave of enemy missiles closed the distance. His interceptor screen met them head-on, engaging the incoming volley with all the ferocity they could muster.

Missiles and interceptors streaked past one another at incredible speeds. Garrett's gut clenched as he watched icons shift and vanish on the display. Ten enemy missiles disappeared from the plot, their fiery trails extinguished in a flash. Five of his interceptors also vanished, replaced with debris tags... Each lost craft represented a crew, lives he had sent into harm's way.

"Tell CAG to order the interceptors to break off," Garrett said. "They've done all they can. The rest is up to us."

"Yes, sir," Shaw said and relayed the orders.

Several moments later, the interceptors began to break away, burning out of the combat zone just as fast as their gravitic drives could propel them.

"EW active. Point defense firing," Cassidy announced, her voice cutting through the hum of the bridge.

Garrett's gaze shifted back to the HTD. One missile swerved off course as the electronic warfare suite did its job, spoofing its guidance systems. Then the rest began falling— kinetic rounds and maser fire systematically cutting through the volley. The screen flickered as one by one, the missiles were hit and taken out, small flashes of light indicating their destruction.

Garrett felt an odd detachment. The situation felt both crushingly real and strangely distant, like he was a spectator in a high-stakes game he couldn't walk away from.

"All missiles destroyed," Cassidy announced, her voice filled with plain relief.

Garrett allowed himself a rare moment of satisfaction. "Good job. Excellent work."

"Thank you, sir," Cassidy replied.

"Enemy PDS fire detected," Krebs called out, his voice cutting through the momentary calm. "Enemy EW active."

"Guns"—Garrett's focus snapped back to the task at hand—"are the masers ready?"

"They are, sir," Krebs replied. "When we pass, they will fire automatically."

Garrett gave a nod. The enemy's formation loomed closer, their PDS systems lighting up as they tried to swat down the incoming missiles and prepare for close engagement.

"Very good," Garrett said. The bridge crew held their breath as *Surprise* hurtled toward the enemy formation. The moment of truth was upon them.

Garrett leaned forward, narrowing his focus on the HTD as the display detailed the impact of his surviving missiles. One moment, a battleship icon was present, solid and unyielding, and the next, it flickered and transformed into a navigational hazard tag. The missiles had done their job. Another battleship on the plot staggered wildly, not from a deliberate navigational maneuver but from catastrophic failure in her gravitic drive. He watched, almost in disbelief, as the crippled vessel collided with another battleship in the formation. The HTD registered the explosion—a massive flare—and then both ships were gone, their tags replaced by swirling debris fields.

Garrett felt the tightening knot in his stomach. They were closing at an incredible speed now. He drew in a deep breath, steadying his nerves. His fingers gripped the armrests of his command chair as the final seconds ticked down, the tension on the bridge mounting with every heartbeat.

"Hang on... course change," Heller called out.

"One of the dreadnaughts is changing course!" Cassidy called out. "She's trying to ram us!"

Garrett felt the tug almost instantly as the gravitic drive exerted power and force. It started as a subtle shift to the right but grew more pronounced as *Surprise* began her sharp maneuver. The inertial compensators strained to keep up, and the ship groaned under the stress of the rapid course adjustment. The deck beneath him vibrated almost violently, the entire structure of the Mothership protesting the extreme forces at play.

Then they were on the enemy.

"Firing," Krebs announced.

Everything happened in the blink of an eye. The ship continued to shake violently. The maser cannons unleashed their fury, firing in synchronized bursts. Garrett was jolted in his chair as the enemy shot back at them, hammering into and through *Surprise*'s shields at close range. The vibrations and shaking only increased, along with a gut-churning groan as his ship strained under the immense pressures of combat. Alarms blared, and the lights flickered, momentarily plunging the bridge into semi-darkness before coming back on. Somewhere in the ship, the muffled crump of an explosion sent a deep shiver through the hull.

Garrett blinked hard, trying to steady himself as the ship leveled out. The vibrations and jerking stopped and for a moment, apart from the blaring alarms, everything seemed to still. He sucked in a deep breath and exhaled slowly, the realization dawning on him.

They had survived.

The thought struck him like a hammer blow. Against all odds, they had made it through.

"The dreadnaught missed us," Cassidy fairly shouted. "She missed!"

They had survived.

He exhaled a breath, allowing himself a moment of relief. His hands relaxed, though the tension in his shoulders remained, like a coiled spring that refused to unbind.

How hard had they been hit?

"Report," Garrett ordered, his gaze snapping to the status board, which was lit up in red. Alarms blared as multiple systems flashed critical. A low, ominous rumble echoed through the ship—another explosion, likely secondary, or perhaps even an entire section depressurizing. Smoke wafted through one of the ventilation grills near the ceiling.

"Shields are down on the starboard side, sir," Keegan reported, his voice clipped.

"Significant damage," Shaw added, scanning his station. "The pressure hull has been compromised in multiple locations. Engineering and damage control are responding."

"How's the gravitic drive?" Garrett asked, forcing his voice to remain steady.

"Functioning, sir," Heller replied without hesitation. "I still have control."

That was a lifeline. Garrett allowed himself a moment of gratitude. They could still maneuver.

"McKay, reactor update?" Garrett pressed.

"Reactors are nominal," McKay said, his tone almost reassuring. "No issues to report. We have power."

Garrett nodded, letting out a slow breath. "We can maneuver and power the ship," he said aloud, more for his own reassurance than anyone else's. "Guns, how are we doing?"

Krebs was silent for a moment before responding. "Still assessing, sir," he said grimly. "We've lost much of our starboard-side capabilities—maser batteries, point defense systems, and missile pods. I wouldn't count on much from that quadrant. They hit us very hard, sir."

Garrett's gaze shifted to HTD. *Ajax*, battered and broken, was still alongside them. Miraculously, her warp bubble was holding despite her critical condition. The ship was in an uncontrolled tumble and streaming atmosphere. Escape pods were ejecting, tiny bursts of light on the plot as survivors sought to flee the doomed vessel. His heart hurting, a sharp pang of sadness clenched at Garrett's chest. Though he had no confirmation, he couldn't shake the gut-wrenching certainty that Jason was gone.

Forcing himself to refocus, Garrett turned his attention to the enemy formation. He needed to know how much damage he'd inflicted on them. His gaze swept the HTD, scanning for answers. Only four enemy combatants remained: three dreadnaughts and a solitary battleship. They were decelerating hard, their intent to pursue plain. One of the dreadnaughts was streaming atmosphere, but she still seemed capable. The drives on the two others were flickering and clearly on the edge of failure. They might even have cracked drive coils. He had clearly hurt them.

"How's the main battery?" Garrett demanded, his tone direct.

Silence.

His eyes snapped to McKay, who was hunched over his console, brow furrowed as he examined the data streaming across his screen. "McKay, report!"

McKay jerked his head up, his expression shifting as he processed the question. "Surprisingly, the main battery is up and functioning, sir," he said, his voice tinged with disbelief. "Despite the damage we've taken, the wormhole emitters seem fully operational. The railgun is good as well."

"Excellent," Garrett replied. "Krebs?"

"The battery is nearly charged, sir," Krebs added, cutting in with an update. "Thirty seconds until full readiness."

Garrett nodded. "Helm, initiate emergency deceleration—drop us to 10 g. immediately. Now, now, now! Guns, I want a solution on those ships. Load a one-hundred-millimeter round."

"Aye, sir," Heller replied. "Decelerating hard."

"Plotting solution now, one-hundred-millimeter round, coming up!"

Garrett felt the familiar tug as the inertial compensators struggled to counteract a sudden change in momentum. The ship rumbled and trembled under the strain, a deep, resonant groan echoing through the hull as the gravity drive worked overtime. He was stressing her more than any shakedown cruise ever could.

Shaw turned his head, his expression a mixture of concern. "A one-hundred-millimeter round? That's a big load. We only have four of them. We may need that round at some point in the future, maybe even at Indigo."

"I want to make sure we finish the job," Garrett replied curtly, his tone leaving no room for doubt. "We've taken enough punishment for one day."

The deck quivered beneath their feet as *Surprise* continued to decelerate. Garrett watched the velocity numbers on his display drop steadily: 30 g., 25 g., 20 g., and finally 10 g.

"Solution set," Krebs announced from his station. "I've targeted one of the dreadnaughts."

"Sir," Shaw said suddenly. "I don't think we should use the main battery on the enemy before us."

"What?" Garrett asked, looking over. He had not expected that from Shaw, not in the least.

"We still have significant missile and defensive capability on the port side," Shaw said. "I am thinking of Admiral Bryer and the force falling back on Calydra. It's a long shot for the main gun, but I believe we should try, sir. They could really use our help."

Garrett felt himself scowl as he thought on the suggestion. His gaze moved back to the HTD. He scrolled out. The running battle was still ongoing. Third Fleet was suffering badly. Bryer had lost at least half of what had been on the field when *Surprise* had arrived in-system. To say they were in a desperate position was an understatement.

The enemy had taken casualties too, but not nearly as bad, for their point defense coverage was better due to superior numbers. Admiral Bryer had seemed confident he could deal with the enemy, but Garrett could not see how without continuing to take substantial, perhaps even crippling losses.

He rubbed his jaw as he considered the suggestion. It would be a very long shot, more than twenty million kilometers from their current position. Should he take the shot? Could he afford to? What if they missed? The solution... the math alone would be challenging to calculate.

Garrett's gaze went back to the force he was currently engaged with. One of the dreadnaught's drives had just failed. From the fluctuations on the screen, her crew was trying desperately to restart her gravitic system. The dreadnaught had not completed her turn, the braking maneuver ceasing as well when the drive went offline. As he watched, her warp bubble collapsed, and the ship literally came apart from the gravitational shear of the efforts to restart the drive. A reactor detonated a heartbeat later and she was gone, taking the battleship with her. That left only two dreads to deal with.

"Missile launch," Krebs reported. "Thirty-two missiles in space."

"That's all?" Shaw asked, looking up, surprise plain.

"It is," Krebs confirmed.

The incoming volley blossomed on the HTD, flaring brightly and burning in their direction. Just to be sure, Garrett counted the missiles. There were indeed only thirty-two in space.

That decided it.

"Helm, turn our port side to face the enemy," Garrett ordered. "Guns, I want another missile volley. Split it between the two surviving ships, staggered pattern of attack. Fire when ready. Target the gripper cannon on the enemy force engaging the fleet by Calydra. Load a two-hundred-millimeter round."

"Aye, sir," Heller replied, "turning the ship."

"Working on solutions now," Krebs said, "and recalculating gripper cannon to target the main enemy fleet. I am going to pick a target in the middle of their main formation. That should cause maximum damage."

"Very good," Garrett said. "Keegan, how are shields on the port side?"

"Ten percent, sir, and rising."

"Missiles away," Krebs reported. "Ninety-two good launches."

Garrett grimaced at that news. The weight of their volley had been seriously diminished. He could only imagine how bad *Surprise* had been hurt. "As soon as the next volley is up, release it, and keep firing until they are disabled. No need to seek authorization."

"Aye, aye, sir. I will keep on them."

"PDS and EW active," Cassidy reported.

Rubbing his jaw, Garrett leaned forward in his chair and watched as the enemy missile volley steadily bore down upon them. Suddenly, two missiles veered away, spoofed by EW, then a third and a fourth followed a moment later.

A great lumbering beast, *Surprise* was still turning, increasingly showing her port side, and as she did, more and more of her undamaged defensive capability came into firing position and online. Missiles began to wink off the display as they closed in. Garrett found himself gripping the armrests as the volley crossed the last few kilometers. More of the enemy's missiles disappeared, twenty were left, then fifteen... ten...

"We got them all," Cassidy fairly shouted.

Garrett let go a breath of relief.

"Wait..." Cassidy said. "Wait... shit!"

The ship shook, shuddering.

"One missile got through," Cassidy said.

"Shields are down to two percent on the port side," Keegan reported. There was a long pause. "Significant bleed through. I've notified damage control."

A deep shudder went through the hull. Garrett could feel it communicated through his seat... a secondary explosion somewhere. *Surprise* had been wounded yet again, badly. How much more could she take?

"Very good," Garrett said. "Mr. Keegan, get those shields back up."

"Death from a thousand cuts," Shaw said quietly, looking over at him.

Garrett could only nod.

"PDS fire detected," Cassidy called out. "Enemy electronic warfare active."

Garrett's eyes snapped to the tactical display, watching intently as their own missile salvo arced in on final approach. The swarm of icons representing the shipkillers closed the distance like a tidal wave of fury.

"Their point defense network looks lighter, feebler," Shaw observed, leaning forward, eyes locked onto the display. "I think we chewed them up good during that close pass."

Garrett nodded in agreement, jaw tight. "I see it."

On the screen, missiles began to wink out—five gone, then another cluster of ten. Garrett felt the tension knot in his chest. He held his breath, silently willing the rest of the salvo onward. The enemy's defenses were doing their best, but they weren't strong enough. They weren't good enough.

And then—impact.

The first detonation rippled across the display as a missile struck one of the dreads, followed in rapid succession by others. Like hammer blows falling one after the next, the surviving missiles slammed home in tightly spaced bursts. The dreadnaughts, already damaged, simply couldn't absorb the punishment. Both massive vessels visibly lurched on the plot, their icons flaring with damage markers.

"Multiple hits," Shaw said. "Ten, maybe more per target."

Then the HTD flared as a reactor breach tore through one of the enemy dreadnaughts, erupting from its core and shattering the vessel's spine. The blast sheared decks apart in a blinding flash, and a heartbeat later, the massive warship was simply gone—reduced to an expanding cloud of plasma, wreckage, and tumbling debris. Its icon blinked out, replaced by a red navigational hazard tag on the tactical display.

The second ship didn't last much longer. Her already faltering shields buckled beneath the relentless pounding, and then one of the final missiles found its mark—piercing the armored hull and detonating deep within. The explosion ripped through internal compartments, splitting the vessel clean in two. Both halves tumbled apart in slow-motion ruin, trailing gas, plasma and debris into the void.

Garrett exhaled and leaned back in his chair, the adrenaline bleeding out of him in waves. He closed his eyes for the briefest moment. When he looked again, the two dreadnaughts were gone, replaced with blinking hazard icons.

"Targets destroyed," Krebs confirmed, his voice steady.

Garrett allowed himself the barest smile. "Good shooting, guns."

"Thank you, sir," came the reply.

Garrett's gaze went back to the HTD and the fleet fight that was under way. "How is the solution coming for the main battery?"

"Still working on it, sir. I am targeting the center of their formation. It's such a long shot... can we bring the ship to a relative stop in relation to the system star? I want to be certain we hit what we are aiming at."

"Helm," Garrett ordered. "Full stop."

"Aye, aye, sir," Heller said. "Bringing the ship to a full stop relative to the star."

"We only have three two-hundred-millimeter rounds," Shaw said. "Are you certain you want to use one?"

Garrett thought about that. He'd been told it took two years just to gather and manufacture enough exotic material to make and manufacture one of the smaller rounds. How long had it taken the Confederation for the larger ones? "Certain, no. But we need to do significant damage to the enemy, enough so that Fleet has a fighting chance. I think it worth the risk. We will use one of the three we have in stock."

Shaw nodded.

"Full stop, sir," Heller reported.

"Very good," Garrett replied, and then looked back on Krebs. "Guns, how are we doing?"

"CIC is checking my math, sir," Krebs said. There was a long pause. "Confirmation... is good. We are ready to shoot."

"Guns, double-check the firing solution. Be very sure you have everything correct. We will only have one shot at this... and it needs to count. There can be no mistakes."

Krebs hesitated for a moment, then nodded, his hands moving quickly over his console. "Rechecking now." The seconds stretched into an eternity before Krebs spoke again. "Solution looks solid. Do you want CIC to review it again, sir?"

Garrett turned his full attention to Krebs, locking eyes with his weapons officer. "Do you believe it's good?"

A moment of silence passed as Krebs deliberated, his face tightening with concentration and the stress of the moment as he studied the math again. Finally, he looked up and gave a decisive nod. "I do, sir. The solution is good."

Garrett turned back to the HTD, the data tags of the enemy ships glowing ominously on the display. As they pursued and fought their long-range missile engagement with Bryer, the enemy formation was broken up into ten smaller spherical formations clustered closely together. On the plot, the target ship was an enemy dreadnaught smack-dab in the near middle of the entirety of the enemy fleet.

This was the moment. So much was riding on what came next... so many lives... so many futures...

"Mister Krebs," Garrett said as calmly as he could, sitting up straight in his chair, "kindly fire the main gun."

"Firing," Krebs replied.

The ship seemed to hold her breath, then a surge of energy pulsed through her hull. The lights dimmed significantly, plunging the bridge into an eerie, ghostly glow. Garrett could feel the charge, a tangible force that made the air itself feel heavier, prickling at his skin. Outside, space-time warped visibly, creating faint ripples that would have been mesmerizing under less dire circumstances.

Alarms blared briefly as the massive energy release triggered automated warnings. These alerts fell silent as quickly as they'd begun, the shockwave dissipating almost as fast as it had appeared. The wormhole blossomed into existence, a tear in the fabric of space-time. The dart was already moving, accelerated to unimaginable speeds by the railgun. The moment the wormhole fully formed, the dart vanished into its gaping maw, propelled toward its target.

On the far side of the wormhole, the exit point materialized, spitting the dart back into local space. The wormhole collapsed behind it as if it had never been. The dart screamed toward the targeted enemy dreadnaught. It struck with unerring accuracy, slamming into the massive vessel's shields.

For a fraction of a second, the dreadnaught's shields flared brightly, their energy layers desperately attempting to absorb the incoming force. But they failed in that effort. The dart punched through, penetrating the defensive screens and driving into the armor before digging deep into the pressure hull. The neutronium casing ruptured, releasing the quantarite payload buried within—a substance so volatile, its very nature defied comprehension.

The result was... catastrophic. The explosion lit up the void, a blinding sphere of annihilation, a newborn sun that radiated outward from the target with devastating force. It was the most impressive thing Garrett had ever seen. Alarms blared across the bridge as their space-time layer fluxed in reply to the event. The data on the HTD flickered for several moments before stabilizing. Garrett watched as the shockwave of exotic matter tore through the target formation, bathing much of the entire enemy fleet in a wave of pure destructive power. Shields buckled and collapsed under the onslaught. As if it wasn't even there, armor was shredded like parchment paper.

The bridge was silent as enemy ships were swallowed by the energy wave that radiated outward in all directions from the point of detonation. The HTD displayed the destruction in vivid detail, as dozens of ships winked out of existence. They were not replaced by navigational hazard tags marking debris fields, for nothing had been left behind.

They were simply gone.

Garrett exhaled sharply. On the main screen, the blast bloomed larger, a brilliant, expanding inferno tearing through the void—a fiery testament to their gamble paying off. Triumph shot through him, overwhelming in its intensity.

They'd done it.

The tightly wound silence that had gripped the bridge shattered like glass. Garrett's voice cracked through it, raw with adrenaline and joy. "Good shot, guns! Damn fine shooting!"

For a heartbeat, the crew remained frozen, stunned. Then the cheer erupted—loud, visceral, and unrestrained. It wasn't clean or polished, just pure emotional release: a mix of relief, disbelief, and hard-won victory. Officers clapped backs, someone pounded a console in exhilaration, and Krebs let out a whoop. The bridge came alive with the thunder of celebration.

"I read twenty-two enemy ships left," Cassidy reported, when the cheer died down. "Many appear damaged to some degree. Several have fluctuations to their drive and shield systems... make that twenty-one... a ship just exploded."

Garrett had hurt the enemy, and in doing so, given Bryer a real chance, but this fight wasn't over. A portion of the enemy force was still intact, still engaged with Fleet. He'd simply thinned their numbers, shifted the odds. They were bearing down on Calydra, Admiral Bryer still withdrawing to the cover of the gathering forces there and the forts, but Garrett had swung the pendulum firmly in Third's favor. He was certain of that. He'd given them a real fighting chance to come out on top and protect the facilities around Calydra.

Garrett leaned back in his chair and closed his eyes for a moment. He had done all he could. The rest now fell to Bryer. *Surprise* was bloodied, battered, but not broken. She'd weathered the storm.

It was time to recover their birds, their small craft, render aid to any survivors from *Surprise*'s shattered task force, and see to their own—tend the wounded, account for the dead, and begin the grim work of putting themselves back together. *Surprise* was in rough shape, but she could be repaired, refitted, and rearmed. Javelin Station had vast shipyards, trained dockhands that could service his ship and put her back into fighting trim. Garrett no longer had a task force. After the fighting was done, would Admiral Bryer have the ships Garrett needed to pull off his mission?

Garrett did not know.

As his gaze shifted over to the status board, he took in all the red lights and tags, indicating damage and nonoperational systems. He wondered... had it been a mistake to come here? Had he erred?

The HTD suddenly blared several alarms. Garrett sat up. Something was happening with Fleet. He manipulated the display to focus on the distant engagement.

The scene blinked into clarity, but what he saw suddenly made no sense. He rubbed his tired, gritty eyes and looked again. It still didn't add up. He sent it to Shaw.

"Holy shit," Shaw breathed after a long moment. "That's half of Third Fleet. Where in the hell did they come from?"

Garrett's mind raced to process the impossible. Then, like a switch flipping, it hit him. Understanding dawned, cold and sharp. Bryer's confidence at dealing with the enemy suddenly made complete sense.

"Bryer hid them," Garrett said slowly. "He concealed half of his fleet... They've been lying in wait this whole time, and even from our own HTD feed. He must've masked them somehow, removed them from all the feeds, in case the enemy had access to our tactical net—like they did the beacon network at Midway."

He glanced at Shaw, whose plain disbelief mirrored his own.

"The rally point, Alpha Zulu and Calydra... both were bait," Garrett continued, his voice hollow with the weight of comprehension. "Bryer never intended to hold the Beleris jump point. He knew they were coming and let them push deeper into the system—let them think they had the advantage... all to lead them straight into an ambush. Our attack could not have been timed better..."

On the HTD, more than eighty Confederation starships, nearly all capitals, had appeared from literally nowhere, right in the path of the enemy, and were unleashing a thunderstorm of fire at near point-blank range. Lasers, maser beams, and missiles by the thousands lit the display, hammering into the enemy formation, tearing it apart. Ships winked out one by one. The enemy, completely caught by surprise, was being annihilated.

"He knew they would come, that the enemy would hit the system from Beleris," Shaw murmured, his voice a mixture of awe and horror. "He simply hid those ships in stealth fields... and this entire time, they were waiting. That must have been his plan all along to defend Dows... one big ambush. Only he did not expect us to arrive and disable the jump point, trapping the enemy here." Shaw paused. "It's a good thing we deployed the main battery against the enemy when we did... otherwise it would have been a near-even fight. Now... well, now, it is a slaughter."

Garrett conceded it had been a good plan. But it would have been a much more expensive one, had *Surprise* not intervened. Admiral Bryer had lived up to his reputation.

But at what cost?

Garrett's mind spiraled, calculating the enormity of what had happened, what the man had done to set his trap. The frontline defenses at Beleris, the forts, the ships, the lives—tens of thousands of Confederation personnel—had been sacrificed... all to set and bait this trap. Bryer had given the enemy everything they wanted, the appearance of being unprepared... having sent the bulk of the fleet away toward Midway. He had showed them a weak point and drawn them into his web, and now he was killing them wholesale. But if Garrett hadn't interceded... the price Bryer paid would have been catastrophic... Third would have been near-finished as a fighting force.

Garrett suddenly felt a moment of intense triumph. Bryer would have the personnel and ships he'd need to carry out his ultimate mission, the strike at the enemy. Coming to Javelin had been the right move all along.

"That's... cold-blooded," Shaw said, his tone low. "To sacrifice that much, knowing—"

Garrett could not help but agree as his thoughts shifted back to Dows. He too had sacrificed... his escorts, his small craft, his people—all for the sake of victory... to win. In a way, he had made the same cold, calculated choices. And now, watching Bryer's trap snap shut, he saw himself in the admiral's ruthless tactics.

The bridge was silent except for the hum of the consoles and the faint buzz of the air handlers. Everyone was now watching the HTD and the slaughter unfolding in real time, the enemy fleet being torn apart piece by piece in a one-sided fight.

Bryer's plan was brilliant. But it had all come with a steep cost. So too had Garrett's own plan. His throat tightened as a bitter thought surfaced unbidden. He glanced around his bridge. What kind of man had he become since taking command of *Surprise*?

The answer came quickly, a whisper in the back of his mind, chilling in its certainty: *You are a cold-blooded killer. You've been one for a very long time... ever since* Repulse *and* Marlowe.

The bloodshed... the killing wasn't behind him. The worst was ahead, for the attack on Indigo Station was next.

A LETTER FROM MARC

Dear Reader,

Writing *Off Javelin Station* has been an incredible journey—a labor of love and a true joy to create. It's my deepest hope that you find as much excitement, wonder, and connection in its pages as I felt while bringing it to life.

If you did enjoy it, and want to keep up to date with all my latest releases, just sign up at the following link. Your email address will never be shared and you can unsubscribe at any time.

www.secondskybooks.com/marc-alan-edelheit

I want to take a moment to thank you, not just for picking up this book, but for making it possible for me to do what I love most—write stories that inspire and entertain. Your support allows me to live my dream as a full-time author, and for that, I am endlessly grateful.

To those of you who reach out with messages or comments about my work, please know how deeply moving and humbling it is. Hearing how these stories resonate with you means the world to me—it's a reminder of why I pour my heart into every word.

From the bottom of my heart, thank you!

If you enjoyed this story, I'd be so grateful if you could leave a review. Reviews not only keep me motivated but also help new readers discover my books. I make it a point to read every single one, so please know that your words truly matter.

Here's to many more adventures ahead,

Marc Alan Edelheit

instagram.com/marcedelheitauthor
facebook.com/MAENovels
x.com/MarcEdelheit
youtube.com/@marcalanedelheit9572
patreon.com/marcalanedelheit

APPENDIX I: INTRA-SYSTEM TRAVEL

The following is a detailed explanation of both inter-star system and interstellar travel, including how speed and acceleration function and are measured in this universe. If you enjoy exploring the mechanics of futuristic travel and the science behind it, feel free to dive in.

The Gravitic or Gravity Drive

The gravity drive is an advanced propulsion system that moves a starship through space by generating a stable gravitational field around it. This field creates a warp bubble—a localized area of stable space-time—that allows the ship to carry a portion of space and time with it. This technique enables the ship to travel at high speeds without experiencing relativistic effects, such as time dilation. By manipulating the properties of the gravitational field, the gravity drive maintains a set speed rather than accelerating indefinitely, redefining "1g." in this context as a specific speed rather than a measure of gravitational acceleration.

How the Gravity Drive Works

In this context "1g." is a set speed, specifically **2.24 km/s**. Unlike traditional acceleration, where "1g." refers to an increasing force, here it represents a fixed speed. The gravity drive can hold this set speed, scaling up through 2g., 3g., and so on, with each "g." increment marking a consistent increase in velocity.

To reach "1g. speed" (or "cruising speed"), the gravity drive must create a stable warp bubble around the ship, insulating it from the relativistic effects that would otherwise distort time and space at high velocities. This bubble effectively isolates the ship's internal space-time, allowing the crew to experience time at a normal rate. This safeguard enables high-speed travel without experiencing the effects of time dilation.

Calculating Distance Traveled at Constant Speed

If we treat "1g. speed" as a set rate, calculating the distance traveled becomes straightforward. At a constant speed:

$$\text{distance (d)} = \text{velocity (v)} \times \text{time (t)}$$

where:

- d is the distance traveled
- v is the velocity, determined by the "g." setting of the gravity drive, and
- t is the time in seconds

For example, at "1g. speed" over the course of one day (86,400 seconds), the ship would travel:

$$d = v \times 86{,}400 = 2.24 \text{ km/s} \times 86{,}400 = 193{,}536 \text{ km}$$

As the "g." settings increase, the distance covered increases proportionally. For instance, at 10g., the ship would cover ten times the distance in the same period.

Why Travel above 55g. Is Inadvisable

The fastest ship can reach speeds up to 55g., which represents its maximum warp bubble stability threshold. Beyond 55g., the gravitational field required to maintain the drive becomes so intense that the warp bubble risks destabilization. This instability poses significant hazards, including uneven temporal effects within the bubble, as well as potential physical harm to the ship and crew. If the bubble were to destabilize, the ship would be exposed to relativistic time dilation and extreme forces, making speeds above 55g. highly dangerous.

In summary, the gravity drive allows a ship to traverse space at controlled, high-speed intervals defined by "g." settings. The warp bubble provides protection from relativistic travel complications, though the technology requires careful management at higher speeds. The 55g. limit serves as a practical safety measure, balancing speed and stability.

Speed Table for Gravity Drive Settings

G Setting
Speed (km/s)

1g.
2.24 km/s

2g.
4.48 km/s

3g.
6.72 km/s

4g.
8.96 km/s

5g.
11.2 km/s

10g.
22.4 km/s

15g.

33.6 km/s

20g.

44.8 km/s

25g.

56.0 km/s

30g.

67.2 km/s

35g.

78.4 km/s

40g.

89.6 km/s

45g.

100.8 km/s

50g.

112.0 km/s

55g.

123.2 km/s

Light Speed and the Gravity Drive

To understand the impracticality of achieving light speed with the gravity drive, consider that the speed of light is approximately 299,792 km/s. With 1g. equal to 2.24 km/s, reaching light speed would require approximately:

$$\text{g.s for light speed} = 299{,}792 \text{ km/s} \div 2.24 \text{ km/s} \approx 133{,}836g$$

This calculation demonstrates why traveling at light speed far exceeds the gravity drive's 55g. stability threshold, making such travel impractical with current technology.

To calculate the time it would take to travel from Earth to Mars at the maximum speed of 55g., we use the average distance and the given speed.

1. Determine the Distance from Earth to Mars

The average Earth–Mars distance is approximately 225 million kilometers (225,000,000 km).

2. Calculate Speed at 55g.

Given that 1g. equals 2.24 km/s, then:

$$55g = 55 \times 2.24 \text{ km/s} = 123.2 \text{ km/s}$$

3. Calculate Travel Time

$$\text{time} = \text{distance} \div \text{speed} = 225{,}000{,}000 \text{ km} \div 123.2 \text{ km/s} \approx 1{,}826{,}298.7 \text{ seconds}$$

4. Convert Time to Days

$$\text{time in days} = 1{,}826{,}298.7 \div 86{,}400 \approx 21.1 \text{ days}$$

Answer:

At a speed of 55g. (or 123.2 km/s), it would take approximately 21 days to travel from Earth's high orbit to Mars's high orbit when the distance between the planets is at its average.

Light Speed Comparison

For reference, light takes about 12.5 minutes to travel the average distance from Earth to Mars (225 million kilometers):

1. **Calculate Light Travel Time**

$$\text{time} = \text{distance} \div \text{speed} = 225{,}000{,}000 \text{ km} \div 299{,}792 \text{ km/s} \approx 750 \text{ seconds}$$

2. **Convert to Time to Minutes**

$$\text{time in minutes} = 750 \div 60 = 12.5 \text{ minutes}$$

Answer:

It takes light approximately 12.5 minutes to travel the average distance from Earth to Mars, highlighting the significant difference between even the highest gravity drive settings and light-speed travel.

ACKNOWLEDGMENTS

I wish to thank my agent, Andrea Hurst, for her invaluable support and assistance. I would also like to thank my beta readers, who suffered through several early drafts. My betas: Steve Koratsky, Marshall Clowers, Paul Klebaur, William Schnippert, David Cheever, Sheldon Levy, Walker Graham, Jimmy McAfee, Joel Rainey, James H. Bjorum, James Doak, Nathan Hildebrand, Tom Moore, Michael Brown, Dragos Emil Ramniceanu, Kieran Maisonet, Lance Dahl, Lee Adrian, Brian Thomas, Ed Speight, and Dominick Maino. I would also like to take a moment to thank my loving wife, who sacrificed many an evening and weekend to allow me to work on my writing.

Editing Assistance by Hannah Streetman, Brandon Purcell, Audrey Mackaman, and Jack Renninson.

Cover Art by Tom Edwards

Agented by Andrea Hurst & Associates

PUBLISHING TEAM

Turning a manuscript into a book requires the efforts of many people. The publishing team at Bookouture would like to acknowledge everyone who contributed to this publication.

Commercial
Lauren Morrissette
Hannah Richmond
Imogen Allport

Cover design
Tom Edwards Design

Data and analysis
Mark Alder
Mohamed Bussuri

Editorial
Jack Renninson
Melissa Tran

Copyeditor
Helen Hawkins

Proofreader
Angela Snowden

Marketing

Alex Crow
Melanie Price
Occy Carr
Cíara Rosney
Martyna Młynarska

Operations and distribution

Marina Valles
Stephanie Straub
Joe Morris

Production

Hannah Snctsinger
Mandy Kullar
Nadia Michael
Ria Clare

Publicity

Kim Nash
Noelle Holten
Jess Readett
Sarah Hardy

Rights and contracts

Peta Nightingale
Richard King
Saidah Graham

Dear Reader,

We'd love your attention for one more page to tell you about the crisis in children's reading, and what we can all do.

Studies have shown that reading for fun is the **single biggest predictor of a child's future life chances** – more than family circumstance, parents' educational background or income. It improves academic results, mental health, wealth, communication skills, ambition and happiness.

The number of children reading for fun is in rapid decline. Young people have a lot of competition for their time, and a worryingly high number do not have a single book at home.

Hachette works extensively with schools, libraries and literacy charities, but here are some ways we can all raise more readers:

- Reading to children for just 10 minutes a day makes a difference
- Don't give up if children aren't regular readers – there will be books for them!

- Visit bookshops and libraries to get recommendations
- Encourage them to listen to audiobooks
- Support school libraries
- Give books as gifts

There's a lot more information about how to encourage children to read on our websites: **www.RaisingReaders.co.uk** and **www.JoinRaisingReaders.com**.

Thank you for reading.